Mickey,
I hope you enjoy
my literary folly.
I hope you enjoy
reading.
We miss you,
Jerry Cunningham

# No Coin for Charon

Jerry A. Cunningham

*No Coin for Charon*

Big Muddy Press

Published by Big Muddy Press, LLC
111 South Highland, Box 433
Memphis, TN. 38111 U.S.A.
Copyright 2008 by Jerry A. Cunningham

Please visit:
ISBN 978-0-615-21524-2
Cover Design © CB Publishing Group

# No Coin for Charon

# CHAPTER

*1*

January 1824
Harrodsburg, Kentucky

Calvin Cabell squatted low over the fieldstone hearth and extended his hands perilously close to the fire. He rubbed them briskly . . . hoping the friction of flesh rubbing flesh would cause warm blood to course through his veins . . . and thaw his freezing fingers.

He had survived a miserably cold and wet winter day. When he set out for home that morning he hadn't planned to spend the night at Harrodsburg's White Oak Inn. Ordinarily he could make the trip from Frankfort to Danville in eight hours. But today's weather forbade achieving his goal. All day long, wind and sleet relentlessly assaulted him and his horse, Noah.

"Yes sir, Mr. Smithson, it was wretched out there. Somewhere this side of Lawrenceburg I began reminding Noah about his namesake. The freezing rain drenched both man and beast . . . to the point I considered if we should be building an ark. I kept telling him, 'In this awful weather, Noah, there won't be enough time to load all of God's animals . . . two by two. The only creatures I'm concerned about saving are you and me.

"I told him, 'Forget the perpetuation of the species. We need to save our own hides'."

Smithson, the innkeeper, chuckled at his guest's sense of humor. He appreciated the young man's wit . . . honed razor sharp by the day's cruel weather.

"Mr. Cabell, that's why we're in business – to provide shelter and comfort to weary travelers. And, I must say, you're about the weariest one I've seen in some time."

5

"And, no doubt, the wettest one, too, Mr. Smithson. Are you sure Noah's sheltered from the weather?"

"Indeed, sir, and he's no doubt at this very moment in his dry stable stall . . . enjoying a hearty meal of oats and corn."

"Excellent, Smithson, he and I both thank you. Tell me, am I the only guest this evening?"

"No, sir, a man named Collins from Bardstown is staying overnight, as well. He preferred to keep warm upstairs by bundling in his bed. It's almost suppertime. He'll no doubt join us soon enough."

"If he considers it chilly here in front of your fire, perhaps Mr. Collins should be reminded he'd be much cozier if he bundled under a blanket with another warm blooded animal pressed next to him."

Smithson looked confused. "And . . . what man among us are you suggesting should bundle with Collins? I'm certainly not a candidate."

Calvin Cabell roared with laughter. "My word, no, Smithson, I only meant to suggest Mr. Collins might want to sleep in the stable . . . and bundle with Noah."

Both men shared a round of hearty laughter and Smithson slapped Calvin on the back to symbolize his guest had pulled a good joke on him.

"Now, you wait here, Mr. Cabell. I've got a sure-fire panacea to warm your cold bones." Smithson opened the cupboard at the opposite end of the room. "You need whiskey, man. A hundred proof shot of my best bourbon will either make you warm . . . or it'll make you forget you're cold."

"Now I know why I've heard you're such an outstanding innkeeper. You're most accommodating – especially to a man nearly dying from exposure. I hope to one day save your life, as well, Smithson."

Calvin had spent the night before in Frankfort. It was mid-morning when he finally concluded his business with a supplier for his merchandise store. Consequently, he couldn't depart for Danville until about ten o'clock. Leaving that late in the day made it unlikely he could travel all the way home to his wife, Catherine, and his two young children, Cassie and Jamie.

While he stared at the fire's leaping flames Calvin imagined Catherine was presently standing at their parlor window . . . worried sick and hoping to soon spot his and Noah's silhouettes emerging out of the dark mist. But he couldn't worry about her fretting. She knew her husband had the good sense to seek a safe shelter in such inclement weather.

Suddenly the door to the kitchen flew open. Calvin observed a woman carrying a tray laden with dishes. She pivoted her way around to face him while her hip secured the door open. After a quick glance in his direction, she further employed her derriere to close it tightly. The bar maid appeared to be about twenty years old. She was just a shade on the homely side, but she was well proportioned. There was a glum look pasted on her face. But when she spied Calvin standing tall in front of the fire, a faint smile broke out.

The glow from the flames was intense . . . and the bright radiance surrounding his trim body prevented her from clearly viewing the man. Sizing him up was like trying to catch a quick look at the blazing sun. Yet, that's what the woman tried to do. She stood there squinting and peering at this surreal sight. Likewise, Calvin stared back at her . . . even as Smithson handed him an ample glass of whiskey.

"I always keep my promises, Mr. Cabell. Take a generous dose of my medicine for what ails you. Here . . . drink and enjoy."

With Smithson back in the room the girl broke her trance and hurriedly carried the tray to one of the four dining tables. She didn't want her boss to think she was lollygagging when there were guests to feed. First, she removed a stack of pewter plates and mugs. Then she arranged them into respectable place settings. She also placed a woven reed basket in the center which held thick slices of bread.

"That's the way, Dolly. We've got two hungry guests tonight. Is the stew ready?"

"Yes, sir, I'll fetch the tureen in about three minutes. Maybe you might want to call the other guest to dinner before I bring it out."

"Good idea. I'll do that." Smithson walked over to the split rail ladder that was propped up against the square ceiling well that was cut to access the loft. He climbed the crude steps . . . just far enough to peer across the attic's floor before calling out to his guest from Bardstown.

"Mr. Collins . . . Mr. Collins . . . supper's ready . . . if you are."

7

There were five cots in the loft . . . which meant Calvin was lucky this night. He wouldn't have to share a bed with another traveler. For a moment he debated whether that was an unfortunate situation on such a frigid night. Then he drew comfort with the notion he would soon be bundling to keep warm in his own bed . . . just like Collins.

Collins descended the ladder and curiously inspected his fellow guest. He was about sixty . . . with a long gray, stringy beard hanging ten or twelve inches below his chin. Calvin sensed the man was sizing him up. Perhaps he was vicariously reminiscing about his own youth – when he, too, was in his late twenties . . . like the lithe man who stood before him. Calvin extended his hand with the expectation Collins would clasp it in a gentlemanly handshake. He did not.

Smithson offered a glass of whiskey to Collins. But the old man declined with an air of indignation. He seemed insulted the innkeeper would think he had ever consumed even a drop of liquor during his lifetime. Nevertheless, Smithson poured two inches of the amber liquid into Calvin's tumbler and he raised it to his lips. The firelight shone through the beveled cut glass . . . causing its contents to shimmer in the light as if it were some magical, distilled potion.

Calvin noticed the old man seemed intrigued, so he tried to engage his fellow guest in conversation. "Well, Mr. Collins, on a cold, wet night like this . . . I guess I'll have to do the drinking for both of us. But, please know I respect your convictions regarding temperance."

Collins grew a perplexing grin. Calvin wondered momentarily if it was a smile forming on just one side of his mouth. Or, was it a sneer of disgust? He couldn't tell. So, when Collins said he wanted to eat supper quickly and hop back beneath his stack of blankets, Calvin breathed a silent sigh of relief. He was thankful he wouldn't have to share an appetizing meal with such a dreary man.

Calvin told the woman, "Why don't you go ahead and serve Mr. Collins, Miss? I need to continue thawing my bones. I can eat later."

As he sat on a bench at the side of the fireplace Calvin could see Collins was getting his fill of stew and washing it down with the soberest spring water available in Mercer County.

Calvin lingered on the idea of branch water. If he was going to drink any more whiskey, he needed to pace himself. So, he asked Smithson in a low tone which Collins couldn't possibly hear, "My good man, I wonder if you'd dilute my next round of whiskey with some of Collins' pious joy juice."

Staring at a fire's dancing flames can lead a man into some serious, introspective thinking. At home Calvin never seemed to have a solitary moment to reflect. But, on this cold night . . . trapped by the whims of nature . . . it was the perfect opportunity to sort out complex personal issues . . . and take stock of himself.

* * * * * * * * * * * *

After Collins consumed his meal and left the dinner table, the old man spoke with the innkeeper for a bit about matters apparently meant for Smithson's ears alone. His confidential words required Collins to lean into his host's ear and curl the backside of his hand . . . to block anyone in the room from hearing what was being communicated. All the while, as Collins spoke into Smithson's ear, the old man fixed his eyes on Calvin.

"This peculiar man can't go back upstairs soon enough to suit me," Calvin thought to himself.

Dolly, the bar maid, walked into the room again and she stood before Calvin. "Tell me when you want your supper, Mr. Cabell. I've got some steaming stew in the back as well as some more hot biscuits. You can slather them with butter and hot apple sauce. Could I tempt you, sir? Please know this. I can provide you with ANYTHING you need. Everyone knows I'll do WHATEVER it takes to please our guests – especially handsome ones like you."

Calvin hung on to every word she said. There was a discernible tone in her voice – a subtle message. Or, was he imagining it? Sorting it all out rendered him silent. He'd consumed too much whiskey trying to keep warm. He knew it . . . right then and there. Dolly knew it, too. So, she spoke up again. "Mr. Cabell, once again, can I fetch anything from the kitchen for you?"

"No thanks, Dolly, I've been well satisfied."

"Completely satisfied, sir?"

Calvin was perplexed. He wondered if it was the whiskey stoking his male vanity. Or, was there more than an accidental double entendre being broadcast - one requiring a response? Calvin thought about it for a moment

9

and he reasonably concluded the cold weather and the warm bourbon must have twisted his wits. Perhaps he was just full of himself.

Smithson approached Calvin's table with a look of relief on his face. "Well, sir, I've just received a mild rebuke about the sins of serving whiskey to guests. It appears Mr. Collins not only prohibits himself from drinking spirits, he disapproves of anybody else warming his bones with a glass of liquor. He doesn't even want a man who's consumed an ounce of alcohol to sleep in the same loft with him. Imagine that."

"I think I should go upstairs and lodge a complaint with our sanctimonious friend, Mr. Collins. He should be informed that I, too, have standards about those with whom I share accommodations. I dislike sleeping in the same loft with a holier-than-thou teetotaler."

The innkeeper never meant to stir up things. He only thought it would be amusing for his Danville guest to hear Collins' ridiculous reprimands. He certainly never considered that repeating what he heard would incite Cabell's ire . . . instead of his already proven sense of humor.

"I meant no harm, Mr. Cabell. Surely you already know I think Collins is a pompous ass. I shared what he said only to illustrate his bogus piety."

Calvin appeared angry to hear about such unprovoked criticisms from a total stranger. Then he calmed down and soon realized the innkeeper was speaking the truth. Smithson had recounted Collins' conversation . . . merely for fun – for the sport of discrediting old buzzards like Collins.

"I'll tell you what, Mr. Cabell. You don't seem to be interested in sleep at the moment. But I must soon get my own slumber . . . as I have to arise well before sunrise. Why don't I offer you more whiskey? It's on the house. And you can remain down here in front of the hot fire . . . instead of hunkered in the loft under whatever blankets the old man hasn't already appropriated for himself. What say you, sir?"

After just two seconds of contemplating his options, Calvin gave his response. "Thanks, Smithson. I'll take that whiskey. Given my assigned roommate for the night, maybe you'll find me stretched on the floor in front of the fireplace when you arise tomorrow. Indeed, the more I think about this situation, I'd say that's entirely probable."

Calvin noticed the young female flirt walking into the room as Smithson responded, "Very good, Mr. Cabell." He then turned to his maid. "Dolly will fetch you whatever you need before she retires for the evening. Won't you, Dolly?"

"Indeed, Mr. Smithson, I'll provide our guest with whatever he desires."

Dolly spoke with her eyes squarely on her boss. But Calvin perceived her true message was directed to him. There was unmistakable innuendo in her words. He kept wondering if he was pompously cobbling together everything Dolly said . . . simply to taunt his basest instincts. He was sure her intent was to titillate the sort of puffed up pride that lies somewhere in the hearts of all young men.

"How long do you think you'll be, Dolly?" Smithson inquired.

"In about thirty minutes I'll have everything in shape for breakfast tomorrow morning."

"Thank you," the innkeeper replied. "Good night, Mr. Cabell. Enjoy the evening. And be sure to let Dolly know if there's anything you need."

"Am I living out some salacious dream?" he thought. "First, it was Dolly's apparent provocative suggestions. Now, Smithson's words seem to actually encourage his bar maid's flirtation. Or, is all this just a misunderstanding?"

"Remember to keep warm," the host called out as he closed the door to his room.

"Good night, Mr. Smithson," Dolly chimed, in return.

Smithson was a widower whose wife passed away just eighteen months earlier. He dearly missed her and the substantial help she provided running the inn. Yet, Smithson did his best to carry on without her devoted labor.

Dolly was referred to him by Horace Crenshaw who owned the local feed store. Her father back in Springfield asked Crenshaw if he might assist finding a job for her. She needed one desperately. Her family had cast her out of the household when it became apparent Dolly was pregnant.

She birthed a son in a ramshackle cabin on a neighbor's farm where she lived for the final four months of her pregnancy. Her favorite uncle offered his slave woman, named Carley, to stay with Dolly until the child arrived. But he made it clear Carley must return to town and Dolly would have to vacate the premises when the child was six months old.

Carley was eventually summoned home and Dolly continued to live in the shack. She fended as best she could for herself and her infant. But the field greens and turnips were running low. She was ready to move on – set apart from her family . . . forever.

Mr. Smithson gave her a job. But the only shelter he could offer this young mother and her son was a humble room within Smithson's shed situated on the rise behind the inn. Her tiny unit shared a crudely constructed stove with the adjacent room. It, too, was occupied by another staff member at the inn, Rebecca Morton. Rebecca was also an unmarried mother.

So, an efficient arrangement was struck. While Rebecca worked during the day, Dolly tended to the two children. The mothers' schedules shifted after noon. Then it was Rebecca's turn to care for the boys. When Dolly eventually retired for the evening, she picked up her toddler and slept with him through the night - until Rebecca awoke her neighbor before dawn to drop off her own son.

It wasn't a fitting situation for a mother and her infant child. But there were many mothers of fatherless children who were forced to set out for Louisville, Lexington, or Cincinnati to ply the streets . . . looking for men who would pay for the company of a desperate single mom. Dolly and Rebecca considered themselves to be fortunate.

"Dolly, tell me something about yourself. I've had dinner here twice before, but I don't recall ever seeing you."

"That's because I've only been here six months. Me and my baby moved here from Springfield."

"You have a baby, do you?"

"Yes, sir, I have a two year old son. His name is Timothy."

"So, who cares for Timothy while you're working?"

"Mr. Smithson let's me and another worker named Rebecca stay in what you might call a two room shed. It's out back. One room's mine and she's got the other. We take turns caring for each other's boy. I suppose it works out pretty well."

Calvin felt either emboldened or nosey . . . or both. "Would I be correct if I guessed you have a child, but you've never been married?"

12

Immediately, Calvin sensed he had stepped over a well demarcated line of decency. And Dolly, at that very same moment, sensed rage building within her.

"That's none of your business, is it, sir? I'm happy to serve you while you're a guest. But my life is MY life . . . and I don't think it's anyone else's business. Now, if you'll excuse me, I need to clean up so I can fetch my bastard baby. That's what you'd call him. Wouldn't you, Mr. Cabell? My Timothy's just a bastard baby in your righteous eyes. Isn't he?"

Calvin had never felt so ashamed of himself. Five minutes earlier he was cock-sure this woman was flirting with him. And, now, she must think he was the biggest boor imaginable. He had to make things right. It was only decent to do so.

"I'm deeply sorry, Dolly, if I've offended you. I guess the whiskey's affected my usual, clear thinking. It's making my mouth spout out insults that were never intended. Please forgive me."

He bowed his head like a sinful supplicant . . . and Dolly seemed willing to forgive his transgression. She paused . . . biting her bottom lip while her eyes, once again, surveyed Calvin. Then she took three slow strides toward her quarry. He braced himself for a slap in the face, but her arms, instead, wrapped warmly around him. Soon she began to stroke his crotch with her left hand as she placed her right hand on his shoulder.

She knew within seconds what lay ahead. No man would permit such intimate touching to continue if he wasn't willing to push forward . . . seeking even more excitement.

"Now, once more, Mr. Cabell, is there ANYTHING I can do for you . . . anything at all?"

Dolly started to massage the back of his neck while her slow fondling below continued – only, now with a firmer grip on his privates.

Calvin was confused. This had never happened before. He didn't have a clue how to react. He needed some time to gather his thoughts . . . and his wits. So, he told her what he often said to Catherine when he wanted a few minutes alone.

"Let me suggest this, Dolly. I've suddenly got some personal business requiring my attention. Nature's calling, if you know what I mean. I think I'll step outside awhile and tend to it. Then, when I return, we can talk some more. How does that sound?"

"I'll be done with my kitchen work in five minutes. I hope we can ratchet up this enjoyable encounter when you come back inside."

"Excellent . . . that's excellent . . . let's meet back here in a few minutes."

Dolly picked up her tray and carried it through the doorway. This time Calvin held the door open for her. Then, he went outside and stood on the ledge of the inn's raised wood porch. He unbuttoned the fly of his pants and he pushed hard on his bladder. He arched his warm stream upward and out into the frigid air . . . until it finally plummeted to the frozen earth and vanished in a gray haze of steam. All the while he thoughtfully gazed at the flickering constellations above.

"Well now, what DO the heavens have in store for me tonight?" he murmured under his breath. He exhaled a blast of warm air that surged from his mouth. It immediately condensed in the night air forming a languid, white cloud. "What DO the stars foretell tonight?"

He stood there thinking about the possibilities for adventure that awaited him inside. He thought about Catherine, too. And he thought about the vows they made with one another. He even revisited each of the Ten Commandments . . . just to check if one of them addressed the pitfalls of this particular situation.

"Thou shalt not commit adultery," rang forebodingly in his head. God's law was clear and Calvin Cabell wasn't about to break a commandment – much less, his wedding vows.

"There's no chance in hell I'll be lured to have sex with that woman – no way in the world."

It was time to leave the twinkling of the starry heavens behind. He resealed the last button on his fly and he went back inside. Dolly was there . . . standing in front of the ebbing flames.

"Well, Mr. Cabell, are you going to make the most of this night? I know you have some urges that need to be met, don't you? And you're sure, aren't you, that I can fulfill those needs? Isn't that right Mr. Cabell? And for such a pleasurable experience I trust you're willing to help a poor unmarried

14

barmaid earn some money to care for her child. Am I right about that, sir?"

Calvin offered no response, but he had plenty to say to himself. "Surely, you must be a damned fool, Calvin Cabell, if you thought you were so enticing that this girl might service you . . . just for the sake of worshipping what a handsome man you are. You knew it all along, didn't you? But your pride thought you would succeed on good looks alone. You're a fool, Cabell. That's not the way the world works, is it?"

Dolly knew her mark was thrashing about in a sticky moral quagmire. She had seen the look before. It was time for the siren to sing again. "You have what I want. And I have what you want. Isn't that the sum of it all, Mr. Cabell? Would the pleasure I can offer you be worth two bits from your pocket?"

"As interested as I may be in your proposition, Dolly, there's no way there'll be a coupling here tonight. I just can't do it. I won't do it."

Dolly had heard this before, too – this effort of a gentleman to make one last attempt to pledge to her . . . and to his Lord . . . that temptation will never undo sacred vows solemnly made unto God. Her response to this sort of piety illustrated that she considered oaths to be mere words. She slowly pursed her lips and extended her teasing tongue . . . so its wet, pink tip glowed from the firelight. It resembled a sensuous snake that slithered rhythmically to and fro . . . so as to moisten her lips in a counter-clockwise series of circles.

"It's too cold for coupling tonight anyway," she purred. "But there's nothing that can warm a man's bone more than a hot mouth working its magic."

"What do you mean?"

"I mean, I know you're married. And I know a true gentlemen like you could never be tempted to lay with somebody like me. But what I'm suggesting isn't sex. There'll be no fornication tonight – only gratification. You'll return home to Mrs. Cabell just as pure as when you left her."

Calvin thought about what she was saying. It made sense. At least, it seemed logical at the time.

Dolly spoke again to close the deal. "Did you notice I have a very talented tongue, sir? My lips and my tongue are like no other you've ever known, Mr.

Cabell. All I ask is for a small contribution to care for my poor son. Surely two bits would seem a worthwhile investment?"

Calvin's heart was racing faster than any thoroughbred in the Bluegrass had ever run. He could feel the muscle pounding wildly in his chest. And, he could almost hear the sounds of the cogs in his brain . . . grinding fiercely up in his mind as he processed everything Dolly was saying.

He was resolute when he told Dolly sexual intercourse wasn't an option. But this proposal deserved some consideration. He'd heard college mates and laborers in Lexington brag about it. Yet, he always discounted the claims. Some of these boys said it was far better than conventional sex. And he had often daydreamed about experiencing it.

But fellatio wasn't suitable behavior for a Christian couple like the Cabells. He and Catherine had never gone to that place. And he was certain they never would. Consequently, Calvin had filed away such aberrant urges. But now . . . now he was being offered the opportunity to turn sensuous, elusive day dreams . . . into reality.

"But where, Dolly? We couldn't do it here . . . with Mr. Collins and Mr. Smithson on the premises."

"My room's just up the hill . . . in back. Meet me there in ten minutes. Knock lightly."

While he waited Calvin Cabell's mind mulled over more questions, more concerns, and more anxieties than he had ever processed. A decision had to be made. Momentarily, he thought about Catherine and his babies. But they had to be thrown out of this debate. Their presence in his consciousness only mucked things up.

After all, what lay ahead of him wasn't a sacrilege to his marriage vows. He wouldn't be "sleeping" with this other woman . . . and there surely wouldn't be any emotional attachment. So, there could be no validity to one's claim he was committing adultery. This was just an enterprising woman – a woman with a son. And Calvin would be providing much needed financial assistance to the two poor souls. That's what was going on here. He would be contributing to the coffers for two needy individuals . . . who could significantly benefit from his money.

But Calvin knew all his convoluted logic was a sham. He'd already made up his mind. He wasn't going to squander this rare opportunity to experience such forbidden pleasure.

\* \* \* \* \* \* \* \* \* \* \* \* \*

As he trudged up the hill he remembered Dolly said she lived in a room adjacent to the quarters of the woman who kept her son. But he didn't recall which door was Dolly's. He tried to remember specifically what she'd said. But details escaped him – especially out in the dark of night where he was so cold . . . and so nervous.

"Which one is it?" he thought. "The one on the right?" He tried to remember if Dolly told him which door was hers. Yet, if she told him, he had forgotten. His odds were only fifty-fifty.

He stood inches away from the door on the right. His knuckles lightly tapped on its unpainted vertical wood panels . . . held together with a sturdy "Z" reinforcement on the front. He heard nothing. So, he tapped again. Just as his fingers completed their last thump, the door opened – but, barely far enough for a face to peer out at an unexpected visitor. It wasn't Dolly.

Calvin didn't know what to say. Yet, he needn't have worried. The woman immediately spoke and filled the awkward silence. "Dolly stays next door."

And . . . with those four words . . . she closed the door and he could hear the metal fastener on the inside grind shut and secure.

"You fool," Calvin reprimanded himself. "She saw me. She saw me . . . and that wasn't part of the plan." Then he rationalized his best case - that Rebecca actually hadn't seen his face. After all, it was a very dark night. And he was wearing a black coat . . . as well as a hat with a wide brim that dropped low over his eyes.

At last, a little common sense struck his brain. "I could see her plainly. Why couldn't she have seen me? Of course, she saw me."

He walked the four steps toward the left door. And, just as he clenched a fist fit for knocking, the door cracked open a few inches. Only a hand extended through the opening – a hand whose index finger curled upward, wiggled seductively, and silently signaled its "come hither" command to proceed.

And so, he did.

It was a dreary room - sparsely furnished with a sturdy oak table, two armless

17

chairs, and a crude metal coal stove doing its best to warm the draft-riddled space. He spotted the bed and examined it. It was small and layered with wool blankets. And beneath those covers Calvin spotted Dolly's son. He was sound asleep and curled up with his knees almost touching his chin.

"Now, Mr. Cabell, I believe I've made you a promise . . . and you've made one as well. If you'd kindly place the four bits on the table, then I'm ready to send you on an exciting adventure."

There was no turning back - even though any lust that might have earlier swelled up within Calvin had, by now, fully subsided. Actually, it had evaporated. And, left in its place, there was an unsettling nausea in his stomach and an aching impulse to walk out the door.

But there was no turning back. He reached into his pocket and pulled out several noisy coins. They amounted to more than five bits. He felt cheap as he looked at them. So he placed all of the coins on the table and piled them neatly atop one another . . . shaping a tidy tower. As Dolly descended toward the floor, Calvin was unnerved that her eyes were focused upward on his.

His mind was jolted by a disturbing thought – as if a lightning bolt from heaven had struck him. How could a lifetime of unimpeachable moral integrity be subverted by just a few seconds of seduction? What price would he have to pay for a momentary moral lapse? He recalled how Eve chose to pluck the forbidden fruit after such a brief moment of temptation. Calvin recalled the consequences. She and her family were cast from grace . . . forever.

He was chilled by the thought . . . and its inevitable analogy. He considered if he, too, might be foolishly sabotaging the course of his life . . . as well as the lives of his family . . . on an uncharted and perverse path through a lost paradise.

"And now, sir, it's time for your treat. Trust me. This'll be worth twice the money?"

Calvin sat on the firm table and arched his back behind him. He stabilized the position with his arms which were ramrod straight. His torso was supported by his splayed hands . . . securely affixed on the table's surface. There was a single candle on the table. Its flame flickered in the unavoidable draft that swept through the chinks of the shed. He noticed his stack of coins haphazardly catching the meager candle light. It made the shiny metal glow dimly . . . in fits and spells.

Both parties in this wretched transaction, Calvin and Dolly, had nothing else to say to one another. Her clever insinuations had evolved into flirtations . . . and her sensuous words had eventually developed into seduction. And now, there was nothing but silence – cold, eerie silence.

Dolly unfastened the lower four buttons on his shirt and parted the cloth. She gently blew around his navel. Calvin looked down and saw his sparse brown abdomen hair bend at her breath. Then she placed her tongue in his navel and she circled the edges of the crevice until he could feel it turn uncomfortably cold from the moist bath.

All the while Dolly continued unfastening buttons. She moved to his pants' front. Working from top to bottom, she nimbly released them all so she could part the gap and pull down the waist band. Calvin raised his hips off the table while his trousers were pulled down. When he rested once again, his cold, bare bottom was pressing against the table's splintered wood surface.

Finally, Dolly employed devices she had obviously practiced many times. Her experience belied this was her first go at oral sex. She licked and blew and touched just the right places. Calvin responded. But he didn't have his heart in it.

And then she began her contractual ministrations. Instead of feeling the ecstasy all her flirty parlor games had promised, Calvin thought he had never felt sadder in his whole life. This was not what he bargained for. He had anticipated the effect of Dolly's service. However, he never expected . . . that when fantasy finally evolved into reality . . . he'd desperately long to be anywhere but here - here in this unkempt place with this devious woman.

So, as he peered down and observed how the intermittent light made Dolly's homely face look mottled and surreal, his only thought was why she was gorging herself for the lousy five bits of coins on the table beside him. And then – when Calvin realized it was futile to wish anymore he had never come here - he could only yearn that this tawdry episode would soon be over.

Yet, his regret still hadn't hit bottom. Just as he thought his own self esteem and his moral integrity had plummeted to its lowest level, he looked to his right. He realized why he wouldn't be able to bleach away this sinful stain for a long time to come.

Suddenly Calvin wasn't even aware of Dolly's handiwork. His eyes and his thoughts were consumed by the boy who lay on the bed . . . and peacefully

19

slept through it all. The child would wake up tomorrow morning with the same pure and innocent soul he had taken with him to bed earlier that evening. The boy was presently in a cherub's dreamland – far removed from the hell where Calvin presently found himself. Yet, he knew he would wake up tomorrow morning – and every morning thereafter – painfully regretting each second of this sordid experience.

But soon . . . he wasn't even conscious he was looking at Dolly's son. Mysteriously, it was Jamie Cabell he imagined was lying in that filthy bed. Jamie, his dear son, didn't deserve living in these quarters and sleeping six feet from the kinds of activities to which no child should be exposed. Neither did Dolly's Timothy. He felt sad – as sad as he'd ever been before.

He had no further consciousness of Dolly. His focus was directed solely at that blameless child who reminded him of the boy he would joyfully hold tomorrow. Calvin wished he were with Jamie then.

"I'm going to pick Jamie up when I return home tomorrow . . . and I'll send him soaring high above my head . . . while he looks down at me and laughs uncontrollably. Oh, how I do relish in that joy. And I'm going to hold him and Cassie in my arms . . . and kiss them both with all my might. Then Catherine will curl her arms around us and embrace me and the children. And I'll tell all of them how much I love them.

"That's what I'm going to do tomorrow as soon as I return home. That's exactly what I'm going to do."

# CHAPTER

# 2

Danville, Kentucky
March 1824

It was said throughout Central Kentucky that Thomas Jefferson left out an important caveat in the Declaration of Independence. God may have, indeed, created all men equal. But he created the members of the exclusive Athenaeum club "more equal than the rest of us".

There were eight members of the Athenaeum and none wanted to ever expand the group. Athenaeum was a "book club." But it was, without a doubt, far more than that. Its meetings often served as the region's innermost sanctum of power and intellect – the place where decisions were made that affected everyone in the Bluegrass. Each of the members was held in high esteem.

Henry Caldwell was a "farmer", although it had been many years since he himself tilled the soil. He owned three thousand acres of the most fertile land in the region and its annual bounty had made him rich.

Dr. Ephriam McDowell was a respected physician who was known for his remarkable surgical skills. He was also the son-in-law of Isaac Shelby, Kentucky's first governor.

Governor Shelby was clearly the most prominent member of Athenaeum. Indeed, he was the most revered citizen in the entire Commonwealth. He first gained public recognition as a war hero. When the Revolution broke out, the state was known only as Kentucky County, Virginia's huge county "over the mountains". Similarly, Tennessee was the westernmost county of North Carolina. Consequently, the two states shared a similar history as well as common heroes.

Early pioneers in both these Colonial counties were called "Overlanders", because they had traversed the Appalachian Mountains to settle in what was then called the "Western Frontier". When war broke out with England, Isaac Shelby assembled volunteer soldiers from Kentucky . . . as did his friend, John Sevier, of Tennessee. The two units eventually joined forces and successfully defeated the British Army at the Battle of King's Mountain, located in the northwest corner of South Carolina.

The victory was vitally important to the Revolutionary War effort, because the defeated English never again were a threat to the Colonies south of Virginia. John Sevier and Isaac Shelby remained fast friends from their shared military experiences. And when Tennessee became the sixteenth state in the newly independent United States, Governor Shelby's fighting friend, John Sevier, was selected as his state's first governor.

Other Athenaeum members included D.G. Cowan, a successful lawyer and a man known for his eloquence in the courtroom. Folks throughout the region would take time out when they came to Danville. Many traveled great distances . . . just to listen to him eloquently plead his case.

Dr. Averill Hempstead was a professor at Centre College. He was a Classics scholar who taught Latin and Greek.

Josiah Denton was educated at Princeton College. He settled in the Bluegrass Region in 1808. Denton was the President of the Security Bank of Danville.

Dr. Robert Chamberlain was the President of Centre College. Chamberlain was a native of Pennsylvania. He graduated from Dickinson College before studying religion at Princeton Seminary. He accepted his Presidential post in 1823 . . . four years after the college was founded.

The Kentucky territory was a haven for Presbyterians and the Athenaeum members were all members of the local church . . . except for Mr. Denton. Presbyterians had fled Virginia to escape the political and social dominance (many called it the "tyranny") of its state religion, the Church of England. Presbyterians in Virginia were forced to pay taxes to the Anglican Church and they were abused in countless other ways, as well. Their only hope to escape this unjust dominance was to separate themselves from the Anglicans with a high, impenetrable natural wall - the Appalachian Mountains.

Consequently, it was Presbyterians - largely of Scotch-Irish descent – who were among the first settlers in the Kentucky Territory. They valued education and personal achievement. Consequently, Presbyterian men usually owned most of the communities' businesses, much of the land, and they were prominent in the professions of medicine and the law.

At the age of twenty-six, John Calvin Cabell was the youngest member of the Athenaeum. Calvin's father served as a Colonel in the Revolutionary War. Like many of the officers in the nation's fight for freedom, Colonel Cabell was awarded a land grant in consideration for his service. The grant consisted of one thousand acres located along both sides of the Kentucky River. The road between Lexington and Danville crossed through the property. Therefore, Colonel Cabell operated a ferry service across the river. Calvin was just nine years old when he began working aboard the vessel.

Because the ferry was essential to the region's travelers, everyone who traveled along the busy Lexington Road knew him. Each passenger was impressed with his charm, his intelligence, and his diligence in meeting each customer's needs.

\* \* \* \* \* \* \* \* \* \* \* \*

One of the Cabell Ferry's regular customers was James Barry. Barry moved from Northern Ireland with his family when he was a lad of ten. Many of the family's acquaintances had emigrated earlier. They came to settle in the countryside around Lexington. The Barrys eventually followed in their wake. Yet, when he was only thirteen years old, James Barry was orphaned . . . along with his brother and sister.

The close network of fellow Presbyterian immigrants offered to raise the Barry children. Three different families offered to adopt and educate one of the children. But no family offered to adopt all three siblings. James was determined to keep the brothers and their sister glued together as a tight family unit.

To earn money, Barry took household supplies on consignment and he went from door to door selling them. He was so successful that by the age of eighteen he had opened a general merchandise store along the Lexington Road at Nicholasville. By the time James Barry was twenty-two, the number of stores he owned had multiplied to four. In addition to the first store, he established branches in Harrodsburg, Danville, and his largest store was located on the south end of Main Street in Lexington.

In 1798 Barry married one of the more eligible young ladies in the Bluegrass,

Julia Simmons. In 1800 the couple welcomed a daughter whom they named Catherine. Catherine grew – like her mother – to be a lovely, gracious, and intelligent young lady. She was educated at the Harper School for Young Ladies. She was also immensely popular with all the boys in Lexington.

Late one afternoon in October of 1818 Calvin was steering the ferry across the Kentucky River. The river's steep limestone canyon downstream seemed cold, dark, and clammy - even though the autumn rays that afternoon were brutally intense. He remembered his backside was chilled, while his face was seared by the sun. Calvin thought he heard a carriage approaching from the southwest. But when he tried to look toward the sounds of galloping horses' hooves, he was blinded by the afternoon's brilliant sunlight. He cupped his hand over his eyes - like a visor. Only then did he catch the first glimpse of the man who would mold his future.

James Barry was returning home that fall afternoon after visiting his Danville store. He drove a snappy two-horse carriage. As usual, Calvin latched a hemp rope to the bridles of the horses, threw a gunny sack over each one's head, and he calmly directed the team on to the ferry. Then he secured the wheels of the carriage to the deck. As the boat began to slide across the smooth-as-glass surface of the river, James Barry ambled to the front of the boat and he began to chat with the helpful lad. This was certainly not the first conversation the young boatman had with the successful older gentleman. But Calvin could sense that Mr. Barry was being particularly friendly this afternoon. He was almost solicitous.

After the raft docked on the river's east bank and Calvin freed the carriage from its leather bindings, Barry turned to his young ferryman.

"Calvin. I want to extend a sincere invitation to you . . . to be our houseguest one Sabbath. You could arrive on a Saturday evening and then join us on Sunday for services at the McChord Memorial Church. I know Mrs. Barry would want to invite a group of church members to Sunday dinner. I think you deserve some carefree time in Lexington. I also think you'll be able to meet a number of our friends who might one day be important contacts later in life."

Calvin was taken aback by the sudden, but generous invitation. He restrained his initial emotions and his face demonstrated no visible sign of surprise. He could buy some extra time to consider what he had just heard while he led Barry's horses and carriage down the ferry ramp. Finally, he turned to Mr. Barry and extended his hand.

"Mr. Barry, your invitation is mighty kind. I'm overwhelmed by your hospitality." He paused for just a fraction of a second and then he broke into a smile. "I would be honored to meet your family and your friends."

James Barry gave Calvin a friendly pat on the shoulder with his left hand while his right hand grasped at the reins. "Excellent, Calvin, let's agree here and now that your visit will be the weekend after next."

"Yes, sir, I can be there then . . . and I will."

"Excellent . . . we shall expect you for supper that Saturday evening at about seven o'clock."

During his Lexington visit, Calvin Cabell - whose good natured presence had warmed the hearts of so many of his ferry passengers - just as quickly melted the hearts of the Barry family and their acquaintances. But one family member was especially smitten with the weekend visitor. Catherine Barry was dressing for church with the assistance of her mother when she looked straight into Julia's eyes and blurted out, "Mother, dear, I truly believe our striking houseguest will one day become my husband."

The three-year courtship of Catherine Barry and Calvin Cabell began during that weekend visit. Calvin soon enrolled at Transylvania University in Lexington so he could be near his Catherine. The couple were betrothed in January of Calvin's last year as a student and they married the following June.

Calvin and Catherine settled in Danville. His father-in-law appointed him manager of the Barry General Merchandise Store. James Barry said he desperately needed a man with good sense and a personal magnetism to grow the business in Danville. Then, in 1821, after the birth of the couple's son, James Barry Cabell, Barry announced he was going to make Calvin a partner in the growing chain of stores.

\* \* \* \* \* \* \* \* \* \* \* \* \* \* \* \*

Following the death of Dr. Malcolm Reed, Calvin was enthusiastically issued an invitation to join the Athenaeum. He might have been far younger than the other members of the venerable club, but his sharply honed intellect impressed all of the elder members.

Governor Shelby was particularly impressed with Calvin. The two often spent hours together wandering about his large farm. They both enjoyed philosophical conversations . . . even while loading pigs to take to market or inspecting Shelby's burley tobacco crop.

Isaac Shelby had made it clear to one and all that his days in politics were over. Yet many people still made the trek to the Shelby farm where they tried to sway the Governor's influence or seek his patronage. Governor Shelby knew Calvin Cabell harbored no hidden agenda. He trusted him. Likewise, Calvin looked upon Isaac Shelby as his mentor and his good friend.

The March meeting of the Athenaeum was at the home of Dr. Chamberlain. There was no official residence for the Centre College President. Five years after it was founded the college was still trying to survive from one term to the next. Fortunately, Henry Caldwell allowed Dr. Chamberlain and his family to reside in a moderately grand residence he had built on West Main Street . . . one block from the college's sole building, Olde Centre.

The house was a brick, two-story structure designed in the Federal style. Caldwell originally built the residence for his daughter and her husband. However, his son-in-law accepted a teaching position at Transylvania University, so they never lived there once it was completed. President Chamberlain and the Board of Trustees were deeply grateful for Caldwell's gracious generosity.

As was her custom every night, Mrs. Chamberlain lit candles which she sat on the home's interior window sills. She thought her home should appear inviting to one and all – especially to students who were welcome to drop by at any time of the day or night. On each side of the front door were large mounted oil lamps which glowed brighter inside the bevel edged glass box .

All the Athenaeum members arrived promptly at six o'clock. Each of Dr. Chamberlain's guests walked to the dinner meeting except for Governor Shelby. He made the trip from his farm located south of town in a liveried carriage. Shelby was now seventy-two years old and he had grown noticeably feeble in recent years. But his mind was still sharp and his wit was without parallel.

President Chamberlain watched for Governor Shelby's arrival from inside the parlor window. When he spied the approaching carriage, he whisked out the door to greet his aged guest. Shelby emerged ever so gingerly, as he had recently taken a fall while negotiating the three metal steps that descended from his carriage's floor.

"Welcome, Governor. It's always an honor to have you visit our home. You

26

look especially hale and hearty tonight," President Chamberlain exclaimed with a smile as he extended his hand toward Isaac Shelby.

Everyone always made on over Governor Shelby. But, since Isaac Shelby was Centre College's Chairman of the Board of Trustees . . . as well as one of its founders . . . Robert Chamberlain was expected to be especially attentive to the esteemed statesman.

"Everyone has arrived, Governor. Allow me to assist you up the front steps."

"I still can manage by myself, President Chamberlain, so long as I use my cane."

Chamberlain glanced at the cane's oddly shaped staff and its curiously curvaceous handle. "Your cane is quite unique. There must be a story behind it."

Shelby had two more steps yet to negotiate. His right hand clutched the wrought iron railing while he propped himself up with the unusual staff in his left hand. He rested momentarily and turned toward Chamberlain. "Well, this pathetic excuse for a walking stick is a newfangled contraption that was given to me by Senator Crittenden. It's called a shillelagh. It comes from Ireland. Apparently, all the members of the U.S. Senate were presented one of these hopelessly gnarled sticks by the Ambassador from Great Britain.

Shelby's son-in-law, Ephraim McDowell, emerged from the house and stood at the threshold of the open door. He extended his helping hand. "Good evening, Governor," he said. "I've already poured you a glass of some special medicine I concocted. It may taste like President Chamberlain's sherry at first. But I'm certain if you drink every last drop, you'll likely throw away your new cane and skip merrily home tonight."

"Ephraim, I know I should be thankful my daughter has married a renowned physician. But, I still question your medical qualifications when I hear you speak such blarney."

"Blarney?" responded the doctor to his father-in-law. "What's 'blarney'?"

"It's a new Irish word the British Ambassador taught Crittenden and his fellow Senators. It means . . . well, it means the sort of aromatic substance that fills your back yard privy."

27

All the Athenaeum members were within hearing distance of this quip and Isaac Shelby's candid explanation was met with much laughter. The men all went inside and congregated by the fireplace in the home's parlor. The floor was made from random width oak panels that had been pegged together. They glistened from repeated waxing, so the floor's reflection of the firelight glowed just as intensely as the fire itself.

Promptly at six-thirty Mrs. Chamberlain stood in the front hallway. She announced the meal would be served in the dining room, the other large room located at the front of the house. Chamberlain sat at one end of the table with Governor Shelby seated to his right. This was the seat he always reserved for an honored guest. The meal consisted of a rich beef burgoo accompanied with fried hominy and turnip greens.

It was the responsibility of each month's host to moderate the discussion of the book that all were to have read prior to the meeting. This month's book was *The Pioneers*, by James Fenimore Cooper. The novel was published in 1823 and it was recommended to Chamberlain by a friend in New York City as well as by a former colleague in Pennsylvania. Cooper wasn't a well-known author, but both men touted him as being, perhaps, the first truly American novelist. Clearly, this hype piqued the interest of all the Athenaeum members.

The moderator always began the discussion by summarizing highlights from the novel which he thought were important and should be discussed. Furthermore, he was responsible for fielding and directing members' questions, arbitrating any literary comments, and inviting all other contributions that might merit sustained intellectual intercourse.

Chamberlain asked the members to consider the symbolism of the novel's protagonist, Natty Bumppo. His ethnic background wasn't fully clear, but he was the product of both European and Native American stock.

Indians were ordinarily demonized by writers as hostile savages. Attorney Cowan speculated Cooper was intimating that Natty's white blood . . . mixed with the Indians' savage blood . . . had made him superior to both races. Or, did Natty represent the best of both worlds? Why was Natty Bumppo, at the age of seventy, still serving as a scout for white pioneers in 1793? Was his elderly age advocating the collective wisdom a man of great experience can only accumulate over many years living harmoniously with nature?

Jeremiah Denton expressed his opinion. "Surely, any reader would conclude Bumppo was a noble person – perhaps, a noble savage. He resented and

28

chided the white settlers for needlessly killing off the animals in the New York wilderness. They hunted for sport – for the thrill of the kill. Yet the Indians hunted solely to sustain themselves. Isn't it, therefore, reasonable for one who lives a life professing and protecting the balance of nature . . . to suspiciously regard any man who doesn't? Where's the connection to God among white people who slaughter animals relentlessly? Natty considered them to be Godless. These are the themes I think we should discuss this evening."

Ephraim McDowell turned to his left to address Hempstead. "Professor Hempstead, allow me to give you a quick pop quiz. The subject is etymology. Are you game?"

Hempstead blurted out a laugh, but anyone at the table could tell that beneath the chuckle lurked the formative stages of terror. The scholar had no interest in flunking a surprise test in front of members of the Athenaeum.

"My word, a spontaneous translation request", he thought to himself. "And he's demanding a translation here in the presence of the President of the College and the Chairman of the Board of Trustees. I'll be run out of town if I make a fool of myself. But I have no choices here."

Hempstead cleared his voice and responded to the challenge. "The professor is ready, Dr. McDowell. Fire away."

"I'm curious about the derivation of Mr. Cooper's title. The word, 'pioneer', stumps me. My Latin and Greek abilities have grown rusty. What's the root word . . . and its meaning, Hempstead?"

Hempstead was immediately relieved. He had just come across the answer less than two weeks earlier. "Dr. McDowell, the Latin root word is a relative of 'ped' or 'foot'. Hence, the Latin word for a foot soldier sent out ahead of his fellow warriors is "pio". Hence, a pioneer is one who proceeds into uncharted country ahead of the general population."

"Aha, Hempstead, you've done it again," exclaimed Dr. McDowell. "Actually, I was less curious to know the word's derivation as I was hoping to stump you."

Hempstead chuckled and feigned a modest look following his latest achievement at root word derivations. But he knew McDowell spoke the truth. For the doctor and many others, playing a game of "stump the professor" was pure sport. And it was a sport in which he was always the prey . . . and never the predator.

"Dr. McDowell, I think in the future I shall require you to submit your derivation questions in writing . . . with the expectation you shall receive a response within one week. Is that fair, sir?"

President Chamberlain was among those who laughed out loud. He then spoke to end this etymological debate. "Good job, Professor Hempstead. It appears you continue to read the Holy Bible in the original Greek and you're still sharp as a tack. Congratulations."

The President paused in a manner that foretold a quip was coming. "What else could explain such Divine intervention this evening? Almighty God has once again swooped down to save your reputation as a Classics scholar."

"And," Denton volunteered, "saving your job, as well."

The laughter swelled around the table and Hempstead was chuckling as jovially as anyone.

Calvin Cabell was unusually intrigued during the novel's discussion. He sat silently. Suddenly he realized that each of the men who sat around the table – except for him - had been, at one point in their lives, a "pioneer". They had been American "foot soldiers" in the Kentucky Territory who paved the way for others to follow . . . and settle.

Each of the men had immigrated to Kentucky from some homestead east of the Alleghenies. And each had played a part in taming the 'western frontier'- as Kentucky was known then. Cabell suddenly felt out of place . . . as if he were, somehow, inferior. He was well liked by his Athenaeum friends. Could any pioneer who settled and shaped Kentucky truly respect a younger man who grew up privileged in a gentrified family? Calvin wondered if he merited any admiration from an enterprising group like the older Athenaeum members.

After reading *The Pioneers* Calvin had a newfound regard for each of the Athenaeum "pioneers". However, he felt as if he had lost some of the regard he had for himself. The experiences of this evening were unsettling . . . like an unexpected epiphany.

When the gentlemen concluded their discussion and Chamberlain adjourned the formal meeting for the evening, most of the men ambled toward the front parlor where they lit their tobacco pipes and began casual conversations.

Laughter peppered the atmosphere.

Governor Shelby lingered at the dinner table next to Calvin. They were the only two members who remained seated, so the young man seized the opportunity to have Shelby listen to the issues he had been mulling over in his mind for the past few minutes. He spoke before Shelby could rise and join the others. "Governor, this has been a most provocative evening for me. Might I share some thoughts and concerns with you before we join the others?"

"It's always my pleasure to chat with you, Calvin. Surely you know that."

"Indeed, Governor, and I appreciate your friendship. But at the moment I hope to seek your guidance . . . and to tap into your wisdom."

"My wisdom, I fear, is ebbing. But I'll try summoning up some sage advice for you."

Calvin revealed to Shelby his sudden concern. Had he had played his life safe – perhaps, too safe? Possibly, he had stayed too close to home. He had enjoyed the fruits of his father's pioneer spirit as well as the many benefits of his father-in-law's achievements. He asked Shelby to offer a retrospective of his own pioneer life. Had being a pioneer and settling a frontier enriched his spirit . . . more than if he had grown up and remained with his family in Virginia?

"What crossed my mind tonight, Calvin, as we discussed Mr. Cooper's novel, was just how recently the pioneer days actually were. It seems as if Kentucky was the frontier just the day before yesterday. To a young man . . . twenty-five years is an eternity. But to an old man looking back on his life, it's merely a flash in time. And twenty-five years ago, Kentucky was just transforming from a wilderness into a regional community that needed to separate itself from Virginia . . . and go it alone.

"If you're lucky enough to live a long life as I have, Calvin, you'll also look back and say that a quarter of a century passed by very quickly. You have to understand that many of us you're calling 'pioneers' weren't necessarily attracted to an untamed frontier that we thought we could develop. Most of us were escaping something. Some of us were escaping our families. Some were escaping an oppressive state religion. And, I think it should be pointed out that some of us were even escaping ourselves."

Calvin was intrigued by what he was hearing. Governor Shelby was being unusually philosophical. He was drilling through the bone . . . to strike at the marrow of this young man's self-searching.

"Unless I'm mistaken, you have no reason to flee further west into the wilderness, Calvin. Once one has enjoyed the comforts and freedoms made possible by his pioneer forbearers, it becomes easy to be complacent. I understand that . . . and I have no problems with it. I'm sure I speak for the others as well."

Isaac Shelby had struck a raw nerve within Calvin. Was the Governor unintentionally categorizing him as a "complacent" slug? Surely, this wasn't an intentional slur, or, was it?

"But, sir . . . there are vast territories in this nation that cry out to be settled. Who will these settlers be? Where will they come from? There's still a need for pioneers, isn't there?"

"The settlers of this century, Calvin, will be people just like you. Indeed, our nation desperately needs men like you to pave the way in the West . . . to establish further settlements for future generations. Consider the impact of President Jefferson's Louisiana Purchase. This country doubled its already significant size with the mere stroke of a pen. Thousands of square miles were bought at just three cents an acre . . . and not one ounce of blood needed to be shed. I'd venture to speculate the next generation of pioneers will be rugged individuals who aren't fleeing something as many of us did. They'll move on and seek their fortunes in the West. And, Calvin, I have no doubt there are fortunes to be made. Very few of the pioneers who passed through the Cumberland Gap into Kentucky expected to become rich. To my mind, it's these 'pioneer' motivations to become rich which will be the greatest distinction between my generation and yours."

"So, in your estimation, Governor, where in this Louisiana Territory do you foresee are the greatest opportunities for the modern day pioneers you describe?"

President Chamberlain and Henry Caldwell had returned to the table by this time. They were wondering why Calvin and the Governor hadn't joined them in the parlor. Both men could detect a very serious conversation was taking place between the youngster and the old statesman.

"Gentlemen, didn't we enjoy a thorough discussion of *The Pioneers*? Are the two of you sitting here still debating the complexities of Natty Bumppo?" quipped Henry Caldwell. "Won't you now join us and the others in the parlor?"

Isaac Shelby gave Caldwell's teasing no consideration. He looked up at Chamberlain and asked his host, "Dr. Chamberlain, might you have a map of the United States here at home - one that illustrates the Louisiana Purchase Territory?"

"Yes, I do, Governor. Would you like to inspect it?"

"If it's not too much trouble, I would appreciate you fetching it. Calvin here has asked me a most provocative question and I need such a map to adequately explain my response."

Chamberlain moved toward the large oak chest that stood in the hallway. He stooped over it to remove from the bottom drawer a paper scroll that was rolled up and bound by twine. As he made his way back to the table, Henry Caldwell found himself so intrigued with the suspense of what appeared to be forthcoming, he had already seated himself on the other side of Calvin . . . who now sat in the middle.

Chamberlain unfolded the curled up document and spread it on the table directly in front of Calvin. The edges of the map were feisty. They kept springing back toward the map's center. President Chamberlain placed one of the water glasses over New England and the other over the new Northwest Territory. Chamberlain was somewhat curious himself about what was going on at his own table. So, he stood behind Calvin and awaited Governor Shelby's impending tutorial.

"Gentlemen, Calvin and I have pushed beyond our discussion about Mr. Cooper's pioneers in New York State. We're now peering into the future of the American frontier - the land west of the Mississippi. Calvin has inquired about my opinions regarding where the best prospects for economic success await present day pioneers. He's asked my opinion where on this map I believe fortunes can be made by today's young settlers."

Henry Caldwell sat up . . . then he leaned over the western part of the large map. "Well, I don't intend to miss such sagacious counsel. I'm sure Governor Shelby will offer us a tip from which we can all make some money. Please, continue, Governor, as you certainly have my attention."

"First, gentlemen, we must recognize we live in an entirely new era. Things are far different from the time when settlements were established along the Atlantic coastline over one hundred years ago. Boston, New York, and

Philadelphia grew because each became an important port for ocean shipping. Today, however, it will be steamboats plying along inland rivers that define which locations along America's waterways will grow and prosper. Rivers will be the highways for commerce now . . . and forever. My strategy is, therefore, to peer into the future and locate these new inland ports."

The Governor leaned over the map and instructed his student. "Look at the scale of this map, Calvin, and tell me the distance between St. Louis and New Orleans."

Chamberlain and Caldwell were calculating silently along with Calvin as he measured the scale of the map's legend. It indicated each cross line represented fifty miles. Calvin kept his thumb and middle finger rigid as he marked off each fifty mile interval. "There are approximately five hundred and fifty miles between the two cities, Governor."

"An excellent mathematical mind you have, Calvin. And five hundred fifty miles is a lengthy distance, wouldn't you say?"

"Yes, sir, five hundred miles is a substantial distance between cities. But there'll eventually be many cities that spring up along the Mississippi River between New Orleans and St. Louis. Surely, anyone would predict the same?"

Isaac Shelby took on the look of the cat that swallowed the canary. "My silly Socratic questioning about this map's scale was designed to both make my point and to answer your question. There's a flaw to your logic, Calvin. Almost the entire length of the lower Mississippi River is surrounded by a vast, flat, alluvial flood plain. Flooding along the Mississippi makes the width of the river - at some points - as wide as seven miles . . . or even more. Only the rare highlands along the river banks are safe from flooding. They are few . . . and far between. They're known as the Chickasaw bluffs."

"A fact about which you have personal knowledge, Governor," spoke Henry Caldwell.

"Indeed," Shelby replied.

"I still don't understand your point, Governor Shelby."

"Here's the point, Calvin. Surely you must know I'm a good friend of General Jackson. The two of us represented the United States in the purchase of the Chickasaw Territory. We paid those red rascals far too much money. But that's another story for another day. Once the title to the land along the Mississippi was cleared as a result of the purchase, General Jackson and two of his Middle Tennessee friends bought out the claim to a parcel that was filed by a white man prior to the Chickasaw purchase. These claims were 'clouded', as they say, because the Indians actually owned the land.

"But Jackson and his friends, Judge Overton and General Winchester, established a partnership. With the land in the Chickasaw Territory now cleansed of title disputes, they bought a large tract on a high bluff. They've surveyed it and they'll soon file a City Plan with the State of Tennessee."

"They've named the town Memphis," interjected Dr. Chamberlain. "There was a large advertisement placed in a Louisville newspaper I recently noticed and read. Of course, such advertisements are commonplace and I always consider their optimistic rhetoric to be hyperbolic."

Caldwell added an additional comment. "Wasn't there an Egyptian city bearing the name, Memphis?"

"Yes, it was the ancient capital of Egypt," Chamberlain continued. "The great pyramids were located nearby. However, the Egyptian Memphis didn't survive. Sand is all one will find now where great buildings and temples once rose above the Nile."

Governor Shelby nodded his head in agreement. "That's correct, Dr. Chamberlain. Mind you, there are only three things I know about this new city's prospects. First: It's situated on one of the very infrequent bluffs along the Lower Mississippi. Second: General Jackson and his partners appear very positive about their investment. And third: General Jackson's well-known aspirations to become the President of our country have forced him to sell much – if not all – his interest in the investment. Memphis is barely a hamlet at present. But his political enemies cite his ownership as a serious conflict of interest . . . given his government role in the Indian sale. I think land prices there are presently a buyer's market."

Finally, Calvin Cabell asked Isaac Shelby about the very heart of the presentation he had laid before them. "So, Governor, you consider General Jackson's investment called Memphis to be an up-and-coming city – one where a contemporary pioneer would have realistic prospects for financial success?"

Shelby turned to Calvin Cabell and responded as he began to push himself away from the dinner table. "You've heard the evidence. You can weigh the logic of my little dog and pony show, Calvin. I make no warranties about the quality of my reasoning."

Governor Shelby then stood and leaned forward toward Calvin. His hands held the back of his wooden chair. "But if I had an itch to be a pioneer, I'd give General Jackson's enterprise some consideration. Call it a 'research project'."

Governor Shelby looked down once again at the map and everyone could see he was contemplating something. After several seconds he looked up again at his young friend. "If you'd like, Calvin, I'd be happy to write to General Jackson on your behalf. I could ask him for updated information about Memphis . . . and I could inquire if there might be an opportunity there awaiting a 'pioneer' such as yourself. Does that seem like a suitable plan of action to you?"

"Governor, I'm humbled by your kind offer. Yes, such information from the General would be very interesting . . . and much appreciated."

"Well, then, I shall write to Jackson in the next few days. I'm actually curious to know for my own sake what's happening along the Lower Mississippi Valley."

Isaac Shelby put his hand to his mouth to stifle a yawn. "Gentlemen, the time is getting late and I have a considerable distance to travel home. I thank you, Dr. Chamberlain, for your hospitality. Please, extend my thanks to Mrs. Chamberlain as well. The meal was outstanding."

Governor Shelby moved slowly toward the hall where his cloak and hat were offered to him. Dr. McDowell assisted Shelby as he put on his outer garments. By now all the Athenaeum members had assembled around the Governor to bid goodbye to their friend. Chamberlain opened the front door and helped Shelby negotiate the steps and the walkway leading to his waiting carriage.

Just as Shelby was prepared to make the first step up into his compartment, Calvin came running out of the house waving the warped cane the Governor used upon his arrival.

"Governor . . . Governor . . . you've forgotten your shillelagh. Here it is."

Isaac Shelby beamed fondly at Calvin. It was a look that showed his appreciation, but he also seemed perplexed. "Calvin, do you remember how I defined the Irish word, 'blarney'?"

"Yes, Governor, I do."

"Well, my friend, I've fed you a lot of blarney this evening. Why don't you keep my shillelagh as a reminder of this dinner . . . and, also, as a warning to beware all the blarney you'll inevitably hear in the future from fools like me. I think I'll stick with my tried and true Kentucky oak cane. Good evening, Calvin. Come see me . . . anytime . . . about anything."

"Thank you, sir. I'll remember that and I'll cherish your gift. I'm, thankfully, not quite in need of a good shillelagh, but I'll enjoy keeping it as a gift from a valued friend."

Isaac Shelby turned again to climb into his carriage with the assistance of Ephraim McDowell. Then McDowell climbed in and the coachman closed the door.

Calvin Cabell stood alone on the curb as he watched the rear mounted lamps on Shelby's carriage get dimmer and dimmer as it moved east on Main Street. He considered everything this great man had accomplished in his life. If wisdom is derived from experience, then Calvin considered he had been blessed by Shelby's lecture.

Governor Shelby had . . . perhaps, unknowingly . . . infected Calvin with a notion that began to prickle just beneath the surface of his skin.

It was a nagging sort of itch. And it was an itch that, most certainly, needed to be scratched.

# CHAPTER

# 3

March 1824
Memphis, Tennessee

Marcus Brutus Winchester stood so close to the sharp edge of the river bluff, his toes could have curled over its rim. One step more would send him free falling down the steep ravine and into the river . . . forty feet below. He breathed deeply and gazed, as usual, with amazement at the vista he saw. Today wasn't the first time he stood there in awed silence. Over time, he had made it a ritual – a veritable religious rite.

This promontory was located about one mile south of the Wolf River's mouth. Marcus looked north for a time. He daydreamed about where all the water meandering below him had begun its journey. He knew the Mississippi River basin was immense. Rainfall – even rainfall in parts of the state of New York - flowed into creeks . . . that fed streams . . . that flowed into the Allegheny River which emptied into the Ohio River. Then the Ohio, in turn, contributed its liquid lode to the Mississippi. So, presently, far away New York and Minnesota rainwater was now continuing its journey below him – along its lazy journey toward the Gulf of Mexico.

He had carefully studied everything he could learn about the river's great tributary basin to the north . . . and to the west. The Lewis and Clark expedition discovered and mapped new, distant rivers. They proved even melted snow from a thousand miles away in British North America or the great Rocky Mountain Range followed the natural pull of gravity ever downward - until this once frozen water from the snow-capped peaks of the Rockies was also passing below where he stood.

Winchester rotated his attention to the left about ninety degrees. The river made a sharp turn toward the west beneath where he stood. He was never able to decide which panorama was more majestic than the other. Was it the view toward the north . . . where he could observe much of the continent's water surging toward him? Or was it this western perspective . . . after the flowing water had already passed by and saluted him with twinkling sparkles atop the slow moving current? When the sun set low into the southwest horizon, it painted this westward view of the river with a coat of glimmering orange. For miles the rusty river water shimmered in the twilight while its once fiery color grew ever grayer . . . until it eventually shaded into the darkness.

He could never make up his mind. And when he finally turned to leave behind the bluff's glorious gallery, he carried home with him the same thought as always. "There is, indeed, a powerful deity who presides over the earth. I've seen His work – and I've worshipped Him and His creation this day. Glory be to God."

As Marcus walked away from the river he passed by the ancient Indian mound that was built long, long ago. The huge hump stood just one hundred feet from the edge of the bluff. He knew he could enjoy a better vantage point at the higher elevation a climb to the top would afford him. But he had always considered this earthen edifice to be sacred to the Indians – and, thus, to him as well. It was beyond his comprehension how Indians using the crudest of tools could transport such massive amounts of dirt to this site. The top of the mound was thirty feet above its base. And the base had an approximate diameter of fifty feet. It must have taken years to build. But, for what reason, he did not know.

This river promontory was hallowed ground in other ways. Winchester had no doubt other men . . . who were either praised or reviled in legends . . . had also stood here.

It was a confirmed fact Hernando DeSoto brought his Spanish gold seekers to the mouth of the Wolf River back in 1541. Marcus did the math. Almost three hundred years had passed between then and now, 1824.

The Spaniards spent two grueling years traveling north from Tampa Bay. Then they headed northwest through the Florida and Mississippi Territories. They were a merciless lot of white men. They were convinced the Indians were concealing from them the location of vast gold deposits. The conquistadores in Mexico had become rich from the gold and silver they confiscated. DeSoto must have reasoned there was gold waiting to be plundered here, too, in the middle of the North American continent.

Again and again the Spaniards tried to either annex or annihilate the Indian

40

tribes along their way. They never succeeded . . . and many of DeSoto's men died in the effort. DeSoto crossed the Mississippi River at this same point. On the Arkansas side, he and his men wandered aimlessly through the bayous and the brush. But there was no gold to be had. And, threatening or killing innocent Indians who couldn't show them where non-existent gold deposits lay was an exercise in futility.

There was no doubt DeSoto looked up and down the river from this very vantage point where Marcus stood. No doubt DeSoto was dreaming the yellow sunsets he saw reflected on the water were premonitions that veins of gold were ripe for the plucking . . . just over the next river . . or around the next bend.

Father Marquette and his merchant friend, Joliet, also passed by the bluff as they made their way in tiny pirogues from Lake Michigan to the Gulf. Marquette was a missionary. But instead of evangelizing the Indians he met along the way, he paved the way for Joliet and others to follow in his path. Near the mouth of the Mississippi Joliet raised a crudely constructed wood cross and laid claim to all the land that lay in the Mississippi River Basin for the Sun King, Louis XIV of France.

"How could it be possible that the French explorers journeyed down this monstrous river and hadn't stopped at this place on the bluff to marvel at the view? Surely, both Marquette and Joliet had, also, once stood at this very spot."

But it was presently 1824 and Marcus Winchester was just one of a handful of white men who claimed as their home a newly minted town named Memphis. There were a few white men who had lived in the area during the past hundred years. They survived by trading with the Chickasaw and Choctaw Indians who lived and roamed over most of West Tennessee, Mississippi, and Alabama. The bluff at the Wolf River mouth had been a place where tribes for many years rendezvoused to barter with one another . . . in peace.

Marcus Winchester's father was one of the three founders of Memphis. General James Winchester served ably in the Continental Army. He was granted land twenty miles north of Nashville where he built a fine home he called Cragfont. Marcus grew up there.

General Winchester's friend and the hero of the Battle of New Orleans, General Andrew Jackson, spent much of his career fighting the Creek and Seminole Indians in Florida and Alabama. When the Indians were either killed or forced into submission, Jackson then turned his attention to the peace loving Cherokee, the Choctaw, and the Chickasaw Indians who lived and hunted farther north. He wanted them permanently removed – far, far away from the white settlers spilling over the Appalachian Mountains.

To claim much of this land by waging war would have cost many white lives. And those settlers who survived the fight would probably, in turn, try to massacre the Indians. So the United States Government authorized Jackson to negotiate a sale of the Indian land east of the Mississippi. President James Monroe asked the first Governor of Kentucky, Isaac Shelby, to assist General Jackson in the negotiations. In 1818, after employing clear threats and intimidation that these tribes would face the same fate as the Creeks and Seminoles if the U.S. Government's offer wasn't accepted, Jackson and Shelby brokered a deal in which the Indians would receive $400,000 over twenty years.

Jackson and his Nashville business partner, Judge John Overton, recognized the strategic value of this bluff. It was doubly blessed by geography. Settlements here would never endure flooding . . . unlike almost every inch of shore line along the lower Mississippi. Furthermore, the bluff was luckily situated at the mouth of another navigable river. But there were claims, cloudy at best, that had been filed on the same plot of land Jackson and Overton wanted to control.

John Rice visited the same strategic location years earlier. In 1783 he returned to Hillsboro, North Carolina, where he filed a claim for five thousand acres for which he paid the state a nominal consideration. There was also a claim for an adjacent five thousand acres filed by John Ramsay. The Ramsey claim adjoined Rice's land to the south.

Marcus Winchester's father was invited to join Overton's and Jackson's investment group. General Winchester's responsibility was to survey the Rice parcel and its adjoining land. Winchester selected the name, Memphis, for this real estate investment. He was a great admirer of history - especially, the ancient Egyptians. His first choice of names was Cairo. But that name had already been taken. Memphis, the ancient capital of Egypt, long ago had wasted away into the desert sand. Winchester relished the thought that this once great ancient city would rise again - like the mythical Phoenix – here along North America's version of the Nile River.

Neither Jackson, Overton, or Winchester had any interest in settling on this promising parcel on the river. So, it was important that a capable representative of the owners devote his efforts to promote the little town and to sell the lots that had been subdivided.

General Winchester's son, Marcus Brutus, (another example of his father's fascination with historical figures) was assigned this responsibility. So, Marcus moved to Memphis in 1820. Everyone who met the young man praised his keen mind, his refinement, and they remarked about what an unusually handsome man he was.

Marcus Winchester buoyed his hopes he could create a viable city based upon several recent developments. He kept repeating a two pronged mantra.

First, westward settlement of the Louisiana Purchase Territory would surely swell and Memphis' chances for survival and growth would swell with it.

Second, the city's future lay in its unique relationship to the Mississippi River and the technological breakthroughs in river transportation that had advanced in recent years.

"Steamboats," Marcus repeated over and over. "Steamboats will be our salvation."

By 1824 steamboat traffic along the Mississippi was steadily growing. At last, there was hope a boat could travel upstream . . . against the strong river currents. In 1815 the 'Enterprise', an eighteen by twenty-nine foot vessel, succeeded making the first successful journey. It managed to travel all the way from New Orleans to Louisville. But the boat plied mostly through shallow flood waters along the way. The current was minimal. Those conditions wouldn't likely apply to any other vessel which tried to replicate this elusive transportation milestone.

The first steamboats of the era continued to incorporate the deep hull design of keel boats . . . that traveled only with the current. The steam engine that propelled the original boats' design was located beneath the deck . . . and within its arching hull.

Then, Henry Shreve had an idea that was quite simple, yet revolutionary. He decided to place the steam engine and the drive shaft of the boat on the main deck. This relocation negated the need for the deep hull. In its place, Shreve designed an almost flat hull . . . so a vessel would experience very little resistance against the strong river currents.

As a bonus to this important engineering advancement, Shreve was able to greatly expand the deck space on board. The boat's deck dimensions could be significantly expanded . . . and Shreve also added a second level atop the main deck. This doubled the boat's surface area and its capacity to carry freight.

Fortunately for General Jackson and the fledgling nation, Shreve's first steamboat was ideal to quickly transport hundreds of troops to the Battle of New Orleans. Jackson called Henry Shreve "a national hero". He said the battle against the British might not have been won without Shreve's invention.

Shreve then tackled the last obstacle pilots traveling the Mississippi routinely encountered. Snags of stumps and trees often sealed off a river channel from navigation. Consequently, he designed a boat he named the "Heliopolis". Its sole purpose was to clear the channels from such natural barriers. The U.S. government employed him to remove snags up and down the river and Henry Shreve became a very rich man.

Everyone living along the nation's navigable waterways was excited about the potential commerce and population growth their communities would experience in the wake of Shreve's new technology. But two years after the Memphis 'Plan for Subdivision' had been filed and approved in Nashville, only seventy-nine persons resided in the new municipality. Moreover, this population count included three Negroes and two Indians.

Steamboats were still too expensive to ship a farmer's crops down river to market. But now a farmer could easily afford his passage from New Orleans back up the river. The inexpensive passenger fare dramatically increased the number of flatboats bound for New Orleans. Instead of hundreds of boats passing south on the river each year, now there were thousands. These rafts and keel boats continued to stop in Memphis for provisions and to sell whatever cargo they carried to the locals. But their visits brought little economic value to the new Tennessee city.

Marcus Winchester forecast that all of Shreve's advancements would eventually make Memphis economically viable. Shreve's steamboat, 'Washington,' was able in 1817 to make its way from New Orleans to Louisville in just twenty-one days. This was a remarkable achievement and one Marcus thought bode well to promote investments in his town.

Winchester relied on his reasoning and his instincts as he promoted the city's subdivision plan . . . wherever he could . . . and to whomever he could. But he had to cope with a "chicken or the egg" riddle. Steamboats would make Memphis accessible for freight and passengers to be transported throughout the vast Mississippi River basin. However, until he could convince a significant number of people to settle in the area, there would be no freight or passenger traffic to warrant making Memphis a port of call for steamboats.

"Which piece of the puzzle would come first?" Marcus often debated with himself.

Winchester wrote to the three Middle Tennessee investors and told them a balanced synergism of businesses must be operating in the city before it could be expected to grow. He cited the need for businesses such as a blacksmith, a lumber mill, and a brickyard. Without these commercial components, he reported, there was little to offer permanent settlers.

He also included in his letters some reasoning about the need to identify some specific local natural resources. He couldn't think of any abundance of resources – other than the river – which could be profitably exploited.

"What resources are nearby that could make someone rich?" he reasoned.

Parts of Illinois had lead deposits. When Henry Shreve was twenty-one years old, he grossed $11,000 taking seventy tons of lead down the Mississippi on a flatboat, and then around Florida to its destination, Philadelphia. Nashville, likewise, had sufficient deposits of iron ore to warrant a foundry being established there. Marcus knew of no ore deposits that lay beneath the land he was promoting.

Then, suddenly he realized the natural resources he was seeking weren't located below the surface of the land. They were to be found at and above the surface.

The entire region was replete with hardwood forests of oak and cypress. He knew Georgia's pines were a blessed natural resource. Even Middle and East Tennessee had abundant forests. But none of the wood in these regions was like the timber around Memphis. The United States was growing rapidly and there would be, at some point in time, a huge demand for the strongest hardwood available. The country would need to construct buildings, bridges, plank roads, and all the other improvements a growing nation would require. Hardwood forests abounded in the region surrounding Memphis.

Marcus also realized the richest topsoil in the nation lay beneath the forests in the Arkansas and Mississippi Deltas. He was certain of it. Alluvial flooding over thousands of years had deposited thick layers of rich sediment.

He decided his marketing efforts should be directed to attract lumbermen to

Memphis. After all, they would doubly profit from their land purchases. After the hardwood was harvested and sold, the cleared forests could be converted into the most fertile cropland one might ever imagine.

Marcus Winchester rode his dappled horse, Marty, north along the bluff as he was considering his "Eureka" moment. He had a marketing plan now. But would the plan attract investments? Was there something he was leaving out of the equation? As Marcus approached the little settlement consisting of seventy-nine persons with big dreams, he was still contemplating if there was an Achilles' heel to his reasoning. He couldn't think of one.

The sun was just minutes from setting over the river as he unsaddled Marty and scooted him into the crude paddock he had made with his own hands. He considered everything he had done that day.

"Well, if lumber and rich farm land won't attract capital investments and settlers to this one-horse town, maybe I can catch the attention of folks who are compelled to stay . . . if only to enjoy the river sunsets."

# CHAPTER

# 4

March 1824
Danville, Kentucky

It was conventional wisdom among folks in the Bluegrass that John Calvin Cabell was a man destined to become a paragon of propriety as well as a leader in business, government, and the church.

But to Calvin Cabell, anyone's prediction about his future lofty status in life wouldn't be predicated on popular opinion. He attributed his assured, high place in society to the Presbyterian doctrine of "pre-destination" which was at the core of the Calvinist teachings of his Scottish Reformation namesake, John Calvin. In short, Calvin Cabell believed he was not only pre-destined at birth to an after-life of eternal salvation as John Calvin preached. Cabell was resolute in the belief he was also pre-destined to greatness DURING his lifetime.

A stranger was quickly captivated by Cabell's charming, confident, and courteous manner. And his physical appearance added to his impressive aura. Surely God Almighty took special care creating John Calvin Cabell.

At the age of twenty-six, he was finally filling out into a young man who projected an image of physical strength in a body measured at six feet one inches tall and weighing one hundred eighty pounds. But everyone considered his eyes to be his distinctive feature. They intrigued all who gazed into them. They looked like a pair of almost mystical, azure blue pools. No one who met him could avoid being captivated by their allure. Some even said his eyes were like a spy glass that peered directly into his unsullied soul.

Everyone was thrilled when Catherine gave birth to their first child, James Barry Cabell. They called him Jamie from the day he was born. And when Jamie's younger sister, Catherine, was born three years later, in 1824, people quickly started referring to her by the name Jamie called her, Cassie. The toddler was unable to enunciate "Catherine" . . . and "Cassie" was just fine with the rest of the family. They rationalized Jamie's mispronunciation should be considered a blessing. It would forever resolve any confusion addressing either mother or daughter.

Catherine Barry was tall at five feet seven inches. Some even referred to her as statuesque. She walked about and interacted with others with an air of confidence and grace. She wore her hair in a bun tied immaculately behind the crown of her head. And when she wore a headscarf or a lace bonnet, her framed face gave off a regal radiance reminiscent of the finest Italian Renaissance portrait. Her temperament was kind and gentle . . . and, sometimes, even meek. She was known as a caring mother and wife by everyone living along the Lexington and Danville Road . . . over which she regularly traveled.

Calvin had broached Catherine about his new-found interest in relocating west within days of the Athenaeum meeting. However, he discussed it in a light, almost whimsical manner. His tone reflected one who was on a lark – teasingly insincere. Catherine laughed at his apparent frivolity. Within minutes the subject was dismissed and the two turned their conversation to another issue.

Then in early March, Calvin cleared his throat and broached the subject again. This time he made it clear he wasn't joking. Catherine was appalled.

"You aren't serious, are you? Have you lost your mind? Do you know the kind of life even gentrified folks have to endure on the frontier? My father has taken you into the family business. He counts on you. He's provided you with any consideration you've required. Even the cockeyed thought of giving up all of this is a slap in the face to him . . . and, to me. What about our children? Jamie will be requiring an education soon. I shall not sacrifice his well-being for your foolish fantasies."

Calvin was merely suggesting the two of them discuss the pros and the cons of his "itch". He dared not mention he had already met with his own father . . . who had lent his endorsement to whatever decision Calvin might choose.

"Mrs. Cabell, I haven't the foggiest idea where in the West we might even want to consider relocating. I just wanted to make certain you were aware of . . . and understood . . . how persistently this matter has been in my thoughts. I can't seem to shake away this notion."

"Well you can flush it out of your numbskull brain. Our families came across the mountains to establish a better life for their children. They've struggled mightily and I appreciate their toil. Quite obviously, you do not."

"To say this discussion isn't going well is a grievous understatement," Calvin silently fretted as he listened to his wife rant.

He mulled over her rhetoric in his mind. Yet, the effect of his wife's vitriolic babble curiously served only to bolster his premise and his determination to investigate this matter further. Catherine dwelled on how her parents and his parents had the gumption to move to a completely remote part of a nascent nation. She dwelled on how she intended to be content enjoying the good life they had provided. There was a weak moral foundation to her outbursts. And "weakness" is exactly the sort of moral character Calvin Cabell was determined to shun.

"Mrs. Cabell, you must surely know you're a valued partner in this marriage. I would never make a major decision that might have an effect on our lives without consulting with you and gaining your approval. On that you have my pledge. However, I've wrestled with this subject since my discussion with Governor Shelby. I intend to investigate what sorts of opportunities lay to our west. That investigation might even require a bit of traveling. But, I repeat. I will respect you and your role in this marriage. And I'll also respect and honor the judgments of your father . . . when and if there's the need to discuss this matter with him. For now, I trust that you'll cool down . . . as it should be clear there's no imminent threat to either your present life or lifestyle."

Catherine smartly closed the shawl around her shoulders. She was clutching its fringes so it completely covered her chest. She did it in a manner Calvin thought mimicked a warrior covering his body with thick armor . . . in anticipation of a long and fierce battle.

Suddenly, the beleaguered husband and his wife heard Cassie crying. She'd been taking a nap in her crib in the next room. Catherine turned in a huff and walked away - still holding her protective, lacey suit of armor firmly in place and ready for battle.

"Now . . . are you proud of yourself? You've awakened the baby."

* * * * * * * * * * * * *

The first thing Calvin Cabell heard as he strode through the front door of his store was Jamison Jeffries' voice. It was modulated especially low this morning . . . as he was trying to affect an aura of doom.

"Beware the Ides of March, Julius Caesar. There's always a Brutus out there . . . armed and prepared to kill you."

"Thank you, Mr. Jeffries. If I decide to take a stroll through the Forum today, I'll keep your warning close to my Shakespearean breast."

"'*Et tu, Brute*.' Don't say I didn't warn you."

"Yes, I understand and appreciate you've warned me it's March fifteenth. I thank you for saving my life and, in turn I might add, saving your job."

"That was my hidden motive, sir."

"Jeffries, last night's rain left a muddy muck for customers to trudge through. Would you be sure to have Marshall purge all that mess from the planks with several buckets of water? And then, be sure to have him mop the walkway clean with a soapy brew."

"Anything you command, Caesar."

Jeffries bowed low so as to imitate the most obedient of courtiers. Calvin was piqued by his employee's insubordination . . . and his response was immediate. "Enough . . . enough is enough. Friends, Romans, and Jeffries – lend me your ears. Stop this preposterous behavior . . . immediately. Now, let's get to work. We both have duties to perform."

"Very well, sir, I'll begin by stocking the bolts of cloth we received yesterday."

"And I need to go to the bank. I'll return in fifteen minutes."

Calvin grabbed his hat from the coat tree behind the counter. Two women shoppers had already begun examining the assortment of bonnets on display. Calvin offered them a cheery "Hello" as he walked out the front door and turned right toward the Security Bank.

Two paces beyond the bottom step he heard his name called out. "Mr. Cabell . . . Mr. Calvin Cabell . . . I need to have a word with you, sir."

He turned toward the voice. It was Dolly.

Calvin was stunned when he spotted her. His jaw dropped and he had the sense all his blood was being drained from his body. His first thought shook him to his core. He instinctively realized . . . at that precise moment . . . his life was about to be turned inside out - all in a mere flash of time. Nothing would ever be the same. He felt doomsday in his bones.

"Mr. Cabell. We need to talk. Do you wish to talk with me here in the alley . . . between the buildings . . . or would you prefer to have our conversation out in the open . . . in front of the store?"

Cabell darted his head in all directions to determine if there was anyone in sight. The only activity he observed was a horseman about one block away.

"Yes . . . yes . . . Dolly, let's chat for a minute in the alley. What on earth brings you here?"

Dolly stood erect holding the handle of a small wicker basket that Calvin could see contained two sandwiches. Her bonnet was luckily tied in a manner that concealed most of her face. She wore a moth eaten wool coat. It was tattered so badly there were holes large enough one could see straight through to her dress. She also wore an old pair of high topped boots that were covered in mud. The shoes were so worn they looked as if they couldn't tread another mile. The bottom of her dress had a six inch border of black, wet mud. And there were splotches of dried mud splattered elsewhere – even on of her face.

As Calvin walked ever so tentatively toward this woman he thought these few paces to confront his unexpected visitor must surely be akin to the final steps a condemned man must walk to his ultimate fate, the gallows. He knew this conversation was going to be a gruesome ordeal. And, the sooner the discussion could be resolved . . . so this pesky peasant could be on her way again, that was all the better.

"Why have you come here? How did you travel from Harrodsburg? What is it you want, Dolly? There's got to be a reason for all this."

"Oh, there's a reason alright. And I walked here from the inn . . . left out at three in the morning. I walked through several fits of showers and four gentlemen's carriages passed me by with nary an offer for a ride. No respectable man's gonna give a helpless pregnant bar maid a ride. But I made it here anyway."

51

"You're pregnant . . . again? Is that why you're here? There's nothing I can do for you, Dolly. Who's the father? If you need something, then why haven't you gone to him instead of coming all this way to talk to me?"

"Because, it's YOU. You're the father . . . and we need to have an understanding how you're gonna provide for this kid AND his mother. That's why I'm here."

Calvin's mind wallowed in stunned confusion. "That's impossible. This is absurd. There's not one chance in a million I'm responsible for your pregnancy. You've got to be out of your mind, woman."

"I wouldn't talk like that, Mr. Cabell. I wouldn't say something that's gonna stoke up the heat of this chat . . . and cause it to be moved out there on the street. I don't think any high and mighty leader in this community . . . like you . . . would want that to happen."

Once, about three years earlier, Calvin was standing on the narrow bank of the Kentucky River at a spot that was beneath a high limestone canyon. Without a warning there was a spontaneous rockslide. A large stone fell crashing on his head. He remembered the oppressive pain came later. The first sensation he had was feeling stunned and woozy. If Frank Nichols hadn't been with him he very well could have tumbled into the river and drowned. Fortunately, Frank sat him down and tried to soothe him with words of encouragement and deeds . . . such as soaking up the blood with his shirt. It took a while – maybe thirty minutes – before Calvin started to feel the intense agony.

"That's what's happening now," he silently reminded himself. "I'm still in the 'stunned' phase. Dolly's a walking rockslide. She's dangerous. And she's deceitful. The pain that's about to follow soon enough is going to be excruciating."

"Don't tell me you haven't sired this foal. A woman knows about timing and when she got pregnant. And the timing for this baby commenced back in January – on the night you stayed at the inn."

Suddenly Calvin sorted through his confusion. There wasn't a word of truth being spoken. This charlatan wasn't a woman with a faulty misunderstanding about the birds and the bees. This woman had pegged him as an easy mark. This woman had plans from the very start to extort and threaten him with a public shame . . . a public humiliation like Danville had never known. He could literally sense his family fading away from him. He felt very, very lonely . . . and scared.

"Listen to me, you harlot. You know darned well one of your many customers is responsible for your predicament. And you can damned well know that I won't stand for this sort of extortion. Besides, nobody else knows about that night at the inn except us. I should think Smithson would want to take a strap to you and give you a flogging . . . until you finally admitted the father of this baby is anybody but me. Your lies will scare away all his customers. It's my word against your bogus claims. I have credibility, Dolly. And you . . . have nothing. There's no witness, so there's no liability I bear."

"You must've forgot? Were you so cold that night your brain froze up? My friend, Rebecca, knows very well it was you who came up to my place. She'll vouch for me. You wait and see."

Calvin thus far had played to a hand that contained no third party witness who could validate her preposterous claim. But Dolly was right. He accidentally knocked on Rebecca's door and the woman looked him square in the eyes – even if it was only for two seconds. He could no longer play those same cards in this game with Dolly. He had been trumped.

He was on the verge of losing all of his life's stakes in this poker game with Dolly. His family's future was put into peril . . . and nothing held more value to him than they did. This predicament required some fast thinking.

"Alright Dolly, this is a big surprise . . . as you well know. I've got to give this some thought. I need some time. I need to get back with you . . . in about two or three weeks."

Dolly began to puff up and fill her lungs with air that would surely be exhaled in a loud, angry scream. Calvin could already hear her harangue before a word crossed her lips.

"Two or three weeks is out of the question, Mr. Cabell. You're going to deal with me . . . here and now."

Calvin had to diffuse this quandary immediately. There were decent folks out on Main Street. They were customers of his store. And they would gossip about this scene until everyone in Lincoln County was talking about it. He desperately needed to buy some time.

"Money," he thought. "Money is the cure-all most of the time . . . and it's all she wants today."

"How about THIS proposal, Dolly? Let me give you some cash this morning. Let's agree on five dollars you can take home with you right now."

"Five dollars," she cried. "I've walked all this way in the mud to get you to give me some respect and do the responsible thing . . . and you think you can quiet me down for five dollars? Well, not on your life."

"Then what will it take, Dolly, to give me some time to calm down . . . to gather my wits so I can give this matter the consideration it deserves?"

Dolly calmed down. She knew she was going home with a pot full . . . and there would be more of it to come soon enough.

"I'll tell you what, Mr. Cabell. You give me ten dollars and I'll give you three weeks. That's a fair exchange under the circumstances, don't you think?"

"Ten dollars is a lot of money, Dolly. I can't just print money, you know? I'm not a magician."

"Well, Mr. Cabell. I don't know if you can create money, but I DO know you can create a pregnancy. And that's what you've done. Ten dollars it is, sir. But if we can't come to agreeable terms in three weeks, then this fall I'll be bringing a baby here to Danville. I'll march right up to your front door. And I suspect he's gonna look just like young Jamie, his big brother."

Calvin was incensed. This tramp knew his son's name. She had the gall to speak his son's name. And she intended to use Jamie as a helpless pawn in this blackmail. He remained mute. But he was still fuming inside. He couldn't risk Dolly ratcheting up these negotiations out there on the street.

"Very well, then . . . very well. . . I'll go inside and get the money out of the till. You wait right here and I'll return in three minutes."

Since Dolly didn't reply, Calvin figured the deal was done. So he pivoted around and moved back toward the street - glancing left and right to determine if anyone might have seen or heard this confrontation. He climbed the four stairs to his store and he returned in just shy of three minutes. He handed the money to Dolly . . . who had opened her small purple, satin purse. She snapped the money from him and sealed the purse shut with a faded red ribbon she drew taught around its opening. Then, one last time, he promised to come to Harrodsburg within three weeks.

She didn't need to admonish him about keeping his word and telling him what would happen if he didn't meet with her. Dolly already knew she could count on seeing him again . . . as well as more of his money.

This mud speckled woman turned about and walked toward the rear of the alley so no one would spot her. She had a good distance to walk back home, unless she could get a ride. She looked over her shoulder one last time. What she saw was a sad, dejected Calvin Cabell walking back toward his store.

But Dolly didn't escape without someone else seeing her there. Governor Shelby's nephew . . . of all the luck . . . was walking up the alley toward Main Street. Calvin had always despised him. He was a nosey busybody as well as a loose lipped gossip. He noticed that Dolly's lavender purse fell to the ground as she whipped herself around toward Calvin. So, he ran forward to fetch it for this bedraggled woman who seemed in such a huff.

"Excuse me, miss. You've dropped your satin sack."

The lad rushed toward Dolly and placed the well worn bag in her hand. And after he inspected her from top to bottom he said, "I know you from somewhere, Miss. But for the life of me I can't remember how or where."

"You must be confusing me with someone else, young man. I've never been to Danville in my life. But," she turned toward Calvin, "I might soon be coming to town more often."

She was as convincing as any grifter could possibly be. "Thank you for your help, Mr. Cabell. I'll count on getting that merchandise you promised in about three weeks."

* * * * * * * *

Jeffries stood behind the counter assisting the same two ladies who were browsing when Calvin left the first time. His boss looked distant and dazed. Jeffries noticed his stunned demeanor.

Then Calvin turned about again and walked toward the door. He called out, "I'm going to the bank, Jeffries. I don't know when I'll return."

"I thought you already made your trip to the bank, Mr. Cabell."

"I did, Jeffries. But I've got to go back."

55

Then the plucky young salesman defied his employer's earlier warning. He called out to bid his farewell. "Don't forget to beware. It's the Ides of March out there, Mr. Cabell."

Calvin stopped cold in his tracks. His head was bowed low . . . heavily laden with worries. Jeffries' stunt had turned into grim prophesy. Calvin couldn't get the cruel coincidence out of his mind.

"Beware of the Ides of March, indeed. Beware the Ides of March," he repeated under his breath as he walked out the door and turned toward the bank.

* * * * * * * * * * * * *

Catherine's antagonism about Calvin's attempts to discuss becoming modern day pioneers distressed him. He didn't dare mention it again until Isaac Shelby received a reply from Andrew Jackson. So, when Ephraim McDowell invited Calvin to ride with him to pay a visit with his father-in-law, Isaac Shelby, Calvin eagerly accepted. Since Dolly's visit and ultimatum, he had found a second – and more pressing - reason to leave Central Kentucky. And, if Catherine ever found out about his tryst, Calvin imagined circumstances unfolding that would force him to move to the southwest wilderness . . . all by himself.

The Governor's home was a showplace. Farming was his passion. He often said how much he loved to walk among the hundreds of sheep and cattle that grazed in his fields. Each was bordered by four-to-five-foot high stone walls.

Shelby once cleverly remarked to Calvin, "Many of my livestock look strikingly like my former constituents. But, happily not a single one of these beasts has ever asked for a favor . . . or filed a complaint."

The stones used to build the walls on Governor Shelby's homestead came from the same source from which hundreds of miles of stone walls in the Bluegrass had originated. They were gathered from the fields of all the farms in the region. Rocks were plentiful to the point of aggravation. They littered the landscape and they were a big nuisance to farmers . . . intent on tilling the soil and planting crops.

These stones were the residue of the region's geological history. Glaciers once slowly crept across the land . . . moving mountains of rock and dirt within them. The substantial power of the ice scooping across the earth pared the terrain clean and smooth. When the Ice Age finally came to a close, these nettlesome stones were all that remained as a reminder of the enormous frozen instruments that sculpted the gently rolling fields of the Bluegrass.

These surface stones were either thin, flat rocks . . . or they were rectangular cubes about the size of a large loaf of bread. The rectangular stones were cobbled together to form a wall's foundation. Then, along the top of the wall, farmers used the flat rocks to increase the height of the barrier as well as to prevent livestock from escaping over their sharp edges The flat rocks were vertically crammed together, so their jagged ridges riddled the top of the walls like the razor sharp teeth of a comb which stretched as far as the eye could see. Governor Shelby, all together, had about two linear miles of stone walls that framed his fields.

As the men walked about the meadows, Calvin asked if General Jackson had responded to the Governor's letter. He had not. But Calvin's inquiry caused Dr. McDowell to broach the subject of politics.

"Governor, last week I spoke with a close friend of Henry Clay who tells me Andrew Jackson is hell-bent on becoming our President. The man said that throughout Washington, there's constant talk about 'Old Hickory this' and 'Old Hickory that'. It appears his political strategy is grounded upon his military record . . . both fact and myth. Do you hear similar reports?"

"Dr. McDowell, this is hardly news. General Jackson has been running for President for the past twenty years. He's diminutive in stature. But in his own mind . . . he's eight feet tall."

Shelby considered his comments and concluded he had been too subtle. "Make that as tall as a tree – a hickory tree."

It was unusual for Isaac Shelby to belittle anyone. And it seemed clear to Cabell and McDowell he wasn't belittling Jackson . . . so much as he was poking fun at an old friend. Nevertheless, the Governor was clearly in a playful mood that evening. He continued his train of thought.

"When President Monroe asked the General and me to negotiate the purchase of the Chickasaw Territory, I chose to serve my country by accepting the post - even though I knew I would be hog tied to General Jackson . . . like one Siamese twin is tethered to the other. The man showed little fiscal discipline. The negotiations reached what I considered to be a mutually acceptable sum of $300,000. I can tell you the Chickasaw Chief was an outstanding trader. He could sense in me that this was the absolute limit to offer him."

Governor Shelby was beginning to speak in ever more righteous tones of voice.

"But the Chief also sensed in Jackson that he would be willing to offer more. When Jackson raised the government's ante to $400,000, I was livid. I didn't want the nation to think I was frittering away its money when I knew $100,000 was being needlessly thrown at the Indians. So I walked away and I began making arrangements to return to Kentucky – immediately. I admit that Old Hickory – as he is now widely called – played me like a fiddle. $400,000 was on the table and it would not decrease or go away. So, I relented and the Chief returned to his tribal council with a broad smile on his face."

"Well, Governor, despite the inflated price, it seems certain that clearing the title to all this land between the Tennessee and the Mississippi Rivers was worth the added price," Calvin said with hopes his comments would be interpreted as a tribute to the old statesman.

They were. So, Calvin continued. "Of course, I must say I'm perplexed why Kentuckians must refer to our state's portion of this deal as the Jackson Purchase. It would've been more appropriate to call it the Shelby Purchase."

Governor Shelby broke out into almost riotous laughter.

"My dear Calvin, Andrew Jackson would have his name plastered on a pig if he thought the exposure would promote his personal mythology. Now, don't misunderstand me. He's my good friend and he's a model American, but his legend is tantamount only to his vanity. When he and his two partners seized the investment opportunities from the Chickasaw sale, soon thereafter they purchased the fourth Chickasaw Bluff for their planned city. Old Hickory would have named it Jacksonville . . . or some other variation of his name. After all, there's already a Jackson, Tennessee. But General Winchester wisely convinced him that, since the Mississippi River is the River Nile of America, the city should share the glorious name of the ancient Egyptian capital."

Isaac Shelby was one never to puff up with pride about himself. His two visitors knew his next comment was purely in jest.

"Winchester, in my view is the partner who insisted the county in which Memphis lies should be called Shelby County – in my never-to-be-humble honor. But he probably pasted my name on the county's map as a tactic to cut off the General from memorializing the Jackson name, yet again."

"So, Calvin," interrupted Ephraim McDowell, "it appears General Jackson pastes his name on a sizeable portion of Kentucky, my father-in-law's home state. And the Governor's name – as part of this conspiracy – was affixed to a small county in the wilderness of Tennessee. I would call that a fair trade. Wouldn't you?"

"No, Dr. McDowell, I DON'T think that's very equitable. But I believe the inhabitants of this insignificant county whose name honors my good friend, Governor Shelby . . . well, I think they should consider themselves blessed."

*No Coin for Charon*

# CHAPTER

# 5

June 1824
Danville, Kentucky

The Presbyterian Church of Danville was an institution of great influence in Danville . . . as well as within the broad southwest quadrant of the Bluegrass region.

One of the reasons was attributable to the size of its congregation. It was large for its time. At the beginning of the War of 1812, the membership hovered between forty and fifty. Then the Reverend Samuel Kelsey Nelson became its pastor. Within the next fifteen years the rolls swelled three fold – to over one hundred fifty members.

Secondly, the list of communicants included virtually all of the region's respected names in law, medicine, education, and other professions.

Lastly, the Presbyterians were hard working, flinty, and highly successful settlers. Their endeavors left a lasting impression on the community.

There were good reasons this Christian denomination began to settle together in the Kentucky County of Virginia. Presbyterians in Virginia resented paying taxes to support the Anglican Church. And there were other social abuses and slurs that continued to grow. They were regarded as second-class citizens . . . simply because of their Scotch-Irish ancestry.

Most of these Scotch-Irish immigrants arrived in America at the port of Philadelphia. They drifted south and west to places like North Carolina and along the Shenandoah Valley of Virginia. Many families eventually crossed through the Cumberland Gap into Kentucky and Tennessee to flee the unjust policies of the Church of England. But they didn't migrate west without an occasional battle – especially along the southern and western borders of

Virginia where Anglican dominance could more easily be challenged.

Presbyterians in Danville loved to tell the story of Reverend Charles Woodmanson, an Anglican priest. His was a story of Presbyterian retaliation against Anglican influence in South Carolina. It was taken from the "Journal" that Woodmanson later published. It read:

"They (the Presbyterians) changed the dates on my posted announcements of when and where I would preach, carried off the keys to my meeting house, distributed whiskey two hours before my services to get the congregation drunk. If all this wasn't enough, they hir'd a band of rude fellows to come to my service who brought with them fifty-seven dogs (for I counted them) which in Time of Service they set to fighting and I was obliged to stop."

Each time this tale was told it generated gales of loud laughter. However, all the Presbyterians in Danville felt assured God would forgive their rowdy forbearers for such sacrilegious sins . . . given the circumstances.

Presbyterians were among the first to act upon Daniel Boone's news there was a Cumberland Gap that cleaved a pass in the impenetrable Appalachian Mountain range. Boone began to clear the Gap's densely forested terrain and within the period of time from 1785 to 1800 over 300,000 settlers passed through the narrow Wilderness Road. Because the Gap is situated on the border shared by Kentucky and Tennessee, most who passed through it either headed north into Kentucky or south into Tennessee. And when Kentucky became the fifteenth state to join the Union, these 'Overlanders' were, at long last, free and sovereign in every respect.

Resettlement to seek freedom of religion and freedom from government abuses was nothing new to these westward moving pioneers. Their escape from Virginia's repression via the Gap was just the latest migration many of the followers of Calvin and Knox had faced over the past two hundred years.

The Protestant Reformation was championed by theologians other than Martin Luther. Two of the most prominent of these were John Knox and John Calvin. The Calvinist doctrines which flowed from their philosophies were adopted by many of the Scottish people who later called their particular Protestant faith, Presbyterian.

In the 17th Century the Church of England was known as the Anglican Church. When the Protestants eventually secured the British throne, this Anglican Church became the official state religion throughout Britain.

Scotsmen began to be harassed about their Protestant church as England sought to stabilize its governmental rule over them. In 1673, Parliament passed the Test Act. It restricted all military officers, civilian government leaders, teachers, and college students to only those who had taken an oath of allegiance to the Anglican Church.

Twenty-five years later during the rule of Queen Anne, Parliament allowed the Anglican Church to strengthen its stranglehold on residents of Britain even further. A law was passed that stated marriages would only be recognized if the union had been sealed in an Anglican ceremony. These laws were retroactive. Violators were subject to arrest. Consequently, many of these Scotsmen moved west . . . to Ireland.

In Northern Ireland they thrived once again. Their successes began to economically and philosophically arouse the British. Even though these Presbyterians had stood side by side in battle with the English against the Roman Catholics in the south of Ireland, Parliament, once again, took action to harm the Scotch-Irish. They restricted the importation of beef, lamb, and dairy products produced in Ireland. And, if that wasn't severe enough, Parliament later passed the Woolen Acts that enlarged the contraband list of imports from Ireland to include woven cloth and other manufactured items.

The culmination of these many injustices motivated several hundred thousand Scotch-Irish to flee to America. There they continued their tradition of hard work. Their emphasis on education molded America perhaps more than any other social institution in the colonies. The College of New Jersey at Princeton is just one example of the sort of intellectual environment American Presbyterians founded and fostered.

And when the Anglican Church's lock on colonial citizens was essentially thwarted as a result of the American Revolution, many of those men who contributed to or authored the United States Constitution were Calvinists. They were determined to include in this new Constitution assurances such as Freedom of Religion and they were dedicated proponents of a separation between Church and State.

The U.S. Constitution is a testament to their Calvinist beliefs and their significant influence.

* * * * * * * * * *

Sunday Services at the Presbyterian Church of Danville had just concluded with the Benediction. The worshipers stood in line to shake Reverend Nelson's hand as they filed out the front door. There was a large brick paved area in front of the church and, as was custom, the members sorted themselves into small groups to chat about the service or to discuss matters that were less sanctified topics.

Calvin Cabell held baby Cassie in his arms while Catherine clung to the hand of Jamie . . . who had fidgeted throughout much of the service. Happily, the boy now seemed calm once he was enjoying the outdoors.

Along the edge of Main Street there were over a dozen horse-drawn carriages with Negro liveries in the driver's seat. They awaited those members who lived beyond walking distance to the church. Of course, there were a few carriages owned by members who could have walked home in ten minutes. But alighting from his own liveried vehicle on Sundays allowed a man to make a statement about his prosperous station in life.

All but two of the Negro liveries had attended the morning service where they looked down at the white worshipers from the balcony. They generally slipped out of their pews and down the steps to the narthex during the last hymn. Consequently, when their masters exited, each would find his carriage already attended and waiting to whisk his family away.

By 1824 about thirty slaves were also members of the Danville church. These Negro church members had developed skills which illustrated the enlightenment of the church. They were not ignorant, illiterate folks. They could read . . . and they were grateful for their literacy as well as for any other forms of education afforded to them. Their education was no accident. It was a direct result of efforts by the founder of the church in Danville . . . back in 1794. The first minister of this Central Kentucky flock was Reverend David Rice.

Reverend Rice was an early and vocal advocate of abolishing slavery. If he couldn't end bondage within the boundaries of Kentucky, he was determined to give the Church a voice to denounce the system and to start a sincere discussion of its issues. He was one of many citizens who attended Kentucky's constitutional conventions which were held in Danville.

The night before the first convention met in 1792 he distributed a publication with the title, "Slavery. Inconsistent with Justice and Good Policy". He fought a hard battle to include a provision in the new constitution that would end slavery. His tactic, like the sensible strategy of all who wished to free slaves, was to emancipate slaves gradually. Despite his efforts to have this clause incorporated into the document, Reverend Rice failed to win sufficient support. His proposal failed.

Rice had another opportunity to improve the lot of slaves two years later. He had played an important role in establishing not only the church at Danville, but his leadership there also caused Presbyterianism to spread throughout Kentucky. Therefore, when the Transylvania Presbytery met in 1794, he was able to push through a doctrine which was highly unusual. The resolution stated that all church members who were under the care of the Presbytery "shall teach every slave under fifteen years of age to read the word of God and to give them such education as may prepare them for the enjoyment of freedom."

Those persons who were proponents of emancipation realized early on that freeing slaves without giving them the slightest amount of a primary education would, effectively, sentence that person to be released from one set of shackles . . . only to be enslaved and bound by other "economic" shackles.

Rice fired the first shots aimed at bringing about emancipation. But debate within the church was growing and most church members foresaw the day when, absent resolution of the slavery issue, the Church would be adversely impacted. In 1822 about twenty families who were members of the Danville church owned slaves. No doubt, these slaves were among the most educated of all the Negroes living in Kentucky.

The rented pews in the sanctuary served to stratify each member's wealth and social significance. Those with the greatest wealth and status rented the first few pews and the lowest ranks of members sat in the back.

The same economic totem also was evident outside the church as well. There was an unofficial pecking order that dictated where each carriage would park. And, certainly, no one enjoyed more respect within the church community than Isaac Shelby. His carriage awaited him directly in front of the church's front doors. No one would dare park his vehicle in this space.

Out on the sidewalk, Calvin was chatting with John McElroy who served on the Diaconate with him. One of the responsibilities of deacons was to visit the sick and shut-ins. John had been assigned to keep in touch with the Widow Wilson and Mrs. Wilson's brother, George Garner, was the responsibility of Calvin. The two deacons were exchanging information about each of these elderly folks . . . so that the brother and sister could be briefed on the activities of the other.

Isaac Shelby approached the two men. He was so revered that his mere presence could be viscerally detected by most citizens. In a room full of people everything stopped and the premises fell silent when he arrived. McElroy and Calvin both ceased their discussion as soon as Governor Shelby had finished his chat with the preacher and he began the walk toward his carriage. Calvin and McElroy turned their heads to offer him a smile intended to show their respect.

McElroy spoke first. "Greetings, Governor, you're certainly looking fit as a fiddle on this fine day."

"I endure, Mr. McElroy. I endure."

Calvin took his turn and tried to turn the conversation away from being trivial.

"Reverend Nelson preached a fine sermon, I thought. For a moment it appeared my boy, Jamie, was soaking in every word. However, I was mistaken; as it became evident he was only staring at the bright pink ribbons that wove through the hair of Edward Trapp's daughter. How are things going at your farm, Governor?"

"We scythed our first stacks of hay last week. With the fine weather we've been enjoying, I believe it's fair to say my livestock won't go hungry next winter."

Shelby then turned to address Calvin. "I wonder if I might have a solitary word with you, Calvin."

John McElroy feigned not feeling marginalized by Shelby and he quickly spoke. "If you gentlemen will excuse me, I promised my wife we wouldn't linger after the service as usual. She's prepared a pot roast for Sunday dinner and we must set out for home."

"It's good to see you, John. Have a good day . . . and I trust the roast will be tender and moist." Isaac Shelby sealed his farewell with a handshake for McElroy and a tip of his hat to Virginia McElroy as they began their walk home.

If Governor Shelby appeared to be caught up into a conversation with a single individual, no one would dare to interrupt him. Isaac Shelby posed such an appearance this day. It was clear to everyone he was focusing intently on Calvin.

"Calvin, I received a letter from Andrew Jackson on Friday."

Calvin's eyes grew wide with anticipation. He remained silent . . . as if afraid to ask what Old Hickory had to say.

"Well, lad, do you have any interest in learning about his reply?"

"Yes, Governor . . . yes, by all means. What did General Jackson report to you?"

"He was most encouraging. It was quite a lengthy letter. He wrote in great detail about the status of his interests in Memphis. When you read it I think you'll agree he offered sincere encouragement that several opportunities to make a fortune might be awaiting you on the Mississippi."

"Please tell me more, sir."

"Well, first of all, this real estate investment was only surveyed and subdivided six years ago. Yet, I think I should be honest and tell you that Jackson and his partner, Judge Overton, are not pleased with the slow sale of lots . . . or the interest the nation has shown in their investment. They've spent money for advertisements in newspapers along the Ohio Valley that tout the opportunities awaiting settlers in Memphis."

"Yes, I remember you pointing that out to me, Governor. But I sense you're saving the most significant information until I'm forced to beg for it. If that's so, then I'm begging you. What did Old Hickory tell you specifically about my objectives?"

Isaac Shelby couldn't contain his glee at seeing Calvin Cabell squirm like a schoolboy waiting to see if his report card would verify if he had passed or failed. He prolonged his silence a few more seconds before continuing. Then he broke into a small grin and Calvin concluded the Governor's upturned mouth meant the news would be good.

"What I think is remarkable about the General's reply is what he had to say regarding the three investors' interest in attracting to the town the very sorts of businesses in which you're well versed. In particular, Jackson stated there was a desperate need for a lumber mill in the community. The population is small, but Jackson reports their man on the scene, General Winchester's son, seems confident that rapid growth is soon coming. Winchester's son has invited you to visit him there . . . and General Jackson says the partners are willing to offer you any assistance you might need to get established. Once again, Calvin, a saw mill is at the top of the list of businesses the investors hope to attract. Your experience working with your father's mill appears to pique Jackson's interest in you."

The news was bittersweet to Calvin Cabell. On one hand, he felt as if providence had bestowed on him a rare gift – an extraordinary investment opportunity. Yet, simultaneously, his anxiety level rose and a lump formed in his throat. He knew he'd be compelled to pursue this fascinating opportunity. Dolly's extortion had been increasingly eating at his innards. After all, he might need to relocate for other darker reasons that still required resolving.

But he dreaded bringing up the subject, once again, with Catherine. If she sensed even the remotest possibility he might eventually ask her approval to relocate their family to "the wilderness" - as she referenced any land either on or west of the Mississippi River - then she would say, "Count me out." Calvin knew he would have to speak much more persuasively than had been required before.

As Calvin pondered these conflicted thoughts, he noticed out of his peripheral vision that Catherine was eyeing the discussion he and Isaac Shelby were having. Dorothy Emmons and Mrs. Chamberlain completed the threesome that included Catherine in their after-church chat. Calvin didn't want her to know he was conscious of her glances.

"She's sure to have a fit - a bloody fit," he thought as he devoted a second or two to think what his reply to Shelby's news should be . . . as well as how and when the news should be disclosed to Catherine.

Calvin turned and looked Governor Shelby straight in the eye. He coated his face with as solemn a demeanor as he could muster. "Governor, I'm humbled by your generosity as well as General Jackson's optimistic report and Mr. Winchester's kind invitation. But may I ask, sir, if you were walking in my shoes . . . with a certain wife . . . and two young children whom you can see over my shoulder, what action - if any - you would take with news of this sort?"

Isaac Shelby's face became as solemn as Calvin's. "Take one step at a time, Calvin. The first step was making an inquiry. The second step is this. You should characterize any future actions as 'due diligence'. Catherine, I trust, will be reasonable . . . if she's presented reasoned logic."

Shelby paused . . . as if to await a reaction from Calvin whose head was bowed now while he was contemplating the herringbone design incorporated in the brick courtyard.

"And, on a personal note, Calvin, I can tell you that . . . as I live out the last days and months of my time here on earth . . . I look back with amazement at how exciting my life has been. I'm blessed to have played a small role freeing the colonies and establishing a democracy that's unlike any government the world has heretofore known. In retrospect, it's merely a vague dream – but it's a satisfying one. I hope you'll one day enjoy looking back on your own fulfilled dreams."

Calvin raised his head up and looked Isaac Shelby straight in the eyes as the Governor continued. "Today, almost fifty years after the Revolution, this country has managed to survive and flourish . . . wherever hardy people have moved to settle. They plant not only their families' roots, but also the roots of a free nation that's still in its formative years. When I fought at Kings Mountain, never in my wildest dream did I imagine fighting for anything other than for an independent government. The government I fathomed was simply a body politic for the people in the thirteen colonies. I could never have imagined what our victory that day over Colonel Ferguson would mean to the Revolution . . . and to this nation. We Kentuckians were merely determined to unshackle the oppression WE endured. Now, we live in a country that might well expand all the way to the Pacific Ocean."

"I never thought about the fact Overlanders probably got more from the victory than you originally bargained for," Calvin stated with a look of wonder on his face.

"At the time of Kings Mountain, Governor Sevier and I . . . well, we were of a mindset that pervaded everyone's thinking of the day. We could only envision the faint possibility that the Mississippi River would be the eventual western boundary of a United States. At that time it appeared to us the French would forevermore be our nation's neighbor west of the Mississippi. France was our friend and our ally in the Revolution. So, we surmised the French would continue to be our friend and ally as a neighbor . . . since they owned the land adjoining Kentucky and Tennessee?"

Calvin had been intently listening to everything Isaac Shelby was saying. He noted to himself, "What a remarkable perspective he has on life and history. I'm in the presence of a great patriot."

Then Calvin's silent thoughts were unleashed as spoken words. "Governor, I feel compelled to perform this 'due diligence' as you call it. It would be

69

impossible for me to pass up this opportunity to see what might lie ahead for the Cabells . . . as well as for the country. I don't know how to convince Catherine of the wisdom in all of this, but I'll do my best."

"Pray over it, Calvin. Pray for your family and pray for this new nation. And pray that this new generation of pioneers . . . your generation . . . moving ever westward . . . will settle and govern communities with wisdom, justice, and an abiding faith in God."

Governor Shelby took a brief pause and adjusted his tone of voice almost as if he were pleading to Calvin. "Calvin, the western frontier needs people just like you. Where will these community leaders come from if not from the educated gentry in former frontiers . . . like Kentucky and Tennessee? Talk to Catherine about this matter. Then, let me know if I should arrange for a discussion with her."

"Governor, you've been a good friend to me and my family . . . as well as a valued mentor. I thank you. We all thank you. But I must tell you that . . . while we've been talking . . . I've noticed Mrs. Cabell spying on us with an air of great personal concern. She's intuitive. She knows more about what we're talking about than you might think. It's time she and I should walk home to have the talk I've been postponing. I don't know if I can be convincing, but I'm certain our discussion will result in Catherine erupting with all of her pent up frustrations. Nevertheless, I'm up to it."

"I know you're up to it, my friend. And I, too, must climb aboard my carriage and head home to my trusting sheep and cattle. As I wander about the pastures with them this afternoon I'll be pulling for you . . . and, I'll be looking heavenward and saying a prayer."

Shelby began to walk toward his carriage. His movement prompted his driver, Cornelius, to open the carriage door and stand at attention for his master. On his way, Isaac Shelby took a short detour. He veered to the left and approached Catherine and the children. She held out her gloved hand . . . so as to pay tribute.

"Good day, Governor Shelby. I hope you won't mind if I ask Mr. Cabell to debrief me about the subject of your discussion?"

"Not at all, Mrs. Cabell, indeed, I would welcome it. You Cabells are a family who've been blessed. It's my wish that all of you enjoy a long and exciting life . . . just as I have. And now I mustn't keep Cornelius waiting. I look forward to seeing all of you . . . soon."

With that salutation, Isaac Shelby took several more tentative steps toward his carriage. His walk had become less stable over the past few months. This clumsy ambling seemed to illustrate his life was at its twilight.

Catherine, Calvin, and the children stood still until the Governor was seated in the carriage. Cornelius flicked a crackling whiplash above the horse's head. The vehicle jolted forward and the Governor leaned into the side window and waved goodbye.

"Mr. Cabell, let's start our journey home. The children are hungry and I, too, am famished. But my hunger is mostly a gnawing need to learn about the conversation which just transpired between you and the Governor."

Calvin lifted up Cassie into his arms. He held Catherine's right hand while she still gripped Jamie with her left. He was still thinking about what tack he should take with his wife. This was a sales pitch at which he couldn't afford to fail. Because of Dolly, there was much more at stake now than when he caught the "pioneer bug".

"The sooner the better," he thought. "Let's get this argument over . . . and out of the way."

So, as the Cabell family began its homeward stroll east on Main Street, he turned to Catherine. "My dear, Mrs. Cabell, we need to have a talk."

Still silence followed his words. Only the rhythmic clomp of heel to toe footsteps could be heard. Calvin knew this peace would be short-lived. It was going to be a long afternoon.

* * * * * * * * *

Since the Ides of March came and went, not a minute went by when Calvin Cabell didn't think about his "Dolly predicament". He rattled his brain searching for a viable solution - one that could cure this predicament . . . for good.

He was listless at the store and Jeffries finally asked him if something was wrong. "Is there anything at all I can do for you?" Of course, there wasn't.

Catherine was concerned, too. Calvin acted aloof, despondent, and moody. She assumed the problem lay in "this pioneer fantasy", as she confessed to

71

## No Coin for Charon

Virginia McElroy.

Athenaeum members also thought something seemed awry with Calvin when Governor Shelby hosted the April meeting. He seemed agitated and anxious. He fidgeted with his water glass by revolving his finger around its rim. Deaton commented about it before he left the Governor's house.

"The tip of Calvin's forefinger must have a blister by now. Surely, it made ten thousand revolutions around his glass's rim. I thought either his finger would fall off . . . or the glass would melt into a glassy puddle."

Calvin wasn't eating much and he certainly wasn't sleeping well. He'd lie in bed and try to catalog all the possible solutions. But hours later . . . as the first light of dawn appeared . . . the verdict was always the same. He couldn't come up with a single fix . . . with the exception of one.

It was a diabolical notion. But he increasingly began to be more and more comfortable with it. "After all," he rationalized, "it was Reverend Nelson who hatched this idea. And he did it while preaching the word of the Lord."

John Calvin was a theologian who believed in the principle of pre-destination. He preached it was God's way of determining salvation - who would be saved . . . and abide in heaven with his Creator . . . and who would be cast away from His kingdom . . . and dwell for eternity outside of God's grace.

It all made so much sense to Calvin Cabell . . . a man, after all, who was named as a tribute to the doctrine's creator.

"It was a sign," he reasoned. "Reverend Nelson's sermon was an unmistakable sign that God was transmitting directly to me. God . . . with the help of John Calvin . . . had cleared up everything that was a vexing muddle before the sermon. It all made so much sense.

"I'm an integral part of God's creation. And I know the Lord is counting on me to do His work here on earth. Look at what He's invested in me." Calvin's logic about this matter seemed to be unbounded. "When you think about it, it's abundantly clear. God gave me superior intelligence. He also made me attractive to look at. I'm articulate. And I'm a man whom people naturally respect and admire. God has, indeed, pre-destined me to lead His people. He wants me to expand these United States in places where men with God-given talents like me can ably lead others . . . who aren't born into salvation – forsaken folks, like Dolly.

72

"God doesn't want my destiny to be derailed by a cheap, lying, conniving tramp. Who could possibly imagine that Dolly - or anyone else of her ilk - could be so evil that she'd try to ruin me and my life? How dare her. She essentially seeks to murder a man whose fate has been pre-determined by God. Essentially, she's challenging God's divine plan for His people. The magnitude of this girl's sinfulness cries out for retribution – either by God . . . or by someone who's been blessed by Him."

Now that Calvin could finally see God's will after it had stubbornly eluded him for those many sleepless nights, he reasoned it was his duty as a Christian to plan a strategy that would put an end to this bar maid's criminal injustice.

Yet, he thought he owed it to the Lord to first see if Dolly would confess her sin. Of course, she'd have to document her confession in a manner that assured Calvin the storm clouds that had hovered over him the past couple of weeks would disappear - forever.

"But what if she can't be reasoned with? What if she fails to see the will of the Lord . . . and she's determined to sack a man who's pre-destined by God?"

John Calvin Cabell was certain he now had all the puzzle pieces in place. His Calvinist Lord had revealed them to him. But he had to make a decision – a decision he knew the Lord would eventually lead him to. And then – or so he thought - the Lord spoke to him.

"An eye for an eye . . . and a tooth for a tooth," Calvin repeated over and over like an apocryphal chorus. "Thank you, Lord, for revealing Your wise counsel through the Holy Scripture."

Calvin felt like the weight of the world had been removed from his shoulders. He could carry on. He WOULD carry on . . . and he would carry on to fully utilize the gifts God had bequeathed to him. He would use them to serve God's will – whether it's in the wilderness of West Tennessee or in Danville . . . where God had first planted him. He repeated the refrain over and over.

"'An eye for an eye . . . and a tooth for a tooth'. Thank you, Lord Jesus . . . for showing me Your way to right this wrong."

* * * * * * * * * * * *

73

It was Wednesday, April 11. Calvin told Catherine on Monday that Henry Caldwell asked him to ride up to his farm near Burgin. He said Henry was spending the week with his daughter and son-in-law in Lexington and he wanted Calvin to check and see if everything there was operating smoothly. In truth, while Henry did ask him for this favor, Caldwell wasn't cognizant his invitation was, essentially, planted by Calvin. His subtle suggestion had a purpose. Spending a night alone at Henry's farm was an important part of his . . . and God's plan.

"Spend a night or two at the homestead, Calvin. You've been looking pretty ragged for several weeks. I think the peace and quiet you'll find there would do you a world of good. Mansel will take good care of you. He'll see you have everything you need."

"That's a splendid idea, Henry, and a very kind gesture on your part. I believe I'll do exactly what you're suggesting. You're right. It'll do me some good. Noah and I can take long rides over your pastureland. The peacefulness of a solitary horse ride always clears my mind."

As soon as Wednesday's dinner came to a conclusion, Calvin gave both of his kids a big hug. But he reserved the grandest one for Catherine as he walked out of the house and headed toward Noah.

"Always remember, Darling, I love you more than words can say. You're very dear to me. Take care while I'm away."

"And you take care, too, Mr. Cabell. Use this opportunity to re-create yourself. After all, that's what recreation means. There's nothing wrong with playing around for several days if you come home renewed and restored."

"And that's what I intend to do – come home renewed . . . and unshackled from any demons that might have been responsible for my recent melancholy."

As Calvin reined Noah's neck around, he smiled one last time at his wife. It was a brighter smile than Catherine had observed on her husband in a long time.

"Good bye, my dear."

"Good bye, my knight in shining armor."

"That's it," Calvin thought. "Catherine hit the nail squarely on the head. I'm a knight . . . fighting for God's Kingdom. It's a knight's quest to right wrongs . . . like Dolly's wicked extortion. I'm on a quest - a holy quest to purge the world of evil sinners . . . like Dolly."

He rode north on the Burgin Road. As Noah cantered and rhythmically kicked up puffs of road dust behind him, Calvin fell into a more somber mood.

"There's no turning back from here, Sir Calvin. You must complete your quest. Your Almighty King requires it of you."

* * * * * * * * * *

When he struck out on the road toward Harrodsburg, it was just after seven o'clock. Calvin was startled at how serendipitously good luck kept falling into his lap. He hadn't realized until nightfall that the moon had fully waned and only a faint glimmer of light ringed its darkened mass. He had difficulty seeing more than one hundred feet ahead.

There were patches of a netherworld fog that cuddled within the numerous dips in the Harrodsburg Road. The weather had been unseasonably warm this day and the temperature of the evening air was quite chilly. Calvin knew the moist, gray ground cover would spread even more as the atmosphere continued to cool.

Mansel had also been the perfect unwitting accomplice. He was now a free man. Henry emancipated the Negro after serving him ably for ten years. Now he lived in a small house that served as headquarters for the southwest quadrant of Henry's three thousand acre farm. Mansel greeted Calvin at the main house when he arrived about four o'clock. The two men shook hands exaggeratingly and Mansel told his boss's guest that he would be at Calvin's beck and call. Whatever Mr. Caldwell's guest needed, he would arrange for it. Calvin assured the aging servant he'd be fine on his own. By five o'clock the caretaker rode home.

Before dark set in, Calvin inspected the barn and the stable. He was scavenging for equipment – any materials at all he could use to pull off his plan. He found three black tarps that measured about ten by fifteen feet. He tested one to determine if it might be folded to look as if it was covering a rolled up rug. It appeared ideal.

At the last minute Calvin incorporated Henry's dappled draft horse, Nell, into the plan. He put a bridle on the animal with reins that could be easily extended when tethered to a rope. There was no need for a saddle. He could drape the two tarps over the animal's broad, curved back.

And, into Noah's saddle bags he stuffed three burlap bags, leather gloves, several instruments for cutting, and a long thin leather lanyard that Calvin found draped over a cross beam in the stable.

He took inventory at least three times. All the gear he needed seemed to be accounted for. But he dwelled off and on whether this important expedition was led by a man committed to achieve his goal. Was he an individual who was sufficiently fortified – a man who had the backbone to do the deed that must be done? He decided the answer would only be known in due time.

Calvin and his four-legged partners in crime traveled just shy of four miles between the Caldwell farm and Harrodsburg. To Calvin's amazement he didn't pass a single traveler along the route. The muffled clops of his horses' hooves . . . as they plodded down the dirt road . . . was the only sound discernible along this pitch-black roadway. The only exception to the silence was an unusual amount of nervous whinnying between Noah and Nell. It was as if each animal sensed its felonious role as an accomplice to a crime. Both were skittish.

By quarter past nine Calvin stood in the dark grove that sloped down to the White Oak Inn. He tied the horses in a secluded spot about one hundred yards away. He carried with him only the materials he suspected he would need.

Dolly and Rebecca's quarters sat on another slope about fifty yards away – a safe distance. The time spent waiting in silence passed ever so slowly. An extended watch such as this tends to make a man think . . . too much. But this was no time to debate with oneself. He would remain resolute. He had a mission to accomplish.

He saw two guests exit the back door and relieve themselves standing on the edge of the porch. Each man laughed riotously. Then, they both quickly buttoned up again and headed inside. He hoped his luck would hold out and no other guest would sense the call of nature when Dolly headed home for the evening.

Calvin was most worried about Rebecca. She had mucked up Calvin's rendezvous back in January and he feared that Dolly's only eyewitness would somehow emerge as an observer once again. It was still too cold to leave cabin doors open. Each one seemed sealed tight. Calvin wondered if Dolly's boy, Timothy, was in Rebecca's care . . . according to the arrangement Dolly had described. He remembered being solely focused on that sleeping child while he foolishly set himself up for Dolly's extortion. It was innocence and evil – all mixed in the same small room.

Calvin wondered if his own son, Jamie, was also asleep this night. He was prepared to take whatever action required to insure that . . . come tomorrow morning . . . his Jamie would awaken without the threat of his father and his family being torn apart by the contemptible deeds of a lowly bar maid.

About quarter after ten Calvin spied Dolly opening the kitchen door. She was carrying a bucket of dish water and she heaved its contents over the back porch. Then, fifteen minutes later she opened the door once again. This time Calvin was dead certain she was about to head up the hill.

His good luck continued as Dolly detoured toward the privy that was located half way between her room and the spot where Calvin waited. The time was now. He had to make his move quickly and quietly. So, he emerged out of the shadowy grove and walked fast to intercept Dolly before she arrived at the out house.

"Dolly . . . Dolly . . . over here. Come over here . . . please."

"Mr. Cabell, is that you? What a surprise."

"I told you I'd come within three weeks. And here I am. I think you need to know I'm a man of my word."

"Yes, you are. You are, indeed, a man who keeps his promise."

"Dolly, I'm prepared to talk with you now – to negotiate with you right here.

But I wonder if we might step into the grove where our discussion can remain private."

"I don't know, sir. I think it's best to talk right here . . . in the dim light of the inn. I'm not too keen on putting myself out of sight."

"I understand, Dolly. But I'm asking you to appreciate that the whole premise of you coming to see me and my coming to see you revolves around a need for secrecy. I'm prepared to deal with you. But I can't be exposed. Surely, you understand that, don't you?"

The bar maid had some silent thinking to do. Ordinarily, she would never relent and step into the dark woods. But the esteemed Mr. Calvin Cabell was right. He'd kept his word to come and talk with her again. Confidentiality was essential to limit his vulnerability. And, after all, he was one of the pillars of the Danville community. If she couldn't step into the woods with this man, then she couldn't imagine anyone else she might trust . . . given the circumstances.

"Very well, sir. I understand . . . and I recognize your need for secrecy. But it's chilly out here and I first need to go up to my room. I'll tell Rebecca to keep my boy a little longer. I can fetch my coat at the same time."

"No . . . please, no. I don't want Rebecca to become involved in our business. She's already served her purpose to you. She's your witness to all this, after all. I'm ready to get this matter behind me, Dolly. But this time I don't want Rebecca to become involved. You understand, don't you?"

Dolly appeared to understand his rationale, but she was far from convinced.

"The coat problem . . . what can I do about it?" Calvin thought. "Here, Dolly, take my coat and drape it over you. You'll stay warm and I can endure the chill for awhile."

Calvin removed his long black leather coat. It was slit up the back - all the way to his waist - so he could ride a horse unencumbered. He put it around Dolly's shoulders as he also guided her up the short incline. Within seconds they had stepped into total obscurity. And just as the two stepped out of sight, Calvin heard the inn door open once again. A commotion ensued. The same two guests who had been enjoying a laugh together had decided to take an argument outside. Each spoke loudly to the other. Soon there must have been a resolution between them . . . as they peacefully returned indoors.

Calvin was ready to make his speech. He had rehearsed it in his mind and during the afternoon while riding to Henry's farm. He even went through his planned discourse out loud for Noah as well as for all the eavesdropping cattle grazing along the roadside.

"Dolly, are you still bent on holding me ransom for a situation I'm not a party to?"

"I'd say you're very much a party to this situation, Mr. Cabell. Indeed you have a leading role in it, don't you?"

Calvin knew at that moment there wasn't going to be any reasonableness exhibited by this wench. Of course, he wasn't expecting any from her. So, he wasn't disappointed.

"What is it you want, young lady? It's my objective to keep my family free from this absurd scandal. But you've got to understand that I can't pay just any arbitrary amount. I'm far from wealthy, you know."

"I think we can arrange something, sir. I think we can do business."

"Well, tell me the amount of 'business' we're talking about tonight."

"I'd say it would be most gracious of me if I kept my financial demands low. What do you say to that?"

"I'd say there's no need for any payment at all. But, given this situation, I'm sure that isn't an option."

"You know, I like you, Mr. Cabell. I like your sense of humor. And I like your smooth style – not to mention your good looks. As a matter of fact I care about you so much that I'd like for you to come up to my place again . . . right now. I can arrange for my boy to spend the night with Rebecca. You and I could nestle and wrestle all over my bed. After all, you still haven't experienced all of my many talents."

Dolly foolishly thought she had another chance to dally with Calvin. She was sure he could be as easily lured into her web as he was back in January. "Did you know I have a special fondness for doing the dirty deed . . . just like a bitch in heat? You know . . . on all fours. I'll betcha Mrs. Cabell's too tightly wound up to give you those kinds of favors."

"You leave my wife and my family out of our discussion," Calvin snapped at this strumpet. Now, what is it you want?"

"Testy tonight, aren't we, Mr. Cabell. Well, I'm gonna tell my testy stud you need to make a payment of sixty dollars at the beginning of each year."

The dye was cast and Calvin wasn't going to waste another moment negotiating a blackmail fee he never intended to pay. But he did have one more question for this charlatan.

"Let's say I agree to pay your price . . . in cash at the beginning of each year. What happens when you later on decide that's not enough – that you want more money . . . and more . . . and then . . . even more?"

"Then I suspect we'll have to negotiate again. Why, I'd be happy to bring your baby to Danville. You and me and Mrs. Cabell could sit in your parlor. I'll bet the three of us could reach a compromise in no time. And the more I think about it, such a homecoming would offer Jamie the perfect opportunity to play with his little brother or sister. Don't you agree?"

Calvin feigned the act of considering what had just been said – as if he were prepared to dance to any tune she played. He turned to the side and contemplatively stroked his chin. "Well, now, let me think this over."

But he slyly lowered his hand into his left pants pocket . . . and he slowly pulled the long leather lanyard out from its hidden burrow.

"Come on, Mr. Calvin Cabell. It's getting late and I'm heading across the glen unless we can arrange something in the next minute. I've had a long day . . . and pregnant women tire easily, you know."

Her mocking, her insolence at calling out his family members by name, and her insidious plotting to tear him down and ruin his life stoked Calvin's rage beyond the boiling point. He remained standing with his left side hidden in the night.

It was time. He slowly rotated around to face Dolly and he looked her squarely in the eyes. Quick as a striking rattlesnake, he lifted the tightly stretched lanyard high over his head and he lurched at his prey. It didn't take a second for him to snare her neck with the leather cord. Tightening it caused a deep purple furrow to swell up around the leather string.

Calvin spoke to his victim in a low voice – all the while gritting his jaws together and forcing his shrill words to escape through the spaces between his teeth. "You want to ruin my life to suit your lying schemes, do you? I don't think so. I think you've met your match. And, more importantly, you're about to meet your Maker."

Dolly never said a word. It was impossible. Calvin was sure she heard him curse her. And he hoped she had spent at least several seconds regretting her wicked devices. But she only uttered muffled gurgles as he tightened the thin noose more rigidly than he ever thought he could. Dolly's face turned blue . . . and then purple. He could see these dusky death hues . . . even in the unusual blackness of the night.

Calvin had, indeed, packed enough gumption within his gut to pull off his crime. But what amazed him was how much he was enjoying strangling this woman who had initially tried to choke out of him all the status and personal relationships that defined him as a man.

"In other words," he thought. "You tried to snuff out my life, woman. So, I'm totally justified to kill you first."

He could sense the end was near. But he had more to say while she might still hear him. "How dare you challenge life's natural order of things. You forgot who I was, didn't you? I'm John Calvin Cabell . . . who's traveling the path of a destiny the Lord planned for me long before I was even born. Consider what He's bestowed upon me . . . and how He cared not one particle about you. But you insisted to fool around with God's grand plan.

"Haven't you heard about pre-destination, woman? If God ever had a plan for you, you mocked Him . . . and disgusted Him with your wicked ways."

Dolly's eyes rolled back in their sockets. Calvin knew the exact moment when her life relented to suffocation. He sensed when it fled her body . . . to who knows where. She went limp. Her body's tense muscles melted into the consistency of mush. She was so flaccid Calvin thought even her rigid skeletal structure had vanished from her flesh with her last breath.

Nevertheless, he still wouldn't let go of his hands that twisted the noose. He continued to clutch at both ends of the lanyard - pulling violently in opposite directions . . . so hard he thought the leather strings might even break. There could be no mistakes made . . . and no mercy shown.

At last he released his two-handed grip. But he maintained his thumbs' pressure against her throat. For all he knew the devilish demon that had turned her heart hard and motivated her scheming . . . still might renew itself and surge vengefully out of her mouth to taunt Calvin and to turn him in. He couldn't be too careful.

Now, time was of the essence. Rebecca would begin wondering why Dolly hadn't come to pick up her sleeping child. She would only wait so long until her curiosity would evolve into concern – concern enough to look for her inside the inn. Probably, Rebecca would also wake up Smithson . . . and all the other guests. Calvin envisioned a posse forming soon - combing every square inch of the expanded premises.

"Of course," he reconsidered, "Rebecca might just as well assume her neighbor had met another mark among tonight's guests at the inn. Perhaps Dolly had contracted with both the men who retreated earlier to the porch. Possibly, she was the source of their argument. Rebecca's concern would be allayed by the justifiable assumption that Dolly was somewhere in the inn, or somewhere in the woods, or - even at that very moment - she might be servicing a stranger right next door. That logical presumption should ease the busybody's mind and buy me some time. But I must move quickly."

Only after all this hypothetical reasoning did Calvin, at last, release his grip. Dolly plopped to the ground. He could feel her body's temperature falling while, at the same time, he felt his own anxiety rising. He raced toward the horses and threw one of the tarps over his shoulder – the one that didn't already wrap around Henry's rolled up barn blankets. He had used his best effort to mimic the bulk inside the roll he figured Dolly's body would shape. He moved quickly back into the grove. Only his toes touched the ground so as to maintain the quiet peacefulness of the night.

Calvin unfurled the canvas cloth on the ground next to Dolly until it lay in a perfect rectangle. Then he picked up the limp body and placed her at one edge of the tarp. On his hands and knees he rolled it over and over until one edge reached the other. With a muted grunt he then lifted his cargo up and threw it over his shoulder.

Then he sped off – but not after inspecting the ground still strewn with last fall's leaves. It was a vital part of his plan. He had to look for any clue that might be used as evidence of a crime. Calvin knew he would have to rake smooth the leaves with his foot so the murder site would look tidy and unremarkable. His inspection confirmed that every square inch of the area looked just as pristine as it had appeared earlier in the day.

Within two minutes Calvin was heaving the roll of tarp across Nell's broad back. Then he placed the other two rolls on either side of the body. Finally, he took the hemp rope he found in Henry's barn and he laced all three rolls around the belly of the draft horse . . . so as to secure them. He wrapped the rope two additional times around Dolly's tarp - just in case.

Then Calvin, astride Noah and holding the extension of Nell's reins, set off east on the Harrodsburg-Lexington Road. Everything was still and silent except for the constant chatter in his mind. The solitary conversation's purpose was to ensure that no part of the plan had been left undone.

"My biggest fear now is I'll pass a horseman or a carriage making its way back to Harrodsburg. Luck and the Lord have both been good to me thus far.

I just don't know if I can continue to enjoy such good fortune."

This internal prattle persisted as the two horses moved along the road at a fast walk – but a walk, nevertheless.

"The fog – it's remarkable how helpful it's been. God must have willed this unexpected blanket to settle on the earth so as to conceal this crime. I think it'll be easy to remain obscure, even if I encounter another traveler on the road. In fact, the fog's become so dense I think sensible travelers might pull off the road and seek shelter in a barn or in a house. They might even set up a camp on the pasture side of the stone walls. That'll prevent anyone from spotting me."

Suddenly he sensed sound ahead. A quivering shiver flashed up and down his nervous system. He was frightened more than at any other moment during the night. Others were on the road as well. Potential witnesses were on the road. And he would have to pass them . . . to confront them. He could hear them approaching, but he couldn't see them. His only method of estimating their whereabouts was going to have to be his sense of hearing - as his sight had been rendered worthless on such a foggy night.

There were two of them. He was sure of it. And the voices of the men, while intermittent, were getting louder and louder. The noise was peppered with raucous laughter - likely due to an off color joke or a humorous reminiscence of the evening.

"These are certainly two rowdy souls who, no doubt, lingered too long at a bar and consumed a big bottle of whiskey."

Calvin veered his two horses far to the right of the road in anticipation the men would pass by him down its center. They wouldn't be able to hear his approach. Calvin considered whether he should call out to announce his presence. If so, he knew he needed to refrain from speaking to these men – or, at least, he should keep his speech to a bare minimum.

He slowed the pace of the animals so neither of the men would recall meeting a horseman who seemed in a hurry. He had kept calm and cool thus far. And these characteristics had served him well. This wasn't the time to alter his methodology.

He gauged their voices and calculated they were within thirty feet of him. It was time to implement the only plan he thought might work. He slumped in the saddle as if he were drowsy . . . or even asleep. He kept his head lowered

. . . looking at the saddle horn. He pulled the brim of his hat low over his face.

The revelers were seconds away. He could clearly hear their conversation. "That's the darndest thing I ever hear tell of, Danny. Ain't nobody gonna believe you had your way with that good-lookin' woman."

"I don't care what anybody wants to think. I'm the one she left with and they're just jealous they didn't."

Then the two horsemen emerged from the misty cloud about fifteen feet ahead of Calvin. They had spotted him and they slowed their pace to a crawl. But they never stopped to engage this unexpected man who hadn't yet made a sound. Calvin could tell two sets of eyes were set on him. And the men's sudden silence made him worry they might want to stop and talk a spell.

But, they didn't. The man on the outside of the road spoke up first. Then he was followed by his friend who cried out. "You sneaked up on us feller. Didn't hear nothing out there in the fog."

"Didn't hear nothin' cause you been runnin' your stupid mouth. Ain't no wonder, Danny."

Calvin turned his head toward the two men . . . just enough so they would only see his broad hat brim far more than his face. He said, "Evenin,' gentlemen. You two be careful out here in this soup."

That's all he said. And Calvin feared it had been too much. Just as he finished his single sentence, the two passed by him. He knew he had pulled off the scheme when he heard one of them turn about to speak. "You be careful, yourself, too. Ain't nothin' ahead . . . but more of the same weather."

"That's right. And the worst is ahead of you. Fog's real thick up near the river," the first man's friend said.

Calvin thought he had succeeded. His tense muscles loosened and he released some of the tension with a long, slow exhale.

"Surely if they were going to stop me for a chat, they would've already done it."

His heart was still racing, but every yard he put between them and his victim's corpse was encouraging.

The last thing he heard happened when the two riders must have been thirty feet behind him as Danny was heard saying, "Melvin, I do declare that man's been drinkin' so much he don't know where he is . . . or where he's a goin'."

The ploy had worked. Calvin speeded the pace of his horses. "The more distance I can put between them and me, the better," he thought.

It wasn't until about two minutes passed that Calvin felt reassured. "I think it might be possible they didn't even notice I had a pack horse at my side. So they surely didn't notice the rolls of canvas. It must be well after midnight by now and I've got to hustle if I'm going to make it back to Henry's by sunup."

Thirty minutes later he could sense he was near his planned destination. The Kentucky River was just ahead and he turned the horses left on to a trail he knew led to the place he had decided - after lots of consideration - would be the best site to dump the body. He had been down this trail a number of times just to admire the river view. This spot was where the canyon walls on both sides of the river were the steepest.

He had often stood there and counted the many different horizontal stripes of limestone tiered up and down the cliffs. Each layer delineated one long geological era from others. From this vantage point he had once counted seventeen different shaded bands from the crest of the canyon down to the river. A seventeen layer canyon height is just what he needed this night.

About half a mile from the road, Calvin knew the small clearing he was seeking was near. There was an open space just large enough to unroll Dolly's canvas tomb. And there was also a promontory that allowed him to stand at the ridge's edge and toss the body into the river.

Calvin dismounted from Noah and tied both horses' reins to a tree. Then he began to untie the crisscross web of knots he devised back at the inn to secure the body. He surprised himself to realize how gently – almost reverently – he unrolled the tarpaulin until the lifeless mass of his former enemy was revealed. She was lying face up.

Then Calvin looked down at her face and began to lecture his victim. He scolded this lifeless carcass in a way that specifically suited his needs. There was no hint of regret revealed in his words.

"Dolly, you know you got what you deserved. You asked for this grim end to your treachery, didn't you? But you never suspected it would come down to this.

"You filthy whore, don't you know what a fool you've been . . . trying to topple a man who's been pre-destined by our Lord to lead His people here on earth. Didn't you know about predestination - and the fact you were born destined to only be a lowly bar maid – and a blackmailing bar maid, to boot. You picked me as your mark. But you didn't know that I'm what the Greeks called a 'philosopher king'. God bestowed on me all the many blessings that define who I am . . . and who I'll become. He knows the good I'll do for His kingdom and for our country. It's God who wants me to go into the Tennessee wilderness to serve as a model citizen for Christ. And it's God who wants me to send you along to hell.

"Didn't you know it's not right to challenge the natural order of things that God's made manifest here on earth? And He's made manifest that I've been preordained to greatness. I couldn't allow a sinning slut like you to mess with the world's natural order of things. I have a duty. I've got to ensure His order in the world remains intact."

A harsher homily was ever uttered at graveside.

Then he said a silent prayer – one strangely like might be offered at any burial service. Immediately after the "Amen" it was time to act quickly. He fetched the two hemp sacks and the rope he appropriated from Henry's barn. He had already cut the rope into four sections that measured about eight feet apiece. It was easy to find sizeable rocks on the canyon ridge. Calvin located four that weighed about ten pounds each.

He put two rocks in each bag. He tied the openings tighter than he ever tied one before. He secured one end of the rope below the knot of each bag and lugged each of the rock laden hemp sacks to the ridge. Then he carried Dolly and lowered her about three feet from the ledge. He placed her so one rope could be tethered to her legs and the other end was tied to her waist. He seemed satisfied he had managed to tie these two knots even more taut than the others before.

He had prepared Dolly for her burial. But she wasn't going to be placed in the earth with a priest reciting "ashes to ashes and dust to dust". This burial would be at the bottom of the Kentucky River. There'd be no dust accumulated from her rotting remains. There'd only be a quick deterioration of her soggy mass of flesh . . . weighted down at the bottom of the river. Chunks of putrid flesh would separate from the deteriorating carcass in three or four days as huge catfish swam about and sniffed at such a curious sight.

Calvin laid the body and its two bags of limestone ballast inches from the edge. And, while still squatting over the corpse and holding the bag tied to her waist, he spoke his last rites.

"Remember, Dolly, it's against God's will to challenge the natural order of things. God's clearly pre-ordained you to go to hell. And so, it's with great pleasure that I now send you there."

He picked up the weight at her waist and pushed it over the cliff. In a millisecond, her body was plunging out of sight as the weight securing her legs almost instantly leaped into mid-air and plunged downward.

But Calvin didn't hear a splash. The absence of sound had to mean trouble. He lay on his stomach, he gripped the cliff's edge with his clawed hands, and he peered over it to determine what had happened. Just barely - down there in the fog - he could see there was a thin, rocky shoreline at the base of the cliff. It was, maybe, five feet wide.

The trajectory of the body's free fall missed the river. There was a small tree below that must have washed ashore during the last heavy rain. It had pinned its roots against the river's edge. Dolly's body appeared to have caught the trunk of the tree. Yet, it also appeared both bags of ballast were solidly in the water.

"I knew there was a serious flaw to this plan. Now I must backtrack to a spot where I know I can descend to the river. I think I can negotiate myself along the bank and push the body off the trunk. But now my concern is time. Traipsing around down there would require about two hours. There's no way I can do it . . . and still return to Henry's by sun up."

Calvin went limp from his despondency, just as Dolly's body had been limp when she gasped for her last breath. Suddenly, he remembered a day he was operating the family ferry. It was halfway across the river. He looked upstream and saw danger rushing directly at him. He knew he couldn't avoid his flat boat being struck by a tree swept forcefully at him. There was a pretty girl on board who was certain this rapidly moving battering ram was going to split open the hull . . . and the ferry would sink. She screamed. She was sure she'd soon be going to her death. At first, Calvin reasoned with her. He said she was being hysterical and irrational. He told her all was safe . . . even though that was far from the truth.

And then, on a whim, he huffed and puffed like the wolf in "Three Little

Pigs". He blew long blasts of air at the log with all his might. Miraculously, the current suddenly swept toward the shore and pushed the tree's course away from the ferry. It floated down stream as fast as an empty canoe. The young passenger was delighted and Calvin vainly claimed credit for saving her life. However, underneath his false hubris he was confounded how and why what had happened . . . happened.

If only now he could blow air out of his lungs forcefully enough to push Dolly's body over the branches and into the water. But he couldn't. And he knew it. He needed another miracle right about now – a dark miracle that would save the hide of a murderous "philosopher king".

Calvin imagined his certain humiliation in the Danville community. He realized his relationship with Dolly was sure to be exposed. And the Cabell family would be doubly cursed when he faced trial for murder. He thought again about taking those final steps along the gallows and having his head covered with a burlap bag by the executioner.

He imagined this burly man's face was covered with a black leather hood . . . with cut-out holes through which one could see only his eyes, his nose, and his mouth. His body sweat reeked of onions. The hangman's lips curved into a vengeful smirk and his eyes bore disdainfully down on him. He could feel the executioner lowering the noose over his head. Skin scratches from the hemp rope sliding against his face and around his neck were the last sensation of life he would remember. In seconds he would be dead . . . like Dolly.

Looking down at the foggy current he wondered if his moral premise had been wrong - and if his plan had just this one flaw. However, just maybe . . . he could blow at that body and push it along on its way.

He had no choice. He needed to blow a stream of air . . . strong as the bellows a blacksmith uses to blast dying coals with an intense surge of oxygen. The bellows' life- giving force renews the coals. The blasts of wind transform them from gray to red . . . and then to searing white-hot heat.

There was nothing else to do but blow at the body – some forty feet below. And that's what he did. He blew three times. He thought if the wolf could easily blow down the pigs' houses with his huffs and puffs, then he, too, had a chance. So, he sucked in his breath until he thought his lungs might burst, and he blew hard . . . three times more . . . until he felt faint and dizzy. And while he was waiting for blood to rush back to his woozy head, he looked down. He was stunned to see the encased cadaver sink ever-so-gracefully into the river.

"I told you not to fool around with the natural order of things, bitch." This cruel curse was his final farewell.

\* \* \* \* \* \* \* \* \* \* \*

Two hours later the sun was beginning to rise above the tree line just as Calvin was unsaddling Noah in Henry's stable.

He had already removed the tarps from the draft horse and he had set his four legged partner in crime free in the pasture . . . to rest after a long night of perverse service. Calvin, too, needed his rest. He was ready to retire to Henry's house. He knew he probably wouldn't sleep. But he would know he was safe there – that every detail of his plan was masterfully planned and executed.

But, as he looked outside through the open stable door, what he saw made his blood run cold, once again. It was Mansel. He was fifty feet from the stable. Calvin thought there was no doubt he was doomed. He knew he would be cornered . . . and exposed . . . just seconds shy of success.

"Mornin', Mister Cabell, fine mornin', ain't it? How'd you sleep last night? I hope it was sound. I know that's what Mr. Caldwell wanted for you – a night of sound sleep. He tells me you'll be gettin' on a riverboat in a few weeks and heading down the Mississippi. He wants you to get good and rested 'fore then."

Without missing a beat, Calvin's shifty, criminal mind thought of a solution. "I slept like a log, Mansel. In fact I feel so fine I thought I'd saddle up Noah and we'd go out on an early morning ride."

Calvin reached for the saddle blanket he had just removed from Noah minutes earlier. He placed it, once again, on the horse's back. Noah turned to look at him with flared eyes full of apparent consternation. Then the freshly minted murderer walked over and picked up the saddle sitting over the stall wall and he placed it atop the blanket.

"Well, you shore do look relieved and refreshed, Mr. Cabell. It's like you shed a heavy burden over night. I know Mr. Caldwell's gonna be mighty pleased to hear of it. I hope you and old Noah enjoy a nice ride. The sun's a shinin' – just like God's lookin' down on His creation . . . and He's mighty pleased at what He sees."

"You think so, Mansel? I don't know. I wouldn't venture to guess what God's thinking as He looks down on his creation this fine morning. I, truly, don't know what He's thinking today."

# CHAPTER

# 6

July 1824
Louisville, Kentucky

The coach trip required two days of uncomfortable confinement in a tightly packed compartment that jostled its passengers like dice are shaken before the throw. So, when Calvin Cabell finally stepped out of the four passenger vehicle at its destination his bones ached. But the relief of knowing, at last, he had arrived in Louisville was panacea enough for the pain.

Henry Caldwell had offered to transport Calvin from Danville to Frankfort. Caldwell needed to deliver a load of honey harvested from his bee hives to a wholesale customer. As their wagon approached the Frankfort ferry line over the Kentucky River, they noticed about thirty people gawking at something located upstream . . . along the shore. There were four fishing boats clumped together and the person at the center of the hubbub was a sheriff . . . or some sort of law officer. The onlookers stood about two hundred feet from the ferry line, so Henry and Calvin jumped down from the wagon and walked toward the curious crowd.

"What's going on?" Henry asked a man dressed nicely in a brown plaid suit. However, its intended statement of fashion was diminished by the natty hat he wore.

"Fishermen thought they landed a prize river cat, but what they really snared was a bloated corpse. It's a woman . . . been soaking in the water for a month or so."

"A month," Henry repeated with his nose turned up like he just smelled a skunk. "Most drowning victims . . . especially women . . . are found right away. They're always accompanied by, at least, one party who can report such an incident. This all sounds odd to me."

"Oh, it's odd all right," the man continued. "Sheriff says it looks like she was strangled and all her body bruises were caused when she got dumped into the river . . . probably far upstream, he says."

Calvin began to make his way courteously through the crowd. Henry found it peculiar his friend seemed intent on inspecting the body. Calvin had never exhibited any ghoulish inquisitiveness before. But . . . here he was . . . making a bee line to the corpse . . . even though there was nothing much to see. It lay on the ground completely covered by a gray wool blanket.

"Sheriff, do you mind if I take a look at the body? I heard someone in Danville mention a woman had disappeared. I'd like to have a look, if I may?"

The sheriff was crouched beside the woman. He looked up at Calvin who was leaning far forward . . . as if he were already set in motion to remove the shroud himself. When Calvin saw the look in the Sheriff's eye, he instantly knew he had said something incredibly stupid. He knew he would have to think of something quick to assuage his words. But what would he say that would make sense?

"What's your name, sir?" inquired the Sheriff. Calvin stood there looking so dopey that the sheriff thought maybe he didn't have a name. Or, if he did, he didn't remember it. Finally, he stammered out a response. "My name is Calvin Cabell. I live in Danville and my family operates the ferry upstream . . . along the Danville-Lexington Road."

"And what's the name of the missing woman, Mr. Cabell?"

"I . . . I don't recall. I mean . . . I don't know. I mean . . . I just overheard someone on Main Street mentioning a woman who was missing."

"Well, what description of this woman did the person you talked to give?"

"I don't know. I mean . . . I don't remember. Do you mind if I take a look at the body?"

"Why's that? You say you don't know anything about this missing woman and you want to take a peep at this corpse? What's up your sleeve, Mr. Cabell? I don't get it. This ain't no freak sideshow."

Calvin was doing his best to think through everything he said from this point on. He had already acted way too inquisitive . . . and he had volunteered too many details. Now he had to pass muster with more than just the sheriff. Henry made his way forward and he stood behind Calvin. When he finally decided what to say next, the sheriff had already begun to undrape the corpse. "I just thought I might recognize her . . . you know. I thought I might be of some help identifying her."

"It's that woman from the White Oak Inn," Henry blurted out while covering his nose with a handkerchief to avoid the soggy stench of rotting flesh. "You know her, Calvin."

"I don't believe I do, Henry. Although I heard the bar maid there was missing."

"Of course you know her. I remember you mentioning her to me a month or so ago."

The sheriff was picking up how disingenuous the banter between these two friends had become. He had dredged up very little information so far this morning. So, he tried a different tack.

"Who was this person who told you the woman from the White Oak was missing, Mr. Cabell? Maybe I'll need to look him up in the future . . . and ask him some questions."

Again, Calvin managed only to stumble over his words. "Well, I declare, I'm not able to remember much of anything today, sheriff. My mind's gone blank. Since you have nothing else to go on, give me a moment to get over the shock of looking at such a gruesomely decomposed body and breathing in the stink in the air."

"Oh, we've got some items to begin working with. In the large pocket on her skirt we found this purse . . . and inside it, there was some sort of a note written on a blank receipt from the Barry Merchandise Store. The ink's blurred from being soaked. I can't tell if it's the one in Lexington . . . or Nicholasville . . . or Danville.

"Well, I'll be," Henry began to exclaim at the coincidence of it all. But Calvin cut him short . . . holding up his palm toward his friend and indicating he wanted to speak.

"That's interesting, sheriff, on two counts. I operate the Barry store in Danville and, secondly, it seems strange a store receipt was left blank. We like all our sales slips to indicate a hefty purchase was made." He cackled a nervous laugh.

"Maybe so," said the sheriff. Then the only other thing we've got to go on is this brass coat button. It's a mighty fine example of workmanship. It must have come off a gentleman's coat. How it got in her pocket . . . we'll never know."

Calvin's eyes bugged out despite the fact he tried to keep them planted in their sockets. The button was his. He knew it was missing from his riding coat. But he thought it must have fallen off from wear and tear. Dolly must have pulled it off in the struggle . . . or maybe it just fell off and into her dress pocket. And to make matters worse, Henry had reached forward, taken it from the sheriff, and he was examining it . . . very closely.

"It's fine workmanship, sheriff. It's crafted beautifully. I'm sure I've seen buttons like this, but I can't pin down where that might have been."

Calvin decided it was time for him to take the offensive. He took the button from Henry's hand and looked at it for a brief moment. Then he passed it back to the sheriff who was covering the body once again. "Yes, it illustrates fine workmanship. Well, sheriff, we must be off. Good luck fitting the pieces together. I've got a stage to catch . . . first leg of a long trip."

Then, as if according to a preset cue Calvin devised, he spotted the stage coach coming down the river embankment from Lexington. Its four horse team had slowed down to a slow walk. "Hey, there's the stage. Come along, Henry. We need to fetch my satchels. Good day, sheriff. And, again, I wish you good luck."

As Henry and Calvin unloaded his belongings and made their way to the roadway, Calvin wouldn't let Caldwell get a word in edgewise. He kept prattling on about trivial matters. "Well, here it comes, Henry."

The coach mounted the ferry on the east bank. Then it slid across the silky river looking like a praying mantis clinging to the top of a floating, curled-up magnolia leaf. When its blindfolded horses pulled the vehicle back on to the roadway on the river's west bank, Calvin paid the driver his three dollar fare. He slapped Henry on the back and bid him farewell . . . and, in just a few seconds, the team felt the snap of a whip above their heads. Fast as a flash, they darted off along the Louisville Road.

The coach already had two passengers who boarded at Lexington. Conversation among the men was inevitable. Both men knew Calvin's father-in-law. One of them, Robert Jennings, said he once met Calvin following a Sunday service at the McChord Church. The threesome talked along the route about a broad range of topics. Calvin provided the travelers with a fairly detailed account of the events which led up to his lengthy trip. Neither of his fellow passengers was familiar with a town named Memphis. But both men were knowledgeable about Isaac Shelby's role negotiating the purchase of the Chickasaw land west of the Tennessee River.

Jennings was the younger of the two. Abrams was the portly passenger who began to talk about news that chilled Calvin to the quick.

Abrams brought up the subject of the corpse found in the river. He got his information while the vehicle was loading the ferry on the Frankfort side. "It was decayed something awful, I heard. But it was still recognizable . . . and it could be identified, I'm told. It was a bar maid at the White Oak Inn in Harrodsburg."

Jennings was intrigued at what he heard and quickly spoke to offer a hypothesis. "I'll bet it was that whore, Dolly. I know a man in Lexington she tried to blackmail. Said she was pregnant with his baby. And there wasn't a particle of truth to it. She wasn't pregnant at all. It was just a ruse . . . and a scam. She demanded money from the man to keep his wife in the dark about the sordid affair. But she sure as hell scared the piss out of him for several months."

Calvin said nothing. However, all sorts of thoughts surged through his head. He couldn't believe his ears.

"So Dolly had a habit of using the 'You're the father of my unborn child' trick. She wasn't pregnant at all. Of course, I knew it wasn't mine . . . and so did she. Oh, my God. I killed a woman who probably would've never bothered me again if I'd just given her several monthly payments. Then it would all be over when her belly failed to swell. She got ten dollars out of the extortion . . . and that might have been the end of it. My dear Lord, she was never an actual threat at all."

He wrestled with this information throughout the journey. He said little to his fellow passengers. He just sat there facing the back side of the coach as he silently stared at the passing countryside.

"I've killed a woman who couldn't have even pulled off the scheme," he groaned to himself. Then his mind flashed on the sights he had seen today at the river – the button, the purse, and the store receipt. "As soon as I return

95

home, I'll bury that riding coat. No one will ever be able to match that button if I do that. Oh, how I pray Henry will remain mum about what he's learned."

The coach stopped at Middletown for the night where Calvin and Jennings had to share the same bed. It was a restless slumber. Jennings snored . . . which kept Calvin awake for much of the night. He lay in bed and wondered what other strangers he would meet on this trip and what sorts of future accommodations he would have to endure on his "due diligence" journey. But every time he thought sleep might be his to claim, it was Dolly who stood in the way of slumber. He was certain she'd be responsible for many more sleepless nights in his future.

Catherine had coolly bid farewell as Calvin boarded Henry's wagon. He hopped on to the bench just after he held up each of his children for one last goodbye hug. Catherine was still very upset her husband kept "hallucinating about uprooting his family and moving so far away that, for all intents and purposes, we'll be abandoning Jamie's and Cassie's grandparents."

 Following Isaac Shelby's report from Andrew Jackson, Calvin spent an entire afternoon with his father-in-law explaining what was happening and he sought his moral support. Calvin framed his interest to justify the journey by telling Mr. Barry, "The trip provided an opportunity to investigate further expansion of the Barry family business on the Tennessee frontier."

His father-in-law didn't buy this rationale for one instant. But he knew from his own youthful experiences what it was like to be a bright young man with dreams of his own. Barry reminded his son-in-law that it was a noble deed to continue the nation's westward development. He also reminded Calvin the Presbyterian General Assembly had passed a resolution just after the turn of the century. It encouraged the migration of its members    . . . so the church might spring forth within the new settlements being founded in the expanding West.

In the end, Mr. Barry offered his approval – albeit a tepid one. He also issued an invitation for Catherine and the children to live with him and her mother during the trip. Calvin estimated it would take three or four weeks. Staying in Lexington was the only part of Calvin's journey that Catherine considered to be palatable.

"It was like winning a consolation prize at the county fair," she told her mother.

The next morning the coach departed the Middletown Inn at six-thirty. At last, just before ten o'clock, the two horses began their descent from the highland region on the eastern edge of the city. There was a roadside clearing that overlooked Louisville and the Ohio River. Calvin asked the driver to stop there momentarily so the three men could gaze and measure the growth Louisville had enjoyed since its founding in 1775.

Louisville had a population of approximately six thousand people. As Isaac Shelby had earlier pointed out, it was a geographical certainty some sort of a city would arise right here on the Ohio's southern river bank. The only impediment to navigation along the eight hundred mile Ohio River was here. This geographical barrier – as Governor Shelby had reminded Calvin – was known as the Falls of the Ohio. The falls dropped only about six feet, but its exposed boulders could snag a flatboat and easily slice through the hull of a steamboat.

Consequently, every flatboat and all the other downstream river traffic had to off-load its cargo at Louisville. Crews transported the freight on land for about one-eighth of a mile along the river's edge. Once a boat was cleared of its cargo's weight, it was light and buoyant. Then, it could be safely maneuvered over the falls and pulled to a loading landing. Once there, crewmen reloaded the cargo on the downstream side of the falls so the craft could continue on its journey . . . unimpeded all the way to New Orleans.

In 1783, when Kentucky was still a county of Virginia, Governor Thomas Jefferson commissioned General George Rogers Clark to explore and secure Virginia's interest in the territory's domain. At that point in time, the countryside located on the north side of the Ohio across the river from Louisville was technically a part of British North America. The British were a constant threat to the Americans. So, Governor Jefferson wished to establish a fort at the waterfall in the event there was a need for defense. General Clark built his fort on Corn Island, located just below the falls. Later, two other forts were constructed on the mainland. Louisville was born.

The city's name was selected because in the years following the revolution, the new nation was enamored with all things French. France's alliance – even though it was late in the war – with the freedom-seeking colonists was the source of this infatuation. Kentuckians, in particular, expressed their devotion to the French in the names they selected for new towns throughout Kentucky County, Virginia. Louisville was named for Louis XIV and the list of municipal tributes also included Versailles, Paris, and LaGrange, the French estate of the most idolized Frenchman of all, the Marquis de Lafayette. Lafayette's name was also immortalized when the county

97

surrounding Lexington was named Fayette County . . . in his honor.

Bourbon County was named by the state legislature to honor the French royal family. The manufacturers of the corn-based whisky produced in the region slowly began to refer to their amber spirits as Bourbon. It was a clever marketing tool. It added a touch of savoir faire and elegance to an otherwise ordinary corn whisky. The new name was clearly more sophisticated than the liquor universally referred to as "moonshine".

When the stage's passengers disembarked on Main Street near Seventh Street, Calvin bid goodbye to his new friends and they both wished him well. Calvin hired a porter to fetch his chest that was fastened to the platform on the rear of the coach. The porter was a free black man who used his jimmied up hand cart to serve travelers . . . just like Calvin.

Before he gave instructions to the porter he bought from a newsboy a copy of the <u>Louisville</u> <u>Courier</u>. Notices of steamboat departures and the points up and downstream they served were published in it. The advertisements were posted either by the boat's local agent or it was paid for by the vessel's captain. Calvin read a notice authorized by a Captain Lawrence Moore of the steamboat, 'Lady Luck'.

The notice read: "Bound for New Orleans and all points between, the 'Lady Luck' departs Louisville August 7, 1824 at seven o'clock in the evening. Exceptional food and lodging aboard is provided to all cabin passengers."

Calvin reached for his pocket watch. He knew today was the seventh of August. When he flipped open the cover to his gold time piece he could see the time was presently quarter after twelve. He ordered the porter to follow him down to the wharf where he spotted the 'Lady Luck'. They descended all the way to the base of its gang plank where Calvin asked a crew member if he might speak with an officer. Captain Moore rounded the corner to offer his services and Calvin inquired about the rates for cabin passage. He also confirmed Moore's steamboat would, indeed, make a stop that would allow him to disembark at Memphis.

However, Captain Moore cautioned Calvin about his destination. "Yes sir, you may go ashore at Memphis. But I should tell you there's been so little development there in the past several years, by the time the 'Lady Luck' reaches the 4th Chickasaw bluff, the tiny town might well have died, decayed, and its remains have fallen into the river."

A deck hand guided Calvin to his cabin where the porter placed his trunk on the short stool at the foot of a reasonably sized bed. The room was sparsely furnished. Other than the bed there was a single table on its right side. The table's four feet were secured to the floor with nails and the oil lamp sitting on the table was, likewise, attached to the table's surface. The room's final furnishings were a cane seat ladder-back chair and a chamber pot that sat underneath the bed. Beside it was a wooden ring - a seat to comfortably facilitate the pot's intended uses. Calvin paid Captain Moore the fifteen dollar fare, he tipped the porter half a bit and he told Captain Moore he would return prior to the boat's departure. He wanted to stroll about Louisville in the meantime.

After he ate an early supper at a small restaurant on Eighth Street . . . just south of Main, he made his way to the wharf to board the 'Lady Luck'. As the steamboat pulled away from Louisville and turned downstream, Calvin walked to the boat's stern. He watched the city slowly shrink with each rotation of the paddle . . . until it faded from view altogether. Then he strolled to the bow of the boat and clutched a wooden railing. He leaned far forward and faced the river ahead. The knob hills that bordered both sides of the river's valley looked like mountains compared to the low, rolling fields of his Bluegrass home.

He had never traveled to the western frontier. He wondered if each day would bring an education and an affirmation that these rugged territories would soon be settled - just like his homeland in Kentucky. But until the sun arose again, he thought there was nothing better to do than to return to his cabin and sleep.

"At least," he reasoned, "I won't be sharing a bed with someone whose snoring will keep me awake all night."

\* \* \* \* \* \* \* \* \* \* \*

Calvin's sense of smell awoke him the next morning. His nose reminded him he was enveloped in a mighty river's wet environment. He was struck by the river's pungent smell. He purposefully delayed opening his eyes to savor the unusual aroma. The moisture was palpable as inhaled air passed through his nostrils. He breathed in deeply and processed the mysterious odors of fish and mud and the other distinctive smells of the Ohio River.

"I wonder where we are at this hour?" was Calvin's first complete thought of the day as he sat up and he reached for his pants. With one quick detour to the lounge, where an attendant poured him a cup of chicory coffee, he proceeded to the front of the boat.

The steamboat's engineer, Zachary Thomas, had just concluded his regular morning inspection of the boiler. It was located near the middle of the main deck. When Thomas spotted Calvin looking out over the bow, he approached the passenger to introduce himself. "Welcome aboard, sir. My name is Thomas and I'm the Engineer on board this craft. I hope you enjoyed a restful night."

"I did, thank you very much. Of course, I was due a good rest after the previous night when I shared a bed with a fellow coach passenger. He was the loudest snorer one could ever imagine."

Calvin remembered he was remiss by not introducing himself. "My name is Mr. Cabell and I'm bound for the town of Memphis . . . in Tennessee. Can you tell me where we presently are?"

"We're several miles downstream from Evansville. We stopped there, before sunrise, to take three passengers on board."

"I must have slept more soundly than I thought. I had no sense we landed at a port of call."

"That's the kind of report we want to hear Mr. Cabell. The captain takes pride when he slips silently in and out of a port. We hope you'll pass this information along to others you meet along the way. A satisfied passenger is our very best source of advertising."

"Mr. Thomas, would that be the mouth of the Wabash River I see ahead?"

"Very good, Mr. Cabell, it appears you've studied your maps diligently. Yes, that's the Wabash. It's the last major tributary on the north bank of the river until we reach Cairo. Of course, on the south side we'll soon pass the mouths of the Cumberland and the Tennessee Rivers."

Calvin liked the engineer. He was both personable and he was informative. There was much he wanted to learn about the West. So long as Mr. Thomas was willing to devote the time to share his river wisdom, Calvin considered it a fortuitous opportunity to receive an education from a seasoned crewman.

"I think what fascinates me the most about rivers, Mr. Thomas, is to recognize the sizeable expanse of their basins. Here we are floating along with the aid of rainfall from places far, far away."

"I think about that fact often, Mr. Cabell. It baffles my imagination, too. And when we pass the mouths of the Cumberland and the Tennessee rivers later on in the day, just keep in mind these two rivers drain runoff water from most of Kentucky and Tennessee as well as parts of Georgia and the Mississippi Territory. Then, of course, when we enter the Mississippi, we're riding on top of water that flowed from almost the entire continent."

"How long have you been working on the river, Mr. Thomas?"

"Seven years, sir. Of course, Captain Moore has plied these waterways since keelboats were the big mules on the river. There's so much to learn from the captain. I know you'll enjoy chatting with him along the way."

"Yes, I look forward to learning as much as I can."

At that moment the 'Lady Luck' was approaching the mouth of the Wabash. It drained a considerable part of the Indiana and Illinois territories.

"Mr. Thomas, are there any towns along the Wabash River?"

"No, sir, there are no towns of any size."

Then Thomas' memory realized he misspoke. "Of course, there's an odd community one might call a town – actually a fairly sizeable one. It's difficult even to describe. It's a most unusual experiment in community living – unlike anything I've ever heard of. Its name is New Harmony."

Calvin was curious by nature and Thomas had certainly piqued his inquisitive mind. "How odd, the way you reference it. I come from a world where a duck is a duck and a town is a town. What is it about New Harmony that defies being categorized?"

Thomas had to first ponder the question. There were no easy answers. He stalled for a moment so he could think. "I don't fully understand the social principles that operate at New Harmony. So, describing it would be all the more difficult."

Thomas continued rifling in his brain for words and then he said, "Mr. Cabell, have you ever heard of a utopia?"

Cabell was intrigued all the more. "Yes, the Greek philosophers and ancient mythologies spoke of utopias. I'd define one as some sort of heavenly place . . . that's free from strife and stress."

"That's it. That's a good beginning to describe Mr. Owen's utopia."

"Who is Mr. Owen? Please, tell me more, Mr. Thomas."

"Mr. Owen is a very wealthy man who lives in Europe – Scotland, I think. Anyway, he's apparently so rich and so interested in creating what he calls 'ideal communities' that he bought the town . . . lock, stock, and barrel."

"He bought it. You say he bought a whole town? We're out here on the American frontier, Mr. Thomas. Are you saying that someone prior to Mr. Owen built a "utopia town" out here in the wilderness . . . and then sold it to a European?"

"Yes, the village was constructed by Germans who shared similar social objectives with Mr. Owen's philosophies. But the Germans ran out of money and the living conditions at Harmony - that was the name they gave it until Mr. Owen changed it to New Harmony – began to deteriorate. The Germans desperately needed to sell the property to someone who would, hopefully, continue its utopian social structure. As I understand it, a German walked right into Mr. Owen's office in Scotland and offered to sell it to him. And - what do you know – Owen said, 'Yes'."

"How fascinating . . . a utopia here in the wilderness. Now, what makes a utopia different from a conventional town?"

"I really don't know much more than what I've told you, Mr. Cabell. But it's my understanding that everyone who lives within the community is considered equal . . . despite whatever work he might perform. For example, presently a doctor in your home town makes far more money and enjoys more social status than a store clerk. At New Harmony . . . everyone is equal to all the others. It's called communal living."

While Thomas was telling Calvin Cabell what he knew about New Harmony, the 'Lady Luck' cruised past the mouth of the Wabash. Calvin craned his neck every which way to try to see as far upstream as he could possibly catch a glimpse. He thought for a moment if he looked hard enough and squinted his eyes just so, he could actually take a quick visual tour of the town's premises.

He was intrigued by what he had heard. As the Wabash passed out of sight, he considered what he learned and he thought to himself. "If this sort of unconventional thinking is symptomatic of what I'll find in the American wilderness . . . then I look forward to becoming a part of the western

102

frontier."

* * * * * * * * * * * *

The 'Lady Luck' made a fifteen-minute stop at Henderson, Kentucky. At each city's wharf Captain Moore waited on deck at the head of the gang plank. He bid farewell to those who were departing and he offered greetings and a solid handshake to new passengers as they came aboard.

The first time Calvin had the opportunity to get to know the captain was when the boat docked at Henderson. He estimated Moore was a man in his mid-fifties. And judging from his bearing, Calvin had no doubt he was, also, an experienced river pilot. If one could peer into his mind, they'd no doubt discover he held a solid memory of every turn, every snag, every island, every channel, and every other peril the river ever concealed from inexperienced and naïve boatmen. Moore emanated an air of authority and confidence. He turned out to be extremely personable, as well.

Captain Moore and Calvin were able to enjoy exchanging ideas with one another. Calvin told Moore the reasons he was traveling to Memphis. He asked the captain if he considered the business premise first suggested by Governor Shelby made any strategic sense . . . based on Moore's first-hand knowledge of Memphis and traffic along the river.

"Your premise makes eminent good sense, Mr. Cabell. I've traveled up and down these rivers for two decades. Because of the Louisiana Purchase, the Mississippi River – and particularly, the Lower Mississippi River – will soon be the nation's premier transportation artery. About that, I'm certain."

"You say you've traveled the inland rivers for two decades, captain. That would mean you were a keel boat man in the era before steam, wouldn't it?"

"I began my life on the river as a flatboat contractor for customers in the lower Tennessee River Valley. They were mostly farmers in the region within fifty miles of the Tennessee's mouth. I usually hired others to man a second and third boat. It's best to travel in groups . . . for safety as well as for the collective river wisdom that comes from having more than one mind to cope with a very wily river.

"The Natchez Trace was the only land route back then. From Natchez it was almost four hundred miles to home. Many folks walked it. But I always bought a horse or a mule in New Orleans and rode home. The journey took me about two weeks."

Calvin was nodding his head to illustrate he was interested in what he was learning. There was something perplexing about this pilot. His roots were humble, yet his demeanor and speech illustrated a degree of acquired sophistication. Calvin was fascinated with Moore's accounts of life on the river "in the old days", as the captain had called them. Moore clearly appreciated a good listener, as well. So, he continued to ramble on.

"The best thing about flatboat transportation in those days was the fact a boat cost about fifty dollars to build in Tennessee. After you sold your cargo in New Orleans, you could also sell it for a tidy profit. Hardwood lumber is scarce in that part of the country. The cords of hardwood logs that floated the freight were in great demand."

"My theory, Captain Moore, is that steamboats will revolutionize both freight and passenger transportation. In my judgment there'll be many more fleets of river boats going down the river to sell products at New Orleans. Cargo brings a higher price in New Orleans, because the international trade markets are there. And, furthermore, I figure all of those hundreds of boatmen who previously traveled the Trace northeastwardly toward home . . . and bypassed Memphis . . . well, they'll now travel upstream on a steamer that likely will stop there. What do you think?"

"I think you're right on the money. Fares from New Orleans north are getting cheaper and cheaper as competition drives the price down – especially if you buy a deck passenger ticket . . . which most of the flatboat boys do these days. If you can stand the life of living on a flatboat for a month on your way to New Orleans, you can certainly tolerate being an uncomfortable deck passenger . . . if your trip home lasts just six days. I suspect the Trace will soon grow over with weeds from a lack of traffic."

Captain Moore was enthusiastic about Cabell's interest in the old days. Moore loved to talk, so he continued. "You see, the Trace wasn't just a long and arduous journey. It was dangerous, too. You can bet that robbers will always go where the money is. And farmers heading home with a whole year's revenue in their pockets made them sitting ducks for thieves."

Moore leaned forward as if to emphasize the comment he was going to impart. "You darn well better arrange to travel the Trace with some fellow farmers. At least one person has to stay awake and listen for robbers while the rest get a decent night's rest. Murder wasn't uncommon . . . and many a farmer whose pockets had been rifled through . . . they wound up in a shallow, unmarked grave just off the Trace."

Moore paused again. Then, with a sense of heightened animation he continued. "You know, don't you, that William Clark was murdered – shot to death in the forehead – on the Trace?"

"Well, captain, I knew he died of a gunshot wound. But, as I understand it, many people think he committed suicide."

"Suicide? Why in the devil would one of the most revered heroes in the country want to commit suicide? Look at the great achievement he and Meriwether Lewis accomplished. Mr. Clark's honored by an entire nation. I've heard that tall tale about a possible suicide, too. But it makes no sense – no sense at all."

Just then Calvin Cabell and Captain Moore almost simultaneously spotted a group of flatboats ahead . . . about three-fourths of a mile down stream. After traveling another quarter mile, it was clear there were three of them. They were lined up like two ducklings paddling behind their mother in the pond.

Captain Moore turned to Calvin and asked him, "Would you like to take the time for a leisurely visit with some fellow river rats?"

"How do you mean?"

"I'll stop the paddle up ahead and we can drift for a short time with them. My opinion has always been that everybody on the river needs to look out after one another. There might be assistance we can offer them. And they also might have information that benefits us. I think you'll enjoy the experience. Maybe some of these boatmen can tell you more about times they've spent in Memphis."

Calvin broke into a big smile. "I would very much enjoy such a learning experience . . . and I think you're most gracious to offer to stop the paddle wheel."

When the 'Lady Luck' had advanced within three hundred yards behind the flatboats, the captain ordered the engine to stop. Then he yelled up to his officer in the pilot house and ordered him to maneuver close – albeit, safely close - to the rafts. Slowly, the forward motion of the steamboat decreased to a creeping crawl. Cabell and Moore could see men on each of the three flatboats. They were waving their hats to and fro in the air as a cordial salute. At least, that's what everyone's first impression was. But Calvin slowly began to suspect their hats were waved more as a signal for help. He soon sensed there was an air of despair among the men.

105

"Ahoy, fellow river rats, the 'Lady Luck' bids you a safe voyage on this hot summer day." Captain Moore spoke loudly into the megaphone he held in his right hand. "Throw us a rope and we can visit while we drift alongside one another. I have coffee and drinking water aboard. Any takers?"

It soon became clear the burly man who handled the rudder of the lead boat was the flotilla's leader. He relinquished its steering shaft to a much younger lad. Then, he walked the short distance to the edge of the raft. He was holding a long, loosely wound hemp rope. When 'Lady Luck' was just ten feet from overtaking the raft, the man swung the end of the rope three times in a circular motion high over his head. Suddenly the circles of rope unfurled and stretched straight as it neared its mark. The tossed end was easily caught by a crewman who came forward to assist Captain Moore. The deck hand began to weave the rope into a secure knot around the deck's metal railing.

"Thanks for your hospitality, 'Lady Luck'." The fleet's leader put his hat back on his head as he continued to look up and to carefully inspect Calvin, the captain, the crew, and the other passengers. The look on his face was easy to read. Calvin could tell this tall brawny man had recently experienced a painful heartache. A horrible tragedy must have happened on board. He could sense it in his bones that this was a man who bore the burden of a great personal catastrophe.

"The name's Caperton. We rejoice at your kind assistance."

With the flatboat now attached to the steamboat, Calvin had a good vantage point to look at the craft and its cargo. The wooden rectangle measured approximately thirty-five feet long and twenty feet wide. Just to the rear of what would be the center of its surface area was a crude shack built above the deck. It measured about nine feet by twelve feet. There was an open window on three sides and . . . on the stern . . . there was a single man-entrance that faced the rudder.

The raft was filled with all sorts of cargo as well as some livestock. Calvin was busy cataloging the inventory. The freight was stacked high, or stored in hemp sacks, or contained in bins and barrels. Caperton spoke again. This time there was an emotional quiver in his voice and big tears began to flow down his cheeks. Caperton wiped his face with his forearm, covered by his checkered flannel sleeve. Then, he looked up at Moore and Cabell.

"There's been an accident - a horrible accident. My son fell into the river last night . . . and he's surely drowned." Caperton paused tentatively. "We

106

searched the water as best we could. But a raft can't be turned about easily . . . and the darkness last night was black as ink. We couldn't have seen a body floating in the water if it were five feet from us."

By this time Caperton was surrounded by the crew members of his flatboat fleet. There were nine in all – seven men and two young boys . . . about the age of twelve. They stood together . . . close to their leader . . . as if to buffer him from any further harm. Each of the crew members seemed just as despondent as Mr. Caperton. All the men looked mournfully down at their feet while each held with both hand his broad brimmed straw hat in front of his trousers.

Calvin saw no reason why he couldn't speak up. "How did it happen, Mr. Caperton? And what can we do for you? Naturally, we all deeply regret your loss. Please accept our condolences."

Calvin reconsidered the words that had just flowed from his mouth. He felt like he had sounded trite . . . and that was the last impression he wanted to offer Caperton.

Caperton looked up from his raft and stared directly into Calvin's eyes. "Sir, I thank you for your condolence. But I stand before you . . . a ruined man. My son meant the world to me. I only wish it was me who drowned . . . if it would mean he could've been spared. And his mother . . . his mother will curl up and die when she learns of this tragedy."

Captain Moore spoke gently. "Mr. Caperton, may I ask how this accident happened? You say it occurred last night?"

"Yes, it was late - past midnight. I was manning the rudder, as it was my duty for the evening. Tom . . . Tom's my son . . . Tom was asleep on the bed of straw you can see over yonder in front of the boat house. Even in the dim light from my lantern I could see he had risen from his sleep. Then I saw his silhouette wander toward the edge of the boat. I don't believe he was sleepwalking. I've never known of such behavior by Tom. But he did seem to shuffle forward . . . as if he were half asleep and half awake.

"I called out to him. 'Tom . . . get back from the boat's edge'. He didn't respond . . . and I cried out again with anger in my voice. 'Tom, you know damn well if you need to take a piss . . . you use the privy in the boat house'.

"He surely heard me, because he pivoted to walk toward me along the side of the raft. But he stubbed his toe on the ridge of one of the deck's logs. He stumbled . . . and then he rapidly lurched forward - all at the same time. The jolt of that stumble sent him flailing out . . . and into the river. He didn't stand a chance. I swung the rudder hard to the right with hopes I could turn the raft around and attempt a rescue. I never saw him. But I heard him somewhere in the darkness. He thrashed about in the water for several seconds. Then, he cried out to me, 'Papa . . . Papa, help me . . . Papa?' "

Caperton sighed a deep, long breath . . . intended to gain some control over himself. It was apparent he was reliving in his mind - over and over – every detail about what he had seen and heard.

Then, he haltingly continued. "I gazed frantically at the water on the side . . . and to the rear – beyond the rudder. I kept swinging the rope in the air. I wanted to be prepared to hurl it at him . . . wherever in the darkness I might hear his voice again. I hoped to lasso him to safety. But I never heard his voice. There was no sign of him . . . and no sound of him . . . anywhere.

"My screams awoke all these other crewmen. They, also, frantically scanned the water. No one saw anything. And I thought to myself, 'What kind of a father are you, Caperton? You should've jumped in the river . . . toward the direction of Tom's voice. What kind of feeble excuse for a father are you? Any Dad worth his salt would have jumped in the water to save his son'."

The guilt-ridden father locked his lips in a pained grimace and his face muscles began to quiver uncontrollably . . . while he tried his best to keep from bawling in front of a gaggle of strangers.

Caperton's description of the events that took place seemed to be more of a confession than a recounting of events. It appeared to Calvin that Caperton believed he bore personal culpability for the accident. Caperton was purging himself of his great grief. And he probably hoped his detailed recollection of the incident would slough off, at least, one layer of guilt in the process.

As Captain Moore listened . . . his demeanor grew tense and stoic. He was clearly saddened by what had happened to Caperton and his son. Yet, Calvin sensed the depth of his empathy seemed to be whetted by knowledge of similar death experiences he had known on the river.

"Or, was it just one incident, in particular, he's reliving?" Calvin thought.

Moore finally spoke. But his voice seemed to crackle as he chose his words very slowly . . . very carefully . . . and very tentatively. "Mr. Caperton, I'm so very sorry . . . so very sorry to learn of this accident. I must tell you that only I know the sort of pain you've endured this day. You see, I, too, lost a son in a similar accident aboard a keelboat. I . . . like you . . . warned my son over and over about how very slick and dangerous the deck of a keel boat can become when a fog settles over the river. But my warnings apparently weren't heard – or, weren't heeded."

The 'Lady Luck' passengers and crew were stunned to hear the captain's statement. Here was a tight lipped, straight-as-an-arrow man who wasn't known for wearing his heart on his sleeve. But Caperton's plight must have prompted Moore's sensitive nature to emerge.

Then Captain Moore looked at Caperton and, by now, both men knew they were essentially one – bound by the shared nature of their common personal tragedies.

"My son was playfully chasing his dog. You see, I allowed him to bring the mutt aboard for the trip. I knew before we left home I had made the wrong decision. Robert would run around the deck much of the day playing "fetch" with his dog. My son tossed bones to him . . . and the dog would teasingly scamper away . . . as if to dare the boy to catch him.

"The dog rounded the front of the deck and Robert, my son, slid hard and fast when he tried to make the turn around the bow. Overboard he went - wailing out a frightening scream . . . followed by a splash. I'm certain water surged into his boots as soon as he hit the river. The weight sucked him down . . . below the surface. He didn't have a fair chance at making it. He never came up – not even once. And so . . . he was gone - just like your son suddenly vanished into death's waiting arms.

"I tore my shoes off and dove into the river's black ink. I paddled this way . . . and that way . . . crying out my son's name and swallowing muddy water with each futile shout. I thought maybe Robert might come to the surface – at least, one last time – and I would have a shot at rescuing him."

Tears were slipping down Captain Moore's cheeks . . . even though his voice remained resolute. He had a story to confide . . . a story that might assist another grieving father. It was a story that needed to be purged. This was no time to break down.

"Finally, I realized it. He was dead. I had known it all along while I was floundering about. But I just kept swimming and praying. You see, Mr. Caperton, I think God must have been attending to someone else's needs . . . or maybe He wasn't answering any prayers that evening."

Then Moore paused with a long look of deep consolation which he wanted to extend to Caperton. "Or maybe God wanted Robert to return home to Him. I'll have to wait until I die to have a chance at ever knowing. But I know one thing, Mr. Caperton. My Robert dwells with our Holy Father . . . and he's just fine. I'm sure of it. Your son, too, now abides in heaven with God – and with Robert. I know it. I know it with all my heart."

There was painful silence on the steamboat and the flatboat alike. Both men had publicly bemoaned their tragedy, their guilt, and their unimaginable losses. It was time to move forward and to face the treacheries that lay just ahead . . . along the river . . . as well as along the journey of life. But Caperton had another dilemma. He knew there was only one man who could give him guidance.

"What did you tell Robert's mother, captain?"

Caperton asked the question in a way that all who now stood at the railing of the 'Lady Luck' knew what he was going to say next. "This news will destroy my wife's spirit. She didn't want Tom to travel to New Orleans with me. But the boy wanted to make the journey so bad . . . and I thought it would be a great experience for a son who'd soon be a man."

Caperton then held down his head. His face muscles, once again, suddenly contorted and convulsed frightfully . . . and he began to bawl – lowly at first. But the noise and the tears grew.

"Tom's mother will die of grief. I know it. And she'll hate me for what's happened. She'll put the blame squarely on me. His mother will simply die of grief."

None of his crew members tried to console Caperton. There was no movement among them except for the slow bobbing motion of their bowed heads as they, too, were sobbing in shared grief.

Calvin looked about at the stymied silence. He had to break it. "What can we do for you Mr. Caperton? Can we post a letter to your wife? Can we offer your men any provisions from our pantry?"

Captain Moore once again regained his composure. He desperately wanted to eventually part from these river men knowing they had benefited from this chance encounter – even if it was in some, yet, unforeseen way.

"How did you tell your wife, captain . . . about your Robert?" Caperton inquired.

"I wrote her a letter, Mr. Caperton. I posted it from Natchez. And every night until I returned home to her five weeks later . . . every night I could hear her wailing away. I imagined her crying huge tears that fell on the creases in the letter she held in her shaking hands. I could visualize the paper. It was soaking up her tears. And the ink spelling out the forbidding news dissolved . . . and ran down in faint, soaking puddles . . . as she sobbed uncontrollably over that letter. She read it over and over again - as if she herself was in an endless dream and this message of death was the grimmest part of it. I could hear her cursing me and blaming me, solely, for losing our son."

Captain Moore momentarily gained some composure and then spoke again with a firmer voice in hopes he might help this flatboat captain. "But, Mr. Caperton, I don't regret writing to her straight away, instead of the other option – doing nothing. I could have waited until I returned home so I could tell her face to face. But I think a mother deserves to know her son has passed on - as quickly as possible. She needs to know her son has gone home . . . to our Lord. At least, that's what I reasoned."

Caperton had the look of a man who had already made up his mind about what he should do and when he should do it. He had already given some thought concerning just how his wife should be told the terrible news. His crying abated. But he placed his head down into his hands as if he was mired in deep thought. Finally, he looked up again.

"Captain, I think my Sarah deserves to learn of this tragedy as quickly as possible." There was a long pause. It was a nervous pause. "But Captain Moore, I regret to tell you I cannot read or write. None of us on this trip can write as well. Could you help compose a letter you could send to my Sarah? Could you post it at the next town you visit?"

Moore was touched. But he stared back at Caperton with the blankest stare Calvin had ever seen. Then, it struck Calvin. Moore probably couldn't bear the thought of writing to Mrs. Caperton. He had once written to Mrs. Moore years before. And writing such a letter twice in one lifetime is more oppression than any mortal should have to bear.

Calvin thought, "How many times in one's life can a man write such a letter?"

The young man from Kentucky evaluated the tense predicament before he spoke . . . hoping to resolve it. "Mr. Caperton, please allow me to assist you composing a letter to your wife. I believe you'll begin the closure process all the sooner if you don't tarry telling her."

Calvin glanced over at Moore and he could see his offer was much appreciated by the captain. Moore appeared to be reliving in his mind every single moment of the trauma he endured . . . before, during, and after the death of his Robert.

"If Captain Moore doesn't object, climb aboard and come with me to my room. I have stationery there. We can work together and choose the right words to use in such a letter."

Captain Moore was noticeably relieved at Calvin's suggestion. "Yes, do come aboard, Mr. Caperton. I think Mr. Cabell offers an excellent idea. Take your time. We can post your letter in Paducah. We'll put into port there late this evening."

Caperton climbed up and over the steamboat's railing and Calvin Cabell folded his arm gently around this grieving father's shoulders. He gently led him to his cabin room. They entered and Calvin closed the door.

The two men worked on the letter for more than thirty minutes. And during that half hour, endless crying could be heard coming through the doors of Calvin's cabin. Clearly it was Caperton who was the source of this inconsolable weeping. But more than one passenger who walked down the deck in front of the cabin door claimed Calvin Cabell's crying could also be heard . . . in concert with Caperton's sobs.

At last, Calvin and Caperton exited the room. Slowly they made their way to the deck area where Caperton's rafts remained tethered to 'Lady Luck'. Caperton climbed down on to the deck and the rest of his men returned to their respective flatboats. Their journey was about to continue - without the assistance of 'Lady Luck' . . . and without young Tom Caperton.

Captain Moore ordered the engines turned on and soon the Caperton fleet slowly faded away as it bobbed up and down in the paddle wheel's staggered wake. Calvin held the envelope addressed to Mrs. Caperton in his hand as he waved goodbye to Caperton. He kept calling out. "God be with you, sir. May God be with you. I'll post your letter at Paducah."

And, just when it seemed that shouting might be insufficient to be heard over the churning water the paddle wheel stirred up, Calvin took a deep breath as he leaned over the railing to catch one last glimpse of Caperton. "May God be with you," he cried out . . . in vain. He knew his voice and his consolation were out of Caperton's hearing range. He was only consoling himself.

Moore was in the pilot house when the paddle wheel once again began its slow rotating motion. Calvin looked up at the captain. Moore was standing at the window of his roost looking down upon him. There was communication between the two men without either speaking a word. Calvin took the liberty of moving to the stairwell and climbing up to the pilot house doorway where he knuckled two knocks and respectfully requested, "May I come in, captain?" Captain Moore nodded his head to indicate his silent approval.

Calvin stood shoulder to shoulder beside the captain. Silently both men looked straight ahead at the calm river. Calvin thought about the river's mighty power. It could never be tamed to resist swallowing up young boys. But someone needed to say something. So, Calvin spoke up.

"It was very generous of you to share your own story with Caperton, sir. I believe he took it to heart. No man's consoling words could have been a better balm for his grief than the touching story you told."

Moore finally turned toward Calvin and spoke with quivering emotions still rumbling inside of him. "I deeply regret I had to talk to that man about me losing my son. I hope Caperton didn't interpret what I said as trying to diminish in any way the tragic loss he was feeling. But I suppose that we're put here on earth to help share the burdens of others. I spoke out because only I know how heavy the guilt is that Caperton's carrying. I pray – following all that happened this afternoon – the burdensome weight of Caperton's grief and his guilt is just a little bit lighter."

The two men continued silently looking out over the river for about five minutes. The moist summer air blew against their faces with cool river breezes. The sun was sinking quickly into the horizon. Calvin intended his next question to be one which further peeled away the pall that was cast over the pilot house. He thought it would take Captain Moore's mind away from dwelling on his son. How terribly wrong his assumption was.

"Captain, what ever happened to Robert's dog?"

Suddenly the muscles in Moore's body grew taut – taut as one of the rope knots his crew ties when the 'Lady Luck' is in port. He stood ramrod straight and his face stared stoically straight ahead. Seconds passed. And without looking at Calvin he finally gritted his teeth and spoke.

113

"I caught that dog . . . and I tied his neck to one end of a rope. Then I tied a brick to the rope's other end. I looked down at the dog. Oh, how I loathed that creature. And then, after some time, I said, 'All right, Pup. It's time to play "go fetch". Go fetch Robert for me, would you?' Eventually, I threw Robert's dog up into the air . . . and overboard."

Calvin's mouth was agape. He regretted ever asking the question. He regretted even more learning the answer. And he was galled at the captain's response. It had shocked his senses to the very core. He had lost all respect for the captain. Calvin would have walked off the boat . . . if he could . . . just to separate himself from this demon. But he clenched his teeth and remained silent. He didn't show outward signs of the\ repugnance toward this man that was brewing inside his gut.

At last, after considering all of the evil ramifications of what Moore had just said, Cabell turned and started to exit the pilot house.

"Mr. Cabell," Captain Moore called to Calvin in a low voice as he crossed over the pilot house threshold.

Calvin answered his call by merely turning his neck until his eyes engaged Moore's.

"You asked me what I did with Robert's dog . . . without asking me why I did it."

Calvin was unmoved. But he was willing to listen. So, Moore continued.

"I sat on the deck of that keelboat and I placed the little fella in my lap. That dog knew something awful had happened to Robert. I sensed it. I stroked Robert's dog lovingly – just like Robert always petted him - for probably an hour. With every silky stroke I sobbed . . . and the dog looked up at me as if he understood what had happened and how heartbroken I was about it.

"Robert loved that dog. And as I observed its demeanor, I realized just how much that dog loved Robert, too. They played together for hours and hours at a time. The dog slept with Robert every night . . . despite the fact his mother and I forbade it. That dog stuck to Robert like glue – protecting him from any harm. Robert insisted that his pet travel with us on this particular voyage. And I, of course, relented and granted Robert his way . . . like I so often had done in his life. So, I started speaking to the dog about the hours of fun they both enjoyed when he played with Robert. Finally, I tried to explain to the dog what had happened . . . and I told him how very sad I knew the two of us

114

were – both man and beast.

"And then I thought about Robert floating about lifelessly in that cold dark grave of a river. He was asleep now - for eternity. I was sure of it. But for the first time, he was sleeping alone – without his beloved dog. How could I leave Robert all alone out there in the muddy water?

"I thought, 'Surely, if there's a God in Heaven, then maybe – just maybe – He'll reunite poor, lonely Robert with his best friend'.

"So I talked to the dog about all this. He, of course, didn't talk back. But I swear to you he looked at me with his tongue hanging out – almost aching to do whatever it took to be with Robert.

"And he was saying to me - just like I'm talking to you, 'Cap'n, I miss Robert dreadfully so. I sure would like to go fetch him. We could play 'til nightfall'.

"And I said to the dog, 'I think you should go play fetch with Robert, too.' And you already know the rest. I held the brick in one hand and I held the dog ever-so-gently in the other hand as I bent across the boat's bow. Then I gently tossed the dog into the air and I said, 'Go fetch Robert, will ya'?

"But, in an instant the dog sank below the murky water . . . and I knew he couldn't hear me any more. Nevertheless, I kept calling out to him anyway. 'Go fetch Robert for me . . . and bring him home to me and his mother. I beg of you'."

The tears were pouring out of the captain's eyes. Calvin, likewise, broke down and was sobbing after hearing the desperation of a father who dearly loved his son . . . and a son who dearly loved his dog. Moore kept a firm grip on the wheel throughout his mournful recollection of what happened that night.

Calvin moved toward the wailing man standing there with his knuckles clenched tightly. He put his left arm around Moore's shoulder and, together, they openly wept until the sun's last glimmer had sunk beneath the shadowy trees along the river's banks.

Calvin held on to Moore's shoulder. And there could have been no doubt he was conveying to the captain the fact that Calvin was silently repeating to himself, "There, but for the grace of God, go I."

Then the captain sniffled and cleared his throat . . . and began, again, to speak. "But there's something else I did to the dog I haven't told you."

Calvin squelched every muscle in his body at the mere thought that there were even more regrets to this gruesome tale. Haltingly, he said with a whisper, "What was it, captain? What didn't you tell me?"

"Just before I tossed the dog into the river, I remembered about Charon. You remember Charon . . . from mythology, don't you? He was the ferryman who carried the dead across the River Styx to the opposite shore from life - where heaven and eternal life awaited his passengers.

"You know, Charon is like the rest of us mortals. He's not likely to work for free. He demands a fee. The ancients knew this. And, just before they would lower a body into its grave, a loved one would raise the deceased's tongue and place a gold coin under it. Everyone knew Charon would know to look in the mouths of his lifeless passengers. That's where he was expecting to find his fare. The survivors knew Charon would carry their loved one - all the way to heaven's gate - on the other side of the River Styx."

Calvin suddenly remembered the years he spent as a ferryman. He could easily imagine a hooded Charon - ferrying bodies across a steaming river of death. Then he remembered he had forgotten about religion – his religion. What about any good Christian's faith in salvation . . . like the Bible teaches? "Are you a Christian, captain? Are you a man of faith . . . even under circumstances such as this?"

The captain looked at Calvin as if his passenger suddenly seemed naive – even ignorant. "Oh, I'm a Christian, church-going man, Mr. Cabell. And . . . I suppose I've said the Lord's Prayer about ten thousand times either in church or at graveside. And I sure would like to believe Robert was scooped up out of that dark river by Lord Jesus and he's up there right now in a Christian man's notion of heaven . . . where mansions line streets paved with pure gold."

The captain's eyes had produced a thick layer of tears. An when he talked about "Lord Jesus" scooping up his Robert . . . the biggest tears Calvin had ever seen slowly rolled down his cheeks. His voice quivered, too. But he still had more to say.

"I ask you, Mr. Cabell, to imagine that it was your son who drifted beneath that inky water. I wasn't going to take my chances and solely rely on a blind faith about the church's beliefs. That's why . . . when I was frantically looking for Robert . . . the ferryman, Charon, made just as much sense to help him and me . . . as Jesus Christ . . . or the Old Testament's vengeful sort of God . . . or any other religion's teachings about whatever God is supposed to be like.

"All I knew was the Jesus who was supposed to be looking out after all us Christians had let my Robert die . . . without even a chance to recover his body and hold a Christian burial. So, I placed two coins under the dog's tongue that day – one for Robert . . . and one for his devoted dog. Then I muzzled his mouth with a rope so those coins wouldn't get lost while he was finding Robert and that's when I threw the pup overboard. If Jesus wouldn't look out for Robert in the hereafter, I reasoned there was a chance Charon would."

Calvin didn't know what to say. He thought he couldn't speak even if words . . . any words . . . would pop into his mind. He just looked horrified.

"You ask if I believe in God . . . in Jesus . . . in everything we were taught about what happens to Christians when they die. I don't know what I believe anymore. I don't know if Jesus or St. Peter is waiting for us at the Pearly Gates. And, I don't know, for sure, if there's a Charon that my poor Robert had to bargain with – to negotiate a ride to heaven - with nothing of value to offer the ferryman.

"But, if it turns out Charon reigns over the dead instead of Jesus, then my Christian faith was pretty useless. I wasn't about to miss the chance to do something to ensure the hassles of getting to heaven wouldn't be a predicament Robert had to face alone. I knew the dog would find Robert. And I sure as hell hope they're spending eternity playing together . . . on the other side of the River Styx."

*No Coin for Charon*

# CHAPTER

# 7

August 1824
Cairo, Illinois

The 'Lady Luck' was about three miles upstream from Cairo, Illinois when Captain Moore summoned Calvin Cabell to the pilot house. It was just after five in the morning. At the rear of the boat one could see the sun was making its first efforts to push above the horizon . . . to conquer the darkness of night.

Moore hoped today's sunrise might symbolize more than just the beginning of a new day. He wished it might represent a fresh chance at life. Yesterday's slate . . . the one that recorded all the choices he had ever made in his life – both bad and good . . . he prayed had been erased. He felt certainty in his bones that the slate was now wiped clean.

Moore stood at the wheel and prayed that the sun this day might renew his soul and ensure that what was past was past - forever. Likewise, the captain was hopeful he could start anew with his passenger from the Bluegrass.

A deck hand awoke Calvin by tapping ever-so-gently on his cabin door. "Mr. Cabell, Captain Moore has a hot cup of coffee awaiting you in the pilot house. He's asking if you can join him."

Calvin was awakened from a deep sleep. So, as he climbed the stairs to the pilot house, he was still groggy. But more than anything, he was curious about what could possibly be so important for the captain to awaken him at the crack of dawn.

"Good morning, Mr. Cabell." Captain Moore almost too cheerfully greeted Calvin as he poured a cup of coffee from a blue speckled pot. It was wrapped in several layers of cloth towels to keep its contents warm.

"I apologize for awakening you at this hour. But I knew I'd have to apologize even more if you learned I allowed you to sleep on and miss the sight of the Ohio River merging with the Mississippi. I marvel at it each and every time I see it."

"Did the letter to Mrs. Caperton get posted at Paducah?"

"Yes, I personally handed it to the wharf master. He promised it would be on its way today."

"Excellent. I've thought of little else except how Mrs. Caperton will react when she reads the news her son is dead."

The captain began to offer Calvin his explanation as well as his apologies about last night's conversation. Calvin had just filled his tin mug with coffee and he held it to his lips to take his first hot sip of the brew.

"No need to make excuses, captain. I was glad to let you unload on me. Truly, I was."

"Well, there's also another reason I wanted to speak with you before the others stirred about. I want to thank you for lending your ear . . . which I bent rather shamefully yesterday. I don't believe it's very professional for a steamboat captain with any measure of integrity to unload such personal and disturbing thoughts on a paying passenger. For that, I apologize. However, at the same time I do want you to know how much I appreciated your compassion, your words, and the comfort you afforded me."

"Captain, there's no need for such talk. Yesterday was quite a day for me, too. I got a good dose of life on the river. Or, should I say, I learned the heartaches the river holds . . . from Mr. Caperton's story . . . and from you. I thought a lot about it last night. I want you to know you gave great comfort to that grieving father. I just know his burden is a bit lighter as he, too, awakens to this sunrise."

"I surely hope you're right, Mr. Cabell. But please know that I'll not soon forget the fact you were, likewise, a comfort to me. I don't believe I'll ever recover from losing Robert and his drowning dog. But I can most assuredly tell you that as you and I stood here in the pilot house last evening, I purged a significant chunk of the sorrow and anger that had been dwelling and gnawing in me each and every day since that tragic night. I thought you'd want to know you were instrumental in reducing my burden. And, for that, I give you my gratitude."

Calvin realized Moore was speaking from his heart. But he also knew the last thing the captain would wish to do was talk on incessantly about such a sorrowful subject. Calvin took the captain's cue. He took charge of changing the subject. The revelations of yesterday would never be spoken of again – at least, not among these two men. So Calvin directed the conversation to what lay ahead . . . instead of what had been sloughed off . . . and left behind.

"I believe I can see the rivers' junction ahead, captain. But I can't believe my eyes. Do they deceive me? The water appears to be churning . . . furiously."

"No, Mr. Cabell, you're eyes don't lie. You see, there's a huge amount of force generated when one mighty river collides with another. You might be surprised to learn the Ohio River contributes twice the amount of water to the Lower Mississippi than the Upper Mississippi contributes. The immense power of water is too often misjudged."

"Yes, I can see what you mean. There's a great deal of turbulence ahead."

"Indeed. But it's nothing like the turbulence Nicholas Roosevelt experienced when he first approached this confluence."

"Who is Nicholas Roosevelt, captain?"

"He was the first man to navigate a steamboat from Pittsburgh to New Orleans. That was back in 1811. It's a fascinating tale. If you haven't grown weary from yesterday's ranting and raving, I'd be happy to tell you about him . . . and the story of his steamboat, the 'New Orleans'."

"And I'd be honored and delighted to hear about it," Calvin replied as he lifted his tin coffee mug to his lips for another eye-opening hit of caffeine. "Please, carry on."

"The Roosevelts are a family with great business and social clout back in New York. In fact, they've been instrumental in the affairs of New York almost since the Indians sold Manhattan Island to the Dutch for a chest full of trinkets and beads.

"So when James Watt and Robert Livingstone became business partners in steam boating back East, Nicholas Roosevelt was eager to join their enterprise. He recognized using steam power to propel a boat would bring about a business revolution in an expanding America."

"I know of James Watt and Robert Livingstone. Livingstone was sent to France by Jefferson to meet with Napoleon. He negotiated the sale of the Louisiana Territory. My great uncle, John Breckinridge, was also a member of President Jefferson's administration. He was Attorney General."

"Yep, Livingstone was the government's key negotiator in France. And it was in Paris that Livingstone first met Watt. They hit it off straight away - largely because of their mutual interest in steam power. They even built a small steamboat to navigate up and down the Seine."

Captain Moore now spoke in hushed tones - as if to emphasize he intended passing on a rare nugget of river gossip. "Word on the river is . . . Livingstone was perversely conflicted in his negotiations with Napoleon. Many say he was determined to conclude that treaty for his own personal reasons. They say his motive to double America's size went beyond Jefferson's instructions. They say he had a conflict of interest. But Mr. Livingstone was clearly not one to agree with such a characterization."

"How could his role in the Louisiana Purchase be labeled, 'conflicted'?"

"Well, the answer lies in the story of steam boating. Today we have free rivers with intense competition from many steamboat companies. That's not what Mr. Livingstone wanted . . . or, also what Mr. Roosevelt had in his mind when he first passed this way.

"You see, Mr. Watt and Mr. Livingstone built the first steamboat to travel the waters of the Hudson River in 1807. Their prototype was called the 'Clermont'. Folks marveled that it could travel from New York City to Albany in just thirty-two hours. The Hudson's an important river in New York. But its currents and its dangers in no way compare to the treachery the Mississippi can throw at you. Many a steamboat will meet its doom on this river. You mark my words.

"Since Watt and Livingstone were the first to introduce steam boats to the nation, they claimed their invention merited a guaranteed monopoly for river traffic on the Hudson. And they succeeded. So, along comes eager Mr. Roosevelt. He wanted to secure a similar exclusive franchise on the major waterways west of the Alleghenies. Watt and Livingstone seized the opportunity. They built the 'New Orleans' . . . just up the Monongahela from Pittsburgh. The boat cost them about thirty-eight thousand dollars.

"The 'New Orleans' was a huge river vessel – especially compared it to the keelboats and flatboats of the era. Of course, the goal of these three New

Yorkers was not just to travel the Ohio and Mississippi to New Orleans. The 'Clermont' could have done that. Their objective was to arrive at New Orleans and illustrate that Watt's steam power could push the boat upstream as well. They hoped to jump ahead of any competition that might arise on the Mississippi. It was the group's intention to secure a monopoly on steam powered vessels - just as they had done at home in New York.

"Apparently Mrs. Roosevelt raised a ruckus about her husband making the long arduous trip alone. She wanted to accompany him. So, she nagged at him so hard he finally relented and said, 'Yes'. I think it's remarkable that a pregnant woman from such an elite family would want to be included in this risky experiment. After all, she was a Latrobe."

Captain Moore knew he was telling his story fast and furious. When he mentioned the family name, Latrobe, he thought he should pause for a moment to make sure Calvin was following this lesson.

"You know the name, Latrobe, right? Her daddy was the architect of the U.S. Capitol. And, wouldn't you know it, when the 'New Orleans' reached the Falls of the Ohio at Louisville, Mrs. Roosevelt suddenly went into labor and gave birth to a son. Finally, in early December of 1811, this growing family left Louisville with hopes the New Year would bring them great financial success from a steamboat monopoly on the Mississippi.

"Then on December 16 . . . right at this very junction of rivers . . . as the Roosevelt's were steaming along, the greatest earthquake to ever rumble America fiercely shook the land. The quake was so ferocious and lasted so long that church bells rang . . . as far away as Boston. It was a disastrous quake and it caused many natural catastrophes. Those who experienced it said the land undulated as if the earth was transformed into a long series of ocean waves. Many portions of river bluffs along the river were ripped away and they plummeted into the water. The river surged along the shoreline so forcibly that it created large lakes far inland . . . where none had existed the day before. River islands and much of the nearby river bluffs were torn apart and swallowed whole."

The captain could see Calvin was closely engaged and he was savoring each of his story's details. His passenger appeared spellbound with what he was hearing. His only movement was to continue sipping his mug of coffee.

"People say the violent river waves the quake set into motion were twenty feet tall. And, the quake even caused the Mississippi River to flow backward . . . for three whole days. Imagine that."

Calvin shook his head in disbelief. So, Moore continued on.

"Of course, the Indians living along the river's banks used the best logic they were capable of conjuring up under the circumstances. It seemed clear to them that such apocalyptic devastation to their homeland must be caused by their religious Spirits. The Indians thought the earthquake was surely a sign of their gods' great displeasure with Roosevelt's steamboat plying the river. After all, the land had always been peaceful. It had provided them a bountiful paradise along the river – at least, up until the time Roosevelt's gigantic contraption was first spotted.

"The 'New Orleans' measured a hundred and sixteen feet long . . . and it was twenty feet high. To the Indians, the floating oddity surely looked like the devil himself - spewing his hot, angry steam into the air and leaving swirling wakes of water behind that lapped menacingly at the river banks. It all defied the laws of nature. They referred to Roosevelt's boat as the 'fire canoe'.

"Anyway, just after they first saw it, geysers suddenly shot up into the air. The earth shook. What else could the Indians be expected to believe except their gods were mighty angry at Roosevelt's unholy invasion of their domain?"

Calvin was fascinated to hear the captain's story of the earthquake, and the Indians, and Roosevelt. At one point he wondered if he was misunderstanding Captain Moore, simply because he hadn't yet consumed enough black coffee. Moore momentarily stopped speaking as he inspected the river to his right - and then to his left. He was looking for driftwood or other floating hazards he needed to avoid. That's when Calvin spoke out to prod the captain along.

"So what happened to the Roosevelts?"

"Well, they miraculously survived the earthquake . . . and they DID finally reach New Orleans in the middle of January. They also got their wish to acquire a monopoly – at least a monopoly to the extent that the Orleans Territory was capable of granting one. The term of their agreement was for four years and the exclusivity of service stretched only from the Gulf of Mexico to Natchez."

Calvin was clearly intrigued by Captain Moore's tutorial. His undivided attention to every word, no doubt, stimulated Moore to ramble on with his story. And Calvin continued to pepper the captain with questions.

124

"But, Captain Moore, I don't recall that steamboats navigated upstream on the Mississippi until several years after 1811. Am I right?"

"Well, you're correct . . . and then, you're also wrong. The Mississippi between Natchez and New Orleans is nothing like the nature of the river north of Natchez. South of Natchez the river's deep and relatively calm. The 'New Orleans' managed to grunt itself upstream. But she just wasn't capable of traveling very far beyond Natchez. So the boat was reduced to, essentially, a novelty. It could only make journeys between the two river cities. It was quite a lark for folks to ride aboard her. The cost of the amusement was sixty-five cents for the fare traveling down the river. But a premium was attached for the experience of steaming up the river. You see, overcoming the current was considered such a phenomenon the fare was set at a dollar and fifteen cents."

"So, the 'New Orleans' never progressed north beyond Natchez?"

"That's right. And thank the Lord Watt's and Livingstone's intent to franchise the river rights . . . all up and down the Mississippi . . . were thwarted. A steamboat monopoly would be a great travesty. I think all of us benefit from the brisk competition among commercial steamboats today. As for the 'New Orleans', she got stuck on a snag in the river and sank. I say good riddance."

By the time the captain had completed his lecture, the dawn had evolved into a beautiful summer morning. The sun was shining brightly and 'Lady Luck' had passed well below the intersection of the country's two major waterways. The thick threads of blue water that intertwined with murky water at Cairo had, by this time, disappeared. The Mississippi was now a solid tawny brown.

Calvin could tell Captain Moore had enjoyed serving as his professor this morning. Yet, there was another benefit that came with the tutorial. The pall cast over yesterday's events . . . as well as the confessions . . . seemed to have been dispelled. The captain confirmed Calvin's hunch when Moore took a deep breath of fresh air . . . and then exhaled it slowly . . . with a subtle, barely audible sigh. One would have thought the man had gone through life without ever consuming oxygen in the air – even though it was always there for the taking.

Moore wondered if the rays of this new day's sunlight had already begun to sanitize his soul. Today he was experiencing a sense of redemption he hadn't felt in many years.

"Calvin, you know, adventures on the river are just like our experiences in life. No one knows where the river originally came from. But everyone knows the river – like everything in life - will come to an end. Along the way there'll be heartaches and joys. Regrettably, the human condition is tender. It's mostly the heartaches we remember. So, our lives flow on . . . like the river . . . responding to an unavoidable gravity within mortals that forces us to slowly sink ever downward . . . until we're unable to flow on any longer.

"We must learn to leave the struggles we encountered . . . along the river bank . . . where they occurred. That way they're behind us. They can't revisit us again."

Captain Moore might have been speaking to Calvin, but all the while he was clutching the pilot house wheel and looking straight ahead. Calvin thought the older man might actually be talking . . . simply to reassure himself. Moore appeared to have passed, at long last, through his own life's dark shadows. He might have even managed to thwart his tenacious demons.

It was time to break this broken man's trance and Calvin seized the moment. "Captain Moore, what perceptive wisdom you offer. It comes from a man who certainly knows about life and death and the river. Now that we're rolling along the Lower Mississippi, I can tell you I can feel the river's power. I feel its history. And I believe there's a future along these banks for me and my family."

Captain Moore broadcasted a savvy grin. "I can feel it, too, Mr. Cabell. I can feel you being seduced by my river. Your life and your dreams lie ahead of us . . . downstream. I would bet the farm on that."

"So, how long until we reach Memphis, captain?"

"This time tomorrow you'll be exploring the 4th Chickasaw Bluff on foot."

"That sounds just fine, captain. That sounds mighty fine to me."

* * * * * * * * * *

Early the next morning Calvin Cabell leaned forward into the river breeze with both hands gripping the rail of the 'Lady Luck's bow. He marveled at the immense width of the river. He wasn't aware the Mississippi had so many islands.

126

As he took a closer look he observed deer quenching their thirst along the river banks. They craned their necks downward to cautiously sip the water. Then, each quickly jerked up his head again to take a long look at this curious, out-of-place paddle wheeler. There were also raccoons, turkeys, and other wildlife he spotted. He had the distinct feeling he was implanted squarely in the American wilderness.

Captain Moore appointed his pilot to take the wheel so he could join Cabell on the deck. "We're passing by Paddy's Hens and Chicks over there on your right."

"Paddy's Hens and Chicks? What in the devil does that mean, captain?"

"That's the name for a series of river islands. See them?"

Calvin looked ahead and squinted at the islands while Moore carried on. "There are hundreds of islands in the lower Mississippi. Any captain worth his salt needs to know the names of every one of them."

"I don't believe I could remember the names of several hundred people. I know I could never remember a hundred islands with such whimsical names. My hat's off to you, captain. You've earned my respect in many ways on this trip. This most recent illustration of your many talents is just the icing on the cake."

The 'Lady Luck' veered to the left so as to hug the east bank of the river. That's where the channel is deepest. Suddenly Captain Moore raised his hand and pointed toward the shore line ahead. "There it is, Mr. Cabell. There's your shining city on a hill. Your river journey is about to come to an end. However, I'd bet a thousand bucks that, in many ways, your journey has just begun."

"I can see the bluff, captain. But I can only see a single building."

"That's Young's warehouse. It's built snugly into the bluff. Take my word, in the next few minutes several small buildings will come into view. But you're not going to find any hustle and bustle on this bluff. The population of Memphis hovers at around fifty people, I'm told."

The mouth of the Wolf River could now be seen. It was approximately two hundred yards ahead. At that point the paddle wheel ceased to turn. Slowly, the boat rotated about. It was facing north now . . . and the wheel was situated downstream. Then, once again, Captain Moore set the paddles turning and the boat began to glide steadily into the Wolf River channel. The landing was ahead. It was a shallow earthen shoreline with no sign of life . . . except for a boy waiting for the boat to dock and to lower its gangplank.

Calvin had already asked a cabin attendant to fetch his personal items. So, standing there above the gang plank with his two satchels straddling him, he gave the clear impression to anyone on shore there was at least one passenger who would be departing the steamboat here. In 1824 there were precious few travelers getting off steamboats at Memphis. Even as the plank was being put into place, Calvin called out to the boy, whom he estimated to be about eleven years old,

"Boy . . . yes . . . you, boy. Do you know a man by the name of Marcus Winchester?"

"Yes sir," the boy smartly responded. "I sure 'nuff do know Mr. Winchester."

Calvin leaned over the railing and tossed a bit piece which he arched high in the air before it landed squarely in the cupped hands of the boy. A smile spread across his face. He looked up at Calvin who followed up the gratuity by saying, "You go find Mr. Winchester. Tell him Mr. Cabell has arrived on the 'Lady Luck'. Then run back here and tell me what he has to say to you."

Before Calvin even finished his instructions the boy had already turned and he was racing barefoot up the hillside. Calvin thought he ran more like a thoroughbred colt than a growing, two-legged boy. Within seconds he had reached the hill top and was out of sight.

Captain Moore ordered his cabin boy to carry Calvin's belongings ashore and deposit them far above the shoreline. The crew member had a harder time negotiating the pocked hillside than the boy had experienced. As the cabin boy began his climb, Calvin knew it was time to bid adieu to his new river friend. As Cabell descended the gang plank the captain stood at its base and extended his hand toward his Kentucky passenger. Calvin, likewise, extended his own hand in friendship.

"Captain, I suppose you and I have reached the end of our shared journey. I want to tell you once again how much I've appreciated getting to know you these past several days. I shall not soon forget the experience. I can tell you with assurance that I'll be remembering you fondly in my thoughts and my prayers. God speed, sir."

Calvin thought he spotted a layer of moisture forming over Moore's eyes. Then, when he finally spoke, the captain's voice wavered . . . just a wee bit. "Mr. Cabell, it is I who've benefited from our shared experiences on the river. I also wish, 'God speed' to you. I'm not much of a praying man. But I'll be keeping you and yours in my thoughts."

Both men shook hands heartily. Calvin placed his left hand on Moore's right upper arm to illustrate his sincerity. "Farewell, friend, I hope you'll ask for me . . . or about me . . . each time you dock at Memphis. Who knows what reports you might hear?"

"I'll inquire about you each and every time. And, when it's time for you to travel upstream again, what a pleasure it would be to have you aboard the 'Lady Luck'."

"That's a real possibility, captain."

"I hope so, my friend. I hope so."

Their farewell was interrupted when the local boy began his descent to the water's edge. He was still speedy, but he had slowed his pace. Calvin sensed the boy had accomplished his assigned task.

"Mr. Cabell, I found Mr. Winchester. I told him you were standing on the waterfront. He said he'd be comin' in an instant. When I told him the news, his smile shore 'nuff spread from ear to ear."

"Splendid, boy . . . and good work."

And without further words spoken, Calvin firmly planted one foot ahead of the other as he climbed up the sandy bank. Then, when he reached its crest, he turned about briefly and gave a salute to Captain Moore – who, by now, had pulled the gang plank aboard. Moore affectionately returned the gesture.

Then both men turned about and moved in opposite directions - toward each man's respective mission. The 'Lady Luck' slid out of port and soon re-entered the river's channel. She turned about once again. Soon, she was steaming south.

Both men resisted the temptation to look back for one last peek at the other. A new chapter was ready to be written in both men's lives. Yesterday's entries in their life logs had already been recorded . . . and the lessons they learned were filed away. Now, there were only blank pages waiting to be inscribed with future successes and mistakes.

Calvin Cabell considered for a moment the sordid sins in his own life's log. Even as he stood here . . . four hundred miles from home . . . all alone . . . in the Southwest frontier of a nation only fifty years old . . . he couldn't get his personal demon, Dolly, purged from his consciousness. He wasn't just a sinner . . . like all his fellow Christians. He was a murderer . . . and that unforgivable distinction would always haunt him. His sin was a mortal sin.

But, at least, he wasn't a murderer who had been exposed . . . caught . . . and brought to justice. Maybe . . . just maybe . . . Memphis was far enough removed from the Bluegrass to shield him from the consequences he knew would always be lurking over his shoulders back at home.

The tales Captain Moore told about his son's death . . . and tossing his dog into the river so Robert wouldn't face death alone . . . rumbled through Calvin's mind as he turned around to see that the "Lady Luck" had traveled far enough to appear like a floating toy on a glassy pond. In minutes it would skim around the sharp westward bend in the river and disappear. He wished the gut-wrenching guilt of Dolly's death would disappear, too.

"I should have had the presence of mind to place a coin under Dolly's tongue," Calvin mused. "She didn't deserve the courtesy . . . but I should have done it, anyway."

# CHAPTER

# 8

August 1824
Memphis, Tennessee

As Marcus Winchester rode Marty toward him, Calvin Cabell was impressed at what he saw. Astride this horse was a man who exuded an aura of confidence and integrity.

"This is a person I can trust," Calvin thought as Marcus dismounted. Instantly, he knew he was about to meet a man who would become more than just a new friend. He was about to cement a longstanding relationship with a trusted confidante.

"Mr. Cabell, we've been expecting your visit, although we weren't put on notice when that day would come. The city's proprietors have each written me a letter to express their joy that you have a genuine interest becoming a Memphian."

"A Memphian?" Calvin thought. The word was foreign to him – much like this part of the country was foreign to him. He supposed being a Memphian meant being a permanent resident of the city. But the sound of the word remained eerie. Furthermore, it seemed odder each time he silently repeated Winchester's phrase.

"I, too, have heard much about you, Mr. Winchester. I'm told you're a most capable and honest man - one whom I can trust."

Winchester gave a self-effacing look in response to the compliment. "I'm afraid my halo was part of today's laundry. It's presently hanging on the clothes line to dry."

Marcus chortled at his own reply. Then, both men simultaneously shook the other's hand and each man's smile beamed from ear to ear. Calvin was relieved his host's welcome was so genuine. He insisted they address one another using their first names. Marcus, on the other hand, was overjoyed that a man of means and determination to settle within the frontier had an interest in Memphis as a place to live and to invest his money. The struggling river town needed all the Calvin Cabells Marcus Winchester could unearth.

Winchester looked down at the boy who had fetched him. "Melvin, you take Mr. Cabell's bags up to Mrs. Winchester. She'll tell you what to do with them."

The boy nodded his head . . . indicating his comprehension . . . and he waddled up from the river holding both bags by each outstretched arm. His small size and the weight of Calvin's satchels made it difficult for him to navigate the hill. The satchels sagged from the boy's arms and came within inches of skimming across the mud-caked ground.

Marcus took his horse's reins in his right hand and he ushered Calvin on a walk toward town with the horse following in tow.

"Calvin, how long do you intend to stay here with us? Please know I'm at your beck and call for any assistance you might require. From what I was told, information for a possible business investment is what you're seeking."

"I'm hoping to get accurate information and solid counsel, Marcus. Governor Shelby has spoken so enthusiastically about the prospects of your new town, I felt compelled to come here and take a look for myself. However, I must tell you, Mrs. Cabell isn't happy about the expedition – not happy, at all."

"So I hear from General Jackson. It's only human nature to resist change. It was pure chance that I wound up living here and managing this property for the proprietors. Fortunately, my wife, Mary, hails from Louisiana. So she's accustomed to the sort of rugged life we lead here. The transition was an easy one for her – much easier than it would be for a Lexington belle."

"Well, sir, let's not talk of a family move just yet. Please, just bear with me and assist me with my 'due diligence'."

The two men arrived at what was clearly the largest house in town - although it would be a rather humble excuse for a residence back in Danville. The two leather bags were sitting side by side on the front steps. The door was open - no doubt to circulate whatever hot air could be forced to flow over one's body in the intense summer heat. Then, stepping out through the threshold was a smiling woman in her mid twenties.

"Welcome Mr. Cabell. Do come in and enjoy some tea I've prepared. We've long expected your arrival."

The threesome proceeded into the Winchester home. Mary Winchester served glasses of room temperature tea garnished with spears of mint. She also offered her guest some small pastries she had baked. The three of them apparently had much to talk about. Their conversation lasted for three hours. Calvin recounted to his hosts all he had heard about the investment opportunities Memphis might offer. He asked Marcus to fill any gaps in his knowledge.

Winchester gave him an overview of the city's history. He went back all the way to DeSoto. Then he proceeded forward – up to the present. He said he attended the transition ceremony when Governor Shelby, General Jackson, and the Chickasaw chiefs exchanged their land for the U.S. Government's $400,000. He earnestly repeated over and again how strongly he felt his city on the 4th Chickasaw Bluff would grow and succeed . . . so as to rival any other city in the Southwest. He unconditionally stated to Calvin that he – on behalf of the three proprietors - was prepared to do whatever it took to bring about a Cabell family investment.

Calvin told Mary and Marcus he had justified his trip with his father-in-law, in part, by telling him Memphis might be a potential location for another Barry store. He said Mr. Barry knew such a half-baked notion was nothing more than poppycock. But he understood the wanderlust his son-in-law ached to fulfill. So, he gave the trip his blessing without acknowledging Calvin's reasoning was only a ruse.

Calvin learned that Winchester operated a small store in partnership with Thomas Carr. They had one commercial competitor, Ike Rawlings. His store was located on "the bridge", a natural causeway that separated Catfish Bay from the town. Catfish Bay was what the townspeople called the "lake" which was formed by an unusually wide basin of Bayou Gayosa as it flowed toward its merger with the Wolf River.

Mary Winchester chased the men out of the house so she could prepare a respectable supper for their guest. Marcus suggested the time had come for him "to give our friend from Kentucky a guided tour of our fair city".

Calvin was eager to inspect whatever Marcus wanted to show him. However, he made a mental note his guide had the tendency to speak hyperbolically about such a small village with such big aspirations.

Winchester carried the city's subdivision plan that had been drafted in 1819. It was rolled up and he pulled at each end to straighten out the curls. Then he laid it flat on the ground so Calvin might have a surveyor's view of what the proprietors envisioned. The tour hadn't lasted five minutes when Calvin noticed Winchester's optimistic voice had suddenly modulated. Now there was a dismal, defeatist tone to his speech.

Calvin looked at his new friend. He noticed a grimace had spread over Marcus' face as if he were saying to himself, "Of all the rotten luck . . ."

Then his sudden sullenness quickly converted into a feigned cheeriness. Marcus called out ahead so he could be heard by the older man who had just rounded the corner. The man was approaching them with a purposeful gait.

"Ah, Squire Rawlings, it's most appropriate I have the privilege of introducing Memphis' finest citizen to my guest . . . whom we hope will be Memphis' newest citizen."

Ike Rawlings' didn't speak and his expression didn't yet show any indication what his next words might be. But Calvin felt sure the old man wouldn't be saying, "Greetings, it's a pleasure to make your acquaintance."

Calvin sized up this old man as a crabby fellow who likely would never crack a smile . . . or show him a single sign of hospitality. Rawlings finally stopped, but he kept a safe distance of six feet between himself and the two men. Marcus continued on . . . trying to break the silence. "Squire Rawlings, I'd like to introduce you to Mr. Cabell . . . who's just arrived this day from Kentucky . . . aboard the 'Lady Luck'."

Without missing a beat Marcus turned toward Calvin, as if the newcomer deserved a fair warning. Everyone else in town knew about the old man's foul temperament. Now, Calvin could be added to the list.

"Calvin, Squire Rawlings has lived here on the bluff long before the Chickasaws divested their rights to West Tennessee. He runs a fine general store on the bridge. He also serves as our unofficial Mayor, Justice of the Peace, and any other occupation that might require wise counsel."

Old Ike Rawlings wasn't a man who hankered to newfangled ideas - much less to strangers who were bent on pushing their way into the existing social structure. Everyone recognized that Memphis was Ike's rightful domain . . . and he ruled over it imperially. Ike Rawlings took a long look at the stranger.

Calvin instinctively knew he was being scrutinized and sized up. So he stood solemnly for this inspection . . . as if to illustrate his immediate recognition of Squire Rawlings' importance. Then, when Ike had seen all he needed to see of the outsider, he turned his jaw far toward the left while still holding Calvin firmly in his sight. He spat to the ground an impressive concoction of saliva and tobacco juice. Old Ike devoted several more silent seconds to inspect this uninvited stranger in town. At last, he was finally ready to speak.

"You from Kaintuck, eh boy? What you doin makin' a special trip down here? Ain't much to see . . . and we're doin alright with just the folks we got. Whatchu got to say 'bout that?"

Calvin, strangely enough, wasn't offended . . . even though he could sense the tension that was building within his host. Calvin had met many a contrary ferry passenger crossing the Kentucky River. Each one of them detested change – any change at all. It was Calvin's experience that curmudgeons like Ike Rawlings were hard shelled on the outside. However, with the right salve applied to their cynical spirits, any ogre he had ever known concealed under his crusty temperament a soft spot that cried out to be exposed.

So, Calvin quickly evaluated his repertoire of soft soap techniques and he shot back at craggy Squire Ike. "Thank you for your warm welcome, Squire. I do hail from 'Kaintuck' where the whiskey and the tobacco are as sweet as summer cider. You want to know why I've traveled here? Well, it's to take a look at life on the frontier . . . and to see if there might be a place in it for me and my small family of four. I think it's an appropriate privilege to make your acquaintance before I'm introduced to any other townsmen. You need to know, Mr. Rawlings, that I offer no commercial threat to your business. I only offer you my friendship . . . and I trust you will accept it in the same spirit it's offered."

"Not a bad reply," Ike thought to himself as he continued to silently scrutinize this Kentucky dandy. Ike sensed Calvin had showed some spunk as well as a good dose of respect for him. Then he spoke again. "I think the two of us can get along . . . if he's determined to move his family from the comforts of Kentucky to this mosquito filled swampland."

It was perfectly clear why the city's proprietors had enlisted Marcus Winchester to sell their city lots . . . instead of Ike.

Calvin quickly learned it was the Squire's habit before speaking to cock his head aside in the same manner as before. Once again, he smacked his lips together thoughtfully. Then he spat abruptly again at the ground before he spoke. Calvin was beginning to wonder if Rawlings was capable of speaking at all . . . without punctuating what he had to say with a stern glare and a spit.

"Cabell . . . you say your name's Cabell, do ya?"

"Yes, Squire, Cabell is my name. Calvin Cabell, sir."

"Calvin? You named after that preacher man named Calvin, son?"

"Actually, my name does reference John Calvin, the Reformation leader. I'm pleased you made that connection, Squire."

Ike still had to continue processing both the assets and the liabilities of this visitor. So, he took a few more seconds of contemplation and then spoke – again, prefacing what he had to say with his obligatory cock-and-spit prelude.

"Well, son, I ain't much of a church goin' man. And I shore don't know nothin' about no Reformation. What I DO know about religion is this. Ever now and agin, we get a scalawag flatboatman who washes up on our part of the river bank and he claims to be a preacher . . . who just happens to be takin' his crops for sale downstream in New Or'lins. Oh, you can be assured that the preacher man will start to preachin' at the drop of a hat and – more than likely – he'll pass around his 'offerin' hat' just often enough to buy whiskey fer hisself. Then, after about four rounds of whiskey, he commences to cussin' and startin' fights – all in the name of the Lord, of course."

The ice was beginning to melt. Calvin and the Squire had found a common bond. Both men hated hypocrites – especially church hypocrites. Calvin seized the connection and proceeded to respond.

"Squire Rawlings, I know many a preacher who fits that description and I know many of them come from Kentucky. Therefore, on behalf of all hypocrite hating Kentuckians, I confess we should have hogtied and locked them up before they could set out from home. I offer you our sincere apology for sending such intolerable 'men of the cloth' your way."

136

Ike continued to be impressed. Maybe this Kentuckian might fit into the community better than he first thought. "So, tell me, Marcus, what's the tour plan for Mr. Cabell here? You seem to change up your sales pitch with every Tom, Dick, and Harry who tell you they're interested in investin' on our bluff?"

"Squire Rawlings, Mr. Cabell's not your ordinary, run-of-the-mill 'Tom, Dick, or Harry', as you put it." Marcus replied with an air of confidence and with a sense of humor that came from just observing the local lion lying down with the lamb.

"Mr. Cabell is a friend of another Isaac you know of. He's Isaac Shelby, for whom our county is named. Governor Shelby has recommended that Mr. Cabell take a look at 'our bluff', as you put it. He comes from a family experienced in the timber and lumber mill business. The proprietors have expressed their interest in promoting a mill business in Memphis. And Mr. Cabell's been good enough to travel here to see what our town has to offer.

"As for my 'tour of the month', let me remind you, Squire, what the definition of insanity is. Insanity is when a man keeps doing the same thing over and over . . . while each time expecting these same tired tactics will eventually lead to success. You see, I keep changing my tour routine . . . 'cause whatever I've been doing or telling prospective settlers during these past few years, it appears my speech hasn't been very effective. My goal is to lure a few more decent people to our town so we can stake a sign on the riverfront that reads 'Welcome to Memphis, Tennessee: Population: over 100'. Now, that would represent quite an achievement. Don't you think?"

"The problem with you young fellers is you just keep stirrin' up change where there ain't no need for change. If it ain't broke, don't have no need to fix it. That's what I say."

Marcus wanted to maintain the good nature that had developed between the three men. So, since Rawlings' quaint colloquialisms demanded a response, he turned to the old man while gesturing to Calvin that it was time to be moving on. Marcus fired one parting shot as he and Calvin walked away.

"What I DO know, Squire, about business is this. If your store is going to be more profitable, there needs to be a growing community to foster new patrons and new sales. It's that simple. And I hasten to tell you, once again, that if you would buy several of the prime lots the proprietors are offering for sale, then I predict your investment will pay off handsomely."

137

As Marcus and Calvin proceeded on, they heard Ike Rawlings summon up another load of spit in his throat that he spat forcefully down at the dusty dirt. "Poppycock . . . you're always the salesman, Winchester. You're always the salesman. Eve'nin to ya, Mr. Calvin Cabell. Drop by my store and we can visit a spell."

By now Marcus firmly held Calvin's upper arm to assure they both were leaving Old Ike behind. Nevertheless, Calvin turned his head over his shoulder and replied with a pleasant enough grin. "Squire, you can count on that. You can count on that."

\* \* \* \* \* \* \* \* \* \* \* \* \* \*

Winchester's marketing plan was to offer Calvin several lots located at the north end of town. They afforded significant frontage along the Wolf River. He reasoned this site was an ideal place where the Cabell saw mill should be located. A mill within the city could be supplied by timber cut at a location farther up the river. The felled trees would be stripped easily, floated downstream, and cut into lumber at the mill.

After their encounter with Ike Rawlings, Marcus continued the tour. He took Calvin to the "mill lots" he had in mind for this much desired investor. Then they walked the short distance to the east bank of the Wolf River. Marcus explained the details of his insightful business plan. Calvin was clearly intrigued and impressed by Winchester's homework and his foresight.

Marcus suggested the two men spend a day or two on horseback to inspect various timber sites up the Wolf River. He suggested his servant, Uncle Bainy, would join them. Bainy could set up and take down their camp . . . as well as cook whatever game the two were certain to shoot.

Winchester had arranged for Calvin to stay at the best guest quarters the community could afford him. Memphis was too small for an inn, much less a hotel. Consequently, Winchester had constructed six "roundhouses" to, at the very least, primitively accommodate visitors. The roundhouses accurately described their shape. But they were more akin to Indian huts than to "houses". A ten-foot-high mast was erected at the center of each building's circumference. It supported a spiral of thin, wood beams that were attached to the circular wall. A roof of wood shingles covered the dome. Then mud and a variety of local vegetation were mixed and intertwined so as to form the core of the exterior wall.

That evening Mary prepared a fine meal for these two new friends. Later, after an animated conversation sitting on the house's side porch, Marcus escorted Calvin to roundhouse number two.

"I apologize for the crude quarters, Calvin. But these roundhouses are all we can offer you presently. There's a chamber pot inside that'll be fetched away in the morning . . . and the privy is located just behind that last building. A water pitcher and bowl sit on a table inside and you'll also find a fresh bar of lye soap. We expect to see you at an early breakfast tomorrow. Then, we'll begin our journey to inspect logging sites."

Calvin detected a sense of embarrassment as Marcus apologized for lodging his guest within a crude Indian hut. Calvin wanted to overcome any shame that was expressed in his friend's hang-dog tone of voice.

"I can hardly wait to tell my friends back in Danville that I stayed in a gen-you-wine Indian hut overlooking the mighty Mississippi. I can assure you they'll be green with envy. I'll be fine here, Marcus. I'm sure I'll enjoy a good night's sleep. And, I'll show up at your door early tomorrow morning . . . eager for your tour."

* * * * * * * * * *

When Calvin slung aside the leather sheath covering the roundhouse door, he could tell the new day was going to be hot and humid. However, he was just as certain that . . . before the sun set . . . he would have cemented all the details that would allow him to move his family to the westernmost city in Tennessee. He inhaled a deep whiff of Memphis air. He was more than willing to allow Marcus to write the terms of the ticket that would break him free from the dreaded ignominy he might face back in the Bluegrass.

After eating some biscuits Mary had packed for the trip, Marcus and Calvin mounted their horses. Marcus led the threesome far up the river to a ford. The water there was shallow and the horses could wade across with the water just skimming along the base of each man's saddle blanket. Marcus told Calvin the site he wanted him to inspect was about one mile ahead. He said the property was owned by an acquaintance of his who was experiencing some hard times. The man was highly motivated to sell.

When they arrived where the property line met the river bank, Marcus slowed the horses' pace. He extended his right arm to point out the various features he thought made the site a good one for timber operations. Calvin was amazed to inspect the large girth of so many oak and cypress trees. At his suggestion he, Marcus, and Uncle Bainy stood around the base of a tree and tried to join hands. They were shy of achieving their goal by at least a foot. The men tried the same experiment on several other trees before they found one that would allow them to complete a circle of locked arms.

Marcus led the group northward and away from the river. About half a mile away, the countryside's elevation began to rise noticeably.

"We don't have any real hills here in Shelby County. That's why I've always been impressed by this ridge line. It overlooks the river valley. But, hold on, Calvin. The best is ahead of us."

The three horsemen meandered up a twisting path through the dense forest. Calvin noticed four springs gurgling out of the ground at different locations just off the trail. One had the sense that native tribesmen had wandered this trail for centuries and they had regularly cupped their hands to drink from these gurgling waters. Eventually, they came upon a small clearing where some trees had been recently felled. About a dozen of them lay on the ground with their treetops all pointing down the hill.

"Calvin, I feel strongly this property is the tract you should purchase. In fact, I thought it was so ideal for you and your timber operation, I sent a crew up here several weeks ago to clear this patch of land. I want you to acquire a sense of the land – to comprehend the uniqueness of Shelby County."

Calvin and Marcus sat astride their horses and silently – almost reverently – gazed over the valley. Moving their eyesight from right to left, the Wolf River's meandering route was visible for several miles – as if God at Creation had straightened His index finger to gently carve out this undulating furrow across the flat plain. Marcus Winchester was right. What was truly remarkable about this spot was its uniqueness in a territory that was generally flat as a pancake. The vista, the spring water, and the spiritually enriching qualities of the valley view caused one's soul to rise up and overflow - just like the springs along the hillside trail.

"How many acres are in this parcel of land, Marcus?"

"Six hundred . . . and they can be had for a song."

"How much does a tune cost here in the West Tennessee wilderness?"

"Four dollars an acre . . . and you can pay for it over ten years. I figure the revenues from the timber alone would bring you a return of three or four times that figure. And then, of course, after the timber's harvested you'd also benefit from the richest alluvial soil imaginable . . . to grow all sorts of crops. What do you think?"

Calvin didn't respond to Marcus' question. He didn't even glance his way. He just sat there on his horse and he looked at the broad river valley. Finally, he spoke. "I think I've caught the bug. I think I've been infected – hopelessly infected. I believe in you, Marcus. And I believe you've created a sound investment plan for me. I'm confident that someday – maybe even someday soon – there'll be a demand for lumber sufficient enough to make a mill profitable. But I don't think I can – in good conscience – uproot my family to swelter down here while we bide our time waiting for folks to settle on your bluff."

Calvin Cabell was ready to offer a proposal. It was a plan he conjured up weeks before he set out on this trip. If he was going to call himself a pioneer, it would have to be under terms that were less risky than those his father, Isaac Shelby, and all the other pioneers who settled his native Kentucky had bargained for.

Calvin addressed Marcus without looking at him. Both sets of eyes were fixed forward - peering at the remarkable, expansive view.

"Marcus. I have a proposal to make. I can recommend to my father we purchase your town lot for the mill and, also, this timberland to supply it. But you yourself know that anyone who invests money on the dreams of even moderate growth in Memphis – well, that businessman would lose money . . . possibly, for years. I cannot recommend that.

"However, what I CAN recommend is the following. We can acquire the properties. We can spend the money to finance a mill and whatever laborers might be required. But I need someone who would oversee this meager operation. Demand might be erratic . . . or even non-existent. When and if the market shows signs of sustainable demand, I can justify relocating my family here. And I will do so. But, let's face it. That might be in several years."

Marcus Winchester relaxed his fixation on the valley view. He was listening and looking intently at Cabell. He desperately needed a saw mill. Memphis needed a saw mill. He, moreover, needed to make a deal before Cabell or someone else was lured to John McLemore's new town or to Randolph, the lively town twenty miles up the Mississippi. He was prepared to compromise his initial demands. Marcus knew it . . . and he knew Calvin Cabell knew it, as well. Consequently, he was prepared to listen to the details of the

Kentuckian's proposal and he knew he would accept it – whatever it was Calvin was about to say.

"Now if I could place this operation in your hands, Marcus, then I believe we'd have a deal. I wouldn't expect you to devote much of your time to get things going. I foresee you finding some reliable man whom you can trust and one you can supervise. That way you can tell prospective settlers a mill is operating and capable of meeting their building needs. I can visit here regularly to determine when and if I, too, will become a Memphian."

Winchester responded in a soft voice. Yet, it was a resolute voice. "I think we have a deal, Calvin. I need you. And you need me. I think we trust each other and I think a friendship has been founded. More importantly, I think we're on the verge of some big developments here on the fourth Chickasaw bluff. And, lastly, I think you'll soon need to buy yet another lot from me . . . in town. You'll need a lot for the Cabell residence."

The deal was done. There were only details to work out. But both men knew that from then forward this would be a mutually beneficial arrangement. After about half a minute of silence, Marcus spoke up again – this time in an upbeat, celebratory tone of voice. "I don't know about you, but I can't think of a better camp site for the night than this spot on the ridge."

He turned toward Uncle Bainy who had dismounted from his mule thirty yards away. Uncle Bainy kept his distance, because he knew there would be important business these two white men needed to discuss. Marcus raised his voice so as to be heard where Bainy stood.

"Bainy, we've found our campground for the night. Why don't you put up the tents and commence setting up the makings for a fire. Mr. Cabell and I are about to spend the afternoon hunting. Only the Lord knows what we're likely to bring you to cook up."

Marcus turned again to Calvin who was still mesmerized by the beautiful view of the valley. "Calvin, let's go see if you're as good a shot with a rifle as you are an astute businessman. If I were a betting man, I 'd say you are."

# CHAPTER

# *9*

May    1826
Memphis, Tennessee

Marcus Winchester was a man driven by a mission. He was hell bent on achieving one singular goal – to create in the wilderness a viable city where none had previously existed. As Calvin Cabell put it, "Marcus Winchester's mission in life is to 'make something out of nothing'."

But six years after General Winchester and his two partners sent Marcus west to peddle property along the Mississippi, he had reeled in just a few purchasers. However, there was no shortage of curious characters abiding on the fourth Chickasaw bluff to keep him . . . and everyone else entertained.

Paddy Meagher was a craggy Irish immigrant who operated the only drinking establishment in the settlement of Memphis. It was called the Bell Tavern. Everyone traveling up and down the Mississippi considered Paddy to be the most colorful personality in Tennessee's newest city.

One afternoon Paddy spied Winchester standing ankle deep in mud. Marcus seemed cast in a spell – oblivious to the presence of anyone nearby. He was holding in both hands the city's subdivision plan . . . drafted by his father six years earlier.

Meagher thought his friend was, most likely, day dreaming that grand stone structures graced each of the subdivision's lots. Or, maybe he was imagining scenes of a bustling crowd . . . shopping at store after store and then heading home laden with purchases.

"Marcus Winchester, You're a dreamer, you are. But, I wager if any man can turn this muddy muck of a swamp into a beautiful, bustling city . . . it's you, lad."

Winchester turned toward Paddy with the blushing face of a man who had just been caught in an embarrassing act of foolishness. He grinned sheepishly and called back to Paddy. "I know the odds are long, Paddy. But you're a property owner and I predict your bet will pay off . . . as well as mine. One of these days there'll be a strong demand for these lots. Prices will rise. I can feel it."

Winchester's job was to pull off this uphill feat in what most Americans considered to be the untamed frontier of West Tennessee. Sometimes – like today – he wondered if he would ever achieve his goal.

Marcus greatly admired young Sam Houston, a protégé of General Jackson. He was presently the U. S. Congressman representing the district of Middle Tennessee. He was doing remarkable work in Washington that resulted in considerable federal funds being appropriated to assist the citizens in his district.

Winchester recognized that he, likewise, needed an ally in government . . . to push along taxpayers' funding of projects that were on his wish list. "What better ally could we ever hope to have than a Representative in Congress from the District of West Tennessee?" he told Paddy over a shot of whiskey at the Bell Tavern.

So, aided by the substantial influence his Middle Tennessee investors wielded, Winchester became the primary proponent to elect a man whom he thought would effectively focus attention in the U.S. Congress on his little town of Memphis. He needed someone who could convince Congress that the U.S. Government should promote increased settlement and make investments in the Lower Mississippi Valley. Memphis needed a huckster who could loosen the purse strings in Washington City.

Marcus eventually met the most spellbinding candidate for Congress he might have ever imagined. His name was David Crockett.

Crockett was born in East Tennessee and . . . over the course of his young life . . . he had moved his home and family several times. Each time he migrated farther west. By 1824 he had settled in the middle of the West Tennessee wilderness. Crockett found the region was abundant with game of all sorts. He considered his new home to be just a shade shy of heaven itself.

If David Crockett could be defined as only one sort of a man, he was – above all else – a hunter. Ordinarily, a woodsman hunter is just about the farthest vocation imaginable from being a politician. Yet, a politician he became. However, it was entirely by accident.

In 1823 he made a trip to Jackson, Tennessee to sell pelts of game he had accumulated from hunting. When he arrived, he realized a large crowd was listening to a speaker in front of the courthouse. This was a day of campaigning by candidates running for a seat in the upcoming Tennessee Legislature. Crockett stood there beside his horse which was laden with furs. He listened with great interest at each of the stem-winding orations. This was the first time he had ever witnessed a "stump speech". He was fascinated.

Each man, naturally, claimed he was the best man for the job. And each pleaded for the public to support him.

"I'm the only candidate up here you can trust," one man said.

"If you elect me as your next representative in the Legislature, I'll fight for your interests like no other man," blared one of the youngest candidates on the podium.

Crockett enjoyed the performances, but he considered each of the candidates to be more bogus than the one who had spoken before.

He commented to several of those in the crowd. "Ever last one of these polecats 'pears to me like some sort of big city aristocrat. The folks I know livin' here in West Tennessee shore ain't no aristocrats. Why in tarnation should we have anyone representin' us who's . . . well, who's just about the exact opposite to all of us?"

With those words Crockett was unwittingly launching himself into a totally unexpected new career.

After the speeches were over, the crowd grew larger and larger around this newcomer with the coonskin cap. He was charismatic as he peppered his discussion of the issues with folksy narratives and humorous tales to make his points. The crowd loved him. He was no smooth talker like the "aristocrats" standing on the courthouse steps. Crockett was one of them. He was just regular folks. When he spoke, people listened to his every word. They thought he made darn good sense while, at the same time, he triggered hearty chuckles from the audience with almost every sentence he spoke.

At the urgings of the locals, Crockett also became a candidate in that election. When the ballots were counted, no one was more surprised at the outcome than David Crockett. He had won the seat.

Marcus Winchester saw in Crockett a noble, albeit, a roughhewn man. Consequently, he became one of Crockett's major supporters when Davy agreed to run for Congress in 1825. The Congressional seat for which he campaigned included Memphis.

"I believe Davy will do more for Memphis in Washington than all the hard work any of us can do to promote this city," Marcus opined.

Crockett didn't win that seat in Congress. But Marcus Winchester and others stood by their man and they swore to fight another day in another election. Two years later in 1827 Crockett was once again a candidate. And this time he won by a hefty majority. The frontier backwoods game hunter was on his way to Washington. And, upon his arrival, Congress would never be the same.

A legend was born. The common folk loved him and the politicians found him to be "unvarnished" and quite "rural". He never purposefully promoted himself as the quintessential frontier character. He didn't have to. He just was . . . the way he was.

People mimicked his speech and his mannerisms. Slowly, the stories about him grew and became exaggerated into the sort of fiction found in fables. By just being himself he became a notoriously effective Representative of his district. Marcus relished the fact that just about everybody up in the Northeast liked Crockett. They concluded he was likely a model for the sort of decent men who hail from West Tennessee. Such good will and fascination by the Yankees had to be useful for his business of promoting Memphis.

Winchester would support Crockett's bid for election wherever he could. One night Crockett had completed a day of campaigning and speech making in Covington, Tennessee. One of the wealthiest planters in the region invited Davy and Marcus to spend the night in his home. Crockett's opponent was, also, a houseguest. He was a lawyer by the name of Alan Huntsman . . . who had a wooden leg. Marcus later told Calvin the story of what happened during that visit.

"When everyone spending the night in the household had finally gone to sleep, Ol' Davy got hold of a stout wooden cane. Ever so quietly, he crept through the house . . . like he was silently sidling up on a deer. Finally, Davy made his way into the bedroom of the planter's daughter. He held the cane tightly and then soundly struck the floor . . . twice. And just as quickly and quietly as he had entered the room – he retreated to his own bed and pretended to be fast asleep. The planter and his daughter were horrified. There was only one man in the house who could have been the culprit. Such a sound could only be made by a man with a wooden leg. Instinctively, the host and his guests concluded the intruder had to be Crockett's opponent, Huntsman.

"Crockett got out of bed. He was informed Huntsman was alleged to be the intruder. Davy indignantly lectured that anybody who would sneak into a young lady's bedroom in the middle of the night was nobody he could ever hold in high regard. The planter agreed with him. The next morning he gave Crockett both his political endorsement . . . as well as a significant financial contribution for his campaign. Crockett won the election handily. As for Huntsman, he never ran for political office again."

Winchester invited Crockett to visit Shelby County. He had faith this accidental politician could win the district's Congressional election in 1827. Marcus wanted to introduce Crockett to as many of the voters in the county as he could. One of those visits took place in the spring of 1826 while Calvin Cabell was spending time in town. He was making arrangements for a home he would build for his family on Monroe Street.

Winchester invited Cabell to attend a dinner he was hosting so he could meet Crockett. "I'm telling you Calvin, this man will be representing you in Washington."

Marcus issued his invitation just hours before the dinner and Cabell accepted immediately. "How kind of you, Marcus, it will be an honor to meet our next Congressman. I shall look forward to this rare treat. Thank you."

Then, Winchester began to bait his Kentucky friend with some teasing. "Calvin, I believe you'll enjoy the evening. And be mindful that a Congressman who is our friend can provide the kind of government support we both need for Memphis to grow. And, if Memphis benefits from Congress's largesse . . . that only benefits your mill enterprise and your investment."

Cabell nodded his understanding . . . and his agreement.

Winchester then continued. "However, I must tell you . . . in addition to Crockett, I look forward to you meeting another special guest."

"And who might he be, Marcus?"

His host for the evening's supper broke into a wry smile that stretched into a broad grin. "Did I say my surprise guest was a man, Calvin? I don't believe I did."

Marcus curtly turned about and began to walk away. His smile was still planted on his face when he looked back over his shoulder. "Your invitation is for six o'clock, Calvin. Don't be late."

\* \* \* \* \* \* \* \* \* \*

As was his custom, Calvin Cabell arrived at the Winchester home punctually . . . at six o'clock. He was greeted at the door by Mary Winchester. As he crossed the threshold, he heard Marcus' voice. "Calvin, my dear friend, come in and meet our mystery guest."

Standing by the fireplace was a woman whom Calvin had never seen before. She was about five feet four inches tall . . . with curly auburn brown hair. She was dressed in a frock that cried out she had come from some distant locale where fashion had progressed far beyond what was known on the frontier. However, the most distinctive feature of this young woman in her late twenties was not physical. It was the broad, inviting aura she emitted. Her presence emanated an air of worldliness and a life of intriguing experiences. She was, also, a woman exuding great self-confidence. Ordinarily, this might have been off-putting . . . had she not shone a delightful twinkle in her eyes and a sparkling smile that could melt an iceberg . . . or, at least, a man's heart.

"Calvin, I have the pleasure of introducing you to Miss Frances Wright. She's a friend of General Jackson. The General recommended that Miss Wright should visit us in Memphis to consider establishing an unusual enterprise in our city."

Then Marcus turned to his female guest. "Miss Wright, Mr. Cabell came to inspect our town last year. He's reached the conclusion Memphis is a sound place to make an investment. Mr. Cabell hails from the Commonwealth of Kentucky."

"It's a pleasure to make your acquaintance, Mr. Cabell. But gentlemen, please, let's forego the formalities. Please, call me 'Fannie' . . . as all my friends do. I trust we will all soon be friends, too."

"Indeed, we shall be," Marcus replied while nodding in agreement. Then he emphasized a point to Calvin. "Fannie's a native of Scotland. I knew this common bond between your respective ancestors would be a source of mutual interest."

Just as Calvin was about to ask all the small talk questions that might illustrate how rapidly the world appeared to be shrinking, Marcus opened the front door once again. There stood David Crockett. He flashed his broad smile to those inside and everyone smiled back at him.

"I'm happy as a plump wood tick to spend this evenin' with all of you. This mornin' I went huntin' and I'm told we'll be dinin' on a fine turkey I bagged. Did you roast the bird, Marcus?"

"The turkey's been roasting for two hours. And, I can further report Mrs. Winchester says her peach chutney will also be on the table. I assure it's an outstanding accompaniment to the meat."

"Excellent," Crockett said as he made his way toward Fannie Wright.

Just like a prospective Congressman, he took her hand and afforded a gentle, but firm, handshake. "Marcus tells me you're among those who accompanied General Lafayette's party on his tour of our United States. It's hard to believe a woman so young could be so well traveled and – I might add – traveling with such a high fallutin' man like Lafayette."

"Yes, Mr. Crockett, I've been fortunate to have visited much of the United States. I was greeted warmly wherever I went. Of course, I suppose traveling in the company of the Marquis was largely the reason for my hospitable receptions."

"How many of the states did Lafayette tour?" Calvin inquired. "Wasn't the number twenty or twenty-two?"

"Well, Calvin, the general visited twenty states. But I saw only eleven. I began the tour with him in Washington and we progressed through Pennsylvania and New York. Then we visited all the states in New England. I remained with his entourage until we traveled to the southern states."

"Why did you take leave?" Mary Winchester asked Fannie.

"I became disillusioned with what I was seeing . . . and the manner with which General Lafayette responded to it. I suppose I should tell you straight away . . . I was shocked to see how the Negro slaves are treated. I find your government sanctioned slavery system to be an abomination. Furthermore, I became increasingly disenchanted with Lafayette and his tacit 'laissez faire' endorsement of slavery. Nevertheless, I expressed my disapproval . . . as well as my contempt. Finally, we both concluded it would be best for all if I parted his company."

Calvin was struck by the young woman's pluck. "I'm impressed by your convictions, Fannie. This nation's got to soon take actions that will curtail slavery and, hopefully, put us in a position to end it. My extended family includes two Presbyterian ministers, the Breckinridge brothers, who've been active in the American Colonization Society's mission. Its purpose is to free slaves and relocate them back to Africa."

"So, do we have in our company a full-fledged abolitionist, Miss Wright?" Crockett asked Fannie.

Fannie was just beginning to respond to Crockett's question when Marcus Winchester courteously interrupted – as if to quell the conversation from becoming a contentious debate. "Our meal is now awaiting us. May I recommend we continue this lively discussion over dinner?"

Everyone nodded and the prospective Congressman extended his arm to Fannie Wright and escorted her to the table. Crockett was seated to Fannie's right. Calvin was especially delighted with his table assignment. It was directly across from this fascinating foreign beauty. He was infatuated by her. Instinctively, Calvin knew this would be a most memorable evening. He wasn't disappointed.

Marcus wanted his guests to know how Fannie found her way to Memphis. "Miss Wright visited with General Jackson at the Hermitage when General Lafayette's tour took him to Middle Tennessee. She described to Old Hickory the nature of her remarkable mission in America. Consequently, he suggested she visit Memphis . . . as it might be just the right place for her experiment."

Marcus could tell everyone around the table hadn't a clue what he was talking about. "Fannie's come to establish a utopia . . . here on the Mississippi."

The oddness of what he said baffled both Calvin and Crockett. Each man was overtaken by a look of puzzlement. Calvin was the first to respond. "Did I hear you say 'utopia' . . . as in the Elysian Fields or, possibly, heaven itself?

Crockett didn't know a thing about the Elysian Fields . . . and he didn't spend much time dwelling on heaven. So, Calvin carried on alone with his thought.

"The term isn't new to me. But I hope to learn more. You see, as I traveled by steamboat down the Ohio River, one of its officers told me about a settlement near where the Wabash River flows into the Ohio. He said it's called New Harmony and he described it as a utopia. But neither of us knew much about it."

"Indeed, Mr. Cabell," Fannie interjected. "I've visited New Harmony. It was developed by a good friend of mine . . . and a fellow Scotsman, Robert Owen. He purchased a utopian village originally conceived and built by German socialists. Mr. Owen is an inspiration to all of us who are interested in the utopian movement. And he's graciously shared with me both his successes and his not-so-successful experiences at New Harmony."

David Crockett was clearly confounded. He wanted to mute any comments that might be interpreted as either audacious or ignorant. So, he placed a good size piece of turkey in his mouth and chewed on it very slowly. Calvin was aware of Crockett's defensive ploy. So, he spoke as if to deflect any unintended insult toward Marcus' worldly guest. He hoped to frame his comments with a continued sense of naiveté.

Calvin wanted to return to the subject of what he had learned about New Harmony on his steamboat trip. "Am I correct, Miss Wright, when I say it's my understanding that in utopian communities all of the men use their skills for the common good . . . and no man is viewed as superior to another? In other words, no man receives financial reward for his work . . . either above or below the labor of someone else. All men who work in a utopia are, indeed, viewed as being truly equal . . . as I understand it."

"And don't forget women, Mr. Cabell," Fannie snapped back. "Women are equal in every respect to men in utopian societies as, indeed, they should be valued in all societies."

David Crockett was sorely tempted to jump into this conversation as he swallowed his now well masticated turkey. Marcus Winchester recognized

151

the impending peril the conversation faced. So, he took command of this uneasy discourse.

"Fannie, all of the unusual social mores you describe are clearly fascinating to each of us. However, could you explain why Mr. Owen's utopia and the one you hope to establish are located far into the American frontier? In other words, why wouldn't you set up a utopian community along the eastern seaboard of America? For that matter, why would two Scots like you and Mr. Owen overlook the efficacy of establishing a utopia in Scotland . . . or some place in Europe? Why the American frontier? It seems more sensible to found a utopia . . . well, any place but here."

"Because, Marcus, we recognize that a revolutionary social structure . . . predicated on the equality of all . . . could never function in Europe. Indeed, such a community couldn't even function in the United States . . . anywhere, that is, except here on the frontier. You see, utopias represent fresh ideas and uncorrupted notions about society. Consequently, budding social principles can best be nurtured in a land that hasn't been debased by traditional concepts about society."

David Crockett couldn't contain himself any longer. "Who in the devil dreamed up such ideas as these?"

"David, I know you're a man who thrives on living in the wilderness . . . far, far away from what we normally call 'civilization'. And I know you're a highly respected man here in America's rural Southwest. Clearly, your natural environment has molded you into a man known for his common sense and straight talk. In other words, you're an organic product of your environment – just like all other mortals."

Crockett was befuddled by Fannie describing him as "organic". He didn't know what it meant. But, he reasoned it was unlikely she would insult him. So, he let the matter go.

"Now, may I remind you that I'm, likewise, an organic product of the British Isles? I've witnessed the so called 'Industrial Revolution' permanently alter the beauty of our countryside. And I've also seen how industrialization has deteriorated the quality of life for much of the population of England, Scotland, and Ireland. Our idyllic land and our stable lifestyle have been corrupted – probably, forever.

"Making money has become the arch idol that's presently worshipped in England. Good rural people are lured to the industrial cities by a false premise that they'll prosper. They soon realize they're inescapably trapped in an industrial culture from which they cannot easily flee. Just to get by, these deluded city dwellers trade the well-being of their children for the prospect of bringing a few more shillings into the household.

"And children . . . seven or eight years old . . . are forced to work ten to twelve hours a day in dangerous factories. Sometimes, they're even shackled to the floor to keep them on task with their assigned work. Mr. Owen and I . . . as well as other utopians . . . seek to illustrate to the world there's a better way . . . and a better life . . . for working people . . . than the one where a worker lives under the thumb of a greedy capitalist."

Mary Winchester had heretofore restrained from being an active participant in this dinner conversation. But what she was hearing fascinated her. She waded into the discussion by asking her guest a question.

"Fannie, you've exposed us to some interesting ideas. I can almost envision such an experimental society existing in a land which is free from what you might call 'conventional living arrangements'. However, I can't imagine ANY sort of society in which women are considered equal to men."

Fannie wasn't one to accept unsubstantiated theories. So, Mary Winchester carried on. "A woman can't fell a tree. And a woman couldn't pilot a flatboat to New Orleans. Who's going to prepare the meals and care for the children? Surely, you'd agree the work of a woman doesn't equate with the value of work done by a man."

Mary got no immediate response from Fannie who was glowering while she surveyed those around the table. So, Mary challenged Fannie once again. "Wouldn't you agree with me, Fannie?"

"Christians – and, please, know that I do not count myself as one of them – like to gloat that God made all of His children equal, Mary. But how could the world sustain itself without women? A world exclusively populated by men is a world that will begin to die away . . . within a mere twenty years. Men can't regenerate the species alone, you know. You point out that a woman can't fell a tree. My reply to that sort of poppycock is a woman CAN pilot a flatboat . . . as well as fell a tree. However, a man CANNOT birth a baby. Tell me this isn't so, Mary, and I'll retract everything I've said tonight."

"Yes, but . . ." Mary Winchester was able to interject in the split second of silence that occurred only because Fannie had stalled to take a deep breath to continue her lecture. But Fannie's lecture couldn't be contained.

"Consider how industrialists purposefully keep women at the lowest rungs of the social ladder. They even use religion to do it. They mock God's word . . . to ensure that women are kept valued little more than chattel. They cite 'Genesis' . . . that 'God made woman from Adam's rib'. They say it was the woman, Eve, who caused all the trouble for mankind when she defied God and plucked the apple from the tree of life. Consequently, these God-fearing Christians insist women must serve men until the Lord's kingdom comes.

"There are hundreds of thousands of women in England today who were raised happily in the countryside and who now live in the slums of a dirty industrial city. Many of these women become impregnated - often by brutal, physical force. It's these same women who then must become the sole provider for their fatherless children. Many of these poor souls are forced into lives of prostitution, thievery, or . . . even worse."

Calvin Cabell, the product of generations of Christian believers, had to step into the fray at this point. "You sound like a woman who puts little faith in our Heavenly Father, Fannie."

"I'm an atheist, Calvin. If there were a God like the God that organized religion worships, then there wouldn't be the spectrum of sins that continue to flourish as a result of the Industrial Revolution."

No one seated at the table had ever heard God so mightily challenged as He was this evening . . . by a total stranger. Perhaps their stunned silence was due to what they were hearing. But Fannie didn't miss the opportunity to espouse her heretical homily. "Then, my friends, there's the sin of slavery in your so-called 'democracy'."

Marcus Winchester was feeling very uncomfortable. Yet, he also felt a strong obligation to General Jackson - as it seemed Old Hickory had wished for him to serve as a gracious host for Fannie. He and Fannie had already made plans to travel up the Wolf River the next day to inspect sites she might find suitable for her utopia.

Marcus was also faced with another critical conflict. The revolutionary ideas of this Scottish woman would be antithetical to the hardy, salt-of-the-earth souls whom he had been trying to encourage settling in Memphis. What kind of pioneer would choose to live among such wildly liberal thinkers as Fannie?

At this point in time he didn't have the foggiest notion if Frances Wright would ever seriously consider establishing her utopia in Shelby County. He wasn't even sure if she had the capital and the capacity to buy land and build a settlement. He decided, there and then, he would be showing Fannie land that was as far away from the City of Memphis as he could guide her.

As the dinner's host, he also needed to diffuse the growing philosophical chasm which – at that very moment – was cleaving apart his guests. He chose to ever-so-gently point out that Fannie's reasoning might be deluded by an understandably false perception - that the American frontier was a suitable place for a utopia to operate and to thrive. So, he exaggeratingly cleared his throat so as to focus everyone's attention.

"Fannie, I've been thinking about what you said about your philosophical premise - that the frontier is free of social prejudice . . . unlike Americans back east in developed regions of the nation. However, I don't believe I've ever considered the social mores here in West Tennessee to be any different from people who live anywhere else where I've traveled in these United States."

Marcus intended to further support his theory. But the mere look on Fannie's face stopped him cold. He knew she had something to say and he feared that anything else he might add would agitate her. It might negatively impact the trust General Jackson had placed in his hands.

"Mr. Winchester, the strong convictions of Mr. Owen and myself . . . that settlers on the frontier are more tolerant to new ideas . . . well, those theories are made manifest here . . . in your household . . . and around this very table."

Fannie was smart and she was cagey. Everyone knew she was prepared to land a knockout punch to this debate as she demurely patted her lips with a linen napkin . . . which she then neatly folded and placed on her lap. Suddenly, she fully extended her left arm . . . straight across the table. She was pointing its index finger squarely in the direction of Mary Winchester.

"Here she goes again," everyone thought . . . except for Mary Winchester whose face took on a petrified expression of horror.

155

"With all due respect, Mr. Winchester, your lovely wife could hardly be characterized as a typical bride by folks back east. My travels in your great country have taken me – once again, with all due respect – to more American states and regions than any of you here at this supper table have visited. I, therefore, know that in New Orleans, my new friend, Mary, would be called a 'mulatto' . . . or, possibly, a 'half breed'. Husbands back east don't have your courage, Marcus – much less your discriminating tastes - to take this beautiful colored woman of mixed races to be a bride. Only on the American frontier can such a stunning colored woman become the wife of a city's mayor."

Mary Winchester turned to Fannie and broke into a warm, tender smile. She was ordinarily uncomfortable talking about her racial lineage. But under these unusual circumstances she dared herself to respond to Fannie . . . and in the presence of the two men who were also her guests. Consequently, she refrained from speaking for a short time while she carefully chose her next words.

"My dear, Fannie, you've indeed made your point. I AM a woman of color. And I agree with you when you say it's highly unusual Marcus would have ever married me if we lived farther to the east.

"You see, many of the trappers who've plied the waters of the Mississippi found native women whom they took to be their wives. The same match making applied to the Spaniards who once occupied our bluff . . . as well as the French. Indeed, lasting partnerships between all sorts of races have been initiated and cherished here in the American hinterland. These mixed marriages were just as sacred, successful, and long lasting as any of the racially homogenous pairings of men and women in the original colonies."

"Indeed," said Fannie, "and what races, may I ask, are represented in your family tree? I see multiple contributions merged together . . . to make you the beauty you are."

"I was told my great grandfather on my mother's side was a Choctaw Indian. And my maternal grandmother was a Negro slave. She met my grandfather while her master operated a trading post not far from the Natchez Trace . . . in central Mississippi. On my father's side, my lineage is more conventional – at least, conventional by the standards along the Mississippi River valley."

"Conventional?" questioned Fannie. "Tell me, what's your meaning of 'conventional' out here on the American frontier?"

"My mother was a light skinned colored slave owned by a family in Natchez. It's my understanding my father was a genteel white man who was a friend of my mother's owner. In any event, my mother died from birth complications when I was three days old. I was nursed and raised by another slave who was a good friend of my mother. I eventually moved to New Orleans . . . to be educated in a school for multi-racial boys and girls. Apparently, there were enough of us 'mixed breeds' with guilt-ridden white fathers who – after thoughtful consideration – wished for their offspring to be both free and equipped with a proper education."

Davy Crockett sat awestruck at what he was hearing for the first time. Naturally, he knew Mary Winchester was a woman of color. Yet, he never had the courage that Fannie wielded so effortlessly to ask for an accounting of Mary Winchester's pedigree. Crockett wasn't the only person who had never asked Mary or Marcus about her ancestry. Not a single soul in Memphis dared to broach the subject.

Crockett knew of many "cross breeds" in East Tennessee. They were primarily folks who were born from the union of a white man and a Cherokee squaw. Many hunters lived so long with the Indians, they had – for all intents and purposes – become Indians themselves.

Similarly, he knew of many "cross breeds" who lived in the settlements of East Tennessee . . . and beyond. To Crockett's mindset, these people were exotic to behold and their uniqueness should be celebrated. Davy rested the fork he'd been holding on his plate. He spoke directly to Mary – only a millisecond before Frances Wright tried to interrupt the momentary silence.

"Mrs. Winchester, Miss Wright has been able - in a very short time - to provoke your heart-rending story. I never once gave any consideration to your lineage. What a remarkable story it is . . . and spoken by a most remarkable woman."

By now everyone's knives and forks were surrendered to rest on top of the plates. Food was of no significant importance to those who came to dine around the table. Fannie Wright had sufficiently nourished everyone's soul following Mary's poignant, personal disclosures. Marcus Winchester didn't speak. But the doting glow that embellished his face as he gazed across the table at Mary . . . spoke volumes.

He was very proud of his wife. He was proud to be living in a place on the frontier where the sorts of "unconventional marriages" Fannie spoke of didn't concern others. Never had Marcus admired or loved his wife so much as now.

The evening's host spoke to his guests while indirectly speaking solely to his wife. "And so . . . Miss Wright, Mr. Crockett, and Mr. Cabell . . . there you have it. Now you know why I chose this remarkable child of God to be my wife. And you've taught us, Fannie, why we do, indeed, celebrate here on the Mississippi a sense of freedom from adhering to actions that are 'conventional' back East in today's modern world."

Marcus took a short pause to catch his breath and he searched for the right words to complete his thought. But Fannie seized the brief silence so she could speak. She held her pewter chalice aloft and cradled it in her hand . . . as if it were the finest crystal she had ever supped from at General Lafayette's table. This modern day atheist was about to offer a very spiritual benediction to the evening's conversation.

"May all of us find here on the edge of civilization the kind of personal integrity, the kind of individual freedom, and the kind of great friendships that we've forged here tonight. May we forever shun the shackles of the industrialized world. And, may we establish here on the banks of America's River Nile a homeland . . . dedicated to freedom from the trappings of the corrupted, mechanized world to the east."

The others at the table had, likewise, raised their cups in a communal salute. Calvin Cabell felt compelled to speak. "My dear friends, could one find such a special communion of souls anywhere but here this night? I want you to know how pleased and proud I am to be among you all."

Marcus Winchester momentarily turned his adoring attention from his wife to Frances Wright, who was seated on his left. "Fannie, tomorrow we'll embark on a search for your utopia." He then turned his head to adoringly gaze at Mary. "You can see that I've already found mine."

Fannie nodded to her host with coy satisfaction as Marcus continued. "Fannie, we have rich alluvial soil here. We have solid citizens with open minds here. We have hope here for a great future. So, surely, we must have . . . in both our culture and our agriculture . . . everything it takes to nourish your dreams of a utopia."

Fannie beamed as Marcus proposed a toast. He elevated his sherry glass from the table and he was joined in kind by his guests and his wife. He spoke with great gratification. "Fannie, tomorrow we'll go in search of your utopia. Deep within the marrow of my bones I feel confident we shall find it."

Davy Crockett, meanwhile, sat with a rather stunned look on his face. Calvin Cabell perhaps best described Crockett's expression later. "He must've resembled the trance-like look on the bear . . . which legend proclaims he stared down from a tree and slaughtered."

Indeed, because Davy Crockett . . . at that moment . . . must have surely been thinking, "This Tennessee wilderness is getting too congested to suit me. It's time to, once again, move on – farther west."

# CHAPTER

# *10*

The next morning's sunrise was breathtaking. Mile long strands of wispy pink and blue ribbons weaved a pattern of delicate celestial lace. But the intricate pastel display in the sky lasted less than fifteen minutes . . . as the hot sun ascended to singe the sky. It was going to be another scorcher today.

Fannie Wright was a guest of the newly constructed Overton Inn. It was the only accommodation in town that even remotely compared to a hotel. Just as he had promised the evening before, Marcus Winchester arrived bright and early to escort Fannie on an excursion into the countryside.

"Fannie, I trust you won't mind if Calvin joins us today. He's arranged for a small packet steamer to take us up the Wolf River. He wants to point out the land he's purchased and to join in the search for property that best suits your needs."

"I don't mind, at all. I'll be honored to be in both his and your company, Marcus. Where is Calvin?"

"He's already aboard the boat and waiting for us at this very moment. Are you ready? You certainly appear to be dressed for the roughest sorts of terrain West Tennessee might offer."

Fannie looked nothing like the cosmopolitan beauty who sat at his dinner table the night before. She had shed her frock. Her attire this day was more akin to a field hand than to a worldly, cultured lady. She wore a riding habit - the sort of attire worn only by men hunting foxes back in Virginia. Her trousers ballooned outwardly along her thighs and the pant legs contoured into a tight fit along her calves . . . so they could be neatly tucked into her high leather boots. She wore a checkerboard flannel, long sleeve shirt and her broad brimmed leather hat seemed more than suitable to shield herself from even the most penetrating rays of the summer sun.

The duo made their way gingerly down the river bank. Calvin, who was already aboard the boat, waved his hat above his head in exaggerated swaths from left to right. Fannie was an independent soul who tried her best to descend the slippery river bank without assistance. Ultimately, she relented and allowed Marcus to lend his secure left arm for stability.

"Lovely day to look at real estate," Calvin called out to greet the approaching pair. "I was able to arrange the use of this little baby. She's the smallest packet I've ever seen."

"Why is the boat called a packet steamer, Calvin?"

"That's because they're built in miniature to the size of ordinary steamboats. They're designed to carry postal packets to plantations and post offices located up even the narrowest and shallowest stretches of navigable waterways. I'm told this one only requires forty-eight inches of water to function. However, I gave her a thorough inspection before you arrived. I predict she could move unencumbered in water as shallow as thirty-six inches."

Calvin already had fired up the steam engine so they could push ahead straight away. As they began churning up the Wolf River, Fannie remarked how the countryside along this wilderness river contrasted with the countryside bordering the small rivers she knew in England and Scotland.

"The terrain along the Wolf River seems more like what one might see along the darkest of rivers in Africa."

Fannie spoke just loud enough to overcome the wet, whistling sounds of the steam engine. Neither of the men wished to challenge whether Fannie had actually been to Africa. She had seemed so well traveled at supper, they both presumed her comparisons were the Gospel truth.

"The reeds and the grasses are so tall. And the trees on each side of the river merge their foliage so densely overhead, I feel like I'm sailing under an expansive, verdant canopy."

"Marcus, how did the Wolf River get its name?"

"She doesn't get her name from any white man. She's been called the Wolf River for centuries by the Indians. Of course, the Indians don't refer to the river in English. They call the river . . . Nashoba. That's their word for 'wolf'."

"Nashoba . . . Nashoba . . ." Fannie contemplatively kept repeating the word with a different emphasis on each of its three syllables.

"I think it's a beautiful name." Fannie initiated a pregnant pause designed to embellish her announcement. "Gentlemen, I've decided, here and now, that today I'll find a suitable site along this river . . . and I'll call my utopia by the river's Indian name, Nashoba."

During the dinner the evening before, Calvin realized he had a thousand questions he wanted to ask Fannie. That's one of the reasons he wanted to include himself in today's activities. He was also quite smitten with the God-doubting, utopia-loving free spirit who had unexpectedly crossed his path.

Yesterday he barely knew what an atheist was. Moreover, he certainly never thought he would actually meet one. So, Calvin found himself overjoyed to be spending an entire day with the most charming atheist imaginable. His hands commanded the wheel. Yet, he wasted little time until he plunged into the list of questions he had been cataloging since the night before.

"Fannie, how did you become acquainted with General Lafayette? And, how did you manage to join his American tour?"

"I admired the man based on everything I read or heard about him. Then I learned that the Marquis had read my book. It was essentially a travelogue based on my first trip to America. I was told he loved it. So, it seemed perfectly logical I should travel to France to meet a famous man who admired my work. My book, you see, served as my entrée.

"I simply crossed the Channel to France and made my way to his estate, LaGrange. Once there, I announced my arrival and introduced myself to the Marquis. We soon became close friends."

Calvin found it hard not to believe such a simple, direct answer to his question. He mulled her response over in his mind. "She wanted to meet General Lafayette, so she just popped in on him? I've never heard of such determination and brazen courage."

He was falling for her free spirit. She was unlike any woman he had ever known.

"My visit to Lafayette's home occurred at the same time he was planning his Grand Tour of America. You realize, don't you Calvin that General

Washington was so enamored with Lafayette . . . he considered him like the son he never had? And, conversely, Lafayette was devoted to General Washington. He even named his only son George Washington Lafayette. He's a delightful and noble young man – just like his father."

Calvin was feeling increasingly comfortable with Fannie. He rationalized it wasn't the least bit impertinent to continue asking her even more personal questions. "Fannie, forgive me if I'm stepping out of line. But it's clear that anyone who travels to France on a whim, who joins Lafayette's American Tour, and who finds herself in West Tennessee . . . on the verge of making a sizeable investment . . . in an unproven social order . . . which requires just as much capital as foresight . . . well . . ."

Calvin paused a second, reconsidering one last time whether he should be as bold as Fannie had been the evening before. "Well, it just seems self-evident to me that you're a young woman with significant financial resources. Is your family one of the richest in Britain? Or, have you succeeded at embezzling the Bank of England with your charm . . . and then run off with the loot?"

Fannie laughed at this Kentuckian's sense of humor. "My parents died when I was very young. My uncle kindly raised me and my sister. He was a wealthy industrialist with manufacturing interests throughout the Midlands. He was also a good friend to Robert Owen.

"Both my uncle and Mr. Owen were deeply concerned about safety issues and other working conditions in factories. These weren't being addressed . . . much less, being remediated . . . by one living soul. My uncle was convinced – as was Mr. Owen – that work days needed to be significantly shorter and decent living quarters should be made available to workers and their families. Both men thought such improvements to the workers' quality of life might actually increase productivity . . . and business profits. And they were right. Their factories became the models for much needed worker reforms."

"It sounds as if your uncle planted the notion of a utopia in your mind."

"Yes, indeed, my uncle thankfully provided me with many ideas, many financial resources, and a solid education. But, more than anything else, he provided me with a strong sense of inspiration and determination."

By now the packet had churned about three miles upriver. That "verdant canopy" Fannie referenced earlier was thicker than ever. The Cabell land was about one half mile ahead. But Calvin had more questions to ask before pointing out his property.

"Can you describe your Nashoba to me, Fannie? I can tell you have a crystal clear image of it in your mind."

"Well, I don't clearly envision the buildings or the layout of the village. However, you're correct. I have a very sharp understanding about its social order and its purpose. You shared with me last night how your family had struck out at slavery through their support of the American Colonization Society. I admire them for taking action against the poisonous pox on this country known as slavery. But I can't imagine the Colonization Society's good work could make even a small impact on the vast number of slaves who need to be freed."

Marcus was listening intently to the dialogue between Fannie and Calvin and it was time he joined the conversation. "The American Colonization Society's purpose is to raise funds to pay for a slave's freedom and then to provide resettlement costs to Africa. That appears to be a sound plan to me – one that could be extremely helpful."

"Nonsense, Marcus, every charitable venture's success is predicated on sufficient capitalization and careful management. There's a lot of money required to free just one slave and relocate him to Liberia. Their plan doesn't address the need for newly freed slaves to have an education or to learn the skills at a trade.

"However, at Nashoba, we'll allow slaves to labor at communal work with dignity. I have no doubt this hard work will turn a profit at the end of every growing season. From the moment they arrive at Nashoba, the black people will no longer be slaves. They'll be considered indentured servants. Over a three year period of service, each person will have produced a share of the profits from farming the land. So, they will have paid off their indebtedness . . . just like European immigrants who freely became indentured servants to pay for their passage to North America. The same principles will apply at Nashoba.

"But these communal workers not only will secure their own freedom, they'll learn a trade and receive a basic education. So, every freed person who leaves Nashoba will also depart with a marketable skill and an education.

"You see, Calvin, the Colonization Society requires quite a bit of money to free and relocate each slave. My plan requires capital to purchase only the initial workers. The profits from their labor will enable me to purchase more and more slaves . . . who shall also be freed."

Calvin was so enthralled by Fannie's plans that he'd forgotten the boat was churning past his property. He turned to point out some of the highlights. "My land is dense with hardwood that I'll cut down and float downstream to the mill. Do you see the ridge about half a mile from the river? That's where I'm going to build a country house. The site is unique, because most of the land in Shelby County is flat."

Marcus Winchester was first and foremost a salesman. And it was his job to promote development in Shelby County. So, he decided to interrupt Calvin's depiction of Valley View's future to reinforce in Fannie that she, too, needed to buy land along this river . . . just as Cabell had done.

"Fannie, we're just a mile or so from Raleigh. Its population is greater than Memphis and it's the County Seat. The property I want you to inspect is about two miles upriver from Raleigh. Judge Robinson owns it and I know he's very interested in selling."

\* \* \* \* \* \* \* \* \* \* \* \* \*

Twenty minutes later Calvin gracefully maneuvered the packet boat along the side of the steep embankment at Raleigh. When they reached the top of the bank, Fannie could see Raleigh was bustling with activity - far more than Memphis.

Marcus spotted a young boy about ten years old who appeared to have no particular chore at the moment. He turned to Fannie. "Shall I send this boy to ask Judge Robinson if he'd care to join us for dinner? We can discuss the property with him then."

"Yes . . . yes . . . let's send for the judge. I throw my destiny into your hands, Marcus. His property is of interest to me – even though I haven't seen it yet. But in the end, I'll be asking you, Marcus . . . and you, Calvin, to evaluate if the land's price is reasonable and if it suits the needs of my Nashoba."

Marcus hailed the boy and he offered him a one bit coin if he would carry a note to Judge Robinson's home which was located about half a mile from town. He pulled a pencil out of his pocket as well as a wrinkled sheet of paper. Then he scribbled out the invitation on a leather notebook he placed on the nape of the boy's bowed neck.

166

"Run on, lad, to Judge Robinson's. Here's your bit. And my advice is to ask the Judge to let you ride with him back to town. Tell him you can lead him directly to the three of us."

The boy darted off as he yelled over his shoulder, "Thank you, Sir."

The intrigue of this female stranger continued to expand . . . "like bread dough rising up from yeast", as Calvin remarked to Marcus later in the day. Neither man had ever met someone so seemingly selfless, so determined, so intelligent, and so worldly.

"I feel blessed to have had this woman cross my path in life," Marcus confided to Calvin. Both men were being drawn into the allure Fannie cast. And they both knew it.

\* \* \* \* \* \* \* \* \* \* \* \* \*

The three friends walked the short distance to an inn. Marcus knew the owner, Mrs. Sally Troutt. She was a widow who had operated the establishment all by herself since the passing of her husband two years earlier. She heartily welcomed the trio and gave Marcus a peck on his cheek for extra measure. This was the second time Calvin had met the Widow Troutt. He received his apt due – only a hearty handshake.

Mrs. Troutt offered her guests the use of the inn's facilities. She pointed out to Fannie where the "ladies' privy" was located. Then she said the guests could wash up using the matching speckled metal wash bowl and pitcher that sat on the porch's only table.

"I've added a lovely fragrance to my last batch of lye soap, Miss Wright. I think you'll find it a treat."

Three rocking chairs sat idle on the other side of the porch from the wash station. Mrs. Trout thought her guests might find comfort in the shade that shielded the rockers. Each person took a seat and began to sway back and forth.

"I trust you have rocking chairs in Europe, Fannie."

Fannie gave a look that indicated she was a wee bit irritated Calvin would think such a fundamental human comfort might have somehow escaped Britain and the Continent.

167

"All right, it was a silly question. But sometimes we Americans can't stifle our provincial perspective and . . . well . . . I truly didn't know the answer. After all, you've traveled more extensively than any person I've ever met. When you return home I hope you'll report that American rockers are far superior to those in your homeland. And remind the Brits the rocking chair was invented by one of our many American geniuses, Ben Franklin."

Fannie chuckled almost inaudibly. An inquisitive look formed on her face and brow. "Marcus, I want to tell you once again how impressed I am with Mary. She's a rare jewel. Words cannot describe how much I appreciated her candor. She spoke with not a single sign of hurt feelings or embarrassment . . . not that there should be any. Nevertheless, her story is one of the most memorable I've ever encountered in America. Please . . . tell me I wasn't too pushy."

"No, you weren't too aggressive at all. But I must tell you, Mary and I rehashed the dinner conversation after our guests departed. As much as it might appear to you she shed light on herself and her lineage, she stopped short of revealing some of the most interesting facets of her life."

Both Fannie and Calvin were noticeably curious. They seemed to be thinking, "How could there possibly be even more mystery to this woman's story?"

So, Marcus offered his explanation as Calvin leaned forward in his chair . . . as if to say, "You have my full attention. Please, do carry on."

"Well, first I must tell you that my Mary not only gave me permission to fill in the blanks of her life's story. She asked me to make it a priority to tell the rest of it to both of you. There are details she stopped short of recounting during her sudden burst of candor last night. And, Fannie, Mary was so impressed with your open-minded and unadulterated nature, she especially insisted you know."

"Know about what, Marcus?"

"To know how she and I met. The circumstances are so unconventional that merely telling it serves to illustrate how your 'wilderness theory' for establishing a utopia here is further supported by the facts I'm going to tell you."

Marcus then turned to Calvin, who was beginning to slide himself back into the ladder back rocking chair. "Mary respects you, also, Calvin. She knows it appears highly likely you, your family, and my family will be fast friends. She wants you to hear what I have to say - from me . . . as opposed to someone's idle gossip."

Calvin and Fannie thought Marcus would never begin. Finally, he spoke.

"Well, you've already learned that Mary represents a mixture of bloodlines . . . and how her father freed her when she was born. And she told you she was privileged to receive an education . . . and to learn the social graces that serve to make her as fine a hostess as ever presided at the foot of any dining table in the country."

"Yes . . . yes . . ." both Calvin and Fannie uttered simultaneously.

"Now I want you to know how our paths crossed. Following General Jackson's victory over the British at New Orleans, an officer from Missouri who served under Old Hickory decided to linger in the city. He is a man of wealth. His name is Thomas Hart Benton.

"After living in New Orleans for awhile he was introduced to Mary, who was then a young woman of nineteen. Benton was smitten by her charm . . . just as the two of you have undoubtedly been enchanted by her. After a time Benton asked Mary to live with him – to which she agreed."

Marcus thought he should clarify a few cultural quirks in the region for Fannie's benefit.

"These domestic alliances are far more prevalent in New Orleans where Creoles, Acadians, and Europeans all blend together to form a rich sort of social gumbo. So, after three years together . . . during which holy matrimony was increasingly discussed between them . . . Mr. Benton grew restless. He was drawn to enter politics back in Missouri. He recognized a union between a white politician and a 'quadroon', as he described Mary, was political suicide.

"So, Mr. Benton – now, of course, widely known as Senator Thomas Hart Benton - and Mary traveled north toward Missouri. They stopped in Memphis. Senator Benton approached me and made a proposition. He asked if I would serve as the trustee of a rather significant amount of funds he wished to deposit in the bank. This trust fund was to be dispersed at my discretion to financially support a new life for Mary – a life without Benton.

"Mary and I thought at the time that Senator Benton hoped to engage in a long distance relationship . . . which meant intermittent trips from St. Louis to Memphis. However, when Benton returned to Missouri, he was quickly swept up by friends and asked to run for public office. Soon he married another woman from a family with important political connections, a woman who would ably serve as a politician's wife."

As Marcus proceeded along with the factual circumstances he was exposing, Fannie and Calvin sat silently with their eyes growing big as saucers. Calvin's lower jaw dropped in amazement. Fannie was less shocked at what she was hearing. But she was, nevertheless, fascinated by the story.

"So, what happened, Marcus . . . after Senator Benton's marriage?"

"Well, as you both can evidently see, Mary and I became close friends. She had relied on me for her financial support . . . just as a wife relies on her husband. This guardianship Senator Benton bestowed on me eventually evolved into a personal relationship . . . more loving and intimate. So, I concluded the right thing to do was to bring our growing love to Benton's attention.

"I met with the Senator and I told him everything. Thankfully, his devotion for Mary transcended the petty jealousies which ordinarily might have arisen. Actually, Senator Benton was relieved Mary had found love and a husband. He kindly gave me his endorsement to make Mary my wife. And, he insisted the money he put into trust for her benefit should remain hers . . . permanently."

Marcus was nearing the end of his story when he looked both companions squarely in the eyes. "All I can tell you, dear friends, is that Providence guided this most unusual romance plot into the most meaningful married relationship I could have ever imagined."

"Amazing," Calvin muttered. "What a beautiful story."

Fannie joined in. "Such a beautiful and romantic story could have only bloomed in a frontier society – one where my Nashoba shall be established."

"Well, maybe you're right. But the laws of Tennessee forbade our union in matrimony. Even Judge Foy across the river refused to marry us. We had to get married in Louisiana . . . where folks are more accustomed to diversity."

Marcus turned to face Fannie. "Maybe Louisiana offers a more nurturing climate for your utopia than Tennessee. Perhaps, you should reconsider securing a site in Shelby County."

Fannie rose out of her rocker and took Marcus' right hand which was gripping the arm rail of his chair. She raised it and kissed his backhand. It was a kiss of admiration and respect.

"No one kisses a hand like that in America," Calvin thought. He reflected on what had happened to his life. Here in the wilderness - a place Catherine had cursed for its dearth of educated people - she would find the most interesting and sophisticated folks she could have ever imagined. And here in the West Tennessee frontier he felt he could find a sanctuary - a fresh start where his past transgressions might never catch up with him.

Memphis had revealed itself as a remarkable place. He was becoming transformed. He was experiencing a refreshing freedom from the rigid structure of society in his beloved Bluegrass. He also knew this almost metaphysical transformation had only just begun.

He wondered what further awakenings within his consciousness lay ahead. He pledged right there on the widow Troutt's porch that he would make room in his heart and his mind . . . ready to be filled up with these new, exciting experiences.

The three friends then heard a boy shouting at them from down the road. Marcus pointed in the voice's direction. "There they are. It's Judge Robinson."

The judge sat behind the reins of two plow horses that pulled a green, wooden wagon with the boy standing upright on its bed - just behind the Judge. As the wagon drew nearer, Marcus stepped off the porch and walked about twenty yards to meet "His Honor", as Marcus often referred to him.

Winchester greeted the judge warmly and offered his hand to assist Robinson. He was clutching a scroll of papers he held in his other hand . . . as he tried to descend from his wagon's bench. But Marcus' gestures were politely rebuffed. Calvin and Fannie stood on the porch. As they waited,

Calvin, once again, tried to tutor Fannie regarding the way things get done in the American Southwest.

"I'm begging you to restrain yourself, Fannie. Judge Robinson doesn't care one twit about social justice or utopias. Marcus told me the man owns twenty-five slaves who work his fields and clean his chamber pots. He's looking for cash, Fannie – not for worthy, ingenious, social experiments. You'll do your cause a great disservice unless you tone down your rhetoric and act the part of a young, rich lady."

"I understand, Calvin. Regrettably, I must tell you that in England we must also put up with magistrates who serve less the Rule of Law than their own rules for self aggrandizement." Then she elegantly extended her hand toward Judge Robinson as he was introduced to the Brit and the Kentuckian.

Mrs. Troutt had suggested the foursome should eat their dinner in the cool comfort of her inn's covered veranda. Wisteria vines climbed its posts and formed a green trimming by spreading horizontally under the eaves. She placed a blue and white checkered cloth on the porch table. Then she replaced the rockers with four cane bottom ladder back chairs. All were identical except for Judge Robinson's . . . which was a bit broader in the seat and modified with a set of sturdy arms.

Everyone in Shelby County – including Mrs. Troutt, who provided meals for the Judge on a regular basis – knew it was unlikely anyone could survive unscathed from an adverse interaction with Judge Thomas Robinson. Robinson wielded legendary political power. He was allegedly able to summon dead citizens from their graves to cast a vote for him or for those whom he endorsed for elective office.

The judge wasted no time getting down to business. He rolled out his plat papers on the table and he began explaining the many virtues of his property. He inferred that anyone with any foresight at all should jump at the chance to buy his land – provided the seller didn't have to finance the purchase price.

Strangely, he asked very few questions about Fannie and he didn't seem to be at all curious why a refined young lady from England would want to move to West Tennessee. He only cared about making this sale. Marcus did, nevertheless, inform the judge that General Jackson was an acquaintance of Miss Wright and it was he who suggested his English friend should look into the prospects of buying land in Shelby County. Marcus' intentions were to emphasize General Jackson's personal interest in this woman. He hoped Robinson might keep in mind the risk of being criticized in the future by Jackson that he hadn't struck a fair sale price with Fannie. There were very few people in Tennessee who wielded political clout like Judge Robinson. But Andrew Jackson trumped them all.

Robinson remarked to Marcus how impressed he was that General Winchester's son had convinced Calvin to stake a claim on Memphis' future growth while, at the same time, facilitating a sale of his property to Fannie.

"Marcus, I shall convey to your father the next time I see him what an extraordinary job you're doing for the proprietors. Someday, the town of Memphis might even become as large as Raleigh. Thankfully, it appears our Miss Wright recognizes building in northeastern Shelby County offers a greater degree of civilized living than she would experience if she settled near those rowdy river men who continuously wreak havoc upon Memphis."

After pompously ribbing Marcus about the superiority of Raleigh over the upstart town of Memphis, the judge turned to Calvin and poured a little more salt into Marcus' wounds.

Winchester was visibly perturbed by Robinson's unwarranted derisions about the quality of life in Memphis. Yet, he didn't want to start a row this afternoon. So, he directed the conversation back to the business at hand. He deftly moderated the negotiations between Miss Wright and Judge Robinson. The deal that was ultimately struck was contingent only upon Fannie's inspection of the property. Judge Robinson proposed to sell her five hundred acres with options to purchase adjacent land he owned at a fixed price.

Fannie was scheduled to depart for England in two days. Therefore, Marcus agreed to serve as her agent in these matters. He would arrange with Judge Robinson the terms and conditions regarding the formal transfer of the deed.

Marcus announced to the group he was obliged to travel that afternoon back to Memphis. He needed to return the steam packet that Calvin had rented from Seth Wheatley. He told Judge Robinson Calvin would escort Fannie on horseback to inspect the property.

"I've made arrangements at the livery stable for two horses. And, I've written a note that Mr. Cabell and Miss Wright will present to Darrell Sweeney, who farms a plot not far from your property. Mr. Cabell says he doesn't mind spending a night in the Sweeney barn . . . and I've asked Mrs. Sweeney to offer Miss Wright suitable accommodations in their home. They should be expected to return tomorrow. I've already asked Mrs. Troutt to provide lodging and food if they should miss the packet steamer that departs for Memphis each afternoon."

Then, all the parties shook hands to symbolize their agreement to the terms of the sale as well as to bid farewell. Judge Robinson was the first to leave. He loaned Fannie his survey of the property with the understanding she would later give them to Mrs. Troutt for safe keeping. As Robinson snapped the reins of his team and the wagon lurched forward, he beamed a broad smile of satisfaction, indicating he had enjoyed this meeting and its profitable results.

Thomas Robinson sorely needed to close this sale. He had been experiencing cash flow problems. He was four months delinquent making mortgage payments on a sizeable tract of land he had purchased along the Memphis & Raleigh Road. Bartley Farney held the mortgage. At first, Farney was patient and conciliatory. He was keenly aware that those who earned the wrath of Judge Robinson often acquired a laundry list of legal and government problems. However, Robinson was getting so far behind with his payments Farney found no choice but to inform the judge it would be necessary to file a suit, which would surely become a horrible public embarrassment.

The judge was prepared to retaliate against Farney and, if necessary, squeeze him like a June bug. But, if Robinson could conclude this sale to Frances Wright, it would solve his dilemma with Farney.

As he proceeded home, Robinson thought he had negotiated a "done deal".

\* \* \* \* \* \* \* \* \* \* \* \* \*

Fannie's and Calvin's horses leisurely ambled east along the Stage Road. There was no need to quicken the horses' pace. The riders were enjoying the companionship and the conversation they shared. Fannie talked some more about her unorthodox views regarding "feminism". She also explained her views about "free love". She saw no reason why women should be forced economically, or otherwise, into a marriage where there was little or no physical attraction between the parties.

Indeed, she made it clear that . . . as for herself . . . marriage was out of the question. Yet, she alluded to Calvin that, even without a marriage partner, she had enjoyed plenty of physical intimacy in her young life. Likewise, she left no doubt her future would be speckled with many other affairs. She hinted that her relationship with the Marquis de Lafayette was just one example of her sexual exploits.

Calvin processed his reactions to this most unusual woman as busily as he could. He tried to overcome the cultural barriers or the prejudices that blocked his full understanding and his appreciation of Fannie. He also realized he was already committing the sin of lust. In his mind he was recollecting his own ancestry and its stern Scotch-Irish, Calvinist traditions. He desperately tried to square everything his upbringing taught him with this thoroughly modern . . . 'fanatic'. What else could he call her?

But the bottom line for Calvin was the fact that most people he knew complained and harped about things they saw wrong with the world. Fannie complained, too. But she followed up her grumblings with a resolve to take action. She had meticulously composed a specific plan that would change the world. And the world had better heed what she had to say.

Calvin also compared Fannie's young life to his own. They were both in their late twenties. He had lived a life most would consider charmed and privileged. He had a wife and two children. He had the wherewithal to leave them behind while he scouted for new opportunities along the frontier. He was respected by everyone he knew and he had been a good, solid defender of the faith – of course, except for his one unforgivable transgression.

Increasingly, he found it easier and easier to skip over Dolly's profound affect on his life . . . and to reassure himself that Divine predestination still applied to his own destiny. He felt privileged. He still felt "chosen" by God.

While he straddled his horse he contrasted his own life's achievements against the accomplishments of this young woman who rode with him along the Stage Road. She had accepted her own privileged life without being prideful. Yet, now he recognized he had never tried to parlay his considerable clout to benefit others who were less fortunate.

Fannie, on the other hand, had utilized her privileges and spun them into solutions to assist those having a hard time in life.

He had been an active church member who prayed to God daily. Yet, Fannie had rejected a God who seemed to squander His power . . . who passively allowed slavery and other unconscionable exploitations of human beings on His earth. After all, didn't God create man in His own image? Then how could He forsake the impoverished and the enslaved? It was Fannie's opinion that the stories of the Bible were just as mythological as the gods Homer interwove into the plots of his epics.

Fannie was striking out at slavery with action. Yet, Calvin's God - this same mythological God of Isaac and Jacob, the God of the Israelites, and the God Calvin Cabell claimed had granted him the license to kill Dolly - regrettably, THIS God hadn't performed a single miracle to stop slavery.

"Maybe," he thought, "there once really WAS a loving God. And now, He's dead."

Calvin cautiously reasoned all of this silently in his mind. Surely, even mulling over the fallacies of church doctrine amounted to heresy. He was ashamed of even thinking these thoughts. But that didn't stop him from contemplating the same heretical premise several more times during the afternoon.

Judge Robinson had given Calvin specific directions to his property. They were to travel three miles east on the Stage Road until they came to a crude crossroad . . . recognizable by a downed tree. There, they turned right and then followed a shabby excuse for a road until they saw a trail splintering off to the left. The trail's threshold was marked by a pile of rocks stacked in the shape of a pyramid. That trail would eventually lead them along the river until they spotted a red cloth attached to the lower limb of an oak tree. This marker corresponded with a symbol they saw on the survey. From that point they could use the plat's metes and bounds to navigate their own tour of the property.

Finally, if they continued along the river trail about another half mile, they would come upon the Sweeney place.

Calvin and Fannie spent almost three hours exploring Robertson's land. Mostly, they walked about while leading the horses by their reins. Fannie wanted "to feel the land". She had plans for its use – spiritual plans . . . that were of a far higher order than most folks devised for their property.

All the while Calvin wondered. "If the Lord could part a sea . . . or raise Lazarus from the dead to illustrate His power over man and nature . . . why is there no evidence of His disdain for human bondage? But if God did, in fact, create the heavens and the earth, He hadn't illustrated much interest in His creation over the past two thousand years."

He continued to muse. "Fannie would sanctify this little piece of the earth with her own brand of righteous indignation – the same kind that God should be employing . . . instead of resigning His might to the challenges of a female non-believer.

"Here was an atheist who . . . through her noble deeds . . . would make this land, her Nashoba, more holy . . . and more sacred . . . than the land upon which any church in the South had ever been built."

It was late afternoon when this man from Kentucky . . . full of questions about the purpose of his life . . . and this woman . . . and filled with what the French call unbounded *joi de vive*, stopped . . . and they looked into each other's eyes. Both felt life's circuitous route had ultimately led them to this shady spot along a wilderness river – a river the Indians called "Nashoba".

Calvin was reflecting on everything that was happening. He was unsettled. So, he did what he had always done since he was a child when he wanted to "think things out". He stood on the river bank and skimmed a series of flat stones along the surface of the water. They skipped and hopped numerous times across the river current before eventually relenting to gravity . . . and to a resting place upon the river's bed. Fannie watched . . . and she marveled at his skill.

Then, Fannie said she wanted to wander about on her own. Calvin knew no harm was likely to come to her. Besides, women have needs for privacy more than men. She returned about forty-five minutes later carrying a cloth filled with large, juicy blackberries. Mrs. Troutt had packed provisions of biscuits, ham, and cooked bacon . . . just in case the pair should get hungry. These berries would make a fitting dessert.

Fannie lay on the ground with her right elbow cocked, so as to elevate her head above Calvin, who now lay flat on his back. He enjoyed the cool breeze flowing across his bare feet. Fannie teased him while she popped one blackberry after another into his mouth. She gingerly held each fruity morsel and circled it slowly above his face . . . like a hawk circles high in still air in search of dinner. Finally – at her own whim – she gave in to his pleadings for a succulent sample.

After about a dozen feedings, Calvin decided to return the mutually pleasurable favor. So, it was he who now gently hovered a blackberry over Fannie's uplifted mouth . . . and made her beg for each one. Calvin held a berry aloft and then he released it . . . to fall and to find its ruby lipped target below.

There was lots of muted laughter. Each of them sensed the berries were nourishing more than just the body. The fruit was providing sustenance to the hungry souls of these two strangers . . . whom fate had joined and serendipitously sent them wandering through this strange land.

Calvin tauntingly held another plump berry over Fannie. He smiled a devilish grin – the sort of mirthful grin one would rarely see on the face of a staunch Calvinist.

Then, before he released the final fruity bomb toward its target, he softly spoke with a wry chuckle. "I don't think you or I will be giving the Sweeney family the pleasure of our company tonight."

Fannie sucked on the sweet missile Calvin launched into her mouth. She painted its black juice over her lips with her tongue. Then she reflected the same wicked smile as her companion's. "I don't think we'll be making the acquaintance of the Sweeneys, either. I think we could find no better lodging for this night than right here along the river – here at Nashoba."

Then Calvin employed a new technique to deploy his berries. He looked into the cloth stained by the blackberries and he selected the biggest one remaining in the bunch. Ever- so-gently he placed the berry between his front teeth, so no part of the fruit was pierced. Slowly, he lowered his delicious cargo downward to Fannie's waiting mouth.

The two partook of the forbidden fruit . . . just as Calvin had planned. It empowered them with a level of passion that he had never known.

The sun was setting at this point in time . . . and the sticky air was cooling. But the encounter of this unlikely couple was, conversely, heating up – to a feverish level.

Calvin Cabell willfully chose that evening to, once again, cast aside his marriage vows . . . as well as the morals that were the basis of every Sunday sermon he had ever heard. He had, regrettably, dallied with Dolly, because she persuaded him her sexual proposition was outside his marital responsibilities. And he remembered everything that mistake had spawned. However, this evening along the banks of a river called Nashoba – quite differently than with Dolly – he was falling head over heels in love.

Nevertheless, inside his conscience there was a moral brouhaha. He found himself swept up in frenetic, silent contemplation. His guilt was at war with his passions and their battle's blows struck at him quickly . . . and often . . . like the afternoon lightning storms over the Bluegrass in the summertime.

If Fannie believed in free love, then Calvin wanted to know all about it. He wanted to experience it. He wanted to become enlightened with the sophisticated wisdom embodied in this very experienced woman of the world.

"Here" he reasoned, "I find myself with a woman who had been the lover of no less an icon than the Marquis de Lafayette. And their intimate relationship was severed by HER decision – not his. She wasn't cast aside because the Marquis decided to sample the favors of another beautiful woman he met along the way . . . while one American city after another feted his legendary fame.

"Fannie had the guts to leave her illustrious lover . . . and the grandest tour anyone in the United States might have ever anticipated. She left his entourage to follow her own conscience . . . and her own destiny. And now it's my privilege to lie here with a woman who could have probably had any man in the world she chose. But she has chosen me – at least for this evening."

Half an hour later their skin glistened with perspiration. Calvin lightly basted the moisture over Fannie's body with the gentle touch of his four fingers . . . so as to convert the heat they had generated into a cooling balm. Then the two held hands. Like Adam and Eve after their fall from grace, they walked hand in hand into the river. They swam and giggled and kissed again. Then they waded toward water that was only waist high. They stood on the rocky river-bottom and caressed one another amid the long thin shadows cast by the setting sun.

That evening Calvin built a fire at this newly consecrated spot on the planet. Fannie commented this was the first fire to light up the sky at Nashoba. She said she would always remember today and she would forever cherish the memory.

They made a light supper of Mrs. Troutt's fare. And, for dessert, they placed the remaining few blackberries on the lower half of a carved biscuit. They delicately nibbled their way to the biscuit's center . . . until their blackberry laced lips touched, once again.

The "Nashoba" River reflected the campfire's glow throughout most of the night . . . until the flames finally consumed themselves. The heat . . . and the bright light . . . and its palpable energy were finally spent. There was nothing left except the embers. And, when Calvin awoke early in the morning to poke at the last of the fire's smoldering remnants, he wondered if more than wood had been consumed the night before. He pondered this sensuous experience. He even wondered if the past day had been only a daydream . . . spun from the whims of a deceitful devil.

Once again, Calvin recalled Dolly's specter. "Have I acted in a manner, yet again, to warrant being cast out of paradise – another transgression by a doomed sinner? First, I strayed into sin with Dolly. And now, I've traveled the same adulterous path with this remarkable woman. Will I be haunted by this most recent lapse . . . like the first?

"Yes," he admitted to himself. "Surely, I'll be denied my chance at paradise."

Then he was struck by a rather perverse sort of reflection. "Or, have I just entered paradise? Surely heaven cannot be as wonderful as lying here with Fannie."

As the morning sunlight began to stretch across America's Southwest, Calvin thought about his Catherine, his Jamie, and his Cassie . . . who were likely rising just about now to live out a new day, too.

"All of us," he mused, "are nothing more than strangers in a strange land. We're all strangers living in a most remarkable . . . strange land."

# CHAPTER
# 11

November 1826

The business arrangement negotiated between Calvin Cabell and Marcus Winchester worked quite satisfactorily during the years following Cabell's first visit to Memphis. Calvin returned during the fall of 1826 with enough cash to purchase the lots on Mill Street . . . as well as the Wolf River timber land – the place he called Valley View.

During this second trip he began construction of the lumber mill's rather crude facilities. In the 1820's wood was manually trimmed and cut into lumber. The process of manufacturing lumber was completed in a "saw pit". It was a rectangular hole dug in the ground measuring about 6' x 15' x 8' deep. Two mill workers were required for the sawing process. Each pair of men had to be both strong and patient. Their only tool was a five foot long crosscut saw with large jagged teeth and a sturdy wooden handle at each end . . . about one foot long.

The team of workers traded positions throughout the work day. The saw's teeth were placed against the base of the timber that lay over the pit. The man in the pit exerted most of the force for the downward stroke of the saw. Then the man above ground used his strong arms to lift the saw upward . . . so the sequence could be repeated over and over. The task of the crew member in the pit was clearly the hardest. The saw's downward thrust required the most physical exertion by the sawyer in the hole. Furthermore, as the saw cut into the wood, the saw dust and shavings produced in the process floated downward . . . and directly into the upturned eyes of the pit man. It was grueling work.

Calvin dug out two saw pits during that visit. He also designed and built two open sheds over the holes with roofs that were ten feet above the ground. Each roof was supported by tall 8" x 8" posts. The area of the roof completely covered the pit, so a crew could work in almost any sort of inclement weather.

One Friday in late November, just after his workers had finished building the second mill shed, Calvin stepped back and admired his creation. He was clearly pleased with his construction crew's work.

Calvin noticed Marcus Winchester was walking towards the men. He could see his friend held a letter in his hand. "Well, Mr. Cabell, I suppose folks in Danville, Kentucky have finally come to the conclusion they've lost you . . . permanently. They've changed your mailing address to Memphis, Tennessee."

Marcus held a posted letter with a playful sense of prideful accomplishment - like a Labrador retriever who had fetched his master's kill. He couldn't contain his unbridled joy as he handed the envelope to his new friend.

"You've gotten your first letter here in Tennessee and I'm proud to serve as the postman who delivers it."

"Thank you, Marcus. I'm privileged to have such a distinguished postman. But I can't imagine who'd be writing to me here when everyone knows I'll return home shortly."

Calvin glanced at the envelope and Marcus noticed a sense of surprise – even shock – on Calvin's face when he read the return address.

"It's not from Catherine, is it?" Winchester inquired as his inquisitiveness quickly evolved into concern.

"No . . . no . . . it's not from Catherine. It's written by a friend from home." Calvin did his best to deflect the possibility of Marcus posing several nosier questions. He wanted to change the subject. And so he did. "I know for sure it's not particularly important. I'll get to it later."

He put the letter in his pants pocket and smiled proudly at Marcus as he directed his friend's attention to the completed pit shed. "So, Mr. Winchester, behold and admire this newest structure at my mill. Not bad, wouldn't you say? We're about ready to call it quits and head home for supper."

"That's the other reason I'm here. Mary's asked that you join us for supper. What should I tell her?"

"Tell her to put another plate on the table. It would be my pleasure to accept. Now, if I could wrap up a few things, I might be able to drop by at a respectable hour. I've got several loose ends to tie down here."

"We'll expect you about six."

"Six it is."

Marcus headed back toward town and Calvin held a brief meeting with his crew. He told them there was just one more pit and shed that needed to be built. He said he'd meet them at daybreak the next morning. All the while his hand was stroking the letter concealed inside his pocket. Just touching it made him hell bent to send the crew home . . . so he could finally open it and read its communication in solitude. He didn't know what it contained. But he DID know he needed to read it without a soul being within a hundred yards.

The men gathered their coats and their tools and they struck off toward wherever their evening meal might be awaiting them. When Calvin was sure he wouldn't be disturbed, he pulled out the letter . . . while he rotated his head for one last three hundred and sixty degree surveillance of the scene. He was sure he was all alone.

He rubbed his thumb over the ink – the script of the addressee as well as the ink that revealed who sent the letter. It was from Attorney D.G. Cowan, the riveting trial orator who always drew a large crowd to the Lincoln County Court House to hear his dramatic arguments before the court.

"What in the world causes Cowan to write? It can't be about any Athenaeum business. And Cowan certainly isn't sending his personal best wishes . . . or passing along local gossip."

The only way to find out was to open it and read it. Even Calvin was surprised at the nerve he had to summon just to pierce the paper and split open its top ridge. As he lifted out the stationery and slowly unfolded its creases, he still didn't know if he was prepared to read it. Butterflies flitted about in his gut.

"This is trouble. I'd bet on it. Well, here goes. "

Dear Calvin,

I understand you will return to Danville about the middle of December. I want you to be aware of developments here, so when you get home you won't step innocently into turmoil about the matters herein.

Last week the Mercer County Sheriff came to town. He dropped by the court house looking for Sheriff Perkins. I happened to be in court that morning and

I was the first person to talk with him. The Sheriff confided in me he was in town to investigate the murder of the bar maid over at the White Oak Inn. While he shouldn't have revealed such information to anyone other than Sheriff Perkins, I was relieved that he leaked to me the purpose of his visit. I was also relieved I could honestly tell him that Sheriff Perkins was out of town for several days. As an officer of the court, I offered him any assistance I could lend.

Sheriff Bonds said he was following some leads in the case that had come to his attention. It seems that you were the focus of his interest. So, I inquired about as much information as I felt comfortable asking him.

The innkeeper, Smithson, has confirmed you spent a night at his establishment last January. He also said a woman who works for him described a man who knocked on the door of her quarters. Bonds was inquiring about the whereabouts of the crime's perpetrator. The man's description, essentially, matches yours.

I assured Sheriff Bonds he could, in good conscience, cross your name off any list of potential suspects. Unfortunately, as Bonds was just about to head home, Isaac Shelby Lancaster passed by and – in his usual weasel way – he managed to include himself in the discussion. With very little information, Lancaster commented he had seen you talking to a woman in a manner he thought might be hostile. He stated he was certain the conversation's tone, at the very least, seemed odd. His description of the female he saw apparently matched the victim.

With the Sheriff's interest piqued at this unsolicited information, I took it upon myself to tell Bonds I would attest that the possibility of your potential involvement was absurd. I also told him I was planning to visit Governor Shelby momentarily. I asked if he would join me – as the Governor would want to be consulted about such accusations of a man he considered a dear friend.

The Sheriff was overjoyed at the prospect of a meeting with the Governor and I was pleased to facilitate it. Governor Shelby is fast failing in health, but he gladly met with Sheriff Bonds in his parlor. The visit lasted fifteen minutes. During that time the Governor was emphatic that you should be immediately deleted from any list of suspects. He said, "I won't stand idle and allow you to implicate a fine man like Calvin Cabell. To name him as a suspect would be an outrage."

Shelby went on to talk derisively about his busy-body nephew. While he

184

didn't say that Lancaster was an habitual liar, he made his point quite effectively that any of his observations should be discounted.

The Governor was adamant that he didn't want to hear any more about this assault on your reputation. And Bonds left the meeting, I believe, quite assured you were not worthy of further investigation. However, that's just my hunch.

Calvin, I have no idea what might have transpired that night at the White Oak Inn, but I want you to know I am doing all I can to ensure that these malicious rumors do not come to the attention of your wife. Nevertheless, I thought you should have some forewarning about trouble that might be brewing prior to your return. I do hope such gossip does not get passed on and I will do what I can to stifle any rumors.

Looking forward to your safe return, I remain your devoted friend,

D.A. Cowan


Calvin felt waves of anxious energy pass up and down his spine. His first thoughts were about Catherine. There was a sense of nausea within this erstwhile Kentuckian . . . who once thought he was anointed by God's principle of pre-destination . . . a man who was bound for eternal salvation. Right then, Calvin's salvation seemed as likely as his chance of walking on the muddy water of the Mississippi . . . all the way to Arkansas. He felt doomed.

"What can I tell Catherine? What SHOULD I tell her if word of this gossip has already come her way? I've got to be VERY careful what I say. I can't slip up with contrasting information I give to one party . . . versus what I say to another.

"Governor Shelby is the key here. No one in the Bluegrass would contradict Isaac Shelby. I'm sure of it. But the Governor's health is deteriorating. He won't be my advocate forever."

Calvin took temporary relief knowing he was hundreds of miles away from home - on the edge of the American frontier. Right then, he wished he didn't have to go back to Danville – even if it meant never collecting his wife and children for a move west. But he knew he needed to digest this information. He needed to read Cowan's letter over and over – tonight, tomorrow, and as long as it took to assure him precisely what should be done when he returned.

The sun was so low in the southwest sky that light was just a shade shy of vanishing. Calvin let out a long breath of air that released with it some of the nervous agitation inside of him. "I've got it. I'll demand Mrs. Cabell to move west. I don't care what I must say or do. Catherine must agree to relocate . . . just as soon as I can speak to her. I will NOT fail to persuade her."

\* \* \* \* \* \* \* \*

Marcus introduced Calvin to the man he determined could best act as the lumber mill's supervisor. His name was Jacob Sperling. Calvin immediately foresaw that Sperling was, indeed, the right individual for the job. He explained to Sperling the agreement between himself and Winchester. Marcus Winchester would be his boss until the time was right for Calvin to move his family to Memphis.

He explained to Sperling his business plan also called for producing barrel staves. Calvin's father produced white oak barrels . . . mainly for the manufacturers of whiskey. His customers aged their distilled spirits in newly charred white oak barrels for at least four years. During that time the whiskey absorbed the woody flavor and the color of the barrel.

The region around Memphis had plenty of moon-shiners. But they consumed or sold their product almost as quickly as it was siphoned out of the vat. None of these mavericks would be potential customers of Calvin's mill. Nevertheless, barrels were needed for the storage or shipping of all sorts of products on the frontier. Calvin wanted to begin his cooperage production before other competitors entered the market.

As it turned out, there was just enough demand for lumber and barrels in 1826 to keep Sperling and his workers consistently busy. The operation regularly turned a small profit.

Likewise, Marcus Winchester's sales of subdivided Memphis lots also picked up its pace. Hence, lumber was in greater demand . . . as more and more structures were being built in the community.

While he always traveled to Memphis on a steamboat, Calvin generally traveled overland on his return trips to Kentucky. He made it a point to spend time in Nashville, the state capital, so he might try to persuade the Tennessee Legislature to invest public money to develop roads in West Tennessee. He made sure the state government knew there was a genuine need for corduroy roads and bridges to span the lowlands of the Hatchie and the Loosahatchie river bottoms. He argued these public works were necessary if Nashville and Memphis were to be adequately connected. Calvin wanted Tennessee's legislators to know his mill stood prepared to meet whatever lumber needs future public works projects in the region might require.

He believed he had the enthusiastic support of Andrew Jackson . . . and many Legislators were aware of this personal relationship. But Jackson was determined to become President in 1828 and he was reluctant to personally speak to officials about Cabell's business objectives. However, Jackson's friend and business partner, Judge Overton, was happy to oblige. Presently, he was the wealthiest man in Tennessee and he proved to be very helpful to Calvin's cause.

1826 was also the year in which the Tennessee Legislature granted Memphis a city charter. This was a significant step forward. But when the citizens who already lived in unincorporated Memphis discovered a charter had been decreed, most were not at all pleased to learn of this development. And Ike Rawlings was the most displeased of all.

"A city charter is well and good for a town the size of Nashville," he grumbled. "But what we have here is 'small potatoes'. Keeping Memphis the way it's been since the Injun days is just fine with me."

Marcus later communicated Ike's resentment to Calvin who responded, "I believe Old Ike's objection can be summarized by one small word - 'taxes'. Now, he's got to pay them."

Winchester served as the city's first mayor. He had essentially acted informally in this capacity for several years. But now it was official. Ike was, as expected, his biggest critic. But a turnabout in 1830 finally reversed Old Ike's discontentment. Andrew Jackson, the nation's newest President, appointed Marcus as the U.S. Post Master of the city. The job forbade him from holding elected office. So, Ike became the Mayor of Memphis, "His Lordship" . . . as common folks called him. Anderson Carr, a partner in the city's main merchandise store summed up most everyone's reasoning.

"Old Ike's been lording over us for nigh on fifteen years. It's about time we legitimized his tyranny."

Calvin never saw Fannie Wright again after the day the two returned from their inspection of Judge Robinson's property. On the packet trip from Raleigh to Memphis there were no goodbyes and no spoken signs of affection communicated between them.   Fannie made the necessary arrangements with Marcus to purchase the judge's property under the terms and conditions which were prescribed on the front porch of the widow Troutt's establishment. Since there was no slave market in Memphis, she headed straight for Nashville to purchase eight Negroes to work the fields of Nashoba in consideration for their eventual freedom.

Fannie rarely came into the city. She worked feverishly with her sister to build and operate Nashoba. During a visit in the spring of 1827, Marcus told him Fannie's health had dramatically deteriorated. She was exhausted from operating her utopian endeavors and from the adverse physical affects she experienced from living in the hot, humid American Southwest. He said Fannie came to town one day only long enough to board a steamboat bound for New Orleans. From there she took a ship back to England where she hoped to experience some rest and recuperation in her homeland's cool countryside.

When Fannie finally recuperated and was ready to return, she encountered a fellow passenger aboard her ship. The two of them bonded almost immediately. Her new acquaintance was Mrs. Frances Trollope, a British widow who was journeying to America to explore it and its people for the purpose of writing a travel book detailing her observations. Since Fannie had earlier published her own book on the same topic, Mrs. Trollope felt she was in capable company in Fannie's care.

Fannie told Mrs. Trollope all about her insights about life in America, her time with General LaFayette, and her passion for Nashoba. She was persuasive in all matters and opinions. She also insisted Mrs. Trollope should travel with her from New Orleans to inspect Fannie's new utopia in the wilderness.

Marcus Winchester was present when the two English women disembarked at the Memphis wharf on Christmas Eve in 1827. It had rained for days and Mrs. Trollope was forced to mush through the cold, oozing mud as she made her way up the wharf's embankment. She was clearly not impressed with her first impressions of Memphis. Then circumstances gradually went from bad to worse.

Mrs. Trollope was the first journalist to inspect and write about the remarkable social objectives Fanny told her were being accomplished at Nashoba. But, what she saw at Fanny's rather ramshackle utopia didn't match what Fannie had told her. Mrs. Trollope was extremely disappointed.

When Mrs. Trollope's book, *The Life and Times of Americans*, was finally published in 1828, Calvin wrote to a friend in Philadelphia and asked him to purchase a copy and to send it to him in Danville. When the book arrived, Catherine was the first person to inspect it. What she read stunned her. The mill business in Memphis was prospering and she was doing her best to prepare herself for what seemed inevitable – a family relocation. What she read sent her reeling into despair.

Catherine discussed the book's shocking revelations about life on the frontier with her good friend, Mary Breckinridge, the widow of Joseph Cabell Breckenridge, Calvin's cousin.

"Calvin has painted a picture of Memphis that in no way corresponds to Mrs. Trollope's account. Just when I was accepting an eventual relocation to the frontier, I read that conditions there are far more primitive and unappealing than I had ever thought. This book says Memphis is some sort of hell hole . . . with streets of mud and manure three feet deep. I feel as though I've been lied to. I don't know whom to believe – Mrs. Trollope's version . . . or Calvin's."

When Calvin finally had the opportunity to read Mrs. Trollope's book, he spoke to Catherine about its accuracy.

"I want you to know, Mrs. Cabell, I don't agree with everything Mrs. Trollope has reported. Yet, I must tell you that rainfall creates mud everywhere I've ever visited. Whether the mud is deeper or sloppier after a rainfall in Memphis I cannot say. What I can say is the sun does eventually come out and it dries up the streets. And when I look at Memphis in the bright sunshine I only have to squint my eyes ever so lightly until I see the future. The future is bright there. The future for the Cabell family is bright there. I ask that you understand both the challenges and the opportunities we face. I ask that you, once again, become enthusiastic about our impending move."

Yet, all Calvin could think about as he gave his best shot at persuasion was the disaster that was sure to fall upon the Cabell family if they remained in Kentucky . . . and he faced a murder indictment. He knew he must close this deal with Catherine. It was now or never.

"Mr. Cabell, I have never been enthusiastic about a relocation of our family to the wilderness - or even to the other side of Danville. I may have been tolerant. I may have even expressed my willingness to follow you there. But I have never – not ever – expressed enthusiasm about moving to Memphis, Tennessee."

Calvin instinctively knew he had chosen the wrong word as soon as "enthusiasm" had crossed his lips. He deserved to be dressed down and Catherine deserved to be accommodated. He thought he might be able to offer a suitable proposition that would, once again, salve Catherine's complaints. But what could he offer? Then it struck him.

"Mrs. Cabell, you've been resilient and resigned to this move. I appreciate you and your support . . . more than you can ever know. I wonder if what I'm about to say will make this move one which can generate some enthusiasm."

"Oh, my God," Calvin thought to himself. "I've done it again. I've set 'enthusiasm' as the expected standard for Catherine's attitude." It was too late.

"Enthusiasm? Enthusiasm? You want enthusiasm, Mr. Cabell? You expect an enthusiastic wife? I don't foresee 'enthusiasm' ever filtering into my consciousness – not now or ever."

She was aggravated. So, Calvin made a proposal that suddenly popped into his head. "What if you and the children returned to Kentucky each May and spent four months of the year with your family and your friends? Is a proposal of this nature something that can make a move more palatable, Mrs. Cabell?"

Then, it was Catherine's turn to silently think about what her spouse had just said. Her face took on an animated look . . . as if her brain was making a series of rapid calculations. Her squeamishness seemed to dissolve after what seemed to be about thirty seconds.

"Four months, you say? Four months in Kentucky? Four months to escape the miserable heat and humidity of the lower Mississippi River Valley . . . and allow the children to enjoy Kentucky summers with their cousins?"

Calvin nodded a silent, "Yes". Catherine thought a bit more and then she asked her husband.

"Mr. Cabell, are you absolutely certain Memphis offers a business opportunity of such magnitude that it's worth risking all our possessions and our very stable, pleasant lives? How can you be so sure the middle of the North American continent will ever be settled? Why would any sane person transplant himself to such a vast, rugged, and hostile territory?"

"Yes, dear, I AM certain this is a great opportunity to make a sizeable amount of money – and, moreover, we can look anyone in the face and honestly say we made our own place on the frontier. Hopefully, we will thrive . . . all on our own. And . . . as for whether I'm certain the Mississippi and Missouri River basins will one day be dotted with bustling, civilized cities . . . I have no doubt about that either. The people of this country have initiated a momentum of western settlement that will not be curbed. They're moving west. Always, they'll be moving west.

In Memphis I heard all sorts of talk about the tantalizing prospects foreseen in Arkansas, Oklahoma, and even California. I predict the nation will one day settle all the territory from the Atlantic to the Pacific except for the land claimed by the Mexicans. And in Memphis I heard plenty of talk about fighting to free Texas from Mexico."

Catherine was listening – and, she was looking directly at her husband while he pleaded his best case. She knew he couldn't resist filling in her silence with his own rhetoric. So she remained tight lipped and, sure enough, her husband kept compulsively making his case.

"We don't have to live in a cottage in town . . . where the streets might sometimes be oozing with mud. We can live outside the city . . . at Valley View. The house there can be modified and made very comfortable. You'll love it. And I know Jamie will love it, too. There's a boys' school in Raleigh where he could enroll. It's only one mile away."

Catherine couldn't, in good conscience, allow Calvin to rant on and on. So, she took a long, deep breath of air that signaled to her husband she was, finally, about to speak. Sensing a possible victory, Calvin's sales pitch eventually wound down and halted. At last, there was silence for a moment or two.

"Mr. Cabell, I married you for better or worse. I fear our life so far has been the "better" part in our marriage vows . . . and a life on the Mississippi will be the "worse". But if the children and I can spend four months a year here in the Bluegrass, how can we stand in the way of your enthusiasm . . . and your conviction?"

Calvin felt immediate relief. Yet, as he glowed about this resolution with Catherine, he was, simultaneously, adulating his wife's capacity to adapt.

"Did I hear you use the word 'enthusiasm' to describe me, Catherine Cabell? Are you possibly also saying that now, you also share my 'enthusiasm'?"

Catherine looked into his eyes and then she held her cupped hand over Calvin's ear into which she gently whispered.

"I share your enthusiasm, Mr. Cabell. And, I love you very much."

The deal was sealed. And, with this triumph of persuasion, Calvin . . . down deep inside . . . breathed a sigh of relief. He had conquered all the obstacles that had stood in his way. He would have his chance to make a new life on the frontier. He would be on his own. And, by virtue of his absence, he would be escaping his association with Dolly's death.

Or, so he hoped.

# CHAPTER
# *12*

March 1832
Raleigh, Tennessee

Calvin and Catherine often met in the overlook he cleared on the ridge at Valley View. It was the same spot Marcus first took Calvin to marvel at the panoramic view. Catherine loved the vista as much as her husband. He had cut a shallow, flat terrace along the hillside and paved it with creek rock to create an idyllic vista for relaxing and reflecting.

The finished site was furnished with four Adirondack chairs . . . sanded smooth and whitewashed. In the center of the seating arrangement was a white, round table, also built of wood. It was the perfect retreat . . . and the perfect place to talk.

"It's hard to believe, Catherine, it was six long years ago when Marcus introduced me to this ridge. It seems like only yesterday in many ways."

Catherine squeezed his hand. "It's time that passed very quickly for me, as well. Six years ago I bitterly protested being transplanted here. Now I've come to love it . . . just like you said I would."

This wasn't the first time Catherine had offered testimony to Calvin that the move from Kentucky had been a good decision. Nevertheless, every time he heard her confession, he glowed a little bit inside. He squeezed her hand in return with a gentle clutch that allowed his thumb to stroke lovingly against the moist palm of her hand. It seemed like this body language was the most effective manner to communicate to her the words which need not be spoken.

"Thank you, Darling. I appreciate your support . . . and I love you."

The fact of the matter was that much had happened to the Cabell family since 1826. And most of it was good fortune. Cabell kept his word after Catherine relocated herself and the children to Memphis in the early spring of 1830. As promised, she, Jamie, and Cassie returned each year to Lexington for a four month visit beginning in May.

Calvin purposefully crafted the timing of the family move to Tennessee in March - just eight weeks before the promised summer visit. He knew it would be advantageous to his cause for Catherine to return home no longer than three months after she arrived. Three months in Tennessee was enough time to get her bearings and to meet some new friends. But Calvin also knew after three months Catherine would begin to long for home. She would start to ask herself, "My God, what have I agreed to? I want to get out of here."

So the summer trip home in 1830 was a great way to wean Catherine away from the civilized life she had known. The spring trip of 1831 occurred just as Catherine was, once again, getting a little homesick. In just three months she and the children would be spending their third Kentucky summer sabbatical. Catherine was only then beginning to talk about it. Calvin knew this was an indication she had made a remarkable adjustment and things should go well for the couple in the future.

Jamie was now nine years old and Cassie was almost seven. When they relocated with their mother, the plan was to live at Valley View for two reasons. First, the country experience would be less of a shock to Catherine and the kids . . . as opposed to moving them directly into a rough river town with muddy streets and rowdy flatboat crews. Second, living at Valley View would allow Jamie to attend the Boys School at Raleigh - as there was no school in Memphis. The Raleigh school enjoyed an excellent reputation and Jamie adjusted well during that first spring term.

But Catherine warmed up to the idea of permanently residing in the house Cabell had built on Monroe Street in Memphis. Mary Winchester had taken Catherine under her wing, so she could be properly introduced to other educated women in the city. They were warm-hearted and hospitable. She wanted to be an integral part of their social circle.

Catherine also liked the members of the Presbyterian Church which was founded in 1828. Presently, it held its services and functions in a room over the Court House building, but there was much enthusiasm about constructing a permanent church. The City of Memphis donated a corner lot – actually, it was a run-down cemetery - at Second Street and Poplar. It was right across the street from the Methodists. This donation spurred the Presbyterians to begin raising money for their building fund.

Catherine seemed to enjoy being in the thick of things when the ladies held fund raising events. Calvin, naturally, was overjoyed with his wife's involvement in church activities. But he was mortified when Catherine was placed in charge of a bazaar selling a variety of articles that were hand-made by the Ladies of the Church. Catherine arranged for the fund raising event to be held in, of all the unlikely places, Royal Hunt's saloon.

Just one week before the bazaar, Calvin could contain his pique no longer. "Mrs. Cabell, why not hold the next bazaar in a bordello . . . or in a gambling den?" he scolded. "This plan of yours is a certifiable act of theological heresy."

Catherine was unmoved by Calvin's scolding. "You moved us here to this decadent spot in the wilderness with few available shelters for us to hold our bazaar. Mr. Hunt kindly offered his facilities. And . . . I gladly accepted."

Calvin seemed unmoved, so she continued. "Besides, my straight-laced husband, I have a plan. You shall see."

After much angst, the day for the bazaar had finally come and gone. Calvin was less angry the day afterward. But he was still somewhat ashamed his wife – who should have made it a priority to play the role of a respectable Kentucky lady – had led the Ladies of the Church astray.

So, when Calvin spoke to Catherine as she counted the bazaar's receipts, he toned down his frustration when he pleaded once again, "Mrs. Cabell, I'm much relieved this bazaar is over. I only ask one favor of you. If you should ever again be in a position of responsibility like this one, please confer with me about planning the details of your money raising schemes."

Catherine looked up at her husband, smiled, and she said, "Mr. Cabell, what would you say if I told you I have a confession to make to you?"

Calvin knew the other shoe was about to drop. And it most likely would be the one that would banish the Cabells from Memphis – forever. He nervously asked, "You mean . . . there's more to this sordid story?"

"Yes, Mr. Cabell," Catherine smugly replied as she began to reach into the cigar box and clutch as much of the money as she could grasp with two hands. "I think you should know the Ladies of the Church thoroughly enjoyed Mr. Hunt's hospitality and the warm reception we received from his bar patrons. As a result of their kindness and their generosity we grossed over seven hundred dollars for the building fund."

## No Coin for Charon

"Seven hundred dollars, you say?"

"No, I said MORE than seven hundred dollars, Mr. Cabell."

Catherine noticed that Calvin's tense muscles were loosening and his apparent high blood pressure was discernibly dropping once again.

"Well, I've always heard that crafty thieves can most likely be found where the money is. While I wouldn't categorize the Ladies of the Church as 'thieves', it does appear that a saloon was, indeed, an ideal place for your church bazaar. I congratulate you, Mrs. Cabell. I keep forgetting what a genius you are. But I must say I also think you're the luckiest chairwoman of a bazaar our church will ever appoint. The entire Cabell family might have otherwise been excommunicated."

Then Calvin showed the face of a man who had just stumbled over a religious afterthought. "By any chance, Catherine, were you ladies able to pick-pocket these sots' money while you simultaneously evangelized them . . . to accept Jesus Christ as their Lord and Savior?"

"Mr. Cabell, I told you we made seven hundred dollars. I trust the Lord will forgive us if we missed saving a few souls."

Both the church Elder and his enterprising wife further reflected on the bazaar's success and they began to laugh with glee. "I suppose all's well that ends well," Calvin admitted under his breath.

Catherine had made her point. Nothing else needed to be said. She just exhaled a haughty sigh of satisfaction.

\* \* \* \* \* \* \* \* \* \* \* \* \*

The other reason Catherine encouraged the move from Valley View into town was the news that a teacher had established a school near Court Square in 1831. His name was John C. Garner and every parent who had enrolled children as students there considered the school to be outstanding. These reviews pleased Catherine, especially since Cassie was ready to begin her education and Mr. Garner's Memphis school taught both boys and girls.

But, during these past five years, there was also the bitter that accompanied the sweet. Catherine's mother suddenly died during the previous year's summer visit. She developed a fever that couldn't be quelled. Ephraim

McDowell kindly rode from Danville to Lexington to offer his diagnosis and his medical counsel. She died three weeks after her first symptoms appeared. Catherine missed her mother deeply, but she took solace in the fact she was at home to care for her and that mother and daughter were able to say their "goodbyes" near the end.

Calvin was grief stricken to learn Isaac Shelby died in 1827. The old man had been a good friend to him. He loved the Governor like a dear uncle. Shelby had certainly played an important role in Calvin's life and he knew the Governor cared deeply about him.

Calvin learned of his death ten days after the funeral. The letter he received from Henry Caldwell informed him the members of the Athenaeum served as pall bearers. Caldwell reported Calvin's name appeared on the funeral program listing him as an "honorary pall bearer." He was pleased to have been included on the printed program. Nevertheless, he regretted he couldn't have been there to assist transporting the Governor's remains from the church to the cemetery.

As Calvin read Caldwell's letter, he reminisced. "My old friend lived a long and distinguished life of honorable public service. What a remarkable legacy he leaves behind." Quickly, Calvin remembered something that brought a smile to his face. "What a blessing it is to live here in Shelby County, Tennessee. I'll always find comfort in the fact I live within the county which bears his namesake and that I was privileged to have known the Governor."

Calvin had another reason to mourn Isaac Shelby's death. He remembered D.A. Cowan's letter that communicated how Shelby had scolded the Mercer County Sheriff for even considering him a suspect for Dolly's murder. Consequently, Shelby's passing also meant his most influential advocate could no longer defend him.

The lumber and barrel making business had done well for the past five years. There never was a quarter when the Cabell Mill lost any money. At first the profits were marginal. But there were no 'red ink' entries in the ledger and Calvin rejoiced at that fact. Then in 1830 the mill experienced a sharp upturn in business. Each time he perused the books he noticed a consistent trend – more and more sales . . . and more and more profit.

The mill now operated six saw pits. Each was so busy that the sawdust and wood chips accumulated at the bottom of the pit so fast that every rectangular hole had to be cleaned out twice a week.

Memphis was still a town on the Southwestern frontier and it differed vastly from Southern towns back East . . . like Atlanta, Charleston, and others. There were few Negro slaves living in the city. However, the number of slaves in Shelby County - outside the city limits - was growing rapidly. The 1830 census stated Shelby County's population was 5,648. That same census showed the population of Memphis was 663. Few of these city folks were black. However, this wasn't the case outside the city, as the census showed 37% of Shelby County's population was Negro.

The planters in the rural areas of Shelby County had cleared timberland and they were growing cotton where forests once stood. Cotton crops . . . like the burley tobacco crops back in Kentucky . . . demanded much manual care. The theory most planters adopted was empirical. One slave should be able to maintain and harvest six acres of cotton. Consequently, as soon as the forests were cleared, there appeared thousands of acres of cotton being cultivated in the region. And the number of slaves had grown proportionately.

* * * * * * * * * *

Calvin carefully watched how the operation of manufacturing businesses was being altered in the established southern states like South Carolina and Georgia. He knew that slaves were no longer exclusively used as agricultural workers. Lumber businesses back east were now replacing white sawyers with much cheaper labor – African slaves.

This was a disturbing development. Calvin had many times repeated the same mantra. "If I can't operate a legitimate business with skilled employees because lumber mills which use slaves spring up and undercut the price of operating an honest business . . . then, I'll just shut down the Cabell mill. I refuse to even contemplate buying slaves to toil on my property.

"The slavery 'problem' . . . everybody calls it the slavery 'problem'. Even those in Charleston and Savannah who are waist deep in slave issues . . . they just pass it off as an irritating 'problem'. You'd think it was something nettlesome . . . like mice in the pantry. Ten years ago they were knee deep in the 'problem' . . . and ten years before that they were just ankle deep. In ten more years, they're going to find their 'problem' has grown so virulently, it's risen above their neck lines. They'll be gasping for air . . . just to survive.

"So, if slavery is a problem – like any problem - there surely must be a solution."

But every effort Calvin could think of to resolve the dilemma had either failed miserably or it had merely made a dent. He remembered a nugget of wisdom Isaac Shelby once passed on to him. "Always remember, Calvin, times change . . . and you've got to adapt to those changing times."

Then, while he was considering all the ways decent people had tried to tackle the slavery issue, he thought about Fannie Wright. "Now, there's someone who tried her best. And she used a 'different tactic' – just like Governor Shelby advised me. She may have failed, but at least she tried a fresh plan."

Even though he had never laid eyes on her since '26, Marcus Winchester briefed Calvin about everything that happened to her . . . and to her Nashoba.

As it turned out, she bought more than five hundred acres from Judge Robinson. He was desperate for cash to meet his own obligations. He later convinced her to buy the other parcels he owned. Somehow, the sophisticated English woman found herself owning about eighteen hundred acres in the American wilderness.

Fannie had bigger plans for the work of Nashoba and its original ten slaves. She considered this was just the beginning. She used her network of social reformers affiliated with Robert Owen's New Harmony. She broadcast her ideas to a wide assortment of other abolitionists. And, to achieve her goal, she left no stone unturned. She even contacted nearby planters who owned slaves and asked that they donate one or two to her new utopia.

What Fannie stirred up was more than she – or anyone – could handle. There were few cash donations . . . and not a single donation of a human slave. Regrettably, what she DID attract to Nashoba was a group of ultra-radical reformers who, by their nature, were eager to join in her noble experiment. They also, by nature, tended to be very opinionated and contrary. Each had his own stubborn perspective on administrative actions that should be taken. Compromise was rare among them.

The planters who were Fannie's neighbors also became increasingly concerned and suspicious about Nashoba. As one of them said, "What in the Sam Hill is goin' on over there?" The white folks talked about little else except the "utopia for nigras" and how its existence would inevitably result in a violent uprising that would eclipse the horror of Nat Turner's rebellion.

Rumors flew throughout the county about "free love" and "relations between the races." Lastly, the slaves whom Fannie purchased were never truly convinced they would be freed after five years of hard labor. From their point of view, this was just another white man's ploy to dupe them.

Marcus said that by 1828 Fannie decided she had enough. Nashoba was abandoned and Fannie paid for the passage for all her utopia's slaves to Haiti where they were resettled and freed. She even accompanied them on the journey to ensure their safe arrival.

Miss Wright's Nashoba never quite caught fire. Most accounts of what went on there were nothing more than 'heresay'. However, Frances Trollope wrote about it in her best selling book, *The Domestic Manners of Americans*. Her book was promoted as "an unvarnished look at life in the new democracy building on the frontier." Mrs. Trollope's account of Nashoba was certainly unvarnished. It was also most unflattering.

Calvin and Catherine loved Mrs. Trollope's book. They considered her evaluation of Americans on the frontier to be hilarious and often cruelly accurate. For example, she described fellow passengers on the steamboat, "Belvedere". It transported Fannie and Mrs. Trollope from New Orleans to Memphis in December of '27.

Referencing the passengers on the steamboat, she wrote, "It is with all sincerity I declare that I would infinitely prefer sharing an apartment of a party of well conditioned pigs."

She was particularly horrified to observe the compulsion Americans seemed to have for spitting in public. She thought it was disgusting and most uncivilized. Then she continued to describe the Kentuckians aboard the boat. The Cabells liked this section the best.

"The passengers were mostly described as Kentuckians, a very noble-looking race of men; their average height considerably exceeds that of Europeans, and their countenances, excepting when disfigured by red hair, which is not unfrequent, extremely handsome. The gentlemen in the cabin (we have no ladies) would certainly neither, from their language, manners, nor appearance, have received that designation in Europe."

"Their manners at the table were startling. The frightful manner of feeding with their knives, till the whole blade seemed to enter the mouth; and the still more frightful manner of cleaning the teeth afterwards with a pocket knife."

Catherine discussed the book with her Ladies of the Church friends and she couldn't help but gloat. "Mrs. Trollope didn't have much to say that was complimentary about our country. But she certainly was telling the truth when she described how good looking and manly are the lads from

Kentucky."

Calvin fondly recalled how Frances Wright had tried her best to eliminate slavery – yet, how she ultimately failed. But there were other attempts at abolition also cataloged in his memory.

There was his Uncle William Breckinridge who was a driving force within the American Colonization Society. But there was never a momentum established to repatriate blacks back to West Africa. And Calvin didn't foresee that much would change in the future.

Reverend Breckinridge had also worked mightily within the church to eliminate slavery. He pleaded his case before the Presbyterian General Assembly. He managed to convince many churches to endorse his proposals. But, the end result was tragic. The Presbyterian Church was split apart by the issue. Those churches in the minority which were proponents of freeing the slaves were called "New School" congregations. Those who wished to perpetuate the status quo were members of the "Old School". The split was just the beginning of more serious church schisms that followed.

Abolitionist sentiments in the North were growing. But Calvin didn't consider their doctrines to be "hard core". Their hearts were, no doubt, in the cause. But abolitionists seemed to find their highest calling when they, for example, fostered runaway slaves who made it across the river from Kentucky into Ohio or Indiana. Calvin considered the situation. They didn't have a clear understanding of what universal suffrage would truly involve . . . and how it would dramatically affect the North.

"What if the trickle of runaway slaves grew so great that communities and states in the North were overwhelmed by their numbers . . . and their social needs? I'll bet that's going to be the eventual solution. When the Yankees start to howl because they're financially sustaining uneducated runaway slaves, maybe that's what it will take to force the federal government to negotiate some sort of resolution."

One thought after another paraded through his mind. He longed to get at the root of the matter.

"It's the blasted U.S. Constitution that's the root of the 'problem'," Calvin muttered out loud. "If the framers of the Constitution only had the gumption to resist the jawboning of the Southern slave states, we wouldn't be in the fix we're in. That's when and where the slavery question should have been addressed and resolved. It's the fault of the framers. If the slave states were given – say, ten years . . . even twenty years . . . to end this social institution, the authors of the Constitution could have nipped all this in the bud.

"Instead, they added insult to injury. They crafted a Constitution that not only endorsed slavery, it mocks the electorate's apportionment of the legislative branch. The Constitution states each slave amounts to three-fifths the representation in Congress afforded a white man. That provision only serves to give the slave owners an unfair, disproportionate stake in the Congress . . . and the government. Virtually everyone agrees that with this added political power, the South has been able to pack the Supreme Court with justices who would never move to meddle with their affairs."

Calvin remembered his own former Senator from the Bluegrass, Henry Clay. Ever since he was first elected in 1810, he cleverly formulated his reputation as "The Great Compromiser".

"Maybe it's such weak-kneed 'compromise' that's at the root of all evil. It sure seems that way to me." Johnathon Lacey, a mill owner from Charleston, visited Calvin's mill earlier in the year. Lacey told Calvin he was going to have to adapt to a slave economy to keep his business competitive.

"Well, that's just another way of saying it's inevitable that I, too, will bend over . . . and, eventually, compromise. So, the question is will I stand resolutely against slavery? Or will I compromise? Will I compromise like the Europeans and their North American colonists had compromised in the past? Will I compromise . . . like the framers of the Constitution? I don't know. But I know one thing for certain. The time's coming when I'll, no doubt, have to make a choice. And I'm certain I'll have to confront the devil, himself. Will I bend just a little . . . or will I bend a lot? In my heart I know that day is coming. But, I can already sense it . . . I'm going to bend."

There was a knot in his stomach and hints of nausea arose toward his gullet. He had, at last, discovered the truth – the truth about himself.

He looked heavenward and murmured so low he could barely hear himself. "I'm ultimately going to compromise my beliefs . . . and everything I've ever proclaimed. Lord, help me. It's my fate . . . to compromise . . . and, therefore, commit yet another horrible sin."

# CHAPTER

# *13*

June 1834
Memphis, Tennessee

The Session meetings at First Presbyterian Church began promptly at seven o'clock on the third Thursday of every month. By 1834 the enrollment at "First Pres" had grown to sixty-two members. Rev. W.C. Blair, who had been the minister since the founding of the church, always attended these meetings. However, only the six lay Elders who were elected by the congregation could make decisions affecting church policies. And . . . sometimes . . . they were required to adjudicate the personal behavior of other members.

Issues concerning questionable personal conduct by members warranted coming before the Session for a ruling. Discipline could be meted out for vices the church guidelines warranted as punishable transgressions. These were defined as, "gambling in any form (which also included buying lottery tickets), attending a theatre performance (as it is a school of immorality), attending a horse race, and dancing - in all of its stages."

Then there were the "Thou Shalt Nots". Each of the Elders believed all ten were derived by Divine proclamation and, therefore, should be upheld to the letter. These "stone tablet" violations warranted swift jurisprudence by the Session. They included intoxication, sexual misconduct, breaches of the Sabbath, quarreling, and malicious gossip.

Given this wide spectrum of punishable sins, one might reasonably conclude the six Elders were sequestered in solemn deliberation for hours at each Session meeting. However, issues of these sorts could generally be privately addressed, counseled, and resolved before they officially appeared on the Session's agenda.

Calvin Cabell often left a Session meeting and returned home to Catherine with the same predictable lament.

"We sat around a table for two hours discussing all the little sins that supposedly remove a sinner from God's grace. But when I consider the Church's prescribed sins of betting on a horse or getting drunk . . . compared to buying or selling humans and forcing them to work for six days of the week with no wages . . . well, it makes my blood boil. Why in the name of Heaven isn't owning slaves considered a mortal sin? Does the fact the United States Constitution condones slavery in certain regions of the country supersede the laws of God? Apparently, it does."

\* \* \* \* \* \* \* \* \* \* \* \* \* \*

Catherine and Calvin had many discussions about how they would live their lives amidst a land of slaves and slaveholders. There was unanimity among them. They swore they would never own slaves. Calvin, likewise, incorporated this same philosophy into an abiding business principle. "If my business can't survive by employing paid workers instead of slave labor, then I'll just shut it down."

Like most of the other wives of successful businessman who lived on the frontier, Catherine didn't enjoy many moments of relaxation. Her life was a never ending series of chores beginning at dawn and ending long after dusk. Nevertheless, she never shirked her responsibilities or complained about them.

She once told Calvin, "I'm no different than our mule, Sam, out at Valley View. I just lower my head down so I can only focus on the row I've got to till. And then, I pull the plow as hard as I can - until it's time to turn around . . . and drag the burdensome load back again."

Most wives living in town had to use every resource that might be available to them. The Cabell home in town consisted of a main house with a separate kitchen building in back. It was a free standing structure, because the heat generated from its fires to boil water or to roast meats was intense. No one living in the main house could endure such heat in an environment that was already sweltering during much of the year.

The Cabells also had a cast iron wood-fired cooking stove installed in the house's rear utility room. It sat idle during the warm months. However, the excess heat it generated from cooking meals during the cold winter was much appreciated.

Each dwelling lot had one or two privies located behind the main house. There might also be other structures such as a hen house, a smoke house, a carriage house, or a barn. City lots were, however, relatively small. They were inevitably surrounded by a picket fence to keep out wandering animals who were lured by the opportunity to raid the vegetable garden. Vegetables were grown in a hodgepodge manner that covered every square foot of soil within the fence.

To make gardening more efficient, different vegetable crops were grown in different sections of the yard. After one variety had finally exhausted its profligacy, the soil was tilled again . . . and a new food species quickly took its place. Thus, many home owners produced at least two vegetable crops a year . . . and, sometimes, more. Parts of the garden where spring lettuces thrived were picked until the heat of May ended their bounty. Then, the lettuce was dug up and replanted with corn, okra, or some other 'hot weather' plant.

Flowers were sown to brighten up the place, but they also had a purposeful function to perform. Bee Balm was planted to lure honey bees intent upon fertilizing the vegetable blossoms. Sunflowers standing erect in the summer sun were a magnificent sight to behold. Yet, they, too, were planted with a purpose. Each one's mysterious, chocolate Cyclops's eye menacingly stared down at would-be animal thieves and successfully frightened them away.

The first section of timber land at Valley View that was cleared during the logging operation was quickly converted to another use. Calvin planted an apple orchard prior to the family making their move in 1832. Catherine brought strawberry plants, rhubarb, herbs, and large packets of vegetable seeds from Kentucky. Each variety added to the bounty the plot was expected to produce. The peach orchard and Concord grape vines were planted in the spring of 1833. All of this agriculture illustrated the Cabell family's intention to be self-sufficient in their new Tennessee home.

Calvin wanted to provide help to ease Catherine's often arduous responsibilities. One year earlier he hired a newcomer named Tim Farley who soon gained Calvin's respect as a hard worker. Farley and his wife, Annie, were among the growing number of Irish immigrants who had settled in Memphis during the past two years. They were respected for their work ethic. But they were also a source of suspicion, because of their Catholic religion. Most people referred to them simply as "Papists" . . . as if to derisively say anyone who followed the religious directives of a mortal in Rome must be a person content with rigidly following the orders given by his boss.

Yet, there were in Shelby County a growing group of people doing the job nobody else wanted to do. Furthermore, their population was growing far greater than the Irish and German immigrants. African slaves were bought in lots from slave traders in Nashville, Lexington, Louisville, and New Orleans. They were shipped . . . or they even walked hundreds of miles to their cruel destiny on the many new plantations that sprang forth on recently cleared land. Indeed, it was the slaves and the mules that felled the trees and cleared the stumps from thousands of alluvial acres around Memphis. Afterward, the same combination of man and beast plowed and planted cotton in the newly exposed fields

When the fertile land was finally cleared, never-ending rows of cotton were planted each April. These weren't fields of ten or even a hundred acres. They resembled oceans of agriculture.

Marvin Himmel, a transplant from northeastern Ohio who grew up along the shores of Lake Erie, described it this way in a letter to folks back home.

"I watched and marveled at the transition the cotton plants made on the Jones' plantation during the growing season. In March I could see nothing but soaking mud. In June there had sprung forth a vast field with verdant rows of cotton plants that blew easily in the meekest of wind. In September the brownish cotton bolls protruded out in clear sight. Then, in mid-October I stood in the middle of Mr. Jones' field and thought I was standing, once again, in a blinding blizzard that had suddenly blown in off Lake Erie. Wherever I turned under the azure blue autumn sun and as far away as my eyes could peer, all I could see was a blinding white. The cotton blooms carpeted everything around me. I thought it was January and I was back at Grandpa's farm outside Ashtabula."

Calvin hadn't noticed the labor market in the City of Memphis shifting toward the use of slaves. But he sensed such a time loomed in the near future. Just outside of town plantations operated largely with slave labor. He knew slavery would eventually seep into the city . . . just like flood waters inevitably flow under the crack of an otherwise secure door.

Initially, these would be nettlesome demographic changes. Nevertheless, Calvin knew if the swell of slaves couldn't be stemmed, then life in Shelby County would be like living next to a polluted pond. The stink would be omnipresent and sickening. Yet, there was little anyone could do about it.

The wealthiest planters in the region tended to have town homes in Memphis where they resided during the winter months. They brought with them their "house slaves". This was an intriguing term intended to denote not only the nature of their work, but it also implied a degree of refinement that every "Massa" and "Missus" had invested in them. They dressed these house servants in clean clothes made so as to conform to contemporary "domestics" fashions. A foreign visitor who was insouciant to the American world of slavery might have easily thought these planter families might be some Rajahs who had moved their families from Bengal or Jaipur.

Calvin would have none of it. In January he came up with the perfect solution to ease Catherine's household responsibilities. It all happened by accident. During the week before Christmas, Calvin assembled his lumber crew one dark night around a huge bonfire. There were eight or nine chickens roasting on a single spit that was evenly turned by a young lad he paid for the job. This was one of several tokens of appreciation he arranged – especially around Christmas – to inspire a sense of unity and goodwill among his workers.

He spied Tim Farley's face brightly illuminated by the leaping flames. Calvin walked around the fire pit to say 'Hello'. Tim was talking with another Irishman as Calvin approached. He accidentally heard Tim say his wife was seeking work. But after three weeks of presenting herself to potential employers, he said she had finally given up.

"What kind of work is she looking for, Tim?" Calvin said as he stepped suddenly from the blackness of the night into the glow of the flames.

"Evening, Mr. Cabell. The fire's light blinds a man. I didn't see you come up on us, sir."

"I didn't mean to sneak up on you, Tim," Calvin apologized in a way he hoped wasn't too condescending. "I just overheard you say your wife is looking for work. I thought I might be able to offer some leads . . . and possibly a reference if it was appropriate."

"That's mighty kind of you, Mr. Cabell, mighty kind of you, indeed. Annie . . . that's my missus . . . is a champion at any sort of household chore. She'll clean the stalls of a carriage house and she'll haul coal, or wood, or just about anything else that a donkey can carry. She's available to work any day of the week. And that means she can work Sundays, too. If you know of a lady in need of a strong back and a discreet tongue, Mr. Cabell, please tell her about my Annie."

As Farley listed all of the chores Annie was willing and able to perform, Calvin began to visualize Annie relieving some of Catherine's workload. She deserved some reprieve. Jamie was now thirteen and he was putting his growing body to good use doing the chores his mother bid him to do. But, like every Cabell, Jamie's first responsibility was to excel at his primary job – being a serious and successful student. Cassie was now eleven and she was also helping Catherine. But she was hardly prepared to cook meals, wash clothes, or pluck the feathers from a freshly killed chicken. The more his mind ran through this long list of chores Catherine had to accomplish during the week, the more he made up his mind that Annie Farley might be just what the Cabell family needed.

"Tim, I can't promise anything, but if your Annie could come by my house one evening this week, Mrs. Cabell and I would like to discuss the possibility she could work for us. Do you think you and your wife would be okay with that?"

Tim Farley's reaction to the proposition bounced between being speechless and shouting for joy. He would have never initiated such a discussion with his boss to promote Annie's need for work. "How perfect", he thought, "that Mr. Cabell brought up the subject on his own."

"Mr. Cabell, Annie will meet with you at any time of day on any day of the week. You just tell me tomorrow what suits you and your wife. And . . . again, Mr. Cabell, we are very grateful to you for my job here at the mill. If Annie could also work for such fair-minded people as you, then she'll be over the-moon with joy."

"Tim, the feeling's mutual. I'm very pleased with you and I'm pleased with your work as well as your work ethic. I haven't had enough experience with you Celts to determine if hard work is an ethnic trait or if it's just a virtuous tenet within the Farley family. I'll speak to Mrs. Cabell this evening. You and I can set up a time for an interview tomorrow morning."

As a sign of respect, Tim was holding his hat over his heart throughout the conversation. When Calvin promised an interview Tim bent forward so that his hat made a broad sweep across his stomach. It was soon hoisted into the air by his outstretched right hand. Calvin thought the gesture to be rather formal. He was uncomfortable with such homage. And just as he was about to remind Tim he now lived in a democratic country where lords and manors are merely a murky reminder of European history, Tim interrupted him.

"Thank you, again, sir. I can't wait to tell my Annie this news." Then, with a sheepish, apologetic look on his face he added, "I understood all that you said, sir, except the part about 'virtuous tenet.' Is that a good thing or a bad thing, Mr. Cabell?"

Calvin burst out laughing so loudly it attracted the attention of all the employees gathered around the fire.

"Yes, Timothy Farley, 'virtuous tenet' is something that's good about you. It's very good, actually."

The pit man clutched a folded cloth to protect his hands from the scalding heat as he slid each golden brown chicken carcass along the metal rotisserie. One by one he freed each bird from its fiery impalement and it fell on to a waiting platter. Steam from the golden poultry flesh began rising into the cold Christmas tide air. Calvin grabbed Tim's hat and he playfully placed it lopsided over the Irishman's head.

"Come with me, Tim. Dinner's ready."

* * * * * * * *

The December Session meeting was tediously long to everyone except Paul Claxton, the Clerk of the Session, who presided over each month's gathering. Calvin could sense discreet fidgeting and squirming all around the table. When Claxton announced the full agenda had been acted upon and the meeting was adjourned, a collective sigh of relief was audible.

Calvin yearned to get out of the stuffy pastor's study and breathe in the fresh cool breeze he knew awaited him outside. Curtis Maplewood shared the same strategy. He clutched Calvin by the upper arm and the two feigned a sudden reason to extract themselves from the other men who chose to linger.

Maplewood and Cabell pushed open the church door and they nearly raced down the four steps to the sidewalk. There they stopped and giggled . . . like little schoolgirls . . . at their artful escape. Neither man recognized that Mercer Watkins had followed on their heels until he, too, walked briskly out of the church and approached them. He spoke with a tone of trumped up humor . . . curiously mixed with a dose of growing anxiety.

"For a moment I thought we might be held captive in the study so long we would all eventually meet our Maker right there . . . around the table."

Mr. Watkins followed his feeble witticism with a nervous chuckle. Maplewood sensed Mercer seemed very anxious. He decided to try injecting a bit of humor. "Mercer, as I judge all the characters who are Elders of this church, I can't think of a single one who will EVER meet his Maker. We're all bound for hell in a hand basket."

Calvin offered Curtis Maplewood a smile for his quip. But he stopped short of laughter.

"Calvin . . . Curtis, I don't mean to barge in on your discussion," Mercer Watkins offered apologetically. He turned to Calvin with a look of desperation. "But, Calvin, I wonder if I might walk home with you . . . to talk about some personal matters you might be able to help me with. But if you two will be occupied for some time I can visit with you later."

Curtis Maplewood spoke before Calvin could. He wanted to grant Mercer his request without putting Calvin on the spot. "Actually, gentlemen . . . it's time I headed for home as well. And since I live along another route, I hope neither of you mind if I bid a fond farewell and start on my way."

"Are you sure, Curtis?" Watkins asked, seeking genuine assurance he hadn't interfered.

"Absolutely . . . I bid good evening to you both. I suppose we shall meet again on Sunday morning."

"You can count on it," Calvin responded to Curtis. "Good night . . . and give my regards to Mrs. Maplewood."

Mercer Watkins chimed in following Cabell's adieu. "Thank you, Curtis. I'll see you here Sunday, as well. And send Emma my best wishes, too."

When the sound of Curtis's footsteps began to grow fainter, Mercer turned to Calvin to speak. He exuded a sense of extreme nervousness. A blind man could see it on his face . . . even on a dark night such as this. "Calvin, I need to talk to you about something that's very private. And, hopefully, it will be held in confidence by you. Do I have your word on that?"

Calvin considered for a moment what could possibly be so private that a well respected businessman such as Mercer Watkins would be so concerned with confidentiality.

"Certainly, Mercer, you have my assurances. But what are you talking about? Are there problems between you and Eloise?"

"Eloise is fine, thank you."

Mercer began to lead Calvin away from the church. "Let's walk while we talk, Calvin. Shall we?"

"What's on your mind, Mercer?"

"I've gotten myself into a real bind, Calvin. Have you heard about it yet?"

"No . . . not a hint."

Calvin thought Mercer might start filling in the blanks on his own. But he didn't. And Calvin couldn't bear the aggravating silence. "What's your problem?"

"I think I may have lost everything, Calvin . . . everything."

"What in the world happened to you, my man? I thought your business was doing just fine. Didn't you tell me you've begun manufacturing wagons and you can't keep up with the demand?"

"Yes, and it's the wagon venture that's at the root of my problem. You see, most of the iron work was manufactured by a blacksmith down in Hernando. He was doing a good job, but he couldn't produce the hardware fast enough. That was causing a backlog of unfilled orders.

"The man's name is Mottel and he asked me to co-sign for a five hundred dollar loan. He said he would use the money to increase his hardware production. I agreed. And that's when I got sucker punched."

"What's happened Mercer? You can pay off a five hundred dollar loan . . . with no trouble at all."

"Mottel rode up to Memphis with the bank note. He brought his brother with him. I met the brother once before and I wasn't very impressed with what I saw. But when the two men came into my shop, everyone was jovial as they could be. I gave the brother a quick tour and then I suggested we step into my office and I would sign the paperwork.

"Well, Mottel said he was in a hurry. He whipped out the note from his overalls and suggested I just sign the papers on the bed of a wagon next to where we were standing."

Mercer's breathing changed to short, rapid, frantic panting. He was clearly getting to the rub. And, apparently, just the thought of saying what went wrong was sending him into a panic attack.

"Mottel pulled a pen and some ink from his overall pockets. And, as I leaned forward to sign, the brother started a commotion with one of my workers. They were about twenty feet away from me. Naturally, I looked up to see what was going on. I focused on signing the note . . . thinking only about how quickly I could get this aggravating Mottel brother to leave my shop."

"So, I still don't know what your problem is, Mercer."

"The problem, Calvin, is that Mottell apparently hid another note under the one I agreed to co-sign. I think the brother timed his antics just to throw me off guard. I signed the note all right. But I signed a note that made me liable for fifteen thousand dollars."

Mercer got increasingly frantic. "Mottel told the Bank of Hernando he wanted to buy three thousand acres of cropland. The bank knew he couldn't repay the loan and they insisted he get a guarantor. The bank told me both the Mottels simply vanished . . . naturally, with the money. I'm told they've headed west . . . probably to California. Now, the bank wants its money . . . and I'll have to liquidate all my assets to settle this debt."

"So why don't you get a lawyer down in DeSoto County and sue the bastard?"

"I did. But there's the smell of home cooking when you get within one hundred feet of the DeSoto County Court House. The bank has a note in default and they want their money. They don't care one particle that I was defrauded. And to make matters worse, Judge Benson down there is the brother-in-law of the bank's president. It was clear as daylight he wasn't about to rule in my favor when their guarantor's problem could be solved so easily . . . by turning to me for repayment."

"It's all so impossible to believe. It's like you were robbed without knowing about it at the time. I can't even comprehend how such a mess could happen."

"Well, it HAS happened. And it's happened to me – just like I told you."

"So how can I possibly help you, Mercer? I don't have the kind of cash you need to satisfy the bank. I'll help in any way I can and, of course, you have my sympathy and my prayers."

"Alright, now I get to the part that's brought me to you. I assure you I've prayed over this matter, Calvin." Mercer Watkins was, at last, going to get to his point. "You know my house servants, Mose and Bettie, don't you?"

"Of course I do. They sit in the balcony every Sunday morning and listen as intently to the service as any of the white folks down below. They're likely even more engaged than most of us."

"And they have a three year old son, too. His name is Jed. They're the best slave help in Memphis, Calvin. I'm here to ask if you would purchase them from me. They'd bring probably twelve hundred to fourteen hundred dollars at a slave auction. And it's to the auction block they're headed if I don't strike a bargain with you."

"Mercer, you know my opinions about slavery. Do you think my moral principles are so weak-kneed that I'll change them on a whim following a Session meeting? Absolutely not, Mercer . . . absolutely not . . ."

A look of desperation overtook Mercer. Calvin recognized his mood change and, for a moment, he thought Mercer would get down on his hands and knees to make his plea.

"Calvin. I'm more than just fond of Mose and his family. They're good people – smart as a whip and dedicated to doing any job I give them. I'm also personally attached to them. I'd do anything I could to spare them from harm. But if I can't strike a deal with you, the Bank of Hernando will take them over as confiscated assets. I have no doubt they'll all be sold to a planter . . . and they'll spend the rest of their lives as field hands. You're the only person I know who might spare them."

Calvin didn't indicate he was wavering . . . at least, just a little. But he did seem sympathetic to Mercer's plight. Or, he thought, was it actually Mose's plight which piqued his interest? There was a gas street lamp at the corner of Third Street and Jefferson where the two men stood. The lamplight shone dimly on Mercer. He was disconsolate and moisture welled up in his eyes.

213

"Here's what I don't understand, Mercer. You bought Mose and Bettie four years ago to the best of my recollection. You bought them as personal property, as chattel, to do your bidding . . . just like you might buy a mule to work for you from dawn 'til dusk. You wouldn't fret selling that mule as part of a liquidation of assets. So, why is it a man who has no compunction about buying two human lives is suddenly riddled with guilt at the burgeoning need to sell his property to raise cash?"

Mercer had a response for Calvin. He had even expected the question.

"Because I've learned something I didn't know four years ago. Back then I never thought I would ever purchase a human soul. I can even say I was, at one time, abhorrent to the notion. But, as times changed, household slaves began serving ever more homes in town. They seemed a natural part of day to day living. So, as I became more affluent and my wife became more plaintive about relieving her chores, it just seemed natural – or, that's the way I rationalized it.

"So, on a trip to New Orleans I went to a slave trader named Vaughan and I asked him to keep a lookout for the sort of Negro who would be suitable to work around the house – to be presentable to guests as well as smart enough to catch on to his chores. Vaughan said he was expecting an order of several dozen slaves he had purchased in Richmond. He said they were being shipped to New Orleans and should arrive any day.

"Well, the next day Vaughan sent a messenger to my hotel with a note that said he thought he had some "stock" he wanted me to inspect before they were sold off to planters. I dropped by his business that same afternoon. He asked me to wait for a few minutes while he fetched the woman he thought would fit my needs. When the door to the rear of the building opened, Vaughan stepped through it. He was followed by Bettie. She was in hand shackles and Vaughan led her with a four foot chain that was attached to the shackles – just like a dog on a leash."

Calvin was soaking in every word Mercer was saying. Annie Farley had told Catherine about the sacrament of Catholic confession. She said the penitent confessant talks to his priest through a carved wood screen. Catherine and Calvin thought the doctrine was admirable. But they both thought that confessing a sin "eye to eye" with a priest would be far more appropriate. Mercer was confessing to him here and now – "eye to eye". Calvin could sense in his bones that Mercer was playing the pleading role of contrite confessant . . . and Calvin was his unwitting priest.

Mercer continued nervously. "Bettie struck me immediately as being different. She didn't hold her head down like others I've seen on the bidding block. She looked right at me. Mind you, she didn't have a defiant look in her eyes. She just looked at me with a kind of personal integrity that impressed me and soothed my growing guilt. Then, Vaughan said Bettie claimed to have a husband within the lot. He said he never likes to split up a couple if he can help it.

"But money is money . . . after all is said and done, Mr. Watkins," he reminded me.

"Vaughan said he would discount the sale price if I purchased both Bettie and Mose. Of course, I hadn't inspected him yet. But I figured that a strong woman like Bettie would likely have a husband with similar characteristics. He said he would bring Mose out for inspection if I was interested. I began to dwell on deep, dark thoughts for a minute or two. It was like a hellish dream I was living. Here I was looking over humans to purchase just like that mule you were talking about a minute ago. I was very uncomfortable. But I was going to go for the bait . . . and Vaughan knew it.

"I approached Vaughan and whispered so low I hoped Bettie didn't hear me. 'Would you return the woman before you bring out the man'?" I asked.

"Vaughan nodded affirmatively and led Bettie back to God-knows-where. Then the door opened again and Mose was led into the office by one of Vaughan's traders.

"I could tell right away that Mose was intelligent. I could see it in his eyes . . . and in the way he was comfortable in his own skin. It wasn't pride I perceived. It was a personal, peaceful resignation that he knew he'd be a slave until he died. But while he was living, I sensed he was going to cling to one personal principle, 'I am one of God's creations . . . nothing more . . . and nothing less'. I was drawn to that sort of self-assurance.

"Maybe Vaughan won me over with his sales pitch, but I returned the next day and I told him to draft the purchase papers. We didn't have at the time a shack built to house them. So, they lived in a tent I set up at the rear of the house. It was Mose's first task to construct his and Bettie's shanty and privy. Then, about a year later, Jed was born."

"What's your point Mercer? Please get to your point. Don't you still consider them to be your property?"

215

"The point is this. It's been nothing but a blessing to have had Mose and Bettie in our lives. I'm not the sort of man who can live with a slave on my property, work inside my house, and still distance my feelings about these people. Mose and Bettie have been devoted to our family. And, without knowing we were going to end up this way, we're devoted to them, too.

"I'm not proud, Calvin, to be a slave owner. But that's just the way things turned out. I compromised my Christian principles when I paid for them . . . and I regret that very much. But I fear what's going to grow inside me if they wind up as field slaves and . . ."

Mercer's quivering voice subsided . . . like he was fighting some force inside that needed to be purged by vomiting it all up and out. Finally, he broke down into loud sobs of self- abusive wailing.

"What I fear the most about the fate of my soul is . . . if Mose and Bettie and little Jed are sold in different lots. There's nothing I can do to prevent it once they're repossessed, Calvin, I can't bear the responsibility of tearing them apart. They deserve better. And, I'm telling you, I confess it's my fault for sliding down the slippery slope of bondage. I'll have to pay the price in the afterlife. But, if I'm bound for hell, I sure as hell am going to try to do the right thing now – the right thing under these circumstances. Please, Calvin, will you consider taking them in?"

"Mercer, what you're really asking is if I'll PURCHASE "them" – not, 'take them in'. You want me to clear your conscience by sullying my own. I don't even know these Negroes. It's just like you . . . buying a pig in a poke . . . from your Mr. Vaughan."

"Well, Bettie and Mose know you, Calvin. At least they know you to be a good and honorable man. Mose told me a few weeks ago how he often peers over the balcony railing and studies you. He's admired you on many a Sunday morning. He would serve you devotedly, Calvin. I'm sure of it."

"There you go again . . . ragging about 'servants' when you mean 'slaves'."

But what Mercer had just said about Mose leaning over the rail from above . . . well, it stuck in Calvin's mind. And it intrigued him. "Mose said that about me . . . to you, did he?"

"Yes, it's the pure truth. I know if I could sit down with them and tell them what's happened . . . and explain they'll be working for you in the future, they'll be just fine with that . . . just fine."

216

"So, you've not told them about your predicament . . . and their vulnerability to being split up?"

"No, I've put it off . . . and I can't bear to summon the strength to tell them. I don't want to cause them anxiety . . . any concerns . . . or fears."

Calvin reached in his vest pocket and pulled out his watch to examine it. He held it just so in the soft shimmer of the street lamp. He could see the time was nine-fifteen. He tried to process everything he had heard.

"Am I being set up by Mercer like the slave trader, Vaughan, set him up four years ago?"

Then he thought about how Marcus Winchester had bought slaves and freed them after they had repaid the purchase price in consideration for their labor. But, he treated them well. He thought about Fannie Wright and how her plan was similar. But it involved providing the freedmen an education and a trade before they set out into the world. And he thought about Bettie and Mose . . . and that small son, Jed, they had. And like Mercer, he shivered at the thought of their family being split up . . . just for the sake of repaying a fraudulent loan guarantee.

He continued to ponder this situation. "I wonder if Mercer's money problems and the devious circumstances that caused them is God's punishment for owning slaves in the first place. Maybe I'll face the same punishment."

Then he dismissed this hypothetical question just as quickly as it had popped into his mind. "Nah, such theology . . . of earthly retribution . . . just doesn't hold water."

As he closed the lid on his pocket watch and burrowed it back into its rightful place inside his vest, he turned to Mercer and stared at him for a few seconds in the night air. Mercer knew he was being examined . . . and judged by Calvin Cabell. He bore the same discriminating look Mercer remembered he had employed as he once inspected and rated Mose and Bettie at Vaughan's slave office. He had regarded them as merchandise. Calvin's grimace indicated he regarded Mercer as less significant . . . than even chattel.

At last, Calvin spoke and gave his answer. "I'll talk to Mrs. Cabell about your predicament, Mercer. I can't say when I might be back in touch – or even IF I'll be back in touch. But I'll consider some options. However, know this, my friend. If I do anything to resolve this situation, it will NOT be to

217

raise capital to repay your indebtedness. It will be to keep a family together . . . with the objective of eventually freeing them. And so, I bid you a good night, Mercer."

Calvin turned sharply and walked purposefully east on Monroe. When he stepped outside the lamplight he was immediately swallowed by the darkness. Mercer lingered there alone under the faint glow. His stomach was painfully aching from the twisting and tightening of emotional knots . . . a gnawing agony like he had never experienced before. He prophesied this wouldn't be the last time he would be afflicted by such a gut wrenching episode. He had considered for weeks the possible remedies he could bring about to save his slaves. Calvin Cabell was his very last option to keep his servants together as a family unit.

Two men on horseback were trotting toward town. They laughed loudly and joked with one another. No doubt they were on their way to the Bell Tavern or Royal Hunt's Saloon to enjoy an evening of drinking and conviviality. They tipped their hats to Mercer . . . and he responded, likewise. As the sound of the men's lively banter and laughter ebbed, he turned and slowly plodded toward home.

However, there would be no conviviality or laughter at his house. The only comfort Mercer Watkins foresaw at the moment was the knowledge he had a full bottle of bourbon in his locker. He knew it was waiting patiently for him . . . like a stalwart friend. He thought if he drank the bottle dry . . . in the sorry solitude of his own company, he might be able to reason how and why he had brought this ethical plague upon himself.

That night Mercer Watkins never felt more isolated from mankind, or his God, or even from himself. "Tomorrow . . . maybe tomorrow I'll get the good word from Calvin," he thought.

"But tonight . . . at least, I have my friend, Jim Beam, to comfort me."

# CHAPTER
# *14*

July 1834
Memphis, Tennessee

Catherine Cabell knew for certain there was bad news in the letter from Henry Caldwell which her husband was reading. Nevertheless, she could sense its contents didn't report something that was a tragedy . . . like a friend's death or some natural disaster that had occurred back in Kentucky. If that were the case Calvin would have flared his eyes and spoken out loud about whatever he was intently examining. His eyes were riveted on the contents of this communication. Catherine knew he must surely be reading the letter for the second or third time. Finally, Calvin raised his head and focused on Catherine with a look of despair.

"You won't believe what Henry Caldwell has asked me to do."

"What? What on earth are you talking about, Mr. Cabell?"

"Mrs. Cabell, think hard about the folks you know . . . or even barely know back home. Of all those people, which one is the most bogus, the most irritating, and the most arrogant of the lot."

Catherine started cataloging in her mind those who might fit this description. "I don't know, Mr. Cabell, I think most folks at home were pretty decent. Maybe I've just filtered out the ones that might match the person you're talking about."

"Let me give you some hints. He's a young man who's quite short in stature. He has a mother who's an insecure, social imposter. He has horse teeth that protrude out like a winnowing filly. And lastly, he's a lousy lawyer."

"I would have to say that paints a picture of Isaac Shelby Lancaster. How did I do?"

"I can't believe what I'm being asked to do for that little weasel. Henry and the others in Danville must think I operate some sort of frontier facility to rehabilitate felons."

"Well, tell me what Mr. Caldwell's asking you to do."

"Apparently young Lancaster has finally gotten his come-uppance in the Bluegrass. He needs to get out of town – to relocate. And, of all the lousy luck, he's moving here. Henry's apparently speaking on behalf of several of my friends who want to banish that horse face. He says it would be a great favor if I would introduce him to some well stationed contacts in the county – particularly to lawyers and judges. Mr. Caldwell tries to make it sound like you and I can distance ourselves from Lancaster if we choose. But, he's coming. And, there's nothing we can do about it, I suppose."

"What do you mean when you say he's being run out of town?"

"In the past year and a half he's been a party to some shenanigans that raised people's eyes about his ethics. How foolish of them. He has NO ethics."

Calvin rolled his eyes back in his head when he said it. "I knew he had no conscience the first time I ever talked to him. What did they expect? Anyway, he's had two serious ethical problems and the last one was apparently the nail in his coffin."

"What did he do?"

"Henry says about nine months ago Lancaster frittered away an escrow account for one his clients. He was almost arrested for thievery, but he managed to somehow come up with the money. Then, a few months later, he represented Franklin Myers in a real estate deal on several thousand acres near Harrodsburg. Squire Lancaster drafted and secured from the seller an option to buy the property. The option expired the first of July. All the while Lancaster knew there was strong interest on the part of some investors from Louisville to buy the land.

"So, when the second day of July rolled around, Lancaster drew up a new option agreement to purchase the acreage in his own name. Then, he contacted the investment group. By the end of July he had purchased the land from Myers and flipped it two days later to the men from Louisville. He made a very tidy profit. It was money that should have accrued to Myers."

Calvin looked down at the letter briefly before he continued. "There were plenty of folks who wanted him arrested. So Judge Boyle is trying to diffuse the situation by having him repay his ill gotten gains and leave Danville – forever. That's the deal he's been offered. And if Lancaster doesn't follow through with it, Judge Boyle says he'll throw him in the state prison. Moreover, the Judge added that this time . . . he'll personally throw away the keys."

"So what in the world made Isaac Shelby Lancaster pick Memphis as his next victim?"

"Apparently he's intrigued that Memphis is in the county named for his uncle, Governor Shelby, He thinks he can make some hay out of the coincidence. Henry swears that our living here has little or nothing to do with it all. But I have my doubts."

Maybe it was inevitable that Isaac Shelby Lancaster would turn out to be a scoundrel. His mother, Clementine, was the Governor's niece. Governor Shelby's sister, Clara Shelby Minot, had one daughter, Clementine, and two sons. "Clementine had been a pain", as Ephraim McDowell used to say, "since she was old enough to talk." That's because when she spoke, she managed to weave her famous uncle's name into every conversation with the intent of putting everyone on notice that she was an aristocrat, a Shelby, and she should be treated as such.

Clementine Minot married Clarence Lancaster who grew up on the outskirts of Lexington. He was handsome, but he had few resources. Soon Clementine could see he had even less initiative  Most people concluded this marital match with Clarence was just about the best marriage proposal Clementine would ever see come down the pike. No one knew how Clementine evaluated her options. But she said, "Yes", for whatever reason . . . only she knew.

The Lancasters' baby boy came into the world within the first year of their marriage. Clementine named him Isaac Shelby Lancaster . . . which most folks considered to be another example of her better-than-thou ways. She insisted everyone address him as "Isaac Shelby" - just so no one would miss the relation he bore to Kentucky's first Governor.

Now, when parents call their children by their first two names it's almost always something like John Henry, Sara Jane, or Billy Bob. There's no implicit pretension that's involved. But when folks address a little bucktooth tyke using the full name of the Commonwealth's most esteemed citizen, it sounds uncomfortable. It sounded peculiarly precocious.

Most mothers adore their children. But Clementine's maternal instincts went beyond devotion and love. She believed Isaac Shelby Lancaster was brought into the world to play out "his destiny as a great leader . . . like his namesake".

In all fairness to the boy, maybe it was his mother's doting and social manipulation that caused him to be so disliked by the children he played with as a young child. Perhaps Isaac Shelby Lancaster never had a chance to develop a normal personality. Instead, he grew into a haughty, braggadocio, skunk of a little man who - like his mother - never missed an opportunity to arrogantly introduce himself.

"Hello. My name is Isaac Shelby Lancaster. I'm named after my uncle, the Governor."

Clarence Lancaster didn't provide for his family. How could he? He didn't work. After he and Clementine were married, Governor Shelby gave him a job as his farm manager. He was great at delegating chores, but his orders tended to be the wrong remedy ordered at that wrong time. The Governor kept him for two years until he could stand no more of his foolishness.

Governor Shelby remembered the numerous times Roscoe Bentley, a farm implement dealer in Lexington, had asked Shelby for a favor here and there. Shelby decided it was payback time. He arranged for Clarence Lancaster to go to work for Bentley as a salesman. His job was to travel around the region to cultivate farmers' interest in his company's products.

This arrangement worked out poorly for Bentley. But it was a perfect situation for Lancaster. He came to personify all of the "farmer's daughter" jokes that began, "There was this traveling salesman . . . "

Bentley put up with seven years of Lancaster's nonsense . . . as he felt an obligation to Governor Shelby. Finally, he fired him. After that, no one could keep up with all the jobs that appeared to fall from heaven into his lackadaisical lap . . . for several weeks or months at a time.

Meanwhile, Clementine was raising the boy using whatever means of support she could connive out of her family. The Mintons had some money, but not enough to provide for Clementine and Isaac Shelby for the long haul. So Clementine began to make jams, jellies, Chow Chow, and other condiments out of her kitchen. She actually prepared some very delicious food. But when she was flattered for her cookery, she demurely replied, "I only work at this

222

sideline, because so many people keep asking me for more. How can I turn them down?"

Calvin had known young Isaac Shelby Lancaster from his days as a ferryman when Clementine would travel between Lexington and Danville . . . looking for her next mark. Calvin always detested the boy and Isaac Shelby and his mother knew it. The snotty little kid had grown into an even snottier little man. Henry said in his letter he was now twenty-four years old.

"I know I can't stop this from happening, but I'll be damned if I'm going to take him around the county like he was my long-lost Kentucky cousin," Calvin bellowed out to Catherine. "He's always been a pain in the ass. We used to tease him unmercifully. NOBODY wanted to be associated with Isaac Shelby Lancaster."

"When is he expected to arrive?"

"Henry's letter was posted on the seventh - two weeks ago. He said Isaac Shelby would be boarding a steamboat in a little over a week. In all fairness to Henry, I think he's just giving us fair warning that a bad storm is blowing down the Mississippi . . . and it's about to get off a boat in Memphis."

"There's nothing we can do, Mr. Cabell. He's not family. He's not even a relative of a close friend. He's just like some anonymous settler moving from the Bluegrass to Tennessee. We'll distance ourselves from him, if you insist. Let's be optimistic though. Maybe this ethical scare at home will cause him to turn over a new leaf."

Calvin couldn't believe how silly his wife was acting. So, to make his point he clenched his teeth together and mockingly said, "A leopard doesn't change its spots, Madam."

Then he turned around and began reading the letter once more . . . hoping that, somehow, he had misunderstood its news the first three times.

"Nope," he said. "A storm's a brewin".

* * * * * * * * * * * * *

A week after Mercer Watkins made his desperate proposal, Calvin walked into his shop unannounced. The two men had seen one another at Sunday services, but Calvin was abrupt, yet polite, when he greeted him. He wanted to let Mercer stew for a little longer.

In fact, he and Catherine discussed this situation every evening. And both thought of little else during the day. Mose and Bettie were a known entity to each of them. They had observed the Negroes in the balcony on Sundays and, individually, each had made a mental note that these two were out-of-the-ordinary sorts of darkies. Calvin believed Mercer when he said Mose had commented favorably about his impressions of him and the Cabell family. He couldn't seem to flush that flattering remark out of his mind.

When Calvin entered Mercer's crude office inside his shop, he caught Mercer by surprise. Mercer couldn't help smiling an optimistic smile. "Surely," he thought, "if Calvin were going to decline the proposal, he wouldn't come to my office to do it." But Mercer's smile was thin and hesitant – and, for good reason. The deal had not been struck.

"Mercer, Mrs. Cabell and I have decided we would like to take Mose and Bettie into our household. Now, mind you, I'll pay the price you quoted. But I don't ever want to hear any talk that Calvin Cabell's breaking his covenant to never own slaves. Is that clear, Mercer?"

"Oh, yes . . . yes, indeed. I'm so grateful to you, Calvin. And I'm so pleased for Mose and Bettie. Mose is smart. He's picked up on my tension and my anxiety. I'm sure of it."

"What do you mean?" asked Calvin.

"Three days ago he approached me. He said, 'Mr. Watkins, I knows you're bearin' a heavy burden. I can tell. If there's anything I can do that could lighten your load, I shore hope you'll give me a chance to help out'.

"Can you believe it? Mose wants to ease MY burdens. So I sat down with him on a bale of straw and I told him everything that was happening to me – and possibly to him. He was worried, all right. But, Calvin, after he thought about it for a moment or two, this black man patted me on the knee in a comforting manner and he revealed his remarkable, optimistic perspective about life.

"He said soothingly, 'Ever thing gonna be all right, Mr. Watkins. Ever thing gonna be all right'."

Mercer's eyes glistened with tears as he repeated what Mose had said. "Now," he thought silently to himself as he continued to stare hopefully at

Calvin, "maybe everything IS going to be all right with Mose and Bettie . . . even though it likely won't for me."

"How long do we have, Mercer? How long before they're taken away by the bank?"

"I'd say ten days or two weeks at the least. Then, who knows what will happen?"

"We're not prepared for a family to live on the premises. I think I'll let them live at Valley View until satisfactory accommodations can be arranged."

Mercer had been the confessant under the street lamp on Jefferson. Now Calvin spoke as if he were the supplicant in the holy sacrament of confession. "I've got to tell you something, Mercer. I've prayed about this . . . and I've thought about little else except the plight of these people. I don't know if God has given me an answer, but my gut tells me this is the right thing to do. I sure hope so."

Calvin remembered the wailing hindsight of Captain Moore after he told him about drowning his son's dog, so he could get the lad a coin for Charon. Captain Moore said over and over, "I hope I did the right thing. I hope I did the right thing for Robert . . . and that God won't hate me for it."

Calvin's conscience was gasping, "I hope I'm doing the right thing. And, God forgive me if I've sinned by purchasing these poor souls."

Calvin put his hat on his head as a sign of his departure. "I'll have the money for you in a week. We can make arrangements for the transfer then."

Mercer approached Calvin with his hand extended for a handshake, but Calvin looked icily at Mercer's palm . . . and he recoiled.

"Mercer, this isn't a business deal we've completed here today . . . where the parties shake hands when they've agreed on terms and conditions. I'm sure I'll feel differently about this in the future. But right now I feel like both of us have unclean hands. As for me, I believe I'll return to the mill and give mine a good scrubbing."

With those words Calvin walked out of Mercer's office. The deal had been done. Yes, somebody could sugar coat what was happening in the terms of this contract. But the raw truth was that three hapless people had, once again, been bartered away to a strange new place to carry on with their lives. They had a new owner. And they had no choice in the matter. There was no denying any of it.

Calvin Cabell couldn't walk fast enough. He maintained his rapid pace until he, at last, was lathering his hands with the bar of lye soap the employees used at the saw pit. His hands seemed soiled and he hoped soap and water would do the trick.

He washed his hands vigorously and, immediately, he felt the need to lather up and scrub them again.

\* \* \* \* \* \* \* \* \* \* \*

When Calvin heard the screeching and tooting whistle of the steamboat, he knew a warning was being issued to everyone within earshot. It was bringing Memphis, Tennessee a boat load of trouble. He was at the mill - about an eighth of a mile from the landing. He often heard steamboats whistle to announce their arrival. Today's steam-driven shriek, however, was eerily discordant. This was a particularly shrill whistle. It proclaimed, "Beware."

Sure enough, early that evening Catherine and Calvin sat in rockers on their small front veranda when they both saw a little twerp of a man sauntering down Monroe Street toward them. He raised his hat and waved it happily. "I'm bringing you a big Kentucky 'Hello.' Hey there, all you Cabells. It's great to see both of you. And it's just terrific to be here in Tennessee."

Isaac Shelby Lancaster ambled through the front gate with his short spindly legs. He turned about to fasten it and he proceeded to walk up the porch steps with both hands extended.

"My word," Catherine trembled as she spoke quietly through her teeth to Calvin, "he's expecting a hug."

Calvin had no choice but to offer him a rocker and the chance to "sit a spell," as he said.

Mercifully, the visitor blurted out the good news first. Isaac Shelby Lancaster had already made arrangements to stay at the Gayosa Hotel. He was prepared, he said, to stay there for a prolonged period of time. Catherine, nevertheless, piped in to emphasize the point that there was no available space in their home to accommodate him.

226

Calvin felt the need to speak out in a manner which the young man would clearly understand. It was essential he address some issues right up front. He abruptly said Lancaster shouldn't expect to be invited for hot meals each evening. And he wouldn't have a standing invitation to Sunday dinner, either. The time to nip any misconceptions in the bud was now. Calvin pulled out his sharpest verbal scissors.

"You know, we barely know you or your family. And Henry Caldwell has written to me and offered a 'no stone left unturned' account of your ethical problems at home. I want to clearly state I'll introduce you to the judges and the lawyers in the county. However, any introductions will also include clear notice that I'm not soliciting a position for you. Indeed, I want people here in Memphis to know there's absolutely no bond between us."

Isaac Shelby didn't flinch or indicate he felt berated – even though he was being brutally dressed down within two minutes of walking through the Cabells' front gate. He pasted a penitent look on his face, wiped his brow with the handkerchief hanging out of his coat's front pocket, and then he spoke.

"President Young at Centre College told me I'm on my own here in Tennessee. I came knowing that fact. And I don't expect any personal relationship to develop between us. I just thought that Shelby County, Tennessee might, after all my unfortunate transgressions, be the place where I truly belong. I'm ready to start fresh, Calvin. I'm prepared to walk the straight and narrow. And I'm prepared to distance myself from the two of you, if need be. But I do want to express my gratitude that you'll afford me some introductions. Yes sir, Calvin, Shelby County, Tennessee and I are going to get along like toast and jam."

"And one other thing, young man," Calvin said interrupting this unwanted pest. "This is Shelby County, Tennessee . . . and folks at home have called you Isaac Shelby since the day you were born. I refuse to incorporate myself in any potential ploy you might have to dupe people into thinking the Governor sired you . . . or that he personally gave you his name. The fact is, he considered you to be an embarrassment. Mrs. Cabell and I have talked about this. You need to pick which of your names, 'Isaac' or 'Shelby', you prefer for us to use. We won't be a party to helping you become entrenched here based on riding on the coat tails of an honorable hero's name."

Again, Isaac Shelby Lancaster didn't take on the demeanor of one who had just been whipped with harsh words He was prepared to make his choice there and then. Back in Kentucky, even strangers recognized his name and he knew it brought with it a certain cache. It took him mere seconds to announce his choice. He considered there must be lots of Isaacs in the world. So Isaac would be of no benefit to him. Consequently, Shelby . . . it should be. In time, he thought people in Memphis would surely make the connection with his august namesake.

"Calvin, please call me Shelby from now on. I've got to tell you, 'Isaac Shelby' has always been a mouthful for folks to pronounce. It's time to trim down my given name. Please understand. I'm willing to make adjustments and amends. I HAVE turned over a new leaf, Calvin. You'll take my word for it, won't you? "

Catherine joined in hoping to mellow this caustic reunion. "Well, then 'Shelby' it shall be. Now, Shelby Lancaster, I have some green beans and ham hocks left over from dinner today. I've also got some cold cornbread. It's not much. But you're welcome to sit down and have your first meal in Tennessee."

"Thank you, Catherine. That's very kind of you. I've got a hankering for vegetables this evening. And I do believe green beans sounds like it'll fill the bill just fine. And Calvin, I've taken to heart every word you just said. You won't have any trouble out of me. That's for sure."

Calvin was standing and leaning against the porch post. All of a sudden Ike Rawlings came to his mind. "I wish I could have it within me to cock my head and spit great gobs of tobacco juice on the ground before I respond to this pecker wood," he mulled over silently as he stared back at Shelby. "But, regrettably, tobacco chewing and spitting just aren't my style."

Catherine went inside and Calvin was standing alone on the front veranda when Shelby stepped forward to join him. He sensed the worst was not over yet. He was right as rain.

"You know, Calvin, I've studied the law . . . and I've practiced the law . . . and there's one thing about the law that continues to intrigue me. It's so simple. Yet, to certain people, it would be profoundly discomforting."

"Yeah, and what would that be, sir?"

"I'm fascinated that unlike any other crime where a perpetrator must be caught and indicted within a specific amount of time if he'll ever be prosecuted . . . there's one, sole exception to the rule."

Shelby added a threatening tone to his words - at least, Calvin thought so. But then Shelby stopped talking and the silence lasted for what seemed to Calvin like an eternity. So, he bit at Shelby's silent bait.

"And what is it that 'fascinates' you so about the law, Shelby?"

"It's this. There's no limit to the statutes of limitation for murder. Did you know that, Calvin? That means . . . however long a man can go undetected . . . or wherever he might flee to . . . he'll never run so far that justice can't be served – not until the culprit's own dying day."

What Shelby was saying was chilling. The runt had pieced everything together. Calvin was certain about it. Lancaster had been in town mere minutes before he threw down the gauntlet and put Calvin on notice that he intended to be his eternal nemesis.

Shelby had made a promise to turn over a new leaf. And Calvin was prepared to tell him truthfully what he thought about this pious pledge. But the banished lawyer was communicating more than just the statutes relating to murder. He was dropping a handkerchief, a warning, that what he knew could bring his Tennessee acquaintance to his knees. Shelby was stating he expected to be regarded with respect. He was out and out demanding it.

However, Calvin didn't dare acknowledge he comprehended the gist of the threat. Doing so would amount to self-incrimination. "We'll see. We'll see how things turn out. The proof's in the pudding, Shelby."

But on his insides Calvin cringed. "This sidewinder will eventually wield to his crooked advantage his knowledge . . . that he spotted me with that mud coated Dolly on the Ides of March. He was the only witness. And Mr. Cowan wrote to report Shelby picked up some more information when the Mercer County Sheriff came looking for me. Isaac Shelby Lancaster knows I'm a suspect . . . and he'll eventually ask me to pay the piper to hush what he could say or do. The only questions are . . . when will he strike . . . and how much will he demand for his due?"

*No Coin for Charon*

# CHAPTER
## 15

October 1834

It was eight in the morning when Owen Winchester tapped on the frame of the Cabells' front door. He pressed his nose into the lattice and called out, "Mrs. Cabell, it's me, Owen. I've got a note for you. It's from my Mother."

He could hear no sound inside. So, he began to repeat himself again. Then, suddenly he saw Catherine's silhouette approaching the door from the rear of the house. She was wiping her hands with a red checkered towel.

"Morning, Mrs. Cabell. Mother asked that I give this to you."

Owen Winchester was Marcus' and Mary's oldest son. His full name was Robert Owen Winchester. For reasons unknown to Catherine and Calvin, Marcus named his first son after Robert Owen, the wealthy industrialist who operated the New Harmony utopia in Indiana.

Clearly, Marcus must have had great admiration for the idealistic industrialist and his objective to illustrate that utopias could be viable, productive communities. However, Marcus had never met Mr. Owen. He had only heard about him from Fannie Wright during her two years in Shelby County.

Later, when Mary gave birth to a daughter, they named her Frances Wright Winchester, in honor of Fannie. Catherine and Calvin thought these choices of names were quite curious, but they never asked the Winchesters about the matter.

Owen was six years old and the top of his head was still several inches below the middle wood brace of the door. Catherine thought he was adorable.

"Owen, what a pleasure it is to see you. I've been working with Sally Farley on the back porch. You say you have a note from your Mother? Well, I can tell you for sure that I've never had such a good looking messenger appear at my door."

Catherine opened the door and Owen reached out and handed the envelope to Catherine. "Won't you come in, young man, and visit for a spell?"

"No ma'am, but thanks. Mother asked me to wait for you to read her note . . . and then come home with your reply."

"I can do that. Let's sit out on the porch. You sit in Mr. Cabell's rocker, Owen."

Catherine lowered herself into her rocking chair and pierced the glued flap of the envelope so her fingernail could slice across its top ridge. She unfolded the stationery and began to read silently.

Dearest Catherine,

I write to cordially invite you and Calvin to join me and Marcus for dinner this evening. A flatboat apparently became disabled and ran aground several hundred yards below the mouth of the Wolf. I'm told it's beyond repair, but it's still in tact. Marcus paid the crew five dollars for it. He said it was worth that much as salvaged wood.

We're planning a picnic this evening on the deck of this forlorn raft. I do hope you and Calvin will be able to attend. I should also tell you that we will be hosting a special guest. Former Governor Sam Houston has stopped by on his return trip from Washington to Arkansas. He must depart tomorrow and I'm pleased to tell you this most reticent of men has agreed to be feted by us and our friends. Mabel and Parker Pendleton have accepted an invitation and we hope you and Mr. Cabell will do so, as well. Our servant, Isaiah, will meet you at the wharf at six o'clock. He will row the boat to our floating picnic ground. Please reply and return this note with Owen.

Yours Affectionately,

Mary

"Well, Owen, what an exciting evening your mother has planned. How could anyone say 'No'? Wait here until I gather my pen and ink. I want her to know right away that we'd be delighted to be her dinner guests."

Catherine picked up the wooden checkerboard that sat on the porch table. She turned its smooth side upward and placed it so its borders rested on the arms of her rocking chair. She laid her stationery on this improvised desk and began to write her reply.


Dearest Mary,

How kind of you to invite us. We look forward to being in your company this evening. Please send me word if there is a dish you would like for me to contribute to the menu. What about some deviled eggs?

Fondly,

Catherine


She folded the letter and gave it to Owen without stuffing it into an envelope. "Here you go, Owen. Take this to your Mother and tell her I said, 'Greetings'."

Then Catherine asked Owen to wait a second more. She said she had something special for him. She made a quick trip inside. When she returned, she held out both hands curled into two tight fists.

"Owen, there's candy in one of these hands. If you pick the correct one, you're in for a treat. However, if the hand is empty, you must agree to sweep my veranda before you return home. Are you willing to take the bet?"

"Candy, you say?"

The boy's eyes dashed back and forth . . . from one clenched fist to the next. "I'll take your bait, Mrs. Cabell. Daddy says I'm a lucky sort of fellow. I'll bet you're about to lose a piece of candy."

Then he bent over to inspect her balled up hands very closely. Their back sides were facing up and he observed her knuckles were white from clamping shut the treasure inside. Owen thought he might be able to spy the concealed loot if Catherine had carelessly left a gap between her white knuckled fingers. But there was no opening he could find. So, he pointed to her right hand and said, "I'll take my chances on this hand."

"Good choice, Owen." She turned her right hand over and unfurled her fingers. The prize was a piece of red and white striped peppermint. Owen was thrilled.

"Well, Owen, you can't be tricked, can you? I guess your Daddy's right. You ARE a lucky boy."

Owen reached for the confection and popped it into his mouth. "Thanks, Mrs. Cabell. I love peppermint. How about if I come back later in the morning? I'll gladly sweep your front porch anyway."

"Well, thanks for your offer, Owen. Let's just call you the winner . . . fair and square. Now you run along home, dear, and you be sure to give your mother my reply."

Owen raced to fling open the front gate and, just as quickly, he sealed it behind him. Then he skipped down Monroe Street . . . sucking on the peppermint prize. Catherine recalled Jamie when he was that age and she remembered how much he loved hard candy. That's why she had rigged the bet.

As Owen turned the corner and skipped out of sight, Catherine unfurled her left hand's fingers. Its palm revealed a second piece of peppermint. She put it in her mouth and went back inside the house thinking, "My word, a picnic on a river raft with Governor Houston. I can't wait to tell Mr. Cabell when he comes home for dinner."

\* \* \* \* \* \* \* \* \* \* \*

Mary Winchester never responded if she needed Catherine to bring any food. However, Catherine boiled some eggs anyway. Within an hour, she had thirty deviled eggs laid out on a tray. Each one of them looked as smooth as alabaster. If any got their surface marred during the peeling process, they were put aside and eventually mashed into egg salad. Catherine's mother always said it was uncouth to serve pocked deviled eggs. The white bottoms needed to be pure and to glisten in the light. Catherine took her mother's lesson to heart and she planned to pass the same doctrine of food preparation on to Cassie.

As Catherine predicted, Calvin was overjoyed at the invitation. He said he would return home early in the evening to get ready.

"Isaiah's skiff is a boat I'm not about to miss," he told his wife. "I recall the last time Governor Houston dropped by Memphis. I thought I might never see him again."

"I remember you describing the day his steamboat came to town. You were upset."

"Of course, I was upset. Houston had just resigned as Governor – in disgrace . . . by most folks' account - after just a few weeks in office. Then, he and Jim Bowie disguised themselves and boarded a steamer in Clarksville. Several days later when they docked at Memphis, Bowie told me the Governor had been "drunk as a skunk" the entire trip. After two more intoxicated days in town, they boarded a boat scheduled to steam up the Arkansas River . . . to the Cherokee settlement near Ft. Smith. When Governor Houston left Memphis he was still drunk. I've got to admit, it was a pathetic sight to see."

"And didn't you say he married a Cherokee Indian squaw . . . just weeks after his first marriage ended so mysteriously?"

"A Cherokee PRINCESS . . . or so I'm told. Remember, I told you Houston lived with the Cherokee for four years as a youth. The chief considered him to be his son. The Governor convinced the chief back in 1818 it was in his tribe's best interest to leave their North Carolina and Georgia homeland and relocate west . . . beyond the Ozarks. He said if the Cherokee didn't move soon, of their own accord, the white men would eventually move them . . . to who knows where."

"I understand President Jackson once took him under his wing . . . like a son," Catherine continued to pelt her husband with her curious questioning. "Tell me again how they met. Wasn't it during the Indian Wars that Jackson commanded?"

"Right . . . the Governor was a junior officer at the Battle of Horseshoe Bend. Jackson didn't know him until one day he spotted Houston lying on the battlefield . . . wounded by an Indian's arrow stuck deep in his groin. Houston had his pistol drawn, cocked, and he had the weapon aimed at a private standing next to him. He told the man if he didn't muster the guts to yank the arrow from his flesh, he would kill the soldier.

"Well, the soldier bit his lip . . . and he eventually began to pull out the shaft. Apparently, it was gruesomely painful. Well, Jackson saw every second of the dramatic scene. He was so impressed with Houston's bravery, he basically adopted him as his protégée. He put him through school, arranged for him to become a member of the bar, and he set Houston up in a law practice in Lebanon – just east of the Hermitage. Before long Houston was serving in Congress and soon thereafter he was elected Governor . . . as Jackson's hand picked candidate.

"He was a single man when he took office, but he took a wife very soon thereafter. The rumors were that Houston's bride was horribly disgusted by the Governor's groin injury – the one the arrow caused. She left him and went home to her Daddy after less than a month of matrimony. What else could have caused her to leave? Nevertheless, all sorts of malicious rumors were hatched and spread."

"But President Jackson isn't so happy with his protégé now, is he?"

"Nope, he's not. Houston returned to Washington claiming he was the full fledged Ambassador of the Cherokee nation – an equal to ambassadors from England or France. He showed up at a diplomatic reception at the White House dressed in all the regalia of a Cherokee chief. He wore leather leggings, ceremonial garments, and he showed no visible signs he was ever once a white man. Jackson was highly upset. He felt betrayed."

"I wonder if he'll be dressed as an Indian chief tonight."

"I don't know. And I don't care. I have such high regard for this most unusual of men . . . and I'm very appreciative the Winchesters invited us to an intimate dinner with him. Dear wife, even though you're not a Cherokee princess, I hope you'll dress like a frontier princess for him."

"Mr. Cabell, you're such a spoil sport. I already had my squaw costume and an assortment of feathers laid out on the bed. Now, I'll have to re-evaluate my wardrobe for something more suitable."

\* \* \* \* \* \* \* \* \* \*

That evening Calvin drove the wagon to the top of the crest overlooking the wharf. The time was five forty-five. There was a rugged, sloping path perpendicular to the channel that declined to the water's edge. A wagon could easily negotiate it. Those on foot, however, often faced a slippery slope.

By agreement earlier, The Cabells were to leave their horse and wagon where Isaiah would be waiting for them. Then, when he rowed back to the harbor, he was to drive the wagon back up the bluff where it and the horse would wait until the picnic was over.

As they peered down at the wharf from Front Street, they noticed several dozen flatboats were moored in the river harbor. It was mid October and the sun would set in about one hour. It was unlikely any of these vessels would venture on until the morning.

Just as the wagon turned to descend the bluff two young men, heavily laden with supplies they had apparently purchased at Anderson Carr's store, were nearing the summit of the muddy trail.

"Let's offer some help to these two lads, Catherine. They're having a mighty hard time carrying their purchases. We've got an empty wagon going to the same destination. Let's show them some hospitality."

He called out to the young men. "Gentlemen, you've got a mighty heavy load you're carrying. Allow me to offer you and your cargo a wagon ride down to the river."

Both men beamed with delight. They were clearly struggling. "Thank you, sir, that's what I call Southern hospitality. We gladly accept your offer," replied the shorter man.

"Mighty kind of you, sir," the tall, lanky man joined in.

"Put your supplies in the wagon and hop aboard. Always glad to offer help to strangers when we can."

Their purchases were placed at the back of the wagon and both men jumped on its bed and sat down on the floor. Calvin turned his head toward the rear and introduced himself. "My name is Cabell . . . and this is Mrs. Cabell. Where do you boys hail from?"

"Illinois, sir," replied the short man.

"Bound for New Orleans, are you?"

"Yes, sir," the tall man said. "It's our second trip down the river. We had a rough time our first time. Maybe your kindness is an omen that this trip will be better than the last."

Catherine was holding her parasol in the intense fall sun. It was made of a lace. "It's the perfect accessory," she had told Calvin, "to meet Sam Houston." The sunlight filtered through the many openings in the cloth's intricate design. Its rays cast a dappled look of shadows and light on Catherine's face. So, when she turned about to greet the men, the tall one said he thought her shadow-splotched face made her look like she had measles. Everyone chuckled at his unsolicited observation.

"Gentlemen, what sorts of bad experiences did you endure on your first trip?" Catherine asked.

The shorter man spoke up first. "Well, ma'am, we had troubles from the get-go. We set out floating down a stream in central Illinois. Our flatboat was loaded with cargo. Just one mile from where we began the trip, there's a small waterfall. Our raft got hung up on the rocks. We had to unload all the freight so we could push the boat over the falls. When we finally succeeded getting past the rocky barrier, we had to load the cargo once again. We feared such a mucked up beginning was a telling sign of what lay ahead."

The lanky fellow then began to speak. "It was my first trip on a flatboat. And while there were many times the river seemed to get the best of us, we managed to get by. But the perils of the Mississippi River weren't the main hazards we faced. One night, near the end of the trip, we beached the flatboat on the Louisiana side of the river to get some much needed rest. We were sound asleep when we were suddenly attacked by about eight black men. Given our location, we could only assume they were runaway slaves."

"Oh my," Catherine said as she covered her mouth from shock. "You've obviously survived the attack. But, were you hurt?"

The short man offered the details. "They ganged up on us pretty awful . . . and the fact we were asleep made us all the more vulnerable. We fought as best we could. But we really didn't stand a chance of beating them away. Yes ma'am, we were hurt real bad. And the men made off with as much of our cargo as they could carry. Come the morning sun, we just considered ourselves lucky to be alive."

"I should say so," Catherine agreed. "These runaways have nothing to lose. Little wonder they're vicious. Mind you, I don't mean to minimize your experience, but my husband and I are deeply concerned how our country is going to get itself out of this quagmire we call 'slavery'."

"Yes, what a shock it was to my senses to be exposed to the bitterness of slavery. Coming from Illinois where all men are free, I simply wasn't prepared to experience what I saw."

Calvin was able to observe the tall man who just spoke. As he talked, Calvin could see that he was, indeed, moved by suddenly being cast into the culture of a slave state. He imagined what his own life might have been like if he had been raised in a free state. What would his reaction be? Being born in the South meant he had grown up just accepting slavery as the way life is.

Then, the thin, tall man continued. "The biggest shock of all came when we finally arrived at New Orleans. We roamed about the city until we came upon a slave auction being conducted in the open air. There was a wood platform about four feet off the ground. Each slave who was being sold stood up there while the white men haggled with each other and the auctioneer.

"There was terror in the eyes of those Negroes – sheer terror. And the women were particularly frightened. I heard the auctioneer speak to the crowd about one woman standing on the crude stage with her two young boys. He said the sons were five and seven. The auctioneer told the bidders if he couldn't get a bid at a certain price for the three, then he'd split up the family. He cajoled the crowd saying these two youngsters in just a few years were going to be able to do the heaviest manual work imaginable.

"The woman cried buckets of tears. Yet, they were to no avail. The boys were sold as a pair and their mother was bought by someone else. I've got to admit, Mr. and Mrs. Cabell, this sight made an indelible imprint on my heart. I'm quite sure I'll never spend a day of my life without reliving that tragedy . . . and, of course, considering the tragedies of thousands more like her. If I could do something to end slavery forever, I would jump at the chance."

Catherine and Calvin shook their heads with disgust. They had seen auctions before and they could visualize every detail the tall man was recounting. They could tell this experience had made a deep, permanent impression on his soul.

Calvin spoke empathetically to the young men. "Well, gentlemen, we don't have many slaves here in the city limits of Memphis, but their population is growing rapidly on the surrounding plantations. We grew up in Kentucky. So we know about slave auctions."

The tall man responded. "I was born in Kentucky and I lived there until I was about seven years old. My family moved to Indiana . . . then, later on, to Illinois. Allow me to introduce myself to you kind people. My name is Abe Lincoln . . . and my friend here is Allen Gentry."

"It's a pleasure to meet both of you," Calvin said as he stuck out his hand to shake Abe's. "You know, I think a lot about the possibilities of finding a solution to this slavery problem. But I truly believe, after all these years, it's permanently entrenched in our culture. There's no way to shed ourselves of it. My cousins are involved in the American Colonization Society. They're the Breckinridge brothers and they're both Presbyterian ministers."

Abe shook his head in disbelief and almost shouted out. "The Breckinridges are part of your family? I've known about the Breckinridge family since I was knee high to a grasshopper. John Breckinridge was an important statesman in the early days of the Republic. He was Thomas Jefferson's Attorney General. I admire him greatly."

Abe then remembered something that just popped into his head and he wanted to explore it. "Say, Mr. Cabell, I recall the Breckinridge homestead was called Cabell's Dale. It's about as famous as Henry Clay's Ashland. Are you folks the Cabells in Cabell's Dale?

Calvin chuckled and replied. "Yes, I suppose I have to plead guilty. My father and John Breckinridge's wife were first cousins."

"Imagine meeting you folks here along the Mississippi. They say it's a small world. I guess there's something to it."

Abe realized they were now at the river's edge, so he spoke again. "That's our raft over there. You folks have been a God-send. We really appreciate hitching a ride – especially with such high-type folks from Kentucky."

Catherine spoke sincerely to the impressive young men. "It was our pleasure. I appreciated hearing your stories, Abe. You both seem like fine gentlemen and I know you'll make a mark on the world."

Abe and his friend jumped off the back of the wagon and reached forward to collect their supplies. When they unloaded the last one, Allen Gentry, Abe's companion, called out, "God be with you, Cabells."

And Abe echoed him saying, "I won't forget meeting you two Kentuckians today. Thank you."

Catherine smiled at Abe. "And I shall not forget you either, Abe. It was a memorable experience and I'm glad we offered you a ride. God speed, young men."

The two raft men then headed toward their flatboat in the wharf while Calvin snapped the reins sharply and said, "Giddyup, Star". As the wagon moved forward, they could see Isaiah up ahead standing next to a rowboat.

Catherine turned to Calvin. "Nice fellows, those two. Abe's story was very touching, didn't you think?"

\* \* \* \* \* \* \* \* \* \*

Isaiah walked toward Catherine and Calvin as the wagon approached his boat. He offered his assistance. "Kin I hep you down, Miz. Cabell?"

"Yes . . . yes . . . thank you very much, Isaiah. Are we the last to arrive?"

"Yes'm, I just got back from rowin' Mr. Pendleton and his wife out to the raft. And I took out Mr. and Mrs. Winchester and Governor Houston, about half an hour ago. Soon as I get back here . . . I'm gonna take your wagon up top of the bluff. Ain't that the plan, Mr. Cabell?"

"Yes, it is. Thank you very much, Isaiah. Here, Mrs. Cabell, take my hand and I'll help you get into the rowboat," Calvin said as he extended his arm to assist his wife.

"Thank you, dear."

But as soon as Catherine managed to sit on the boat's flat wooden seat she bolted upright.

"What's wrong, Darling," Calvin exclaimed. "You're not afraid of being out on the river in such a small boat, are you? We're only going a short distance."

"No, I'm fine. But I left the deviled eggs in the wagon. Would you fetch them for me Isaiah?"

"Sure 'nough ma'am. Deviled eggs are a comin' right up."

When Catherine, at last, held the tray of eggs on her lap, the boat glided away from the shoreline. She looked over at her husband. "You know, Mr. Cabell, if I had a brain . . . I would have given those Illinois boys some deviled eggs. I bet they would've appreciated it. Lord knows we have plenty to go around."

In less than five minutes Isaiah was sidling the skiff up against the abandoned raft. Marcus stood on its edge looming over them. He stretched straight his right arm and lent his helping hand to Catherine.

"Allow me to assist you, Mrs. Cabell. My word, what a lovely parasol you're sporting today. It looks like it was bought from a fine milliner's shop window in Paris."

"Thank you, Marcus Winchester, but I'd prefer you tend to handling these deviled eggs than to foolishly gush over me. And mind you, Marcus, don't be responsible for any scratch marks on the whites."

Isaiah had already climbed aboard the raft and was offering Calvin a hand as Marcus carried the eggs over to a bench being used to display the food. Isaiah stabilized the row boat so Catherine wouldn't wobble as she stepped on to the raft.

Marcus approached them again . . . this time with Sam Houston in tow. "Catherine . . . and Calvin Cabell, allow me to introduce you to Governor Sam Houston. Calvin, you already met the Governor when he passed through Memphis in '29."

"I'm pleased to meet you, Mrs. Cabell." Houston then turned toward her husband. "Hello, Mr. Cabell. How are you?"

"I'm well," Calvin responded. "The question is, 'How are you'? I've been reading about your last trip to Washington. You caused quite a stir up there, Governor. I'm glad you finally escaped the tentacles of Congress. From what I understand, you came close to being put in prison for quite a long while."

"I'll never go back to Washington again, sir. And I should tell you . . . quite honestly . . . this might be my last visit on American soil east of the Mississippi. I'm disgusted with Congress – with the whole country. Last week I spent several days at the Hermitage trying to make amends with President Jackson. He was livid that I attended his White House reception dressed as a Cherokee chief. I tried to make my peace with him and I think he honestly believes I haven't willfully tried to embarrass him. I've acknowledged and thanked him for making possible the major achievements in my life. None of it would've ever happened without his patronage.

"But when I depart Memphis tomorrow morning, I'll travel to Ft. Smith and I'll be reunited with my family. I know my Cherokee relations won't berate and insult me like those white men in Congress I've left behind."

Marcus sensed he should redirect the conversation away from politics . . . toward a topic that wouldn't upset Houston. "Governor Houston, would you kindly tell us about your years living with the Cherokee when you were a youth? I've been waiting patiently to put the pieces of your very interesting life together. Your time spent with the Cherokee is a good place to start."

His ploy worked. Sam Houston immediately seemed less agitated.

"Those were the happiest days of my life, Marcus. And what a wonderful contrast of cultures I observed and experienced. I ran away from home at fifteen to live with the Cherokee. Our white culture craves to control so much of life's many uncertainties. But the Cherokee live from hour to hour and from day to day . . . relishing in the blessings of each moment. And, I assure you their souls overflow with a joyous love of life.

"There's great personal caring for each member of the village. I was most graciously accepted by them . . . and, especially, by Chief Oo-loo-te-ka. He sensed a need I had . . . to conquer my own personal demons. You see, the Chief's name means 'He who puts drums away'. That's rather prophetic, because he was instrumental in me putting away the war drums that were pounding loudly deep in my soul."

Marcus' eyes illustrated he was stunned at Houston's candor about his demons and his need to quell their 'war drums'. "I think I know exactly what you're saying, Governor. I think we've all have felt, at one time or another, that angry drum-like pounding in our hearts."

Governor Houston was now speaking very sentimentally and with great nostalgia. He lifted his bowed head and continued to muse.

"Can you imagine, gentlemen, the peace I enjoyed sitting under a magnificent forest tree situated by a cool, babbling stream . . . and reading Homer? It was under those circumstances I came to love Ulysses. I identified with him and the many obstacles he faced trying to return home from the Trojan War. I realized that I, too, had barriers separating me from discovering my own purpose in life. I always believed God put me on earth

243

for a reason. But I just couldn't figure out what it was. I needed to iron out those issues before I could carry on. Ulysses and his adventures in *The Odyssey* guided me along my journey to manhood."

Calvin appeared fully attuned to what Houston was saying. He was facing his own hurdles in life as he tried to put his own dark past behind him and move on . . . toward the kind of life he once was certain he was predestined to live.

"I think I also understand what you're saying, Governor. All of us are making a journey to eventually reach some unknown and elusive place - a place where we can discover what our life's purpose is and whether we'll ever be able to fulfill it."

"That's the way I see it, too, Calvin. And that's why I decided to bail out of Washington's political system. It's corrupt . . . and the only people it's serving are rich folks with an insatiable hunger to get even richer.

"Hang around Washington and you'll understand that the guiding principles of the Revolution have been forgotten. Everybody's either on the take or trying to pack the courts with judges who'll neuter each and every new idea for reform . . . just to preserve the *status quo*.

"Two years ago I went to Washington as the duly authorized Ambassador of the Cherokee. These people have God-given rights to their land. And the white folks who've traveled west, likewise, believe it's their God-given right to steal it from them. I pissed off my old colleagues when I solemnly conducted my diplomatic business dressed in full Cherokee garb. But, what's an ambassador to do except to illustrate the culture of his people? The white men in Congress saw me as the worst sort of turncoat."

Pendleton, Winchester, and Cabell shook their heads in perplexed agreement. They knew Old Hickory greeted him at his White House reception for ambassadors with the same courtesy he greeted every other foreign official. However, the President wasn't at all pleased with Houston flaunting the Indian culture . . . especially a man whom most folks considered to be Jackson's "adopted son".

"I've grown sick of it all. That's why during this recent visit to Washington I traveled up to New York. There are money barons there. And they're interested in investing pot loads of money in the West – in Texas. And Texas is where I'll soon be bound."

Houston was now looking pensively across the river. His mind was mired in deep thoughts. Then he turned about and opened a door to his personal life. It was a personal matter none of the men would have dared to mention.

"That Congressman I beat with a hickory stick . . . well, he intended to impugn me in a far more hurtful way than telling lies about my service to the United States as an Indian agent. He taunted me with his malicious gossip . . . about my short-lived marriage to Miss Allen. I wonder now about all the vicious rumors that have been broadcast about why my marriage suddenly ended. I realize now I should have candidly responded to the understandable curiosity of all the Tennesseans who had elected me their Governor. They deserved to know why I abruptly resigned after serving just three weeks as Governor."

He looked like a man who was weary of dancing to someone else's tune. Sam Houston grew silent once again. Then he turned to gather his thoughts as he watched three flatboats poling their way into the Memphis wharf. They were fighting the tricky currents where the Wolf and the Mississippi meet. Sam remembered how his own life had been one in which he was often forced to fight against the currents of the public's expectations. He had generally taken a "To hell with them" attitude.

"To hell with them, gentlemen. That's what I say. That two week marriage broke my heart. I was deeply hurt when my wife left me and returned home to her father. But it's all nobody's business. That's the way I still see it."

"We're all in agreement with you, Governor." Marcus Winchester sounded genuinely in concert with what Sam Houston had just said. "None of us here would ever choose to broach the tender subject of your failed marriage."

Houston spoke now in much lower tones - the kind of whispers that make a man lean toward the source of the sound and summon up all his listening capacity.

"I want to tell you something relating to my brief marriage. You see, I was duly warned not to take Eliza Allen as my bride. And I failed to take heed. You all know, I'm sure, that Chief Oo-loo-te-ka welcomed me into the Cherokee tribe as if I were his white son. He gave me the Indian name, Colloneh. It means 'Raven'. A raven is a revered animal to the Cherokee. Its spirituality is much admired. So, bearing this noble name was intended to be a great honor. I can tell you I was very proud to be known as 'Raven'."

245

Mercifully, Houston began to talk a bit louder. But his voice had a bitter edge to it. "You see, I was 'Raven' when I lived among the Indians. Yet, I must have forgotten years later that, in my soul, I was still an Indian . . . obligated to serve as a worthy human incarnation of the bird's glorious spirit. But somewhere along the way . . . while I served in Congress and as your Governor . . . somehow, I must've cast aside my Cherokee soul."

Then he continued. "On the road to Eliza's home in Goodlettsville on my wedding day, I spotted a beautiful raven ahead of my buggy – about a hundred yards away. It was a cold January morning. I foolishly dismissed any significance to the raven's presence. The air was clear and crisp. I felt a sense of confidence that winter day. I felt certain marrying Miss Allen would be the crowning achievement in my life.

"And yet, as I look back, I realize I was wrong. I was foolish. After all, I was a former member of Congress and the Governor of Tennessee. I had only been sworn in as Governor several days before my wedding. I had decided the citizens of Tennessee needed and deserved a Governor who was a married man.

"Anyway . . . back to the raven in the road . . . as my buggy drew closer to it, the bird took flight in a most distressful way. It hovered ahead of me . . . frantically flapping its wings . . . as if to prevent me from passing. Then, it ascended . . . fast as lightning . . . and it looped in wildly irregular circles. It climbed high in the air . . . and then it suddenly fell . . . rapidly . . . toward the ground.

"As if the raven were frantically trying to tell me something, it rose . . . yet again . . . and it hovered in one place above the road. All the while it was furiously flapping its wings. Then it flew high in the air and fell, once again, to the ground. It nosedived fast and crashed on the path before me. And, when I finally reached this beautiful black bird, I was shocked. It was dead.

"So, there stood a proud Cherokee named 'Raven' looking down at the carcass of the same majestic animal for which he was named. I was mightily distressed at the sight. But I was determined to do what I had come to do that day. I rode on to the Allen home . . . and I got married. After all, I had betrothed myself to her. I was obligated to go through with the ceremony. Tennesseans expected me to take a wife . . . and to keep my word."

Pendleton looked confused and spoke out. "I don't understand the significance of the bird's behavior."

Houston gave him his answer. "Any Cherokee would have comprehended the obvious omen the raven was predicting. Surely, it was telling me my proposed marriage was doomed. But I refused to respond to the bird's obvious pleas."

All three of the married couples were stunned at Governor Houston's unprecedented candor. And each was shocked to hear the bizarre tale about this odious prophecy and the promises honorable men sometimes stupidly feel compelled to keep.

Then Sam Houston turned to make eye contact with each of the men. His glare communicated there was a lesson here for everyone. It took Sam Houston many years to mull over the significance of the raven. Tonight he was willing to share this allegory . . . even though all of it was painfully etched in his memory.

"How clear was the message imparted to me by that dying raven. Its death would have been understood and heeded by any of my Cherokee brothers. No one in the Cherokee nation would have lost face from heeding what it was communicating – its very, very desperate plea that said, 'Do NOT marry that woman'.

"You see, gentlemen, I now know in my heart and soul I'm Cherokee – an Indian named 'Raven'. But that day I only viewed myself as the white Governor of Tennessee. I had forgotten the valuable lessons I learned during my four years of bliss with my tribe.

"I had discarded all the important life lessons I learned from Chief Oo-loo-te-ka and his people. That's why I moved to Arkansas and married my Indian wife, Diana. That's why I made my diplomatic calls in Washington dressed in elegant Indian garb. And that's why I'm returning tomorrow to my true race, the Cherokee, far up the Arkansas River."

Parker Pendleton jolted his head as if he just experienced a revelation. "I keep forgetting many Cherokee long ago moved from the Appalachians to Arkansas . . . and it was you who promoted the move."

Houston turned to Pendleton and replied. "Yes, back in 1819 I was instrumental getting many of the Cherokee to voluntarily move west. I wanted them to settle on land that would forever be out of the realm of white men's greed. Regrettably, I was imprudent to think Indians could ever escape the greedy encroachment of the white man.

"I'm telling you, men, if things don't change in Washington, there'll be a dying raven in the path of each Congressman, each Justice of the Supreme Court, and each Senator. The omens are clear. Yet, not a one will recognize the bird's sober warnings."

Suddenly, Sam Houston looked as if he wanted to either clear up something or make an additional point. "I must amend what I just said, folks. There's, thankfully, one Representative who doesn't fit that foolish mold. And he, quite happily, is from Tennessee. Congressman Crockett also appears fed up with his serendipitous career as a Congressman. He seems disgusted, as I have been, with the avarice that corrupts decent men each time a new section of the frontier is settled.

"Crockett and I have talked about the glory we both see in the West. He's also intrigued with the vast expanse of Texas and the bold future it offers."

Sam Houston had thus far consumed nothing except a glass of tea Mary Winchester offered him. But, as he began to speak of the Eliza Allen matter, he folded back his coat and pulled a pint of whisky from its left inside pocket. He took one long swig from time to time while he told his story. Soon, he turned and gazed out toward Arkansas . . . where he was soon headed.

He never placed the bottle back in his pocket. He just gripped it ever tightly as he proceeded to recall the missed lesson the raven valiantly tried to teach him. Finally, when he spoke about himself . . . and Crockett . . . and the fact that both were becoming fascinated with the notion of heading west, he put the thin rim of the bottle to his lips again.

"Excuse my rudeness, gentlemen. I've been sucking on this hundred proof teat at the expense of minding my manners. Anyone care for a taste of my snake bite medicine?"

With that impromptu apology, Sam Houston held out the bottle . . . first to Calvin . . . and then to Marcus. Both of them held up the palms of their hands in a "stop" signal . . . so as to politely decline.

Houston extended his bottle toting arm toward Pendleton and he accepted the invitation. Mabel fussed at him on the way home that night, but Parker explained his reasoning. "I had to sip some of the Governor's whisky, Mabel. It just wouldn't be friendly if a great man like Sam Houston was turned down flat . . . by everyone."

Mabel Pendleton wasn't satisfied with his reasoning. "Well, Mr. Pendleton, reciprocating the Governor's hospitality is one thing. But you didn't have to take three long swallows, did you? Wasn't that just a little TOO much?"

"Gentlemen, our picnic supper awaits you," Mary said softly like the refined hostess she was. "Isaiah ferried out several bales of straw earlier in the day. You may each claim one to sit on, to lean against, or you may choose to ignore them completely."

Then she looked directly at Sam Houston and she smiled. "Governor Houston, you're the guest of honor tonight. Please do come and mark your place . . . wherever you choose."

Houston responded by bending the elbow of his left arm as an invitation for Mary to place her hand in the angle it formed. He wanted to escort her to the dinner table in a proper, formal fashion – even though they were aboard a rickety flatboat so insecure Marcus had bought it for scrap wood.

The "dining table" consisted of three brightly colored quilts laid out on the deck. Each woman had brought her favorite. Pulled pork barbeque was mounded high on a pewter platter and about a quart of Parker Pendleton's "secret" barbeque sauce sat on the tray in a glass bowl. Even though it was October, Mary managed to find some of the season's last green beans. She blanched them and tossed the beans in some of her homemade vinaigrette dressing.

During dinner everyone participated in numerous topics of conversation. They talked about the renowned history of the Cabell and Breckinridge families as well as Sam Houston's trip to New York to find rich land speculators whose money he could invest in Texas real estate. The slavery issue was also debated and Catherine recounted the stories she and Calvin had just heard from young Abe Lincoln. The Governor said Congress wouldn't do a thing about slavery so long as it can keep bringing states into the Union equally split between "free states" and "slave states".

"This nation's afraid to take any actions that subvert the *status quo.* There's a price that'll have to be paid . . . eventually. I fear it will break all our backs."

Catherine broached a new subject. "Governor, tell us about your Diana. I understand you live in a wigwam over in Arkansas. Is that some sort of a thatched Indian hut . . . or is it more like a teepee?"

Houston chuckled as he sought a cloth napkin to soak up a rogue stripe of barbeque sauce trickling down his chin. He wiped the sauce away, chewed the remaining meat before swallowing, and then he replied. "No, Mrs. Cabell, we call our place Wigwam Oswego. And it's not a hut or a teepee. It's actually a pretty conventional Arkansas farm house – probably much bigger than most."

Catherine was confused. "I'm genuinely disappointed, Governor. I was envisioning a structure much more exotic than a farmhouse."

"Sorry to disappoint you, ladies, but 'wigwam' is merely the Indian word for 'home'."

"Well, then, what about Diana? Do you call her your squaw?" Mabel Pendleton asked.

"Yes, Diana is my squaw. And she's a very pretty and patient one, as well. I might add. "Squaw" is another example of language the Cherokee transported west with them. In some cultures, Diana might even be considered a princess. She's a grand niece of Chief Oo-loo-te-ka. She helps me run the Indian supply station for the tribe. But mainly, her job is to look after me and keep me on the straight and narrow path. Believe me when I say that's quite a job for any woman."

Then Houston was asked to report about his visit the week before with Jackson at the Hermitage. All the men began to recount some of Jackson's political appointments – especially those who hailed from Tennessee.

"You know as well as I do, Marcus, you could have asked for . . . and been offered . . . any position of authority in the federal government. Old Hickory would have gladly granted it to you. He thinks the world of you. You know that. Yet, you're still living here on the edge of the frontier . . . apparently content with Jackson simply appointing you the United States Postmaster of Memphis."

Marcus seemed embarrassed and Houston didn't know if his chagrin came from him praising Marcus for the clout he had with Jackson or whether he was embarrassed to have his life defined as a rather lowly postal official.

"Well, Governor, I think you overestimate President Jackson's regard for me. He did speak to me just after the election and asked if I had any interest in following him to Washington. I gave the matter a bit of thought. But Mary

250

and I are quite satisfied to live here . . . with our good friends and our growing family."

Then Marcus turned to Mary and, as if to put the matter to rest, he asked her, "Isn't what I said just about the size of it, Mrs. Winchester?"

Mary Winchester beamed a loving smile at her husband and nodded, "Yes".

This notion of Marcus having the choice of any federal appointment he wanted was a subject the Cabells, as well as the Pendletons, had discussed among themselves. They knew what Sam Houston had said about President Jackson's fondness for Marcus was undoubtedly true. He could be serving . . . right at that moment . . . as a high official in Washington and coming in constant contact with people most folks could only dream about meeting. Yet, Marcus never acknowledged these opportunities everyone knew he had been afforded . . . and . . . had declined.

As much as the Pendletons and the Cabells loved and respected Mary, they often debated whether Marcus had passed up opportunities to move to Washington because Mary was a "woman of color".

Washington was the home to more slave trading businesses than any other city in the nation. Also, there was the matter of Senator Thomas Hart Benton, Mary's former lover. Presently, he was one of the most visible and prominent statesmen in Congress. Calvin and Catherine wondered if the potential embarrassment arising from idle talk about Mary and Senator Benton might have ultimately broken her heart. Certainly, no one in the world would ever want to break Mary Winchester's generous heart.

The sun was setting over the southwest horizon. Above the tree line were thin strips of undulating purples and pinks and various shades of orange. Marcus noticed Sam Houston appeared entranced by the beautiful sunset which presently rested on the same horizon toward which he would make his way come morning.

Marcus spoke as if to offer a toast to his distinguished guest. "Governor, I'm predicting this is the last sunset over the Mississippi you'll ever see. It's not a happy thought. But it's what I foresee . . . based on everything you've spoken about this evening. We wish you much success out West. We're going to be soon missing you . . . sorely.

"But, by all means know this, Governor. You've served this nation and the State of Tennessee with devotion and dignity. It is we who should hang our

251

heads in shame. And maybe – just maybe – you're going to be able to leave behind whatever personal demons you've been toting for far too long. I think all of us tonight feel the same way. We wish you peace . . . and we thank you for joining us on the eve of your departure."

"Thanks, Marcus, but right about now I feel like I'm going into exile. Yet, whatever we may choose to call it, I know it's the right thing to do."

Sam Houston glanced one last time at the thin orange filaments of light about to disappear until morning . . . and then he rose from his bale of straw. "You're all fine people . . . and I've greatly enjoyed your friendship and your hospitality. But it's almost dark . . . and I need to get my rest."

Isaiah's row boat was tied to the raft. Sam Houston began to walk toward him. "Isaiah, would you kindly take me back to town?" the Indian named Raven asked.

"Yes, sir, Governor, climb on into dis boat. It's an honor to be of service to YOU, sir."

"Isaiah, the honor is mine to have you as my able captain."

Sam Houston had an idea and he whipped around his head to face Marcus. "Mr. Winchester, would you allow me to hire Isaiah to ferry me across the river tomorrow morning? Lord knows I can't walk across water like some people in Washington think they can."

"Governor Houston," Marcus replied, "I know Isaiah would be quite pleased to take you to the other side. But there's no need to pay him."

Houston began to place one leg and then the other into the small craft. He patted Isaiah jovially on the shoulder as he sat down on the wooden boat bench. "Isaiah, you might be an enslaved servant, but that's all the more reason I want you to be my ferryman. And I know your master wouldn't begrudge my wish to pay you for it."

Houston looked directly into Isaiah's white eyes which were almost aglow in contrast to the sudden darkness on the shore. And with all the earnestness any of the white folks on the disabled raft had ever heard, Sam Houston spoke to the humble Negro.

"You see, Isaiah, black folks aren't the only poor souls in this country who are enslaved. Some of them even serve in the U.S. Congress. I was one of

252

them, too. So, I know all about being owned by others . . . and about being bought and sold.

"But tomorrow, with your help, I'm going to become a free man. And I know that one day Mr. Winchester here will make you a free man, as well. When that day happens, I invite you to join me in Texas."

Isaiah handed Sam Houston the lighted torch to hold so the black slave could use both hands to row. As the boat lurched away with each broad stroke of the oars, Sam Houston waved to his hosts . . . and they waved back at him.

Calvin turned to his friends who were standing and watching the torch's glow get fainter and fainter. "I don't know what's ahead for Sam Houston. But I do know one thing, for sure. This time tomorrow, all of us east of the Mississippi will be missing that man."

*No Coin for Charon*

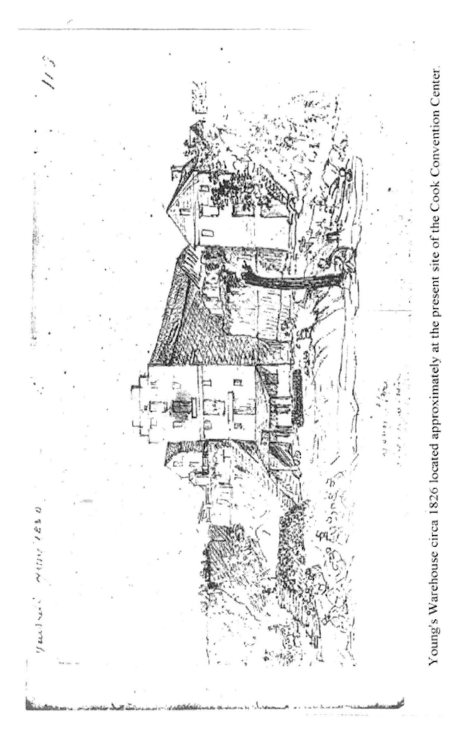

Young's Warehouse circa 1826 located approximately at the present site of the Cook Convention Center.

255

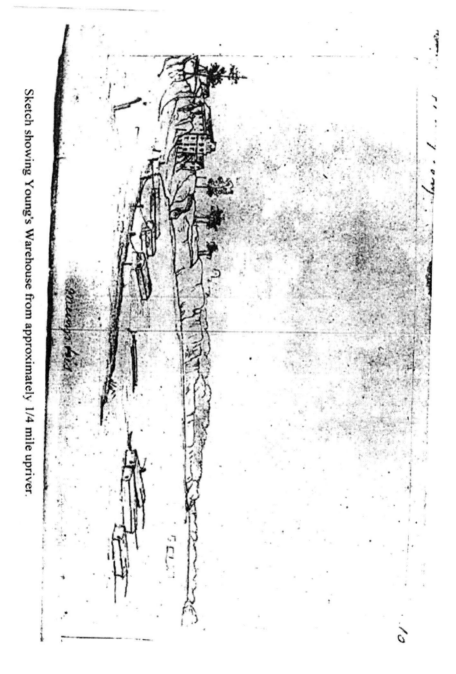

Sketch showing Young's Warehouse from approximately 1/4 mile upriver.

Circa 1825 sketch made from approximately the present intersection of Union Avenue and Riverside Drive showing the village of Memphis in the background.

Sketch of Frances Wright's utopia, Nashoba, circa 1826, located approximately at present day Riverdale Road along the Wolf River.

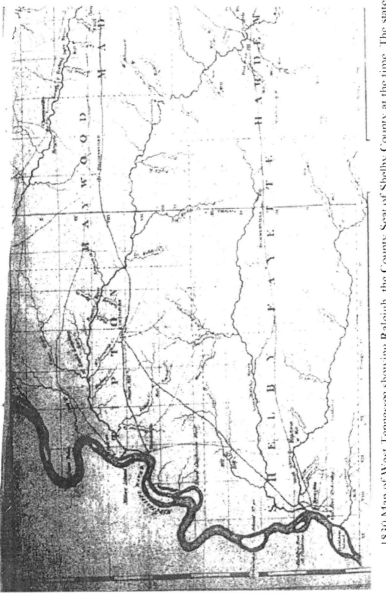

1830 Map of West Tennessee showing Raleigh, the County Seat of Shelby County, at the time. The state line with Mississippi's present day Winchester Road. A subsequent survey showed the state line was, in fact, farther south. at today's State Line road

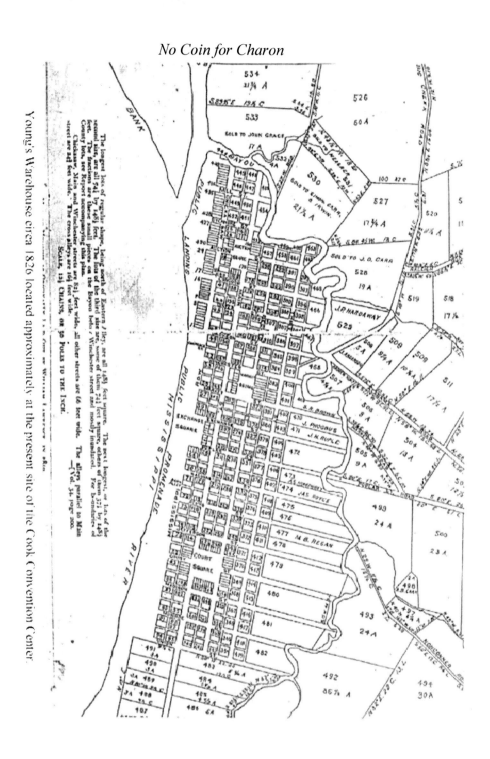

Young's Warehouse circa 1826 located approximately at the present site of the Cook Convention Center.

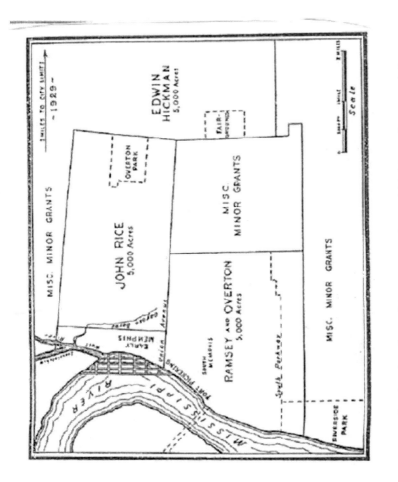

Map showing the Rice and Ramsey parcels on which Memphis was settled

261

Sketch circa 1826 showing a flatboat approaching the Memphis harbor.

# CHAPTER

# 16

November 1834

"Some Sundays . . . I'd just as soon keep the Sabbath in bed – maybe even under the bed. And THIS Sunday . . . is one of those Sabbaths."

Calvin had begun griping to Catherine two days ago. To her great frustration, he ranted on relentlessly ever since supper on Friday. Nothing could please him. The grumbling subsided somewhat on Saturday. But now the Cabell family was dressing for Sunday's service and the head of the household was howling louder than ever. Catherine knew he was angry at himself, because of the invitation he extended on Friday. Now, she would probably have to endure his foul humor . . . at least, until after the Vespers service.

The source of Calvin's foul humor was the same person who had been grating at his innards for the past two weeks – Isaac Shelby Lancaster. Catherine and Calvin agreed they had made their point crystal clear to Shelby. They wouldn't be willing to introduce Shelby as a "friend" to folks in Memphis and Shelby County. Furthermore, he shouldn't expect to be a guest in their home on any regular basis. In fact, he should expect his visits to be few and far between.

But there was still the lingering church problem. And it was a problem for which Calvin couldn't come up with a solution – even though he had spent hours trying to devise an acceptable strategy.

Shelby was a Presbyterian back in Kentucky. The thought of encouraging him to worship elsewhere seemed just as un-Christian a choice as Calvin's second plan. That option was to shamelessly shun him when and if he ever passed through the church's front door . . . as if Shelby were the devil, himself. Catherine and Calvin had discussed the dilemma several times.

263

"Neither one of these tactics seems very Christian to me," Catherine told her husband.

"I'll bet if I scavenged through the New Testament long and hard enough I could find a verse or two that would encourage . . . and even condone . . . decent Christians to use any means they could to prevent pond scum like Shelby from slithering into a church sanctuary."

"No, dear, I don't think you can find a parable or even a verse that advocates anything of the sort. And if you spend even a minute of time researching this cockamamie Biblical premise of yours, then you're a fool."

"Well, I'll bet there's plenty of ammunition in the Old Testament. Those prophets and Biblical kings didn't fool around. They stoned to death urchins like Shelby."

"Mr. Cabell, I do believe you've forgotten everything you ever learned in church. Don't you remember anything you were taught? There were NO Christians in the Old Testament."

"Well, in the New Testament . . . even the twelve disciples didn't know that Isaac Shelby Lancaster would one day walk the earth. If they had, there would be a parable in the Bible whose lesson was, 'Don't let no-good lawyers step inside God's house of worship'."

But Calvin had agreed to assist Shelby in one restricted way. And this Sunday morning he was regretting that, too. He made a promise he would introduce Shelby to the two lawyers who had set up practices in town. But everyone knew they, too, were having a tough time scratching out a living. Anyone with a civil dispute tended to prefer a hearing before Old Ike Rawlings.

Ike was the generally recognized arbiter of disputes long before any semblance of a Tennessee justice system appeared on the bluff. His brand of justice always made infinite good sense. And now that Ike had succeeded Marcus as the town's Mayor, there was added legitimacy to his rulings. With satisfied litigants on both sides of an issue, most Memphians concluded it was foolish to throw away hard earned money paying a lawyer when Ike's services were rendered for free.

The previous Monday Calvin spotted Judge Robinson in town. He had traveled to Memphis for the day to cultivate his political base. Memphis was growing and the Judge could no longer be content to rule imperiously on important decisions solely from the Shelby County Seat, Raleigh.

The judge warmly greeted Calvin and offered an exaggerated hand shake as well as three sound rib-rattling pats on his back. Calvin told Robinson about Shelby Lancaster. However, he highlighted he wasn't asking a favor from the judge to arrange an interview with Shelby. He simply communicated Shelby had arrived in town and he wished to set up a law practice.

Calvin told Robinson he had advised Shelby about the judge's pivotal role in the legal community as well as in all other matters in Shelby County. "Any man seeking to become a member of the bar in Shelby County was duty bound to meet first with Judge Robinson," he quoted himself.

Robinson seemed pleased to hear such an assessment from Calvin. It was important for people of Calvin's stature in the community to recognize the Judge was the "go-to man" in Shelby County for the many indulgences he could dole out.

Even though he framed his comments in a respectful manner, Calvin was thinking all along that a good translation of what he was saying to the Judge could be more aptly put. "I told this scourge from Kentucky he would have to pay a call on you and kiss your ass. And there's no one who's a more prolific ass kisser than Isaac Shelby Lancaster."

"You mean this young fellow's real name is Isaac Shelby Lancaster – the esteemed Governor's nephew?"

"Yes, Your Honor, that's his name. I'd swear to it on a courtroom Bible.

Judge Robinson pondered this remarkable name as he massaged his chin thoughtfully. Then, with a grin expressing the Judge had contrived a plan, Robinson spoke. "Well, have him come out to Raleigh any day this week. I'd like to meet him. I think a name like his could be very useful to him . . . and, possibly, to me. We'll have to see."

"Well, Judge, you're mighty kind. I'll tell him what you had to say. But know that after this conversation, I won't be making any more pitches to you about this newcomer."

"I think I understand, Calvin. I think I understand precisely what you're saying."

Shelby was overjoyed to learn what Judge Robinson told Calvin. The next morning he rented a horse from Tom Bishop's livery stable and set out on the five mile ride to Raleigh. Then, upon his return on Wednesday, Shelby came directly to the mill. He was overjoyed.

"I couldn't wait to share the news with you, Calvin. Judge Robinson arranged for me to clerk for his old law partner, Roscoe Page. He predicted I'd become a member of the Tennessee Bar within six months.

"The Judge said Memphis was growing faster than the County Seat and one day the city's population might even exceed Raleigh's. He says Attorney Page would be crazy if he didn't set up a branch office here in town."

Calvin didn't crack a smile or offer his congratulations. He was too preoccupied thinking about what he had just heard and what it really meant. Roscoe Page wasn't just Judge Robinson's "old law partner". Page essentially acted as Robinson's agent for all sorts of legal and political shenanigans. Calvin was certain Robinson continued to get a cut from the law practice's proceeds.

Calvin considered Shelby's news and silently thought to himself, "If ever there was a perfect professional match of two scoundrels, this is it."

Then Calvin remembered something else that had eluded him. He was prepared to save Mose and Bettie from the slave auction block. But he had forgotten this was an important legal matter. It required bona fide paperwork and documentation.

"Shelby, I'm pleased to say I've never needed an attorney before. But there's a situation I'm involved with presently that requires a lawyer's skill. I'm not proposing that we're establishing a long term business relationship today, but I wonder if you'd draft some papers I need?"

Shelby's horse teeth protruded out especially far as he expanded his mouth into a broad grin. "Calvin, it would be a pleasure to be of service to you. By golly, you're my first Tennessee client. I'll never forget that hallmark."

Calvin cringed at what he had just proposed. He was surely opening a Pandora's Box filled with unimaginable horrors. But he had said it. There was no turning back.

"What sort of document do you need, Calvin?"

"It's a Bill of Sale for two of Mercer Watkins' slaves."

Suddenly Shelby's ecstatic smile of excitement turned into a look of bewilderment and disappointment. "I must've misunderstood you, Calvin. I thought you said you were buying two slaves. Surely that's not what I heard, is it?"

"No, I didn't . . . Yes, I did . . . Well, it's an unusual thing and I want you to keep all of this very confidential."

"You have my word of honor. Now what in the world is going on here, Calvin?"

"Well I'll be a monkey's uncle," Calvin thought. "The little double-dealing donkey has given me his 'word of honor'. I'm doomed now, for sure."

Calvin explained to Shelby what had happened. He wasn't specific about the details of Mercer Watkins' financial problems which had precipitated all of this. He thought Mercer's circumstances should remain confidential. He proclaimed with as much earnestness as he had ever summoned in himself that it was his intention to set Mose and Bettie free. Yet, he told Shelby he didn't know at present when or how that would be accomplished. But he set out the necessary details to be incorporated in the transfer papers. And he said he needed the paperwork in just a few days.

Right then, the notion of personal redemption crossed his mind. He wondered if he and Catherine had been too hard - too callous - with Shelby. Maybe they were dwelling on inaccurate or obsolete memories that were etched long ago in their minds. After all, the Cabells go to church. And they hear the preacher say that everybody can change for the better – even murderers, like himself. If God was willing to forgive him for killing Dolly, surely Calvin should give Shelby a fresh chance.

As he contemplated the notion of redemption – forgiveness granted by God – Calvin revisited the principle of salvation for his own soul. Maybe God would fix matters so Shelby would face Judgment Day with a clean slate. But the Lord would, no doubt, have to hold His nose when He evaluated the soul of Calvin Cabell.

Finally, Shelby's exposure to religion might even dissuade him from pointing his accusatory finger at Calvin. Yes, taking Shelby to church might be worth the agony.

Calvin reflected on all this . . . and in a moment of what he would later call "insane righteousness", he spoke to Shelby. "Do you still consider yourself a practicing Presbyterian, Shelby?"

The little lawyer was noticeably taken aback. Then his lips folded into an impish grin. "Yes, Calvin, I'm practicing to be a Presbyterian. But, I must admit, recently I haven't been practicing very hard."

"Was this the kind of humor I set myself up for – to be Shelby's straight man?" Calvin reconsidered the possibility. In a few seconds he had his answer. "Well, I've got to admit it. That was a pretty clever response."

"I'm sure I speak for Catherine, as well. I want to extend an invitation for you to join us at this Sunday's eleven o'clock service. And please come home with us for dinner afterwards."

Shelby acted like this invitation was an achievement that even surpassed Robinson setting him up with Roscoe Page. He was thrilled.

"Thank you, Calvin. I'd be delighted to spend Sunday with the family."

There was something about Shelby's retort that irked Calvin. "Who does this guy think he is - saying he wants to spend Sunday with 'THE family'. It's MY family, damn him. Lord Almighty, I invite the little buzzard to Sunday dinner and he already thinks we've adopted him. I'm still concerned about his veiled threat . . . about citing the statutes of limitation for murderers. I'm certain he wouldn't hesitate to ruin me and 'THE' family. "

Calvin glanced at Shelby with one brow cocked a tad higher than the other. "Well, Shelby, we're far from being your family, but I thought you might welcome an opportunity to 'practice' your faith Sunday morning. Meet us in front of the church . . . just before eleven."

* * * * * * * * * * *

And now it was that dreaded Sunday morning. And this was the day Calvin would have to pay the piper for his errant evangelism earlier in the week. He looked at the clock on the mantle of his bedroom and imagined it said the time was seven in the evening. But it wasn't. It was seven o'clock in the morning . . . and soon he would have to lead his family to its just punishment – sharing the Cabell pew with Shelby Lancaster.

By premeditated design, Calvin's objective was to delay arriving at church until no more than five minutes before eleven o'clock. Such razor thin timing would eliminate the need for him to chat with fellow parishioners with Shelby attached to him - like some close "member of the family". Then the worship service would lend temporary relief until it concluded . . . usually just after noon. Lastly, after the benediction he would have to vanish before anyone suspected he had an association with Shelby.

But he couldn't devise a plan how to visit with his friends after church and avoid the intimations of association. His failure to devise something satisfactory piqued Calvin's frustration.

"Shelby Lancaster might have to sit with us during the service, but I'd rather spend the hour burning in hell than be seen afterward with a ne'er- do-well whom everyone, surely, will assume is my close friend. Or worse, they'll assume he's part of 'the family'."

At ten fifty-three the Cabell family approached the front door of the Presbyterian Church. Shelby was standing at the base of the steps to the sanctuary. He wasn't standing idle. He was chatting up John and Rowena Cummins. All Calvin could hear was Shelby telling them he was a good friend of Catherine and Calvin back in Kentucky. Calvin winced as he hurriedly greeted John and Rowena. He quickly stretched his arm around Shelby's shoulder and – after just a few spoken words, he essentially force marched Shelby down the aisle and corralled him into the Cabell pew.

As they progressed, Calvin could see Mercer Watkins and his wife were already seated. He quietly bid a good morning to Mercer. It seemed apparent Mercer was nervous about their deal. Time was running short and he badly hoped to complete the transaction before the following Friday. His apparent angst made Calvin particularly fidgety.

He was relieved when he could stand up once again to sing the first hymn, "Faith of Our Fathers". Before the end of the first verse, Calvin was struck with an incredible case of curiosity. "Surely," he thought, "Mose and Bettie must be singing along with him from their usual seats in the balcony. How can I spot them without craning my neck around . . . so they don't notice I'm trying to gawk at them?"

Then he came up with a sensible plan. At the end of the hymn it would be time to pass the peace. Ben Walker's pew was directly behind Calvin's. As he greeted the Walkers he could easily glance up and get a good glimpse of the slaves in the balcony. And since they, too, would be busy passing the peace among the darkies, there was a good chance Mose and Bettie wouldn't know he was trying to observe them.

So, when Reverend Blair held up both hands as if he were extending a blessing, he proclaimed, "May the peace of Christ be with you." And the congregation replied in unison, "And also with you." There was a sudden stir as worshipers leaned over pew rails and bid others their respective blessings to others. Likewise, Calvin pivoted about and nervously stuck out his hand to shake Ben's.

Yet, while he blurted out," The peace of Christ be with you, Ben," he was simultaneously scanning the black folks up above. He spotted Bettie and Mose and, sure enough, they were busy extending the grace of the Lord to those around them.

But when the congregation finally settled down and Calvin, once again, took his seat, he had another problem. Just as sure as his wife's name was Catherine Barry Cabell, he could actually feel Mose and Bettie staring down at him. Their gazes, it seemed, retaliated with sting-like sensations along the back of his neck and head . . . as if he had stirred up a hornets' nest and the insects were bent on attacking him with a vengeance. Or, so Calvin imagined. Surely, the Negroes were thinking to themselves, "So, this is the white man who will own us in a matter of days."

Calvin remembered Mercer told him how Mose had sized him up as a man of integrity and honor. Likewise, Mercer told both Mose and Bettie they were mighty fortunate that a righteous man like Calvin Cabell would be purchasing them.  But, when the congregation concluded this ritual and everyone sat down again, Calvin still had found no peace. Those nettlesome sensations emanating from the balcony were just as irritating as if Ben Walker were leaning over the Cabell pew and sticking sewing needles clear through the backside of Calvin's coat.

Finally, he couldn't withstand the agony any longer. Ever-so-slowly, he placed his right arm along the top of the pew and rotated his head about . . . so that he looked straight toward where he knew Bettie and Mose were seated.

Bettie was staring unashamedly down at Calvin with a sort of, "Howdy, Mr. Cabell" look on her face. But Mose was preoccupied with an open Bible he had placed on his lap. He looked down at its pages as if he were silently reading the scripture from the New Testament as Reverend Blair was reading the lectionary aloud. But since black slaves here in Tennessee weren't

270

allowed to read or write, Calvin thought maybe Mose was simply bowing his head in prayer.

He smiled at Bettie and she smiled back at him. Then she poked Mose in the ribs with her elbow. She demurely pointed at Calvin until the white man's eyes from below locked on the eyes of the black man up above. Calvin smiled at him. But Mose didn't return it. He just stared pensively down at the white man – this pale, Caucasian supplicant who sought God's mercy for the purchase he was about to make – for the sin he was about to commit.

"Who can blame him?" Calvin thought as he, once again, turned to face the pulpit.

The piercing, sharp needle sensations on Calvin's backside continued to prick at him throughout the service. But, somehow, the pain was tolerable, because he had sought out these two souls and offered them a friendly grin. He thought it was akin to "passing the peace" . . . clear across the sanctuary.

The sermon Reverend Blair gave was predicated on the parable of the Good Samaritan. The title prompted Calvin to wonder. "Am I being a Good Samaritan in this deal? Or would the Good Samaritan spit at me if he knew about this sorry saga? I can't believe I've become a party to this convoluted scheme. I haven't even verified if Mercer's telling the truth. Maybe I'm not really saving these black folks from a family breakup. For all I know Mercer's just interested in raising some quick cash without paying a commission to a slave trader."

But there was another moral quandary in which Calvin had also placed himself. And that vexing conflict was gnawing away at him . . . probably more than anything else. The pickle was this. Under no conditions would a tight, Scotch Irish businessman worth his salt ever agree to pay twelve hundred dollars for two slaves and their young son - only to release them a few weeks later as freedmen. Twelve hundred dollars was a lot of money. Calvin Cabell had to formulate a plan to get his investment back – either in cash or in consideration of services rendered. And, both of these options clearly smacked of slavery – hardly the deeds of a Good Samaritan.

Every time he analyzed his moral and practical predicament, he ended up feeling like an even bigger hypocrite to his increasingly muddled mind.

"Now, may the Lord bless you and keep you. May the Lord shine his countenance upon you . . . and be gracious unto you. And may the Lord keep you safe from harm . . . until we meet again. Amen."

271

The benediction meant just one thing to Calvin this particular Sunday morning. He wished he could run down the aisle with the one hundred fifty pound pariah still sitting in his pew. Shelby stood up and, without any interplay by Cabell or Catherine, he introduced himself to Ben Walker and his wife, Helen.

Calvin noticed Mercer Watkins was meekly waving his hand over his head. He seemed desperate to seek some time alone. Yet, all Calvin could recall hearing was Ben Walker's greeting to Calvin's guest. "Well, Shelby, we heartily welcome you to Memphis and we shall count on you sitting in the pew in front of us each and every Sunday. We know Catherine and Calvin Cabell will be offering you their tender loving care. They'll ensure, no doubt, a smooth and successful transition into your new life in West Tennessee."

Catherine said nothing to Ben. She just stood there silently . . . with a knot growing inside her gut and another knot clogging her craw. "Lord Jesus, spare me from all this," she prayed.

The task of introducing Shelby to the other members of the church fell into Catherine's lap. She decided to fib. She claimed Cassie needed to 'relieve herself', so she could scoot on down the aisle and out the door.

"Please excuse us for not taking the time to make proper introductions, Shelby. We have an emergency to deal with," she apologized.

Meanwhile, Calvin had to respond to the look of pandemonium on Mercer's face. The two men moved toward the narthex. Each hastily offered his respects to Reverend Blair and then they walked out the door toward a secluded spot considerably beyond the mingling church members.

"Calvin, time's running short. I talked with the President of the Hernando Bank on Friday. He says he's going to move rapidly ahead to force a forfeiture of my property. Are you still aboard? Can we close the deal before the end of this week?"

"Yes, but I've got to tell you I've fretted over this situation more than you know. I realize from your perspective I'm playing the role of the Good Samaritan . . . that Reverend Blair was praising in his sermon. But I can tell you I'm not. I won't go into detail. But I tell you again, Mercer. I don't consider myself a Good Samaritan. I'm not even a good Christian."

Just as Calvin was confessing his spiritual faults, he spotted Mose, Bettie, and their young son taking a circuitous path around the two white men. Their expressions were unmistakable. They knew Calvin and Mercer were standing outside of the church and bartering them away. Calvin felt like he'd been caught committing a crime.

"My God, there they are . . . just over your shoulder."

Mercer began to rotate his neck.

"No, Mercer, please don't turn around. They've picked up on all of this . . . and I don't feel very comfortable right about now."

"So, when can we transfer their title to you?"

Calvin usually despised euphemisms. He considered them to be the language of cowards. But hearing Mercer use such speech as "transfer their title to you" made Calvin yearn for a gentler euphemism – yes, even a highly hypocritical one.

"I've instructed that bunion on my butt, whom I've inherited from my so-called 'friends' back in Kentucky, to draft the paperwork. He's now affiliated with Roscoe Page. And Judge Robinson has taken a liking to him, as well. You know . . . 'Birds of a feather' . . .

"He'll have the papers ready by Wednesday. I'll bring them to you along with a bank draft on Thursday. As for taking possession . . . my Lord, would you listen to what I just said . . . 'taking possession'? Anyway, we'll make those arrangements on Thursday, if it's all right with you. I don't even know where they can live . . . come Friday."

"All that's fine and dandy, Calvin . . . except for the part about the bank draft. I've got to have cash in the bargain."

"What did you say?" Calvin was livid. "Mercer, I can't go over to the Farmers and Merchants Bank and withdraw twelve hundred dollars in cash. Marcus Winchester and Ike Rawlings are owners of the bank. They'll hear about such a withdrawal within five minutes of me walking out of the bank's doors. All sorts of wild speculation will ensue.

"I'm trying to keep all of this business clandestine. If I do what you ask, I might as well buy an advertisement in the newspaper with bold headlines proclaiming, 'Calvin Cabell has scuttled all of his moral principles and is buying a family of slaves'."

"I'll tell you what, Calvin. Suppose you pay me four hundred dollars in cash on Thursday . . . and two more cash payments of four hundred dollars during each of the two months thereafter? The Bill of Sale will show that full consideration was paid up front. I trust you."

Calvin was getting very frustrated and even more irritable than he had been while dreading the prospect of escorting Shelby to church and enduring dinner with him afterwards.

"My Lord, I've still got THAT painful experience ahead of me," he thought.

"All right, Mercer, I'll pay you four hundred dollars in cash for three months. Now, if you'll excuse me, I've got to go home after all this belly aching and take another hot soapy bath. Negotiating this sale of human slaves makes me feel filthier than a field hand on an August afternoon. Good day, Mercer."

\* \* \* \* \* \* \* \* \* \*

Shortly after noon on Wednesday, Shelby sauntered smartly on to the mill lot . . . while clutching his leather valise. He proceeded toward Calvin's modest office. It was attached to a shed where mill equipment was stored. He looked about and sensed Calvin wasn't on the premises.

"Have you seen Mr. Cabell?" Shelby called out to Tim Farley, who was doing his best to handle the bridle of an uncooperative mule. The animal's harness was attached to the end of a chain forged out of the stoutest iron links Shelby had ever seen. The other end of the chain wrapped around a twenty foot log that Tim was trying to drag over to pit number two.

"He's gone to the bank," Tim called out just as the mule sharply reared his head with displeasure. The jolt to Tim's grip on the animal prevented him from speaking for several seconds. "He should be back in about ten or fifteen minutes."

"Very well, thank you. He's expecting me sometime this afternoon. I'm his attorney."

Tim had seen Shelby about town two times before. Sally Farley told her husband this short newcomer had, in some way, a relationship with his boss. She didn't know what it was. She observed that Shelby wasn't closely knit to the Cabells, but he had visited them in their home at least twice. One visit, she said, took place last Sunday when he came to dinner following the church service.

Tim considered everything he knew about this little man. He was comfortable calling back to Shelby, "I'm sure he wouldn't mind if you waited in his office. It's over there."

When Tim briefly released the mule's bridle as he pointed out the direction of the office, the momentary lapse of attention to the mule provided an opportunity this contrary beast of burden seized upon. The animal shook his head violently from left to right and up and down, so as to separate Tim's left hand from his hold on the leather lead. He bellowed out angry epithets in Gaelic . . . or, so Shelby assumed. And whatever Tim was yelling, Shelby felt confident the mule realized he was being roundly cursed by the Irishman.

A gourd ladle hung from the eave of the equipment shed and a wood bucket filled with water sat on a cleanly sawed stump that appeared to be used as an outdoor utility table. Shelby dipped the gourd into the water and gulped down its clear contents. Then he meandered over to Calvin's office and walked in.

Most folks in Memphis, as well as those back in Kentucky, admired Calvin and his many accomplishments. Shelby was among them. However, he regarded the man more with envy . . . than esteem.

Calvin was tall and Shelby was short. Calvin was liked by one and all. Yet, Shelby was always the last boy chosen for team games. Calvin married a beautiful woman and Shelby was still sleeping alone. He could only lie in bed and dream of female companionship. Calvin seemed quite successful in his lumber business. Yet, Shelby was still sucking up to almost everybody - desperate to secure a foothold in the business of the law.

Calvin's office was more crude than courtly. Shelby looked about the premises. There was an oak file cabinet in the corner and an old chest along the wall that was laden with papers all askew. There were two cane bottom ladder back chairs in front of Calvin's desk and his wood chair behind the desk wasn't the least bit impressive. Nevertheless, it gave notice to visitors that the boss sat there. The desk was the most impressive of all the furnishings. It was also made from oak, but it sat above the floor on four impressively carved claw legs. Shelby thought a similar desk would be quite suitable for him as soon as he could set up a Memphis office for Roscoe Pryor.

The desk's surface wasn't strewn about like the top of the chest. It was clean except for a Bible on the side. And in the middle was a writing mat with quill pens, paper, and ink . . . sitting just off its border. There was also a leather bound ledger book resting within arm's length of Calvin's desk chair. The sizeable iron safe sat on the floor beside the desk. Its door was wide open.

"That's got to be Calvin's bank ledger," Shelby thought to himself. "He must have noted today's deposit and withdrawal. He forgot to place it back in the safe before he left."

Shelby stared at the book all the while wondering what sort of information it contained. "How well IS Calvin doing?" he pondered.

There was little debate in his mind whether taking a peek inside would be right or wrong. "If he's going to be so foolish to leave his ledger unattended while he's away . . . well, maybe he's not so smart after all. Besides, there's no harm that can be done."

Shelby took one precautionary look out the window to see if one of the workers might be approaching. They all appeared to be busy with their duties. Then he went behind the desk and gently lifted the binder's cover. He did so, considering if Calvin might have marked the exact spot where the ledger sat so he would know if it had been tampered with.

Shelby scanned the entries on the first page. Calvin's banking information started in 1830. He turned over several pages at a time until he found the last page with the most recent entry. It showed today's date and a withdrawal of four hundred dollars. Immediately, he turned his attention to scanning over bank balances, deposits, and withdrawals.

"Impressive . . . very impressive," he silently concluded. The bank balance after today's cash withdrawal was $4,238.42. Past deposits that were recorded appeared to range from $50 to $400 and the average balance was in the range of $4,000.

Out of the corner of his peripheral vision, Shelby spotted Calvin about thirty yards away. He approached Tim Farley for a few seconds of conversation and Tim pointed to the office. Clearly, Tim had informed his boss that Shelby was waiting for him inside. Calvin began to walk . . . and, as he got closer, Shelby could read his expression. It was one of concern. He knew he had left the ledger book on his desk and he also knew Shelby was a man who couldn't be trusted.

Calvin had been thinking all week how Shelby joining the family after the church service for dinner was just as unpleasant an experience as he had predicted. After the meal of fried chicken, baked apples, and rice with chicken gravy, Calvin, Catherine, and Shelby chatted almost amicably for over an hour.

But eventually, Shelby purposefully wove into the conversation some anecdotal comments about the bar maid, whom he reminded his hosts, was brutally murdered back home. As Shelby told the story, he never took his eyes off Calvin. He reported everyone in the Bluegrass was very upset about the crime . . . and he had no doubt the murderer would eventually be brought to justice.

"Well, I hope you're right, Shelby," Catherine said. "Such a heinous crime shouldn't go unpunished. I hope they catch that vicious killer and send him to the gallows."

Shelby nodded his head . . . so as to endorse her righteous indignation . . . while he peered at Calvin with the smarmiest smile he had ever seen. "I think Catherine hit the nail on the head. Don't you, Calvin? The monster who murdered that helpless woman will be tracked relentlessly . . . until he's caught. And he WILL be caught. Of that, I have no doubt. I think he should be shackled and carried back to Harrodsburg. And, he should be hung to death before a cheering crowd of law abiding citizens."

Shelby was mocking him – right there on Calvin's veranda and in the presence of his wife. Calvin wouldn't give him the satisfaction of a response. He just stared at his nemesis . . . like his friend, Davy Crockett, had once subdued a bear with his seductive gaze.

Shelby spent the rest of the afternoon playing with Jamie and Cassie while their parents rocked on the front porch and observed it all. Shelby gleefully interacted with the kids. Jamie, especially, seemed to take to him. They played stickball and Cassie joined in for a match of marbles that lasted quite some time. After he let Cassie win, she challenged Shelby to a game of hopscotch. She had placed sticks in the middle of Jefferson Street to mark the game's grids. Shelby was reticent at first, but he was soon hopping clumsily about like a three legged rabbit.

Later that evening after Shelby bid farewell, Calvin and Catherine talked about the day. He told her everything he and Mercer Watkins had discussed and planned for the coming week. He told her he asked Shelby to draft the Bill of Sale. She saw no harm in his choice.

"How can a lawyer botch up a Bill of Sale?" Catherine commented. She said she told Sally Farley that the Cabells were about to become slave owners. "Sally wasn't so much shocked by the news as she seemed to appear threatened. "She's served us well and I see no need to let her go on account of Mose and Bettie."

"Tell her they're going to spend most of their time working out at Valley View. There's plenty of work to do out there and Sally can continue to work for us in town as long as she wants to."

* * * * * * * * * * *

Calvin was recalling every detail about Sunday as he walked into his office. Shelby offered him an awkward smile and a handshake. Calvin glanced around the premises and surveyed his desk to determine whether or not this notorious busybody had looked any place where he should've known better. The company's ledger still sat on his desk . . . just like he left it.

"I should've put everything in the safe before I went to the bank. Well, I suppose there's a slight chance Shelby kept his nose out of places it doesn't belong. But, I doubt it."

Shelby wanted to go over the paperwork with Calvin. However, Calvin was more interested in scooting this irritating lawyer out of his office. He impatiently told Shelby he would inspect the document later in the afternoon when he went to meet with Mercer Watkins. Calvin had all of his conscious thoughts focused on his dread of the rendezvous that awaited him at the Watkins' house. He would, in a matter of minutes, have to look a family of three in their eyes and tell them he now owned them . . . lock, stock, and barrel.

"Why don't I feel like the Good Samaritan now? Why don't I feel like I'm on a rescue mission . . . and saving the lives of a loving family from a life of despair?"

Calvin had plenty of soul searching questions. But he didn't have an answer to a single one of them.

He told his mill foreman he had some business to tend to and he'd be away from the mill until the next morning. Then he climbed into his open carriage, snapped the reins, and turned south toward town . . . toward his waiting slaves.

\* \* \* \* \* \* \* \* \*

When Calvin's carriage turned the corner that led to the Watkins place, he suddenly felt nauseous. There they were . . . sitting on the sidewalk outside the Watkins' picket fence. The three Negroes had their eyes fixed on Calvin. Yet, he couldn't bear to look back at any of them – even the young son.

In unison, the three arose and stood at attention just like this was a previously rehearsed ceremony marking the changing of the guard . . . instead of the changing of the masters. At their feet Calvin counted five gunny sacks with protruding lumps. All were tied with twine. Instinctively, he knew these burlap bags contained all their worldly possessions.

"Is Mr. Watkins here?" Calvin called out – not to anyone in particular.

"Yessuh, he is," replied Mose helpfully. "He's inside de house."

Just as Mose spoke, Mercer almost ran out the door with a curious countenance that appeared half panic and half relief. "Calvin, come inside first, please."

"Are there to be no introductions, Mercer?"

"It's best you come with me, Calvin. It's best you join me inside."

So, Calvin rose from the driver's bench and jumped the four feet to the ground. He walked directly past the three waifs. The only one with whom he chose to make eye contact was the child. The boy held his mother's hand and he looked back at Calvin with the blankest, most enigmatic look Calvin had ever seen. It appeared he had some notion of what was happening that afternoon. He knew this was going to be a watershed day for him and his parents. Yet, he didn't have a clear idea what was going on.

Calvin walked through the door Mercer was holding open for him. As he closed the door behind Calvin, he quickly took another glance and saw the three were following every move Calvin made.

"Do you have everything in order, Calvin?"

"Well, I have the Bill of Sale, the money, and I have a carriage outside waiting to haul these beleaguered looking people away. Yes, I suppose I have everything except a resolute feeling in my gut that what's going on here is within the scope of the catechism we both learned as children. I suppose, Mercer, my feelings could be summarized by saying I don't feel very 'Christian' at the moment."

"Well, if it's any comfort, there are thousands of Christians who own slaves. Many of them are church officers."

"That's precious little consolation, Mercer."

Then Calvin expressed his sole objective. He wanted to get this 'business' over and done. He pulled several items from the side pocket of his coat. "All right, the money's here in this envelope and here's the Bill of Sale that Shelby Lancaster prepared. He's not a member of the bar, just yet, but I figured he didn't need to be licensed to prepare straight-forward contract like this."

Mercer hurriedly opened the envelope. It contained eight, fifty dollar bills. Then he scanned the Bill of Sale so rapidly, Calvin didn't think he was actually reading anything on the page.

"It's all in order. It's all in order," Mercer repeated as he leaned over the chest in the hallway and signed the Bill of Sale over the line marked 'Seller'. "Now let's walk outside and get these people on their way."

"What's come over you, Mercer? You're acting even stranger than I'm feeling."

"Calvin, this is a very emotional time for me. I'd appreciate it if we could carry on with what needs to be done as quickly as possible."

Then Mercer abruptly moved back toward the door and, once again, held it open in the same clumsy manner as before. "Come on, Calvin. Come along, please."

Mercer began the introductions several steps before he even passed through the front gate. "Mose, Bettie, I've just signed the papers and Mr. Cabell here is ready to carry you to your new home."

Calvin had no idea what was the appropriate etiquette when first meeting one's newly purchased slaves. So he winged it. He held out his hand to Mose. "Hello Mose, I'm Calvin Cabell."

It seemed to Calvin his arm was suspended awkwardly in mid-air forever. Mose stared up at him with his lower jaw suspended in a look of complete consternation. At last, he responded to Calvin's self-introduction. "Yessuh, I know who you is." But he offered no handshake.

Calvin retrieved his hand and felt the urge to either stick it deep inside his pants pocket or cut it off with whatever crude implement might be handy. "Oh, you bloody fool," he thought to himself. "This man has the eminent good sense not to clasp my palm in a handshake. He knows he's a slave . . . and slaves don't shake hands with their masters. I should have known that."

Suddenly the tension in the air could be cut with a knife. Consequently, Calvin took the initiative to wrap up this prickly moment in time. He looked at Bettie . . . and then to little Jed. "I assume those sacks are your belongings. Mose. Why don't you put them there on the back of the carriage and you three hop on in. I know Mrs. Cabell wants to meet you, so we need to be getting along."

Once again it was Mose who was forced to teach Calvin another lesson about the protocol for being a proper master. He looked at the empty rear seat in the carriage where Calvin had asked them to sit. Then he gave a perplexed look at his new owner. Mose quickly darted his eyes from the carriage seat to Calvin . . . twice. Finally, he spoke. And Calvin knew whatever was about to be said would be uncomfortable . . . like everything else this afternoon had been uncomfortable.

"Master, we is YO slaves now." Mose paused nervously, but he needed to say what had to be said. "Ain't no slaves in Memphis ridin' in no carriage – 'specially no carriage driven by they master. It ain't right."

He looked down at the ground . . . embarrassed . . . and he repeated more softly, "It just ain't right."

Again, Calvin had allowed his incredible insouciance to be spotlighted . . . and, correctly so . . . by this black man with such wise eyes and such soft spoken speech. Calvin didn't know what to say. He wished he could have the benefit of a quick tutorial right about then. So, he turned to Mose, his teacher in this lesson of "How to be a slave owner", and he meekly asked for guidance.

"How do you suppose we should handle this, Mose. Somehow or another you and your family have got to make your way to my house. How do you propose this rather simple objective might be carried out?"

"We'll walk, Mr. Cabell. We'll walk behind the carriage."
But Mose was a good reader of people. And he had read in Calvin Cabell that if he didn't allow some accommodation . . . so that, at least, one expression of Calvin's graciousness was accepted . . . this inexperienced master would feel both derided and defeated.

"But, Mr. Cabell, I knows all of us be mighty grateful if we could take you up on your offer . . . to toss our sacks in the back of your carriage." Mose looked at Bettie who acknowledged with a nod that, indeed, Calvin's suggestion would be greatly appreciated.

"Very well then, let's follow that plan. Mose, you hurl everything up here in the rear."

Then, Calvin had an idea. Mose immediately detected it was another offer of kindness and grace. Whatever it was, it shouldn't be refused. "You know the way to our place on Jefferson, don't you, Mose?"

"Yessuh, we knows where you stay." Bettie was also bobbing her head in agreement.

"Well, you three walk on over and I'll tote your bags. How about that?"

"Mighty kind of you master. Dat's mighty kind of you."

Calvin was seated on the driver's bench holding the reins. Suddenly, he glowered down at Mose with a look that seemed frightfully angry. In a voice that was low and with a tempo of speech that was slow, Calvin admonished these wary black folks as best he could manage. "Mose . . . Bettie . . . don't call me 'master' again. Call me Mr. Cabell."

Then to make certain the point was imbedded in their minds, he turned toward them and said it again. "Please, we'll get along just fine if you refrain from calling me 'master'."

With that issue cleared up . . . hopefully, once and for all . . . Calvin called out, "Giddy up". His wagon jolted once and pulled away. He could see his new family of slaves had turned around to face Mercer. They said nothing. And their silence at this pivotal moment in their lives was eerily pregnant . . . with thoughts and emotions that had never been uttered. If their sentiments and feelings were ever to be spoken, it was now or never.

"You take care, folks. You take care, now," Mercer said.

"I suppose," said Mose, "we'll see you in church, Mr. Watkins."

"You bet. I'll be there . . . and I know you'll be there, too."

Bettie hadn't said anything thus far. Suddenly she recalled something she thought was appropriate to add. It was a sentiment she had long fostered within her. It was something she wanted to get off her chest. Before she spoke, she paused reflectively. "You been mighty kind to us, Mr. Watkins. I believe we gonna see one another in heaven . . . in the bye and bye. I do believe we will."

A lump in Mercer's throat swelled so large he couldn't easily catch a breath. But, he tried. "I hope so, Bettie. I hope so." He could only hope to choke out the rest. "There's no doubt . . . you folks . . . will make it past the Pearly Gates. I'm just . . . not so certain about me, though."

Mercer looked down at the ground. He couldn't face these fellow human beings any longer, even though he wanted to look at them eye to eye. He didn't even think he could look in a mirror and face himself . . . and glare at the weak-as-water man he had become.

"Yes, Bettie, we'll see what happens . . . in the 'bye and bye'."

As Calvin turned his carriage at the corner he looked back toward Mercer's house. Bettie and Mose and Jed were plodding behind him in the dusty road. Their sight was fixed on the ground. And, as they moved farther away from Mercer, he looked up at them just as Calvin caught a glimpse. Mercer was crying. He wasn't teary eyed. He wasn't mournfully sobbing. He was desolate with despair. He buried his face into his hands and the pitch of his wailing was loud enough Calvin could hear him thirty yards away . . . over the noise of the moving carriage. There wasn't a doubt the slaves he had just sold were also hearing him cry. Yet, they had the presence of mind to not look back.

Calvin couldn't help wondering what was going through Mercer's mind as he stood in front of his gate . . . shamelessly weeping away. Was he crying because - as he had volunteered to Calvin, "These people have become like family to me?"

Or, was he crying because his financial ruin was imminent? He'd soon be served with a Court Order that would freeze all his assets, so they could be liquidated for the benefit of the Bank of Hernando. Was that the pain he felt?

Or, was he feeling his soul suddenly slipping away – draining out of him like the buckets of tears that were now dripping between the fingers . . . of the trembling hands . . . that covered Mercer's face?

Or, was he crying because he knew, there and then, he would never get to see Bettie . . . in the "bye and bye'?"

Calvin remembered how he and Captain Moore - silently, and without any discussion - decided how they would handle such a fork in the road of life. As Calvin climbed the bluff that morning long ago to meet Marcus Winchester and to begin a new chapter in his own life, he didn't turn back for one last glance. And Moore evidently was also determined not to sneak a parting peek at Calvin. It was just better to move on and not look back. The same dynamics were being put into play there on South Second Street. There could be no looking back . . . by any of the disparate parties whose lives were being put into play.

Calvin also recalled telling Captain Moore's tragic river story to Marcus Winchester. He had punctuated its moral when he told it. He emphasized, "In life, there's no good that can come from looking back. But there's one exception to that rule. Every once in a while a man has to look back and take stock of his past. Then, he must look ahead . . . to evaluate if he really knows where he wants to go . . . and how he's going to get there."

Recently, Calvin hadn't been able to resist looking back and taking stock of his life. The retrospective he invariably chose to revisit was the sorriest, most sordid chapter. Each time his mind lapsed into the underbelly of his past, he saw Dolly's bloated body more clearly . . . and he smelled the stench of her rotten flesh more acutely. His new slave woman, Bettie, was looking forward to the "bye and bye" while Calvin . . . her new master, whom Mose had once characterized as a good Christian . . . was peering at an interminable stay in hell.

But this afternoon Calvin didn't have the luxury of looking back and rehashing whether or not he had done the right thing by buying these people. He was now a slave owner. That decision lay in the past. There was only the future that mattered now.

Mose, Bettie, and little Jed most certainly didn't have the luxury of looking back either. They could only speculate what lay ahead for them . . . and pray. They had never had any control over their past. Their lives had unfolded according to the whimsical decisions of others. For them . . . there was still a future of uncertainty ahead. But whatever cards fate might deal them, Calvin thought eternal salvation was a shoo-in. If the New Testament held any truth at all, these slaves were bound for heaven . . . at the end of their cruel time on earth – in the eventual "bye and bye", as Bettie had referenced to Mercer – was assured.

As Calvin's carriage moved nearer to his house, he couldn't get out of his thoughts the executed Bill of Sale sitting on Mercer Watkins' hall chest. To Calvin the papers served as official notice that his own odds of getting to that sweet "bye and bye" . . . after Dolly's death and today's barter with the devil . . . were about as risky as a crapshoot in a dice game with thieves.

\* \* \* \* \* \* \* \* \* \* \*

When Mose, Bettie, and Jed eventually turned the corner and began to walk down Monroe Street, Calvin and Catherine were standing side by side on the porch. Cassie and Jamie stood on the step below them. One family was about to meet another. All of them knew that . . . to some, yet unknown, degree . . . they were about to be wrought together as one.

Calvin arrived three minutes before the Negroes. He used the time to assemble his rather nervous greeting committee. He told Catherine how bizarre it seemed that he felt the need to welcome three human strangers he'd just purchased. The children had been briefed during the past ten days about their impending arrival. Jamie had some marginal understanding of how the household was about to change. But Cassie couldn't quite put the pieces of the puzzle together.

"Okay, children, here they come," Calvin prepped his clan just seconds before they stopped in front of his home. As the three Negroes stood before the front gate, the Cabells just stared at this wary Negro trio. Jamie and Cassie were transfixed upon Jed. And little Jed was focused solely on them, as well.

Calvin and Catherine had been unable to devise a script as to just how these unfamiliar folks would be welcomed and by whom. "What can we possibly say to these people that will put them at ease . . . and put us at ease, too?" Catherine inquired as she and her husband discussed the dilemma.

285

"I've given it a lot of thought, Mrs. Cabell. I don't know yet what should be said. But, somehow, I've got to believe the right words are going to come out of our mouths . . . and out of theirs."

Now, that moment in time had arrived . . . and both were bemoaning their lack of preparation. So, as usual, Calvin severed the silence with some scattershot words. "It may seem odd to you folks, but all of us wish to extend a sincere welcome to the three of you."

He looked at the little black boy while he gently grasped a shoulder of each of his children . . . as if to form a three link chain of hospitable solidarity. "Jed, this is Jamie . . . and this is Cassie. Can you say 'Hello' to Jed, children?"

Jamie offered a tentative "Hello". But Cassie could only welcome him with a confused smile.

"And, Mose and Bettie, may I present Mrs. Cabell to you?"

"Hello. I'm pleased to meet you," Catherine said uncomfortably. "Won't you come through the gate so we can get acquainted?" She wore a genuine, welcoming smile as she looked down at Jed. "Jed, do you like to shoot marbles?"

The boy stood there mute - as he didn't know what to say.

Bettie responded on behalf of her son. "Ma'am, Jed don't know nothin' 'bout marbles. He ain't never seen one. And he shore don't know how to play no marbles game."

Catherine modulated into a much cheerier voice. "Well, then Jamie, why don't you take Jed over to your marbles shooting arena and show Jed how it's done. I'll bet he'll catch on pretty quick."

"Yes, Mama. Come with me, Jed. Cassie and I'll show you all our tricks."

With the children gone and only the two pairs of adults standing face to face, Calvin once again filled the lull. "Bettie, I know Mrs. Cabell would like to show you around the house. And Mose, I wonder if we might go out back and talk a spell?"

"Yessuh, mast . . ." Mose, thankfully, caught himself about to violate the only rule Calvin had laid out so far. "Yessuh, Mr. Cabell. You lead da way."

The two men sat down on wood lawn chairs that one of the workers at the mill made for his boss. The chairs were whitewashed and they sat situated face to face. And face to face is how Calvin wished to speak to Mose.

"Mose, how much do you know about what's been going on . . . and about the situation that's led you and your family to us?"

Slaves are supposed to see no evil, speak no evil, and hear no evil. Mose was a slave. He was a smart one, too – smart enough to say not much of anything. "Mr. Cabell, Mr. Watkins and me had a long talk . . . 'bout two weeks ago. I don't know nothin' 'bout his business. But, he told me you was fixin' to buy us . . . and if you couldn't or wouldn't . . . then, sure as Satan is the Devil, we was likely to be split up." Mose paused reflectively for a moment. "I shore hope things gonna work out for Mr. Watkins."

Then, Mose leaned forward . . . and as earnestly as one man can speak to another . . . he spoke to Calvin. "Mr. Cabell, I knows you stepped in to keep me and Bettie and Jed together. I thanks you for dat. I thanks you for dat, for shore. I seen you in the church. I seen how you carry yerself. I seen that you 'pear to be a good man, Mr. Cabell. And whatever's goin down 'tween you and Mr. Watkins, I want to say, 'Thank you, suh'. Thank you very much."

Cabell felt an immediate sense of relief. Mose had saved him from going over highly emotional and delicate territory. And this new slave had ever-so-skillfully managed to plow through all the thorny issues. The seeds of these two men's precarious relationship had been planted. Calvin was touched by Mose's sincerity. He was impressed with his bearing and his respectful, yet straightforward, speech.

Calvin leaned forward in his chair to match the intense pose Mose had struck. He was able to see every red vein that crisscrossed the whites of the Negro's eyes. And Mose, likewise, could look into his new master's ice blue irises – the azure pools that had fascinated . . . and, even mesmerized . . . most folks who had ever met him. Mose, like so many admirers before him, thought Calvin's blue eyes offered insight into his character. He, too, wondered if he peered long enough into them . . . could he see all the way into the white man's soul?

If he succeeded, he'd have seen that . . . etched into Calvin's character . . . was the indelible stain of a murderer. But, that mark of mortal sin eluded Mose's inspection. Nevertheless, the lowly slave could detect there was a vexing impurity about his new master . . . something akin to a scab-covered flaw down deep in his conscience . . . one that made this rich white man want to frequently peck away at its crusty surface and squirm from discomfort. Yet, whatever the flaw was, he felt certain the overriding essence of Calvin Cabell was a commendable brand of decency. What Mose saw . . . put him at peace.

"Mose, here's what I want to say right now. First, you and I are going to have a long talk. But, it won't be today. And it might not be for several weeks . . . or months. You should know now that I hope to free you . . . one day. But I've still got some thinking to do.

"Second, I'm going to take you and your family day after tomorrow to our place near Raleigh. We call it Valley View, because it overlooks the Wolf River valley. There's plenty of work to do up there . . . and you, Bettie, and Jed can stay in our house until other arrangements can be worked out.

"Lastly, we're just going to have to get through the next several days as best we can. All we can offer you for accommodations is a place on our back porch. It gets pretty chilly these December nights, so we've gathered together plenty of blankets and such. We'll have a few chores to do around here tomorrow. But let's use the day simply to get to know one another . . . and we'll bide our time until Friday. Do you understand what I'm saying, Mose?"

Mose was never one to give a quick response. So, Cabell punctuated his first question with a second one. "Is that okay with you, Mose?"

Mose's answer was to the point. "Yessuh, Mr. Cabell, that'd be fine. That'd be fine." But what he was really thinking was a sentiment that had to be said, as well. "Mr. Cabell, I thanks you, suh. Bettie thanks you, suh. And when little Jed gets old enough to understand what's goin' down here today, he's gonna thank you, too."

Calvin was becoming discernibly emotional. Mose could tell. He was looking once again into his new master's blue eyes. But this time Mose could see the man's soul was churning with anguish. Calvin needed to regain his composure.

"Well, Mose, I don't know how good of a man I am. But I do know Mrs. Cabell has some tasty vegetable soup prepared . . . as well as some of her famous cornbread."

Twilight was upon them. Calvin looked east toward the gigantic harvest moon that loomed low over the earth. Its cream colored glow hovered in the eastern sky. It was impressive . . . and huge . . . and more than a little menacing. One might irrationally fear the Man in the Moon's fierce face had turned hostile tonight . . . like he might vengefully swoop down and devour the planet. It occurred to Calvin this extra-terrestrial monster was probably peeved about the events of the day.

"It's getting late, Mose. Let's get through this night. And, then, let's get through tomorrow. Let's just take this new experience one day at a time." Calvin arose from his wood chair. "Come up to the porch, Mose. Soup is coming soon."

Mose stood at attention just after his new master arose from his chair. He acknowledged the wisdom and the gentle nature in his new owner and what he had just said. "Dat's right, Mr. Cabell, we gonna take all dat's ahead . . . jes one day at a time."

Mose paused once again and looked up at the moon before he began to move toward his temporary home on the back porch. It had been a tumultuous day for his family. He began to wonder. "Jes maybe, dat's the face of the Lord up in the sky. Maybe it's really the Lord who's the man in the moon. After all, it's written in Genesis He created it. Maybe the Lord's looking down on all us sinners. Maybe He's mad 'cause he don't like it when black folks get bought and sold like livestock. But I believe . . . with all my heart . . . the Lord's gonna look after us. I believe it was Jesus what sent us to live with these Cabell folks."

Mose breathed a little easier and he felt the gist of his conversation with Mr. Cabell was worth repeating. "We gonna take all dat lays ahead . . . one day at a time . . . one day at a time."

*No Coin for Charon*

# CHAPTER
# *17*

December 1834

"Sally, I do declare," Catherine exclaimed as she walked toward the front door while glancing at the grandfather clock's hour and minute arms. They were standing at attention . . . precisely on the seven and the twelve.

It was the habit of Sally Farley, without fail, to knock on the Cabells' front door sometime between the clock's first and seventh chime.

"Sometimes I wonder if you're really human, Sally. No one I know is so punctual . . . so dependable."

As Catherine opened the door and Sally walked through it, she continued, "You're simply amazing, Sally . . . simply amazing."

Sally was removing her woolen shawl when Catherine spoke again – this time more softly. "Sally Farley, step into the parlor with me, please."

Sally had a good hunch what was playing out now. She had suspected it was coming. And, she was right.

"Sally, you know I told you about this Negro family Mr. Cabell was going to buy. Well, it was done yesterday afternoon – after you'd gone home. The man's name is Mose. The woman's name is Bettie and their son's name is Jed. I guess you can already smell that Bettie's been making breakfast. Come on back with me and I'll introduce her to you."

Sally smelled the bacon drippings, all right. Yet, something else in the air smelled irreparably wrong this morning. Sally could sense it. She'd been told about the upcoming acquisitions Mr. Cabell was about to make. She even knew he was purchasing the family from Mercer Watkins, whom she had spotted several times on the street. And she also knew that when she heard about this impending news, she was unnerved.

"There'll be too many cooks in the kitchen," she had thought to herself when Catherine first mentioned the impending purchase of the three slaves. Now, she had arrived at her place of work, as always, at her appointed time. And, sure enough, there was already another cook in the kitchen.

Catherine took Sally's hand and led her toward the back of the house. "Come and meet Bettie, Sally."

Bettie was standing in front of the hot cast iron stove when the two white women walked in. Long before dawn Bettie awoke outside on the porch and made her way into the kitchen . . . carrying a load of kindling and some split wood. While the fire she lit was building, she rummaged around the place until she found all the ingredients needed to make biscuits. She spied the salt cured country ham in the larder and she craftily cut even slices which she fried in some of the bacon grease she found in a jar by the stove. By the time the oven was hot enough, the biscuit dough had been prepared, kneaded, and was ready to bake.

So, when Sally Farley walked into the kitchen with Catherine, she saw a veritable breakfast banquet laid out on the table. Still steaming biscuits were stacked on a wood cutting board. A mound of butter and Catherine's strawberry jam were close by. They were the perfect trimmings.

The ham this industrious newcomer fried up was sitting on top of the warm oven. And there stood black Bettie . . . frying eggs in the cast iron skillet - coated with the crackling juices of the country ham she had fried in it earlier.

Sally took one look at Bettie and sized up the situation silently. All the while she posed in the doorway with an imperious air about her. "This nigra," she thought, "is going to be trouble – just as I had predicted."

"Bettie, I want you to meet our loyal help around the house. This is Sally Farley."

Bettie looked at Sally silently, but respectfully. And Sally stared back at Bettie as the first degrees of rage began swelling up within her. Her heartbeat was thumping in her chest. Yet, she was determined to keep calm and to project unmistakable notice to Bettie . . . that she held seniority around the house. And, moreover, she was a white woman.

Bettie nodded her head so as to acknowledge Catherine's introduction. It was clear to Catherine her silence was the result of past conditioning. It was taboo under the circumstances for a black woman to speak to any white woman to whom she is introduced. It would have been unthinkable for Bettie to reply saying, "Pleased to meet you, ma'am."

Likewise, Sally didn't speak. But she acknowledged Catherine's introduction in the subtlest of body language. She thought speaking to Bettie first was a sign of weak character and it would only diminish the natural advantage a white woman loomed over a black woman standing at a hot stove.

"Sally, would you care to sample some of Bettie's biscuits? They're the best I ever had. They're hot . . . right out of the oven."

Sally Farley still had her flared nostrils focused on Bettie. She reluctantly turned to Catherine. "Thank you, but I don't care for any, Mrs. Cabell. I just ate some cornbread left over from last night's supper. It was delicious . . . and ever so filling."

"If you change your mind, let me know. I'm sure if all this food is consumed – as I suspect it will be, knowing my hungry family - then Bettie would be happy to whip up whatever she could for you."

"Thank you, ma'am, but I'm I sure I won't go hungry."

"Well then, Sally, why don't you empty and clean the chamber pots as usual. Later on, I have some work in mind you and Bettie can do together."

Sally Farley began biting her lip. She thought for a second her teeth might even lacerate the lower one and warm, red blood would ooze down her chin. Her clenched lips were holding back a long list of emotions – hurt, rage, and personal marginalization.

She had just been instructed to clean the household's chamber pots while this new Negro stood over the skillet . . . merrily moving eggs about with a spatula. All of this violated the natural order of things. Or, so it seemed to Sally as she tried to make sense out of this unexpected situation.

"I think Mrs. Cabell has forgotten it's the role of a slave to clean the chamber pots," Sally surmised to herself.

Then she dug deep in her consciousness . . . hoping to find a justifiable explanation for her employer's sudden disregard for white supremacy.

293

"I suppose Mrs. Cabell's been disoriented," she reasoned, "from waking up to find the coffee's been brewed and the breakfast was made. And I know for a fact she's nervous about suddenly owning slaves. She told me as much last week.

"Surely she knows the pecking order in a white household. I'll overlook her confused state of mind. Tomorrow we'll return to a more sensible household routine - when this Negro woman is doing the sort of work she's supposed to do. And I'll be doing the work of a proper housekeeper."

But Sally, nevertheless, felt humiliated in front of the entire Cabell family. When Catherine brought her into the kitchen, there sat Mr. Cabell, Jamie, and Cassie. They were seated around a small rectangular table in the corner of the kitchen. And, "faith and begorra", the cook's little black son sat right there with them . . . reaching over Jamie's plate to fetch a second helping of strawberry preserves.

There were looks of contentment all around the table. Today's breakfast was far from the ordinary. There were hot biscuits with plenty of butter tucked inside and oozing out of their flaky, cut crevices. Biscuits like these were an unusual breakfast treat and every one of the Cabells had the look of a satisfied customer on his or her face.

And, to have Mrs. Cabell give Sally her chamber pot instructions in front of Mr. Cabell, the children, and the little slave boy – well, it was an outrageous discourtesy.

Nevertheless, Sally held her tongue and maintained an unflappable poker face. The last thing she wanted to project to this darkie was any notion her esteem within the house had risen . . . at the expense of Sally losing hers.

Yet, the fact of the matter was that Sally HAD lost this contest. And the defeat had "gotten her goat". To make matters worse, she and Tim needed the money she earned. And she never, for a moment, lost sight of the fact that Calvin Cabell was her husband's employer . . . as well as hers. The Cabells were the Farleys' sole source of income.

"This Negro woman may have won the battle, but she doesn't have a chance of winning the war," Sally thought. Nevertheless, it was Sally who was defeated in the initial skirmish. Consequently, she now was required to make her way into Cassie's room and retrieve the stinky chamber pot that surely awaited her under the bed.

"Cleaning my own chamber pot each morning gags me. How I hate doing it all over again at the Cabells," she muttered in defeat.

Calvin assigned Jamie two chores at breakfast. He was to scrub the two English saddles in the shed with saddle soap. Then he was to deliver some invoices from the lumber company to three different residences. "Why don't you let Jed help you with the leather work and then the two of you can make these deliveries together?"

"Alright, Father, that's just what we'll do."

Then Jamie stood from his seat and grabbed one more biscuit off the plate. "Come on, Jed. We'll knock down these chores lickety-split." He walked out to the back porch and then on to the shed . . . with Jed following several steps behind him.

Jamie noticed in the corner of the porch the stacked blankets his mother gathered together last night so the Negroes would have some degree of comfort and warmth during the night. He thought how odd it was these three people had suddenly come into his life. Even odder, his family wasn't prepared to offer them anything except some blankets laid out on the hard wood floor of an unenclosed back porch. It was all perplexing to him.

Mose wasn't inside the house. Calvin had instructed him to head toward the mill where he wanted him to clean and oil the long pit saws stored in the shed. "My manager, Mr. Sperling, is expecting you and he can get you started. You'll find," Calvin cautioned, "they've been neglected and rust is beginning to set in. There's sand paper on the table in the corner of the shed . . . and an oil can is sitting there, as well."

Back in the kitchen, Bettie was cleaning up and wrapping the leftover biscuits and ham in a blue checkered cloth she found in the cupboard drawer.

"Somebody's gonna have good eats later on in the day," Catherine predicted.

Meanwhile outside, Sally backed out of the privy where she had emptied the waste contents of each pot. Then, she used the long handled brush that hung on the back of the out house to clean the containers' nasty residue. Finally, she mixed some sheep dip with water and poured about three inches of the mixture into the bottom of each container. The strong, antiseptic aroma scented the air wherever the pot sat. Each morning she placed them back in their respective places and the air once again smelled fresh and clean.

As she carried the clean pots toward the house the Irish woman heard Catherine call out her name from the back porch. "Sally . . . Sally, dear, when you're finished . . . would you kindly visit with me?"

Sally looked suspiciously at her employer. She reluctantly replied, "Yes, ma'am, I'll be done in a few minutes." Within her gut there was a great crisis swelling.

As Sally passed through the hallway toward Catherine, she was pleased to see Bettie had pulled back the carpet in front of the fireplace and she was just beginning to stoop over a bucket of water. She held a soft scrubbing brush in her hand. Then she stabilized herself on all fours and she began to scrub the floor.

"That's more like it," Sally muttered silently to herself as she momentarily enjoyed feeling quite smug.

"Sally, I've asked Bettie to give the floors a light scrubbing. The weather is balmy and the planks should dry quickly. Go fetch the other soft brush on the porch and help her. I want to get this chore done as quickly as possible. Then the two of you can beat the rug on the clothes line while the floor is drying."

Sally looked completely stunned for a second. She thought she was going to break into tears. But, she managed to compose herself – at least on the outside. "Mrs. Cabell, I've served you faithfully for almost a year now. I thought I had earned at least a small degree of respect for my work and my dedication. But today my heart is broken."

Then Sally looked across the room and pointed to Bettie with her outstretched finger. "Surely you don't expect a white housemaid to get down on her hands and knees with a savage black slave and assist her scrubbing the floor."

Now, it was Catherine who was stunned. She recalled all the tensions she had experienced during the past two weeks. She and Calvin agreed to purchase these people from Mercer. But that only precipitated the stress of not knowing where they would stay, what would be their duties, and wondering if she could even tolerate being in the same household with her own personal slaves. She had been overwhelmed with anxiety. This was not a good time for a housekeeper to tell her she's too good to do what she's done around the house for a year . . . simply because she refuses to work with black Bettie. It was too much to bear.

Catherine thought about this predicament. And with each second that passed, her blood pressure rose higher and higher.

"Mrs. Farley . . ."

Catherine had never referred to her house helper by any name other than Sally. She felt pleased with herself - beginning what she had to say in such an authoritative manner. It clearly scared Sally to hear her surname called out so formally.

"Mrs. Farley, I have appreciated your work. And . . . I trust you have appreciated the wages you've been paid for it. You've scrubbed this floor on numerous occasions during the past year. You've gotten on your hands and knees . . . just like Bettie is doing. And, Mrs. Farley, you have never complained. Why . . .? Because, it was your job."

Catherine thought she was doing fairly well so far. But now she had to formulate an ultimatum and she wondered what it should be and how it should be stated.

"Now, Mrs. Farley, I told you several days ago that we would have some additional help here in the house for a short period of time. In no way did I infer that these three Negroes would supplant needing you as an employee. In fact, I told you they would likely be living at Valley View. But, where they live, Mrs. Farley . . . and what they do for Mr. Cabell and for me . . . is absolutely no concern of yours."

Still, no ultimatum had been conjured up. But, suddenly, one popped out of her mouth. "Therefore, if you wish to continue your day's work with us . . . and, with Bettie here, then I would be pleased to hear of it. On the other hand, if you've determined you wish to cease doing the same work as before, then, please tell me so. I'll give you your wages through today and you'll be free to find a position with another family. Please tell me, Mrs. Farley. What is your decision?"

"Mrs. Cabell has never spoken to me in that manner . . . or even implied she wished to eliminate my job." Sally mulled what she had heard over in her mind. "I wonder if she's seriously telling me to make up my mind right now – to stay or to leave."

Then Sally looked at Bettie still scrubbing the floor. She seemed oblivious to what had just been said by both women. There was no doubt she had heard it all . . . and, yet, she carried on as if she had not.

"I wonder what's going through that nigra's mind right now?" Sally considered. "I'll bet she's laughing heartily on the inside saying to herself, 'Black folks are just as lowly as Irish Micks around this town. Those Irishmen are nothing more than white niggers . . . suitable to serve until their employers can afford to buy a slave to do their lowly jobs for them . . . and eliminate the Irishmen's livelihood."

The more Sally contemplated what was happening this morning, she was filled with ever more rage. All of her human dignity had been stripped from her in less than an hour.

"A body's got to do what a body's got to do," Sally remembered her father saying as he lay on his deathbed. "Well, this body's got to do what this body's got to do. And I've made my decision what that should be," Sally Farley decided under her breath.

"Mrs. Cabell, when my husband and I came to America, the people back East let us know each and every day that the Irish were destined to clean out the chamber pots for everybody else. So we moved here . . . to Memphis. And here, Mrs. Cabell, we were, thankfully, NOT the bottom rung on the social ladder. We found work     . . . and our work was appreciated. We enjoyed, at long last, a sense of dignity once more."

As Sally was speaking, tears welled up with each agonizing sentence she spoke.

"Now, today, you want to remind me that we Irish are still doomed to remain at the bottom of the heap – along with your new black slaves. I have no doubt that, eventually, the Irishman's income will disappear – as you people buy niggers to do our work. But it just ain't right, Mrs. Cabell. It just ain't right."

"So, Sally. What's your decision? I need to know. What's your decision?"

"Well, Mrs. Cabell. It's you who made the decision. If you want me to hunker down on your floor with that nigger woman, then that's something I just won't do. I may not have a job this afternoon. But I'll damn sure have my dignity. And that's mighty important to have when you've been kicked around like a dog  . . .  like we Irishmen have been kicked around in this country. There's just so much kicking a body can stand."

"I take it you're leaving us, Sally."

"Yes, ma'am, I'm taking my leave. I want you to know Tim and I've appreciated your employment. I hope my leaving causes Tim no harm at the mill. But it's time for me to go."

Sally Farley grasped her hat and her shawl from the hall tree. But she didn't bother to put them on as she strode out of the house, walked past the gate, and stomped up Jefferson Street.

Catherine looked down at Bettie who continued swirling the soapy scrub brush in the same counter-clockwise motions – just like nothing had happened. No words were spoken between the two women.

Catherine considered whether she should act as if nothing had happened – as if no one in the room had reminded Bettie that even the lowest caste of white folks considered her to be far beneath them. But Bettie WAS the lowest of the low. She knew it all along. Yet, Catherine couldn't move on with this owner/servant relationship without an acknowledgement of what had just occurred.

"Bettie, I'm sorry about all you've just heard. I've been terribly stressed about making plans for your arrival."

Then, Catherine felt the need to give validity to Sally's dedication to the Cabell clan. "You know, Bettie, Sally's been a good worker . . . and I still can't quite comprehend what's just happened here this morning. I hope you'll understand and remember that about her. She has served us well."

Bettie scooted her stooped body back . . . yet another two feet. She relied on the support of just three limbs as she placed the scrub brush in the pail of water once again before removing it, shaking the excess water back into the bucket, and then continuing with her circular motions.

"Yes'm, Miz Cabell, I understand . . . I understand."

# CHAPTER
# *18*

August 1836

"There's a butt out there to suit everybody. It's just a case of sniffing out the right one."

"I declare, Mr. Cabell," Catherine reacted with a bit of amusement filtering through her shock. "That's the crudest thing I've heard in quite some time. Please, don't go speaking to anyone else in that manner."

"Well, it's true . . . and this news only confirms it."

The "news" was delivered by the little Bantam rooster of a man who had just walked out their front door - Shelby Lancaster. Calvin and Catherine had never seen his buck-tooth grin quite as wide as it was this evening. Shelby told them his "most joyous news". He was betrothed to marry Judge Robinson's spinster daughter, Clarabelle.

"It's hard to believe Shelby's ear-to-ear grin was the result of him being beauty struck by that female hobgoblin. I hear when the Judge hosts his quail hunt every September; he has to hide that hideous beast inside the house. Just showing her face outdoors apparently trips up nature . . . and puts it all out of kilter. Upon seeing her, the birds flutter skyward in a panic and flee to the next county . . . before anyone can even fire a shot."

"Mr. Cabell, please stop. I don't want Cassie to hear you talk so."

Calvin finally heeded Catherine's admonition and agreed she was right. Cassie shouldn't hear him talk derogatively about another female.

"Besides," he thought, "Cassie might develop a case of the 'loose lips' and innocently tell some other girl what I said."

But Calvin despised this pathetic opportunist. As time passed, his once veiled threats became more potent. He knew Shelby hadn't dropped by to share the joy of his betrothal. He came to drive home the point that his marriage to Clarabelle Robinson would cement his desired destiny in Shelby County, Tennessee. He wanted Calvin Cabell to know the power Judge Robinson wielded would one day devolve to him. He wanted to give notice that he would be a formidable force to deal with. And, if Calvin had thought for a moment that he could thwart whatever attempt Shelby might wage to bring him down . . . and bring him to justice, this marriage would tip the scales of any advantage Calvin thought he might have enjoyed over Shelby. The die was cast. The weasel lawyer would soon sit in the catbird seat.

Calvin gradually concluded it was inevitable Shelby would one day take action that would dig up this dreaded specter in his past. Shelby sought to illustrate to everyone in Shelby County that their perception of the highly esteemed Calvin Cabell . . . is only an illusion.

But, for now, he could only attack his nemesis with puns. He looked at Catherine with a sinister sparkle in his eyes. He had a zinger to punctuate his point . . . and, then, that would be the end of it. "Perhaps I should explain the quail's point of view, Mrs. Cabell. You see . . . the fowl find Clarabelle . . . to be quite foul."

Calvin snickered out loud. He knew a pun was the lowest level of humor. "But," he justified out loud, "if Clarabelle is a 'catch', then Shelby surely had to troll the Robinson's pond to catch her."

The fact was that Calvin and Catherine and everybody else in the county knew Shelby vainly considered himself to be quite a desirable bachelor. And, if Shelby was looking for a mirrored match, then he and Clarabelle deserved a crack at symbiotic bliss with one another. Shelby was seeking status and power . . . and his father-in-law-to-be had plenty of it for him to inherit – even before he eventually passed on.

Clarabelle's height was just a few inches shy of six feet - which was an altitude that towered over Shelby by at least seven inches. She was physically stoop-shouldered and gawky with a personality defined by her high-pitched giggling and her inveterate hobnobbing at social occasions. She was twenty five years old - an age at which virtually all spinster women can expect their chances for matrimony to be nearly zero.

Admittedly, Judge Robinson relished the match. Shelby's branch office for Robinson's old law firm had become more prosperous than the home office -

as Memphis' population now exceeded Raleigh's. As was the original plan, Shelby had advanced his law practice by making clients promises of services above and beyond the counsel of the law.

"If you bring your legal needs to me, you're also leveraging Judge Robinson's unquestioned clout on your behalf."

More often than not, Shelby had been able to deliver on that promise - which only served to procure even more clients.

Shelby took particular pride when John McLemore hired him as counsel. He was the nephew of Andrew Jackson's wife. McLemore had cagily parlayed his acquisition of large tracts of the old Ramsay land grant. He used his enterprise and his ingenuity to create another town, South Memphis. And South Memphis began to grow and rival its namesake city to the north.

McLemore had become wealthy. Relying on his business prescience, he was the first man to predict that steamboats would find the Memphis harbor too confining – and, therefore, the landing would become obsolete. And, indeed, steamboats had slowly gravitated to the broad beaches of land that lay at his property's riverfront.

He intended to make lots of money providing a need for the new trend in river transportation called steamboats. They needed to dock at broad beaches instead of narrow coves. But, presently, McLemore had his sights on yet another transportation revolution – the railroad.

Utilizing the invention of the steam engine to power riverboats made no commercial sense for an island nation like England. Instead, the British tinkered with steam technology and created the first railroads.

"Now," McLemore said to Marcus Winchester, "as the United States expands and new cities sprout up inland and away from major rivers, there'll be a natural need to connect them. Railroads will be the new arteries of commerce of our nation."

McLemore set out to build the region's first railroad connecting his South Memphis investment to points east. This railroad needed to acquire rights-of-way along the route to its intended termination point at LaGrange, Tennessee . . . approximately fifty miles away. He needed a lawyer who could acquire those rights – one way or another. Judge Robinson's future son-in-law was the perfect man for the job. The Judge had the capacity to apply pressures to uncooperative owners of land situated along his intended route. Shelby

Lancaster could effectively communicate to a reluctant settler that he placed himself in great peril if Shelby's offers were rejected.

As Shelby's involvement with McLemore's railroad grew, so did his status in the business community.

"The wedding is set for three weeks from this coming Saturday. It'll be at the Robinson home and the Judge and I would be mighty honored if you two would attend this solemn rite," Shelby had told the Cabells as he beamed with unbridled joy.

Catherine had absolutely no knowledge of the blood feud between her husband and Shelby. She was pleased as punch for the happily betrothed couple. She had no inkling that Shelby was her husband's mortal enemy.

"We'd be honored to attend, Shelby. Thank you for asking us to witness this milestone in your life," Catherine courteously responded to his invitation.

Calvin considered his wife's eloquent acceptance and he thought it bordered on overkill. So, he felt justified to ask Catherine, once more, if she would be tolerant . . . and hear just one last pun. She hesitantly agreed to endure one more verbal assault.

"You say this wedding to Clarabelle Robinson is a milestone in his life. I'd say this 'milestone in his life' is more like a 'millstone in his life'. Clarabelle's a burdensome load Shelby will have to wear around his neck for a long, long time."

\* \* \* \* \* \* \* \* \* \* \* \*

There are SOME issues between a husband and a wife that go unspoken. And what didn't need to be said between Calvin and Catherine Cabell was clearly evident to the both of them. Their love life had long ago come to an end – a dead end.

Calvin knew for quite some time that Catherine began to fear relations, because she dreaded getting pregnant. She had lived through three heart-breaking miscarriages since Cassie was born. The experiences only fed her tendency toward melancholy. Catherine was sure another pregnancy was bound to end in still more disappointment and despair. She brooded about the perils of responding to her husband's need for sex. She decided she couldn't live through another failed pregnancy, even if it meant denying her husband what he considered his due.

After a while Calvin recognized her anxieties had grown and evolved . . . into an outright rejection of him. She was disgusted by him and his increasing interest in sex. And she was disgusted at herself for being feebly barren. Increasingly, she was disgusted and shamed with her own morose moodiness. These episodes were happening more frequently and each occurrence seemed darker and lasted longer than the one before.

Calvin wasn't ignorant. He knew she was passing through a rough patch. He was genuinely concerned about her well-being. He was certain she had thought many, many times, "My miserable melancholy makes it impossible for anyone to want to be around me. And, after all, if I can't tolerate living with my despair, how is it possible anyone else can bear to be with me?"

But, over time, Catherine found a source of strength and comfort. And that soothing aid emanated from - to her mind – the unlikeliest person of all. She learned she could rely on Bettie to get through her bleakest days. Bettie seemed to understand . . . as she was becoming evermore devoted to her mistress. She was always prepared to offer comfort.

There was plenty of interaction between a Nineteenth Century wife on the frontier and her house servant. Regardless of each woman's skin color, Catherine and Bettie always had more than enough chores they did together. They were an effective team. Frequently, they joked about their shared sense . . . how each woman often felt tethered to the other.

Catherine grew to appreciate "being joined at the hip to Bettie". She also realized she might tend to sink into one of her "black spells" when she was alone for a period of time. But, with Bettie close by, it seemed slipping down that slope . . . into an emotional tar pit . . . was something that was improbable – sort of like swimming in deep water with a buddy who could keep her partner from going under for the third time.

Bettie, a slave woman, didn't try to cheer up Catherine. That would have been unthinkable demeanor. And she rarely spoke a word, except sentences that redefined her station in the household. "Can I fetch that fer ya, Miz Cabell?" or "We're runnin' low on cornmeal, Miz Cabell."

And when the two women sat on the front porch snapping freshly picked green beans, or shelling Crowder peas, or shucking ears of sweet corn . . . well, those were the quiet times when it seemed Bettie was especially helping Catherine keep her sinking spirits afloat. The only noises one could hear were the soothing sounds of shucking, the snapping, and the shelling. It was bliss. Keeping her hands busy in the company of Bettie seemed to be Catherine's best panacea.

But, just as Catherine knew Bettie's presence held her despondency at bay, Catherine, likewise, knew that somehow the growing rift with her husband was rooted in some secret Calvin was harboring deep inside – one he was afraid for her to know. She could never pin down her theory with fact. She just knew. And, like most women, Catherine trusted her intuition. It was her compass when issues got murky.

And, whatever his secret was, it was growing inside her husband like a wild vine that constricted his thinking and choked out his good nature. The secret was cutting off the sustenance that had nourished their marriage. Whenever she tripped and fell into depression, thinking about Calvin and the demon that lurked inside him only made her malaise fade farther and farther from sanity.

However, there was one day when Bettie's first aid to Catherine led to a remarkable discovery. One stunningly sunny April afternoon, when the children were at school and Calvin was at the mill, Catherine felt the urge to slump forward and hold on to a chair . . . or anything else that would help stabilize her. She felt as if her spirit was free falling inside her mind . . . and her soul . . . and her body was growing limp and listless and ready to collapse on the floor from the oppressive weight of dark forces.

Not wishing for others to acknowledge her dilemma, she shuffled silently to her bed. Before she lay down upon it, she closed the thick window draperies and tucked in both its edges where they met in the middle. She carefully creased the fabric so as to block out every slim, sliver of daylight. When these "black spells" came along, she felt compelled to cocoon herself in an equally black environment. Catherine would have ventured far into the bowels of an eerie, ominous cave, if she thought she could ultimately reach its blackest realm. She was agitated by even the dimmest light . . . or the faintest noise.

About that time Bettie realized Catherine was out of her sight. She wandered throughout the house from room to room . . . all the while softly saying, "You all right, Miz Cabell? . . . Is you all right?"

Hearing these repetitive calls disturbed Catherine more than having shards of sunlight pierce between the drapes. Every time she heard the servant woman call out, Catherine cringed and silently said to herself, "Make that question the last one, Bettie . . . please."

"Miz Cabell, you all right in there?"

Bettie was now calling to Catherine through the bedroom door. She wondered when or if this persistent Negro would give up. She just wanted to be left alone.

"Oh, please, Bettie," Catherine kept repeating to herself. "Make that the last one . . . please. I'm so ashamed . . . and I want to be alone."

Bettie had never spoken of it, but she knew Catherine's secret. She sensed when her mistress felt she was going to lapse into desperate darkness. She knew she had to keep Catherine busy, preoccupied, or anything else that might diminish her consciousness of impending gloom. Yet, Bettie had never spoken about it. Today, however, she knew Catherine had rapidly slipped beyond the barrier. She wasn't about to stand by idly when there was the need for comfort to be administered.

So, Bettie stood near the closed bedroom door and called through the wood barrier, once again. "Miz Cabell, I know you're painin' right now. Let me help you . . . please."

She paused and lowered the volume of her voice so it was just a shade more than a whisper - just barely loud enough to pass through the door. "God bless you, Miz Cabell . . . Jesus'll take care of you. But, is there somethin' I can do fer you?"

Catherine was worn down. She relented. "I'm in here, Bettie. I'm resting. I don't feel very good all of a sudden . . . You can come in and check on me. It's okay."

Slowly the bedroom door creaked open. It was dark as a tomb inside. Bettie could see nothing at first. Then, there she was – lying on her side with her face turned away from the door and burrowed between the pillows. Bettie closed the door without making a sound. She took the liberty of perching herself on the side of the bed . . . inches away from Catherine's back. It seemed to symbolize a wall Catherine wished to partition her from Bettie. She lay on her left side with her hands over her eyes . . . to blind them from any extraneous light.

"Miz Cabell, don't you fret. Ever thing gonna be alright."

"I don't think it will, Bettie. I'm feeling mighty low right about now."

307

"My Mama taught me the touch, Miz Cabell. It's the healin' touch. I think it might help you, Miz Cabell."

There was creepy silence for a few seconds there in the darkness. Eventually, Bettie could hear the rustling of Catherine's petticoats as she began to turn over. No words were spoken. But Catherine placed the palm of her left hand over her lids to shield her eyes . . . while she extended her right hand toward Bettie.

The black slave woman's callous pincers gently grasped her mistress's hand. She placed her thumb on the back side of Catherine's hand and her middle finger made contact with its palm. She gently lowered Catherine's extended hand down on to the bed . . . and then she began her ministrations.

There was no physical movement of Bettie's hand she could discern. But Catherine felt something that only could be described as a soothing, calming, healing energy. It flowed from Bettie into Catherine's fingers . . . and then throughout her body. It eased her aching heart. She lifted the hand from her covered eyes. Then, she turned her head slowly toward Bettie. "Thank you, Bettie . . . You DO seem to have the touch . . . the healing touch . . . I can feel it . . . but, I must rest."

Catherine lay on her back so her head, once again, faced straight up at the ceiling and she raised her left hand to swathe another fleshy protective layer over her shut eyes.

No sound emanated from that room for the longest time. Bettie just kept silently summoning up her "healing touch", so it could be channeled down into Catherine's fingers, her hand, her arm, and . . . so it could ultimately be distributed to every aching nerve. For two hours Bettie sat on that bed applying her gift. No words were uttered. And when Cassie called out . . . announcing she was home from school, Bettie quickly stood and walked to the door. She cracked it just wide enough until she caught Cassie in her sight.

In hushed tones she said, "Miss Cassie . . . you're Mama's in here with me." And with the most soothing tone of voice Cassie ever heard, Bettie reassured the child.

"Ever thing gonna be alright with yo momma. Ever thing gonna be fine, Miss Cassie"

# CHAPTER

# *19*

September 1836

The way Calvin saw things, Catherine's mental malaise and her disregard for his needs would be never-ending. It was a prickly marital gripe . . . about which he never spoke. Nevertheless, he carried on a lively debate with himself about his dilemma. He didn't like the fix he was in . . . and, he wondered if there was anything he could do about it.

Calvin had hoped to sire a family of four or five children. Consequently, it was true he had methodically initiated bedroom encounters to coincide with the monthly cycle when his wife was most fertile. He knew she resented his contrived timing.

He was nobody's fool. He recognized his wife's angst had eventually evolved into anger. And he certainly recognized the suppressed hostility that was seething within her.

Calvin knew about Catherine's desperate bouts with depression - even though he referenced them as her "melancholy episodes". He offered this explanation in the same vein as scholarship in the Dark Ages' . . . which decreed the human condition was governed by the balance of the body's four humors; "choleric", "phlegmatic", "sanguine", and "melancholy".

But like most people of the era, Calvin didn't fully understand Catherine's condition. He simply tolerated it as best he could. Yet, he felt guilty . . . about the sorry state of his marriage and he fretted if the worst mistake in his life might be at the root of her blues. His dreams increasingly evolved into nightmares as he relived tossing Dolly's body into the river or disguising her remains as a carpet on Henry Caldwell's draft horse. And sometimes he lounged in his chair at home and sat up ramrod straight, because he thought the knock he heard at the door was the posse from Kentucky . . . who had

309

finally come to arrest him and haul him back to Harrodsburg to stand trial for murder.

He inevitably broke into a sweat imagining the final scene. In it he was crying while he said goodbye to his children and to Catherine . . . as he was led away in handcuffs and leg irons. He envisioned his family standing incredulous as he was paraded down Monroe Street. Each time he dealt with this irrational apparition, it seemed more real than the last episode. And when Catherine expressed her grave concern about his odd histrionics and asked, "What's the matter, Mr. Cabell?" He offered the same sort of excuse. He told yet another lie.

Nevertheless, Calvin Cabell thought he deserved better. He felt he merited more respect . . . as well as the full support of his wife – at all levels in their marriage. He couldn't cope with these serendipitous sinking spells Catherine went into and, much later, slowly returned to her normal self.

Business was good at the mill and it was inevitable it would get much better. The U.S. Army reached an important decision in 1835 which cemented Memphis' future. It announced the sole military road to be built to Little Rock would begin at Memphis. There would be a phenomenal demand for timber products for the military road as well as for bridges that would be required to traverse the many Arkansas bayous and swamps along the route. It was then Calvin knew he would become very wealthy.

Furthermore, the Army's announcement essentially nailed the coffin shut for the languishing city of Randolph, located forty miles north of Memphis at the mouth of the Hatchie River. Randolph was a formidable commercial foe to Memphis. Its population was larger and its thriving businesses were far more numerous than what Memphis offered to settlers. So, a military road that began across the Mississippi from Memphis quickly precipitated Randolph's demise. The population at Memphis grew substantially as residents of Randolph moved south to the Fourth Chickasaw Bluff.

All of these opportunities to sell lumber kept Calvin busy. But his business demands didn't require him to keep long hours at the mill in the evening. He hung around the office . . . simply because he dreaded the thought of heading home. He wanted to chat over drinks with his mill manager. Thomas Sperling had a family of his own to tend to. But he felt obliged to linger later and later with his boss who never spoke of problems at the Cabell home. But Calvin's actions belied any presumptions that his household was a pleasant and harmonious place.

Only Calvin knew the real reason that explained his long hours, his reluctance to go home, and his hostile moodiness. He had been unable to enjoy a single night of sound slumber in over a month. His nightmares grew more frightening. They always visited him about two hours after falling asleep. And they always were about lies, deceit, murder, and . . . about Dolly.

He didn't know why these haunting episodes occurred . . . night after night. But he had recently begun to think about Dolly's son – who must be fifteen or sixteen now. The boy was a regular participant in these frightful episodes. He cursed Calvin for taking his mother from him. He swore he would hunt him down and bring him to justice. And when Calvin walked those final steps in his dreams to the gallows, the son promised he'd be there at the end . . . to spit on him and remind him he was bound for hell.

But the most upsetting and the most recurring part of these gruesome dreams was something else Dolly's son threatened. He laughed wickedly each night as he dwelled on that ominous Ides of March. Dolly's son said Shelby had poked around after his mother's death and he had come up with evidence from Rebecca, from Mr. Smithson, from Henry Caldwell, from Caldwell's farm manager, and from the two men who encountered Calvin and his mother's corpse on the Lexington Road that foggy night.

Sometime around midnight Calvin would sit up straight in his bed and begin to wail. But his screams were contained, as he soon realized it was all just a dream . . . a miserable, recurring, haunting dream. But it was a dream that was entirely plausible to play out at any time. Shelby had already pointed out that the statutes of limitation didn't apply to murder. And he had seen Dolly argue with him in front of the store.

Over time Calvin increasingly came to believe Shelby did, indeed, have all of this incriminating evidence. There seemed no doubt any jury of his peers would reach a "guilty" verdict.

He rarely could go back to sleep. So, each morning he went to work . . . more exhausted . . . and more irritable . . . than the day before. And at the end of the work day he tried to contain his demons with alcohol – ever more alcohol. He wasn't heeding Governor Shelby's counsel. He was trying to affect change using the same failed methods. It was all a vicious circle. He was living a life that was his own definition of insanity.

Calvin kept some exceptional single malt Scotch whiskey in his office safe. At first he set up glasses at seven o'clock for "after hours chats" with

Sperling. Several weeks later, Calvin "opened the bar" earlier –at about six o'clock. Sperling eventually had to beg to leave. He was certain Calvin didn't depart for his own home until much later.

One evening well before six o'clock, Sperling found Calvin hunched over his desk with a glass of Scotch and water in his right hand. His eyes were glued to the newspaper spread out before him. Sperling had seen Marcus Winchester leave his boss's quarters about thirty minutes earlier. He studied the look on Calvin's face as he examined the print. Calvin seemed just as miserable as Winchester had looked on his way out the door.

"Boss, we're wrapping up operations for the day." Then, Sperling paused to consider just how chummy and bold he should be. "I noticed Mr. Winchester leaving in a fairly glum mood. Now, I see you're looking the same. Is there bad news, boss? Is there something I can do for you?"

Calvin didn't move. He just murmured. "Come on in. Have a seat . . . and pour yourself a drink. I think you might need it."

Sperling began to think of all the possible reasons for his boss's dazed look. The notion of the death of one of Calvin's children or his wife passed through his mind. But that wouldn't be printed in the paper. Maybe it was news from back in Kentucky. But it would be unlikely Marcus Winchester would be the bearer of bad news from the Bluegrass. So, rather than guess wildly at all the gruesome prospects, he concluded he had no choice but to charge on with an inquiry.

"Mr. Cabell, what's going on, sir?"

Calvin looked up from the newspaper and took a slow sip of Scotch. His eyes were the saddest pair Sperling had ever seen. "You know, don't you, that it was Mr. Winchester who introduced me to Congressman Crockett? And I think you also know how much I liked and admired him?"

"Yessir, I know that to be a fact."

"Well, Crockett's dead . . . brutally killed . . . along with everyone else with him. And that includes Jim Bowie, my lumber friend from Arkansas. All were victims of the Mexicans, I'm sorry to say."

Sperling expressed genuine shock. He knew Crockett had gone to Texas to fight against Mexico's claim to the Texas Territory. But Davy Crockett seemed – in his mind, at least – to be tough and wiry. Consequently, he considered himself nearly impervious to injury . . . much less to death.

"Is that what's in the newspaper, Mr. Cabell?"

"Yes, he and everyone else, about fifty men, were killed at San Antonio . . . in a mission they call the Alamo."

"And Jim Bowie's dead, too?"

"Yes, no one survived. It was a massacre."

Sperling's mind quickly cataloged another possible victim. "What about Sam Houston? He's out there in the fight with the Mexicans. What about Governor Houston?"

"He's leading men farther south of the Alamo. Houston's not among the dead."

Sperling knew about Davy Crockett both from his press notices that described this iconoclastic Congressman as well as from the personal stories his boss had recounted to him. "It seems like only yesterday that you and Mr. Winchester . . . and all the others feted Crockett as he headed off to Texas."

"Yes, it was last November. I remember it was the last day of the month. That was quite a memorable evening. Now, I know, I'll cherish my remembrances of that night all the more."

"Would you care to share them with me now, Mr. Cabell? I'd love to hear the details. I find that when a loved one or friend passes on, it's comforting to reminisce about the good times they shared."

"Oh, yes, I could tell you several humorous stories. But, his last night here was special. Crockett spent most of the day wandering about the city . . . visiting with friends. And when word spread he was in town and in rare form . . . even for Crockett . . . well, that set into motion a frenzied night of carousing."

"Tell me what happened . . . if you don't mind."

"A group of Crockett's admirers were drinking and telling tall tales at the Union Hotel when there was a dispute about the bar tab. Davy offered to pay the tab for everyone's drinks. But the crowd would hear nothing of it.

313

Finally, the men decided to move their bacchanal to McCool's place . . . just a short distance away.

"Without any notice, Crockett was hoisted out of his seat at the hotel and placed on to the shoulders of a small band of revelers. He was carried to Neill McCool's saloon as if he were a Roman emperor. Then they lowered him with a thud on to one of the few seats in the place.

"Now mind you, the whiskey was flowing freely. And Crockett had abandoned any political politeness he may have once practiced in Congress. Of course, his critics claimed he rarely showed any signs of diplomacy during his time in Washington."

"So, what happened then, Mr. Cabell? As I heard it, Old Davy gave quite a memorable speech."

"Well, Sperling, I don't know how eloquent it was. But it was memorable, indeed. You know, Crockett served as a Congressman from '27 until last year when he lost his race. His defeat was precipitated largely because he and President Jackson got sideways with one another. Crockett called Jackson, 'King Andrew', and compared Jackson's "imperious nature" to Napoleon, Cromwell, and others of their ilk. Crockett took his defeat hard . . . and, quite personally. He let us know just what he thought about Jackson . . . as well as his former constituents that evening.

"After plenty of drink, Crockett jumped up on to the counter at McCool's wearing a coonskin cap and holding up a vessel of liquor with his right hand . . . as if he were about to offer a toast. A toast it was. But it was intended to scorch those who threw him out of Congress.

"He said, 'My friends, I suppose you're all aware that I was recently a candidate for Congress. I told the voters that if they would elect me, I would serve them to the best of my ability. But, if they did not, they should go to hell . . . and I would go to Texas'.

"Davy upended his glass and drank thirstily from it to the cheers of the crowd. Then he looked at us and offered us his farewell. "He said, 'So, gentlemen . . . as the country no longer needs my services, I'm bound for Texas'."

Calvin held his glass and lifted it toward Sperling. "Mr. Sperling, I'd like to propose a toast."

Sperling raised his glass and he waited for his boss to speak.

"To Congressman David Crockett: He died in a cause he thought was honorable – fighting to defend Texas. May we all die doing what we believe is just."

The two glasses clinked against each other and Scotch whiskey went down smooth as silk. But, that evening was the last time Sperling remembered any justification for a toast during their after business hours' "meetings".

Never again was a swig of whiskey consumed at Calvin's office preceded by a toast. All of the endless alcohol he drank thereafter was solely intended to drown Calvin Cabell's demons. And Calvin Cabell had more demons relentlessly poking at him because of his past than any of Dante's images of hell.

* * * * * * * * * *

Calvin's mill was operating at capacity now that Memphis was finally growing at a rapid clip. There was a strong demand for lumber . . . for houses, as well as for the government's military road to Little Rock. The Tennessee and Mississippi governments were also making investments in their respective transportation infrastructures. Hardwood was in great demand.

There were now twelve covered saw pits. The first shift began sawing at six-thirty in the morning. These workers were replaced by a second crew at noon. They worked until nightfall. Yet, even men strong as oxen couldn't saw continuously for more than two hours without a substantial rest. It was back breaking work.

The supply chain for timber became critical due to a prolonged drought. The Wolf River's water level receded so low that logs couldn't be floated downstream to the mill. As a result Calvin made a decision - a difficult decision that churned inside his gut. He decided to buy timber from a forester who owned property approximately a half mile northeast of the mill. The man's name was Jason Martrell. Calvin's dilemma was the fact that Martrell owned slaves and he used them to do most of the work.

Calvin wrestled mightily with this decision. But he couldn't locate any other feasible suppliers. He had dreaded the day when slavery would impact the way business was done in West Tennessee. That day had finally arrived.

315

Calvin was distressed. He was finally bending his moral resolve . . . just like he had feared.

He hated to see slaves haul timber on to his mill property. His workmen seemed to look uncomfortable when that occurred. Maybe they were expressing their personal distaste about slavery. However, Calvin sometimes feared they were observing the Negroes and wondering, "When will my job be replaced by much less expensive slave labor? They're already doing some of Mr. Cabell's work."

He recalled often swearing righteously he would close down the mill if there was ever the economic need to use slaves instead of employees. But business was booming. While his conscience had been pricked by his quandry, he didn't have the gumption to keep a pledge he had made to himself and his God. There was too much money to be made.

So, Calvin rationalized his reasoning – just like he was beginning to do more and more about his business, his family, his future, and his faith.

"If I shut down the mill, my workers would lose their incomes. Families would be ruined. I've got to weigh their best interests with the consequences of any decision. That's why I'm forced to make this deal with the devil. Surely any reasonable God-fearing person would see things the same way.

"Besides, I've only hired Martrell as a temporary contractor. This man might use slaves he owns, but they're still not MY slaves. Surely, anyone with a grain of sense can see there's a significant difference . . . a huge moral difference."

# CHAPTER

# *20*

October 1836

Calvin never seemed to get around initiating his conversation with Mose – the one that would outline the terms and conditions for his family's eventual freedom. It wasn't that the encounter slipped Calvin's mind. He simply chose . . . time and time again . . . to avoid the subject. But he always carried with him a concern that Mose would suddenly ask him to revisit the discussion that took place during that first discomforting afternoon when Calvin took possession of this black family. But he never did.

There was an uncanny mystery about Mose. And, for Calvin, that enigma sometimes proved to be something of a threat to him. Like most men, Calvin was wary of what he didn't fully understand. And he could never quite figure out Mose.

A part of Calvin's procrastination to discuss his eventual freedom was rooted in the mincing and dicing of his recollections about what he had said that first afternoon. As he recalled - as he often did in the months thereafter – whatever he said to Mose didn't constitute a promise to lay out a specific timetable to gauge when the black family might be freed.

"I remember clear as a bell telling him I didn't know if I would talk to Mose the next day, or the next month, or even the next year about when I might free his family. I even said it might be quite a while before I'd ever talk to him. That's what I said that afternoon, as I remember it. Everyone knows – and that includes Mose and Bettie – when Calvin Cabell makes a promise, you can bank on it being kept. I made no promise."

Calvin replayed this litany so many times in his mind he vividly could recite every word and every nuance of his speech that day in the fall of 1833. Yet, Calvin constantly felt guilt ridden he never followed through. There had been several times – actually, many times – when he could have and probably should have broached the subject with Mose. But he weaseled away from it . . . time and time again.

Two Christmas Eves ago, for example, he and Catherine gave the two Negroes a ham as a present. Calvin arrived at the slave cabin by himself. He was sitting in front of the fireplace of the one-room shelter in the arm chair which was, otherwise, Mose's proprietary seat. Catherine said she was going to follow after him and carry the ham. But, somehow, she got delayed.

While he waited, Calvin lectured to his Negroes about the season of Christmas. He said the Yuletide represented a season of hope and peace for the world. It was insipid talk . . . and he knew it. But he always felt the compulsion to blabber on . . . just to fill in any silence that lasted more than a few seconds.

Mose listened to Calvin with both an air of anticipation and expectation. Calvin recognized from the look in his eyes that Mose thought the plan for HIS freedom would be laid out right there and then. The black man reasoned Calvin's soliloquy . . . about Christmas joy . . . was the perfect prelude for him to build up to that glorious moment when his master would issue his long awaited pronouncement of freedom.

But Calvin just couldn't bring himself to broach the issue. "That would have been the perfect time to have had that discussion," He later reflected about the situation. "But Bettie was there. And Jed was there, as well. And Mose looked at me like he was saying to himself, 'Lord Jesus, Master Cabell gonna give us our freedom dis Christmas'" I could read his mind just as if I might have pried open his skull and looked inside.

"But I wasn't going to give these servants their freedom right then and there. They should have known better. And then . . . when Catherine walked in with the ham after what seemed like hours of uncomfortable waiting . . . I just wanted to toss that ham at them and run."

The fact of the matter was simple. Calvin couldn't firm up in his own mind what sorts of terms and conditions should apply to freeing these folks. He and Catherine were more than pleased with their servants' performance . . . and how well they, quite surprisingly, blended into the fabric of the Cabell family. Sometimes Calvin even deluded himself into thinking these people were, indeed, already freed. They were just sticking around the place and going about their duties out of a sense of devotion and admiration for the Cabells.

It was easy – even comforting – to think such thoughts. But they weren't true . . . and Calvin knew it. The only truth about these black people's lives was that, day after day, every one of them got up before dawn every morning. Then, each worked until evening – except on the Sabbath – when everyone relaxed after the church service.

On Sundays, Jamie or Cassie took on Bettie's chore of disposing the contents of the family's chamber pots. Sunday was the only taste of freedom Mose and Bettie ever knew. Yet, they always were conscious about the cloud of bondage that hovered over every Negro they knew. They were keenly aware on Sunday that . . . come the next rising sun . . . their twenty-four hour "taste of freedom" was over . . . and the nub of their existence would soon commence for six more long days and nights.

Calvin couldn't get out of his mind one particular incident several months ago. It caused him to consider whether or not he would ever emancipate his Negroes.

One Sunday afternoon he was walking to the shed to fetch a bridle that needed mending. The sound of his footsteps treading on the yard's soft turf was naturally muted. And the ordinary noise of walking was hushed even more by the rustling sounds of leaves fluttering in the gentle summer wind.

As he rounded the corner of the servant quarters, Calvin noticed Mose sitting in his prized wood chair. During the winter he sat on it while absorbing the warmth of the fire. And when the weather turned balmy, he brought it outdoors so he could soak in the heat from the sun. That afternoon Mose had situated his chair so the top of its back frame rested against the side of his cabin wall. Its two front legs were reared up, so Mose could comfortably settle back in a reclining position.

Calvin realized Mose didn't hear him approaching and for some unknown reason he paused. He saw something odd. The seconds of his silent, anonymous observation ticked on. He came ever-so-close to speaking up and greeting Mose. But what had caught his eye was so curious . . . his gaze lingered on.

Mose held an open book in his hands as his elbows rested on the chair's wooden arms. It was the Bible Catherine had given to Bettie on Easter Sunday. Bettie had made a comment about how righteous all the white folks appeared when they walked into the church clutching a Bible in their hands. That sparked an idea in Catherine's mind.

319

"Somethin' 'bout that sight, Miz Cabell, makes them white folks appear 'specially sanctified . . . and reverent. You know what I mean, Miz Cabell? It makes me think the dear departed souls must surely be totin' a Bible in their hands when they step up to them Pearly Gates. How else is St. Peter gonna know who was church goin' folks and who wasn't? Seems to me dat Bible in their hands gonna be a sure-fire signal tellin' the gate keeper those who's been saved and those who ain't. Don't you think so, Miz Cabell?"

So, just after the Easter sunrise service – which was always attended by both white folks and darkies alike – Catherine presented Bettie the Bible that had belonged to her spinster aunt. Resting on the Bible was a basket containing her signature Easter treat. Catherine had baked her traditional Easter morning pastry which she called "resurrection buns". They were square shaped rolls with cinnamon swirls inside. The top of each bun was iced with a brown sugar confection and on that dark backdrop Catherine and Cassie emblazoned two broad swipes of white icing in the shape of a cross. Bettie was overjoyed. From that Sunday morning on, she proudly carried the Bible to and from church. It was the most precious gift she had ever received.

When Calvin saw Mose leaning against the cabin wall, his first thought was reasoned. He remembered Bettie might be the one who carried that Bible into and out of the church, but he had often observed it was Mose who controlled the book during the service. As he watched Mose, Calvin puffed up with vain pride as, he first thought, "What a sight. Look at Mose thumbing through the Bible's pages. He's happy to just imagine what the Holy Word might be saying to those who can read. Bless his heart. I'll have to tell Mrs. Cabell about this. She'll be pleased, all over again, she gave Bettie her aunt's Bible."

But Calvin observed there was something peculiar about the way Mose was looking at the Bible. It prompted his master to continue monitoring his slave.

Mose wasn't just meandering through the text like a blind man wondering what parables were on what page in the New Testament and what Psalms lay sequestered in the thicker section of the Old Testament. Mose glared with apparent comprehension at a single page while his focus was drawn lower and lower. Then he gently turned the paper leaf over . . . and, once again . . . he appeared to focus on what was printed on the upper right hand corner of the next page.

In fact, Mose was so immersed in whatever he was observing, he was oblivious to Calvin's presence. What was occurring seemed obvious . . . and

Calvin reached this conclusion silently in his mind. He thought to himself, "Mose can read. I don't believe it, but Mose can read. I'm sure of it."

Reverend Rice back in Danville bullied his liberal proposals through the Kentucky Synod that required Presbyterian masters to give their slaves at least the crude basics of an education. But most slave owners in Kentucky forbade their slaves from learning to read. Knowledge was power . . . and reading was at the core of knowledge.

That was pretty much the same doctrine applicable to each and every slave in Shelby County, Tennessee so far as Calvin knew. White folks thought slaves MUST be kept illiterate. The danger of another uprising like Nat Turner was always lurking in their consciousness. A slave who could read was a danger to the entire agricultural society.

After all, Frances Wright's goal was to provide her indentured slaves an education. That was one of the primary concerns of her farmer neighbors – as well as all the other planters in the region. That's why they shunned her.

"But how did Mose do it?" Calvin considered. "How did Mose learn to read?"

This was a perplexing conundrum. "Surely Mercer Watkins would have mentioned literacy as one of Mose's skills when he talked me into buying his family. So 'when' . . . and 'how' . . . did this remarkable achievement come about?"

Calvin was stumped as he continued to surreptitiously marvel at the sight. He ever-so-gently stepped backward . . . like a panther secretly retreating, so as not to alarm its prey. He didn't want Mose to know he was watching. He withdrew far enough that his presence could no longer be seen. He was certain his spying had gone unnoticed. But it was a close call.

"Daddy . . . come on, Daddy. You promised a carriage ride this afternoon. You said we could go see the Creek Indians camped along the river."

It was Cassie. And it would be clear to anyone that Cassie was addressing her father . . . who was standing just out of Mose's sight. He had to think fast. Should he place his index finger to his lips and mutely mimic a "shhh" at Cassie? Or, should he pretend he was simply making his way to the shed . . . and he had only progressed this far? He chose the latter . . . and Calvin took a few strides forward . . . to where he earlier had stood.

He whipped his head in Mose's direction . . . so as to pretend he unexpectedly caught sight of him out of his peripheral vision. The black man was still seated in the chair . . . and the chair still reared up against the cabin. But the Bible now lay in his lap . . . closed.

"Mose, is that bridle needing repair still in the shed? I thought Jamie and I would work on it this evening on the front porch."

Yessuh, Mr. Cabell, it's hangin' from the rafter at the rear of the shed."

"Thanks, Mose . . . I see you're out here enjoying the mild weather . . . and I see you've got Bettie's Easter Bible, too."

"Yessuh."

Mose was a man of few words . . . and Calvin wanted somehow to broach the subject of the sight he'd been studying. But he couldn't think of a conversational link to make the connection . . . without admitting he'd been secretly scrutinizing Mose's competence at reading the Bible. He mulled over all the potential first sentences he could craft to bring up the subject. Nothing worked. But he was determined to charge ahead.

"Mose, just before Cassie was calling to me I had walked beyond the corner of your cabin . . . far enough that I could see you. Then, when Cassie spoke I moved out of sight . . . without you knowing I had rounded the turn."

Mose knew Calvin was minimizing what he saw and he also knew what was coming next.

"You know, Mose, back in Danville our church members abided by a denominational directive. It stated every church member who owned slaves would ensure they could read and write . . . as well as do some basic mathematics. While I didn't own slaves at the time, I thought it was an enlightened way of addressing the education black folks are going to need one day."

By this time Mose stood up and he was walking toward his master. He postured himself in his typical manner – standing erect and respectful. He was holding the Bible in his left hand. But, as was always the case, he played the part of a slave who was exceedingly docile. He didn't offer any response. That would only invite his master to shift his inquiring monologue into the realm of a dialogue between the two men.

Cassie was still standing on the porch and she was impetuously eager to get going. What she had called out was true. Her father had promised her a ride to view the Creeks . . . and Calvin Cabell was a man who always kept his promises.

"I'll be ready to go in five minutes, Cassie. Find Jamie. I know he wants to go with us. I want you two to see for yourselves the way our government's treating this Indian tribe. It's just sinful to abuse human beings that way." Then he walked back toward the porch while he continued his comments.

"It's just sinful to abuse human beings like our government's doing. You can't call it anything but 'sinful'. It's nothing, but sinful."

Mose couldn't believe his master was telling his children that moving Indians off their ancestral land was a serious sin, when the same government . . . as well as Mr. John Calvin Cabell . . . condoned humans being bought and sold if their skin favored an ebony hue.

He shook his head in disbelief and then opened the Bible again. He thumbed through its pages until he reached the passage he was looking for . . . in St. Matthew.

"Blessed are those who hunger and thirst for righteousness, for they will be filled."

*No Coin for Charon*

# CHAPTER
# 21

November 1836

Something dark and despondent often seemed to be brewing within Jamie Cabell. Everybody who knew the youngster at one time or another wondered what disturbing thought had recently taken root and was growing down deep in his soul.

Catherine increasingly became more and more concerned about him. She tried her best to conceal her own malevolent moodiness from family and friends. But Jamie had a sixth sense. He knew his mother's shame. And he knew his father had a secret, too. He didn't know, yet, what it was. But, eventually, he was certain it would be revealed to him.

Jamie's intuitiveness was especially attuned to sensing the soft, dark underbelly of those around him. He disregarded the positive, joyous moments in people's lives. He only absorbed and fed on their anxious moods and furtive fears.

Catherine's concern about Jamie was magnified by a sense of guilt. She was frightened it was she who had passed on to Jamie her dark hereditary legacy of melancholy as a family trait – like Calvin passed on blue eyes to Jamie and she passed along large brown doe eyes to Cassie. The longer she considered this perverse theory, the more volatile her own emotions became. She constantly dreaded if another of her mood swings lurked with the next full moon . . . or sooner. She feared that Jamie might one day be incapacitated by the same dark curse which constantly haunted her. That would be the cruelest fate of all.

"The problem with Jamie," Calvin often told Catherine, "is I fear he's exceptionally bright – too bright for his own good."

Jamie excelled at his school subjects and he voraciously read all sorts of fiction and non-fiction genres. Perhaps it's the human condition that for every blessing there's a curse. And, in Jamie's case, intellect was certainly offset by the curse of his keen perception about the dark side of humanity.

Cassie was one of only two individuals who managed to occasionally fling open the doors to the cobweb-filled closet located within Jamie's brilliant mind. It was she who could command his dark spirits to escape and fly away . . . at least, for awhile.

She could lovingly nudge him toward a brighter outlook. "Just open yourself up. Allow some sunshine into your life, Jamie. Sunlight has an amazing capacity to cleanse and clear what's clogged up inside your heart."

Cassie was exceedingly bright, too. But every adversity that came her way, she let slide effortlessly off her back . . . like water rolling off the roof. Jamie envied her optimistic temperament. But he didn't covet it enough to adopt her positive point of view.

When Jamie was just fourteen, Calvin decided his son needed to be put through a Spartan training regimen at the mill. He thought if Jamie was going to be the heir apparent to his prospering business and ascend one day to Calvin's august stature in the community, he needed to show his father and others he was worthy.

Calvin considered it was his paternal obligation to cultivate and prune his son into his own model of an ideal man. From his perspective, it would take considerable time and a lot of work to whip Jamie into shape. Calvin thought he was weak and needed to be toughened up.

He put the boy to work in a saw pit and paired him with one of his most prodigious workmen. It was cruel. Jamie was still developing his physical power. He was no match for his partner's productivity. Jamie did his best to replicate his oversized saw partner's capacity to cut through endless stacks of wood and to never tire. He perceived this assignment was a planned, personal humiliation his misguided father devised to shape him up - to toughen him to suit Calvin's standards. He knew he would have to endure. And he did.

Jamie stuck to his task and stood tall under the circumstances. He stayed in the saw pit for hours while he lugged his end of the saw downward . . . and then grunted to push the saw's teeth upward once again . . . only to begin the routine over and over. Sawdust fell like splintered raindrops and stuck on the moisture of his upturned eyes. They filled up with tears. But these pools of tears were merely the body's natural defense to protect his eyes from the invasion of extraneous materials. Jamie shed no tears because of the degrading ordeal. God made it his lot in life to be Calvin Cabell's son. And he was determined to prove – if only to himself - he had the gumption to fulfill that destiny and do it with dignity.

But the experience had its effect – yet, not the effect Calvin had intended. Jamie's labor enabled the boss' son to gain great respect from the mill workers. But, in the process, his father lost a measure of esteem from his men.

Increasingly, Jamie was drawn to another serious, somber person – someone whose nature was more similar to his own. He was an individual who seemed to share Jamie's intellect, his perspective about life, and his contempt for the way the world was. He was a man who appeared to trudge through each black day knowing that the morning would surely bring with it the same malaise as the day before. That person was Mose.

Calvin eventually recognized his plan for Jamie to labor at the mill was ill conceived. Yet, he remained convinced Jamie needed work experiences where he would use his hands instead of his intellect.

That summer Mose began to work almost full time at Valley View and Jamie spent much of his time working on projects with him. The two were born into wildly divergent statuses in life. But when they labored together, they took on traits of the best team of mules that ever pulled a plow.

When Calvin first brought the three Negroes home, he and Catherine decided the small kitchen building behind the house was the only available place for them to live. Fortunately, it was December and they had already "fired up" the Cabells' inside wood stove for the winter. The kitchen in the out building was largely abandoned until spring. So Mose, Bettie, and Jed called it "home" and they used the summer kitchen's fireplace to keep warm.

During that time Calvin instructed Mose to build a small addition on to the north side of the kitchen building. It would be his family's quarters. The room's dimensions measured ten by twenty feet.  It was during this construction project that Jamie first became fond of Mose. After school and on Saturdays Jamie ably assisted him. "Jamie's like my carpenter's apprentice," as Mose would say.

Calvin was so pleased with Mose's carpentry skills, he directed him to move out to Valley View and enlarge the kitchen building there. The main house at

Valley View was built of logs. While its exterior walls looked much like the wood and chink layered sides of a rustic log cabin, no one could ever mistake the Cabell place for a cabin. The house was shy of being what one might call "grand". Yet, it also exceeded what anyone would consider "humble."

* * * * * * * * * * *

After three weeks of Jamie's tenure in the saw pits, Calvin dispatched his son to assist Mose at Valley View.

During that summer, he and Jamie spent many days building a smokehouse, a barn, and hundreds of yards of split rail fences. The pair bonded so well that little conversation took place while they worked. There was no need to give instructions or chatter on the job. Each knew what the other was thinking without the burdensome need for spoken words.

Mose remained the more reticent of the two. His wisdom was deeply imbedded and muted. He knew far more than what he said. If Jamie wanted Mose to impart to him some insight or information, he approached the black man . . . "like I was posing a question to the Oracle at Delphi".

And, like the Oracle, Mose's responses tended to be oblique – offering only tiny pieces to complete a complicated jigsaw puzzle.

One of the questions on Jamie's mind concerned the extent of Mose's literacy. During a break from splitting wood for fence rails, Jamie sat with Mose in the shade of a willow oak tree. Jamie purposefully held an open newspaper in his hands and began to read the front page. He noticed Mose paying attention to its headlines.

"Mose, my Daddy says he thinks you can read. I think he's shy about asking you directly about it. But I'm not bashful at all. So I'm asking you now, Mose. How much of this paper can you read? I'm certain you can read some of it"

Mose at first looked away. Then he turned to face Jamie and curled up his lips into the semblance of a sly smile. The black man had little in life to smile about and Mose didn't smile at anybody else but Jamie . . . and that occurred only when the two were completely alone.

"Well, Jamie, I'll tell you this . . . and no one else is to hear about it – 'specially your Daddy."

Jamie nodded affirmatively to pledge his confidentiality.

"I suppose I can make out a lot of words on that page. But I need lots and lots of practice 'fore I could tell you I can truly read. 'Bout the only thing I got to read at all is that Bible your mother give to Bettie. It's that Bible that taught me how to read."

"Did somebody give you some lessons? Surely you didn't just pick up that Bible and start reading it chapter and verse . . . like one of Jesus' miracles."

"Nope, nobody give me no lessons." Then, Mose quickly reconciled the accuracy of what he had just said. "Well, if I had a teacher, I guess it was the preacher . . . Reverend Blair."

"You're telling me Reverend Blair helped you learn to read?"

"Well, Master Jamie, he helped me. But he never give me no lessons. I just picked readin' up from him while I'm sittin' up there in the church balcony."

Jamie still didn't understand. So he persisted. "You're gonna have to spell it out for me, Mose. How did Reverend Blair help you to read?"

"At first I couldn't follow along the printin' I was seeing in the Bible . . . with the words Reverend Blair was sayin'. But I listened hard – real hard – to each word he was readin' . . . from the Old Testament and the New Testament, too. I put ever one of those words into my head – ever single one. Then I'd come home after church and I'd open up that Bible to the passages he said he was readin' from. I didn't recall ever last one of his words, but I remembered enough so I could pick out a buncha the written words that matched what I remembered him sayin'."

Jamie could comprehend Mose's line of reasoning. But one question needed to be answered. "I don't follow you, Mose. How did you find the exact passage in Bettie's Bible to match what the preacher read?

"Well now, Jamie. I thought you was a smarter feller than this. You know the preacher announces where in the Bible he's gonna be readin'. So, I learned what each book of the Bible looked like in print. Don't you see? When he says, 'The Old Testament reading today comes from the book of Chronicles beginning at Chapter 3, verse 10' . . . then it's not too hard to flip through those pages 'til I come to that very spot."

Mose feigned a looked of being insulted. "You know, Jamie, even Negroes can count. So after I learned what Chronicles looked like, don't you think even an ignorant darkie like me could count out the chapters and the verse to get to the start of the passage? How dumb you think I am, boy?"

Jamie was embarrassed on two counts. Not only should he have figured out on his own that it's easy to know where the preacher begins his lectionary text, but he was humiliated he might have unintentionally insulted his friend.

He had a blush to his face when he tried to make amends. "Of course I don't think you're an ignorant fool, Mose. I'm the one who's acted foolish. So, you matched up Reverend Blair's readings with the printed text, huh?"

"Well, there's more to it than that. There's all those things we say every Sunday – things like the Lord's Prayer and the Apostles Creed. All those are in the Bible. And don't forget the words to the hymns we sing over and over."

"Amazing, Mose, you're amazing."

"Yep, and that word 'amazing' you just said . . . well, I learned it from singin' 'Amazing Grace'. I got lots a reading practice from just learnin' the Lord's Prayer. Did you know, Jamie, that prayer is part of Jesus' Sermon on the Mount? It's written down in St. Matthew. So is those Beatitudes. You know, all those 'It's blessed to do this' and 'It's blessed to do that'."

"Yes, Mose, I DID know the Lord's Prayer was part of the Sermon on the Mount."

"Then I put to my memory the 23$^{rd}$ and the 100$^{th}$ Psalm . . . and I read these passages over and over 'til I learned what ever last one of those words looked like. If a man takes his time matchin' what he hears to what's printed, then a body can set up his own dictionary . . . up in his head. And, that's what I did."

"The Lord is my shepherd. I shall not want," Jamie repeated the Psalm out loud so he could better understand Mose's lesson plan. "Our Father, Who art in heaven, hallowed be Thy name."

Jamie was counting the verbs, the nouns, and the adjectives in each of these Biblical passages. He could see how there might be a treasure trove of useful words one could claim as his own. "So, you CAN read . . . and you've been hiding that from all of us all this time."

Then Jamie mustered up a look of stern scolding. "You're nothing but a 'sneak', Mose. You're a low-down 'sneak'."

The two enjoyed a wicked laugh together. Then, Mose began to rise up off the moist grass.

"Let's get back on the job, Master Jamie. Our break time's long over and I'm worn down 'splaining to you how to read. Remember, I'm a slave. I ain't no white boy, like you. I gots plenty of work to do around here . . . and I best be gettin' to it."

# CHAPTER

# 22

December 1836

Calvin and Catherine decided at the end of 1835 to build a much larger house. Ten years had passed since he began to persuade her to relocate along the Mississippi. The new house was designed to better accommodate the Cabells – including Mose's family. But Calvin was planning the house to be, in large part, a testament to his wealth and status in the community.

He purchased two large lots known by street address as 425 Adams. Its frontage along Adams was two hundred feet and its depth was one hundred seventy-five feet. The lot afforded plenty of room for the main house, a respectable cabin for Mose's family, a hen house, a carriage house, and a handsome looking stable for the Cabells' four horses.

After the plans and specifications were drafted, construction began in March of '36 and the family planned to reside there before Christmas.

Calvin wanted a grand home, yet one which didn't appear to be ostentatious. It had a red brick exterior and at both corners along the front of the house there was a tall, round turret . . . capped with a pointed, metal dome.

Catherine requested for the house to have as many large windows as possible. She and Bettie had noticed a pattern. They reasoned her melancholy episodes might be triggered when her exposure to sunlight was marginal. It was just a hunch based on their recognition that her "spells" occurred more often during the short days of winter. But if the home could be laid out to let in lots of sunshine, there could be no harm experimenting if increased exposure helped stabilize her temperament.

Accordingly, Catherine's sitting room was planned on the second floor at the southwest corner of the home. That was at the rear corner of the house where the winter sun loomed low over the horizon and it would shine directly into her room.

The master bedroom was situated at the northwest corner of the house. It was connected to the sitting room by traversing through three large closets used for all sorts of storage. The reference to a "sitting room" and the "master bedroom" belied the uses intended for them. Everyone in the household knew Calvin was the sole occupant of the master bedroom while Catherine, on the other hand, resided each day AND night in the "sitting room".

There were three additional bedrooms upstairs with a wide hallway passing in front of their doors. Jamie would soon go away to college, but Catherine wanted him to have a room he could call his own. "Perhaps," she thought, "this large room might be an inducement to lure him home to live when he graduates college."

Privately, however, Cassie and her mother believed Jamie would never return to Memphis – especially if he had to work for his father.

Downstairs there was a spacious grand foyer stretching from the front door to the wide staircase that arose twelve steps until one reached a broad landing. From the landing there were two parallel sets of stairways to continue the climb. Both led to the second floor hallway.

Situated above the landing there was a large stained glass window Calvin had commissioned. It channeled both summer and winter light through its panes. The window featured an imposing, beautiful angel wearing bright, white raiment. Her two hands were held forward in an intriguing – almost seductive - manner. Cassie remarked that the angel seemed to be beckoning, "Come and let me wrap my arms around you and give you comfort." Geometric designs bordered the angel's field. Everyone thought it was very impressive. The window was a true work of art. It illustrated the owner of the house, most certainly, had lots of money, but he also harbored a hearty dose of refined culture.

On the right of the grand foyer was the parlor. It was connected by a hallway to the library. Its walls were covered by shelves displaying shining leather books that glistened . . . even when the sun had almost disappeared for the night.

At the left of the grand foyer was the music room furnished with a fine piano and a gold harp that leaned precariously on its staff in the corner. Behind the music room, was the large family dining room . . . capable of comfortably seating twelve guests. Then, as one crossed the back of the house, there was the kitchen, an alcove for the servants to eat, and farther beyond there was a sizeable pantry and larder.

Calvin demanded that the interior of the house would exhibit the finest wood moldings, floors, window sills, and other wooden accoutrements which – in their entirety – made a clear statement to visitors that a lumberman of great renown resided within.

Mose, Bettie, and Jed, who was now nine years old, were also thrilled with their new home. Its only disadvantage was the fact the south wall of their cabin adjoined the alleyway behind the lot. This meant there was no place on the property where their presence could be sequestered from view by someone in the house. While they were grateful for the well landscaped and fastidiously maintained grounds in front of the cabin, they knew they were going to miss the opportunity to enjoy some solitude and privacy.

Their new quarters had outside walls covered with wooden clapboards and the interior walls were genuine plaster. There were three wood steps to climb to reach their door. On the inside there were wide, oak plank floors that shined from repeated waxing. A fireplace was situated at one end and a table and three chairs were located at the opposite side. Behind the front room there was one small room for sleeping and Calvin included into the design a lagniappe feature. He had a wood ladder built in the large room that climbed to a small loft. Jed was delighted having "my own secret hideout".

Mose and Bettie considered themselves blessed when they were bought by Mr. Cabell. Sometimes one of them would recall those nervous days of wondering who would be their new owner.

"Bettie, you seen Mr. Watkins at the church last week, didn't ya? My, oh my, how pained he looked – just like somebody done sucked out his blood and put turpentine in its place. Why, I don't think the man's gonna make it through another Christmas. He looks turrible – just turrible. I can't imagine the load he's a bearin'."

Mose often reflected on the past as he glanced at his new place. "We could've just as easy wound up livin' in a tar paper shack in the middle of a cotton field . . . where the cold winter air swept inside right through the slats. We're blessed, Miss Bettie. We're doubly blessed. And we sure don't deserve nothing like this. Praise the Lord."

\* \* \* \* \* \* \* \* \* \* \* \*

335

As the Cabell family became prosperous, each member began to lead a life that was more isolated from the others. Jamie was eager for the day he would leave home and go to college. Cassie followed the regimen of a typical school girl. Their parents' lives, likewise, continued the sad progression of drifting apart. Each member of the family had settled into his or her own respective routine.

Jamie was very bright and quite advanced in his learning, but during his last year at Mr. Magevney's school, he became lax and lazy. Mr. Magevney encouraged him to redeem his growing reputation for sloth by reading well over two dozen of the classics he recommended. Jamie was fascinated by these works of literature and the academic experience whetted his appetite for his upcoming college curriculum.

Cassie, now fourteen, was budding into a beautiful young girl. She may have inherited her mother's brown doe eyes, but she clearly didn't inherit any of her mother's melancholy. Her auburn colored, curly hair framed a pair of sparkling eyes and a heart-melting smile. Cassie had a small group of close friends and a far wider spectrum of acquaintances. Everyone seemed to adore her for her outgoing, rambunctious energy. Where there was fun, Cassie was likely to be found at the center of it.

Calvin was now thirty-seven. Most Memphians considered him to be the quintessential example of a man who managed to "have it all". He was distinguished looking with just a few gray flecks speckled in his hair.

For the past two years he had sported long sideburns with a thin, trimmed beard that ran along his jaw lines . . . then merged with his chin where it was set off with a miniature goatee. Shortly thereafter, he added a mustache to his sartorial appearance. What was once an almost rakish face had dimmed . . . and settled into middle-age convention.

He still was a handsome man. But the glimmer of his enthusiasm . . . about himself and his circumstances . . . was fading. He gave off a discernible air of disappointment. His youthful vitality had evaporated as the years progressed.

Nevertheless, beneath this middle aged veneer, Calvin still considered himself to be a very healthy man - still in the prime of his life. And THAT, he thought, was the problem. "Things aren't always what they seem to be . . . and that surely is the case with me. If they only knew. If they only knew."

Memphis had always been a fairly rough and tumble town. Flatboat men described themselves as "half horse and half alligator." The river traffic of flatboats had swelled in recent years. Now, there were thousands of rafts that floated down to New Orleans each year. At any given evening during the warmer months one could expect to see between one hundred and five hundred rafts residing temporarily at the wharf.

There was increasing civic concern about their arrival *en mass* for two reasons. First, they refused to pay any wharf fees for the privilege of taking up space within the city's primary asset – its port capabilities. Second, when they came to town, drunken brawls sprang up everywhere and ordinary citizens often felt their safety was being endangered.

But the class of people who were most reviled were the gamblers who set up shop wherever there were drunken fools to prey upon. Actually, it was semantically incorrect to refer to these charlatans as "gamblers". Those men they lured into their card games never had a "chance" at winning. They were "con artists" who illicitly rigged the playing field in their favor.

These swindlers were generally despised by the solid citizens of every river town. But in the summer of 1835, the residents of Vicksburg expressed their disgust with gamblers in a manner that was quite shocking to their colleagues in crime. The people of Vicksburg held a hasty tribunal and hung to death five of them before a cheering throng.

These executions promoted a mass evacuation of the scoundrels plying this profession. They soon scattered – mostly up the river - to Memphis. However, Memphians were determined they wouldn't operate within their city limits. So the scalawags set up shop across the Mississippi River in a town known as Hopefield, Arkansas. Hundreds of years earlier the Spanish built a settlement there. They named it "Esperanza." It means "hope". It was a most appropriate name . . . as one must be fortified with a stout sense of hope just to live there – on low land that is subject to flooding by the Mississippi. The most notorious of the buildings these bandits built was the Pedraza Hotel. The place was ramshackle and its clientele was rough. It was infested with thieves and whores.

Calvin, like all up-standing men in Memphis, knew what went on in the buildings near Foy's Point, Arkansas. He sometimes even daydreamed of sampling the vices Hopefield had to offer . . . until the reality of his life set in. An elder in the Presbyterian Church of Memphis would be publicly shamed into ignominy if he ever patronized such an establishment. Yes, he would be shamed . . . IF he got caught. Nevertheless, Calvin's physical and emotional frustrations made his imagined pleasures at Hopefield increasingly tempting. Ironically, even the slim chance of being recognized there only served as spice to his daydreams about finally committing the carnal sin – enjoying an uninhibited romp with the women who made the Pedraza their residence.

Yet, the close proximity and the lures of the flesh at the Pedraza didn't mean Memphis was left devoid of either gambling or loose women. Bordellos operated within houses in the town until they were eventually raided. Inevitably, they closed down and soon sprouted again nearby. The Chelsea area to the northeast of the city was a neighborhood where these houses were less likely to be of much concern to anyone. Consequently, Chelsea became the recognized haven for prostitution.

Most people considered the vices within Chelsea to be essentially harmless - so long as these women didn't show their faces in town. Woe would befall those who did. The sanctimonious citizenry of Memphis wouldn't stand for it. One particular foray into town by these ladies of the night illustrated the townspeople's resolve.

Late one afternoon in November, Calvin spotted a fine carriage parading up and down the streets of the city. Enjoying the horse drawn jaunt were two drunken men, each with their arms snuggled around the necks of two flashy, loose women. These "painted ladies" behaved both loud and loutish. Decent folks were disgusted. Then, someone had an idea.

Fire was a constant threat to towns on the frontier. Bucket brigades were the most efficient means to fight them. But a brigade's efforts were usually too little and too late to quell a blaze. However, technology to put out house fires had advanced, just as the technology of steamboats had revolutionized river traffic.

In 1834, a horde of curious citizens showed up along the riverbank to catch a glimpse of a fire fighting device that had just arrived by steamer from Cincinnati. It was a crude pump designed to suck up and hurl arcs of water directly into the center of a fire. This device was affectionately known as "Little Vigor". Memphians were thrilled it had arrived, because virtually everyone had a vested interest in its promised firefighting capabilities.

After the bawdy passengers in the carriage paraded up and down Main Street several times, someone had a bright idea. "Little Vigor" could be put to work in another community minded manner. It could fight more than fires. It could fight vice.

338

As the carriage crossed the intersection of Main and Poplar for the fourth time, "Little Vigor" took aim at the vehicle's passengers with one intended goal – to extinguish their vile language and to wash away the women's tawdry makeup. The intent was to express the disgust of peace loving citizens as well as to encourage these painted ladies to quickly retreat back to Chelsea – never to be seen in Memphis again. Two men fortified "Little Vigor's" water lode with boot black and soap suds and the machine hit its target with perfect accuracy. The stream of polluted water surged through the air and landed smack dab on all four of the carriage occupants. The onlookers laughed uncontrollably as they witnessed the hilarious harassment of these rowdies.

The two painted women were particularly amusing as they screamed for mercy . . . all the while dodging the constant surge of liquid. The deed was done in just a few seconds. The black liveryman roused the horses with a crack of his whip. Soon the carriage passengers' loud cussing at the bystanders faded away. One could only hear the gleeful crowd congratulating themselves because "Little Vigor" proved it had multiple civic uses.

Nevertheless, the spectacle these two men and two women presented was titillating bait for a big fish like Calvin, who observed the women in the carriage and found them to be far more inviting than they were iniquitous.

"I wish I could muster the gumption to go out to Chelsea and engage in some much deprived love making," Calvin thought at the time. "A roll in the hay with either of them would be utter joy." Eventually, he returned to his senses. "But I don't have the nerve to risk being caught and exposed as a cad to my family and to the members of my church."

As the days wore on after "Little Vigor's Revenge", as folks called it, Calvin replayed over and over in his mind what he had seen that day. He began to evaluate the risks versus the rewards of making a trip to Chelsea.

He also imagined what a trip to the Pedraza might be like. After all, Foy's Point was farther away and more remote than Chelsea. But Calvin seemed certain he would be spied there, too. "With my luck, I'd probably be caught by another Elder of the church.

"I wonder what it would be like - me running into Paul Claxton right there in the second floor hallway of the Pedraza? I'm sure we'd both be mortified at the encounter? What would each of us say?"

Then Calvin appropriated his skill to rationalize problems away from the zones of reasonable concern. "But then, there's a good chance we'd both break out laughing, latch on to two sultry ladies, and head to the bar squiring both bawdy babes on our arms."

The prospect of such an unlikely vision provoked him to laugh out loud. The temptation grew . . . as well as his "death wish" - the act of being caught and publicly exposed as a rogue and shameless lothario. On one hand, it made no sense he would relish both these dissimilar outcomes. However, only Calvin Cabell could reason that, regardless which fate he might face, he would, at least, know he was still alive – that he was still a red-blooded man. For many months, he hadn't felt as if there was much of a spirit dwelling in his soul anymore. He felt lonely and disheartened.

Calvin knew if he continued to fantasize about experimenting with the seedy underbelly of life, he'd eventually act on the impulse. He felt certain the opportunity would eventually arise to visit Hopefield and to explore the pleasures these women could offer their clients.

"I might be rich and folks may look up to me as an example of Christian piety. But I have basic needs that cry out to be met . . . just like any other man."

# CHAPTER

# *23*

July 1837

Catherine insisted that each member of the Cabell family be present for the Sunday worship service and for the dinner that followed. Consequently, during the summer Jamie and Mose worked at Valley View, they wrapped up their work before noon on Saturdays and set out on horseback for home. They always traveled through Raleigh where they could ferry across the Wolf River. One Saturday they needed to drop off a bridle to be repaired at the livery stable and to place an order for some grass seed. They rode into town just before noon.

Raleigh was abuzz on Saturdays. Many of the farmers within a wide swath of Shelby County came to town to buy and sell produce and livestock . . . as well to visit the bank or conduct other business matters. So, Saturdays afforded the time and opportunity for rural white folks to mingle. News and gossip was disseminated. Weather and crop reports were discussed. And, inevitably, conversations turned to politics. Every wannabe politician in Shelby County - as well as those who already held office - made it a point to meet and greet as many folks as they could.

Judge Robinson always was in attendance. He received his many courtiers at the Court House or sometimes on the front porch of Mrs. Troutt's inn. She kept a large pitcher of tea beside the broad chair he always appropriated as his throne. Anyone who was asked to "take a seat and chat for a spell" considered himself honored. And the paramount achievement one could ever hope for was if the Judge offered a sycophant to share a glass of tea with him during a rare personal audience.

Shelby Lancaster, likewise, wasn't about to miss an opportunity to use a Saturday to remind everyone that the imperious Judge Robinson was his powerful father-in-law and that Shelby would ascend to his political throne soon enough. In the mean time, he made it clear he was a formidable force to reckon with.

Of course, with so many planters coming to town, they brought with them slaves upon whom they were reliant. These black men and boys loaded the purchases on the wagons and performed other chores. So, while the white men clustered here and there to gossip and trade stories, so did the black slaves.

Calvin Cabell encouraged Mose to interact with groups like this. Servants had information and insights into situations that Calvin knew were relevant to a lumberman who needed to keep abreast of local news. And a man with a presence like Mose was greatly admired by these Negro men. Over time he had emerged as the preeminent oligarch among his race. They all trusted his judgment and sought out his advice.

Usually Mose was at the center of the group of slaves who often mingled underneath the oak trees next to the livery stable. But as Jamie exited the hardware store with some hinges and bolts, he noticed Mose was standing at the rear of Shelby Lancaster's carriage and he was intently listening to something Shelby's man servant, Tyrus, was saying. Jamie immediately sensed this was a conversation out of the ordinary. Tyrus seemed to bear a heavy burden he bore and he had the good judgment to confide in Mose. Jamie knew Mose was known for giving sage advice to his own kind. However, he perceived his black friend's wisdom was being tested by whatever Tyrus was sharing with him.

Jamie waited patiently for several minutes until Mose noticed he was watching the two black men. He spoke a few more words to Tyrus before he placed his right hand on the young man's shoulder . . . as if he were bestowing a blessing upon his charge. The two men bowed their heads for a few seconds of prayer. When the prayer ended, Mose gave his young friend a consoling pat on the arm as he began to walk toward Jamie.

Little was said as Jamie and Mose walked down the Wolf River embankment and boarded the crude ferry that required less than two minutes to cross the churned up waterway. When they led their horses down the ramp on the Memphis side, Jamie steadied his animal and prepared to mount. However, just as he placed his left foot in the stirrup, Mose spoke to him in a reluctant, tentative way.

"Master Jamie, if it be alright with you I wonder if we might walk a spell down the road . . . 'fore we set out for home? I got sumpin' on my mind –

had it steepin' up there for the longest time - and I think I gots to share it with you, sir. And I gots to share it with you soon, 'fore it eats away at my innards."

"Well, sure, Mose. We can walk a while. Whatever's on your mind? Does this have something to do with your talk with Shelby Lancaster's boy? What's his name? Thaddeus?"

"Tyrus, Master Jamie, his name's Tyrus. And Tyrus was tellin' me 'bout sumpin' what reminded me you best hear – as I been puttin' off tellin' you for the longest."

Jamie looked around and saw the ferry crossing back toward Raleigh. Then he looked all about to make sure they were alone - despite the fact he knew darned well no one was anywhere within hearing distance. Mose had his eyes fixed down at the dusty road . . . as if he didn't want to face Jamie while he spoke. So, Jamie began to walk leading his horse. He waited fifty yards or so before he broke the silence.

"Okay, Mose, I'm all yours. Tell me what you've got to say."

"Master Jamie, it's all 'bout our talk the day when you was testin' me with that newspaper of yours . . . you know, bout me figurin' how to read a little bit at a time. Well, sir, I come to learn that readin' can sometimes bring on burdens – heavy ones, too. And it's a burden that's come from readin' that's at the root of what I gots to tell you, sir.

"You see, Master Jamie, one day several months ago I was runnin' an errand for your Daddy. He had me carry a deposit down to the bank. That's when I seen Mr. Lancaster . . . as I was headin' out the bank door. Well, Mr. Lancaster gets this real relieved look on his face when he sees me . . . he called me over . . . and tells me I wuz jes the person he needed for a chore.

"He talked real low-like and he pulled some folded up paper from his inside coat pocket. I seen it was a letter written on good paper stock and I could see it was a right lengthy letter, too. Mr. Lancaster say he needed to get this letter delivered to your Daddy and he asked me if I'd fetch it to him right away. Mr. Cabell was up at the mill at the time and I had to return the deposit slip to him anyway.

"Mr. Lancaster said, 'You wait here, Mose. I got to run inside the bank and get an envelope. I couldn't find one at my office and I don't have time to buy a box right this minute. I'll fetch one from the teller and send you on your way.'

"Then, no sooner than he finished tellin' me all about needin' an envelope, he give off this big grin and he reaches out his hand with the letter in it. He chuckled as he looked at me real haughty and he said, 'Well, I suppose I'd be wasting my steps fetching an envelope when I got an illiterate darkie here who couldn't read a single word that's written down . . . even if he tried. Here, Mose, you take this to your master right away . . . and you tell him I said he'd better read every word . . . carefully, 'cause, I mean everything I say in it and he needs to know as much.'"

Mose stopped talking . . . like he feared the two horses snorting at each other as they followed behind were tattling about what they had already heard and each was speculating about what was going to be said next. Jamie could tell Mose wanted to continue, but whatever was coming was going to be painful to say. His friend needed some encouragement.

"Come on, Mose, what happened? What happened next?"

"Well, Master Jamie, I'm comin' to the part I ain't so proud 'bout – not proud at all. But when you hear me out, maybe you won't be harsh on me. I shore hope so anyway."

"So, what is it, Mose? Tell me."

"As I headed toward the mill, I kept hearin' over and over in my mind what that little squirt of a white man had said to me – 'specially the way he said it. It was like he was sayin' no black man – no black man on the face of the earth, mind you - could ever learn to read a single word in that letter I was clutchin' in my right hand. Of course, I was thinkin' that squatty white feller didn't have a clue – not even a hint of a clue – that I picked up more than a few words of readin' at the church house. And the more I thought about it, the more the devil tempted me to do what I did."

"So, now the devil worms his way into the story, does he? My word, Mose, do carry on."

"Yessuh, the devil filled me with evil pride . . . made me hide behind Hinton's Pharmacy and open up that letter . . . all just to spite Mr. Lancaster for talking to me like I was a ignorant field nigger. Oh, I could read what he wrote all right. But when I pieced the words together, I wished I was struck dead . . . right there. And when I think about that letter today . . . a part of me still wishes I'd carried it straight away to your Daddy and put it directly into his hand. But I didn't. The devil shore had his way with me that prideful day. And now a part of me wishes I'd be struck dead now . . . and right here on the road . . . just so I wouldn't have to tell you what it said."

For the first time since he began this story Mose stopped walking. He raised his head up . . . and he stared right into Jamie's eyes. Jamie sensed he was signaling that what was about to follow was so painful for the Negro to say, he wanted his friend to know that when he said it, he was looking Jamie squarely in the eye . . . like a man prepared and willing to accept the consequences for such sinful impertinence.

"Master Jamie, that Shelby Lancaster says your Daddy killed a woman . . . back in Kentucky."

Jamie's eyes shot open like he just saw a ghost. He was speechless, but it was Mose who had all the talking to do.

"And he says he can prove it . . . and he would jump at the chance to send Mr. Cabell to the gallows . . . all cause he thinks your Daddy's been uppity and hateful toward him ever since he come to Memphis . . . and long before then, too. He said he'd get great pleasure takin' down a rich man like your Daddy . . . and havin' all the white folks in town know Mr. Cabell's a killer."

Jamie stood stiff as a statue . . . with his mouth dropped wide open in disbelief. He was thinking that if anybody but Mose had told him such a tale, he wouldn't have given it a moment's credence. But this was Mose talking . . . and telling him a first hand account of what he knew. Mose would never lie. About that, Jamie had no doubt.

"Mr. Lancaster says even if the law back in Kentucky don't come down here and haul him away in chains, he'd be pleased as punch to tell ever single soul in Tennessee what he knows. He says folks love to hear how high fallutin' heroes are just sorry sinners like the rest of us. And they're waitin' like wolves to tear down men like your Daddy – tear them into shreds of scrap. He says if your Daddy don't want to ruin his life – and he shore 'nough said he'd gladly ruin all the lives of his family, too – then he'd better start givin' Mr. Lancaster some serious respect."

"Did the letter say anything about this dead woman? Did Shelby offer a motive?"

"If a 'motive' means 'the reason', I remember the letter said she was a 'whore' who was goin' to let everybody in Kentucky know Mr. Cabell was a shameless rounder. He said his whorin' would have broke your Mother's heart and caused a partin' of the ways with your Grandfather Barry."

"This makes no sense. It's incredible. Everybody knows Calvin Cabell represents the epitome of Christian morality and integrity. I'll bet Father read the letter and sized it up for what it was – a pack of lies."

"Well, Master Jamie, maybe it was the devil still stirrin' in my soul, but I lingered for a good while after I give the letter to your Daddy. I wanted to see for myself if he was angry . . . or sad . . . or put out with his lawyer friend. And what I seen was a man lookin' like he jes saw a ghost – a ghost that was goin' to haunt his ever wakin' moments. He wuz scared, Master Jamie. Your Daddy was scared as scared can be. And I gots to tell ya, I think there's more than a little truth to what wuz in that letter. I think it was all true."

"Why . . . that low-down scalawag is a bigger maggot than I ever thought. I never did like him . . . and I know Father always felt the same way. But 'murder', Mose, is a serious charge . . . and one sure to ruin a man's reputation and his business. Besides, how can anyone prove a negative?"

Mose didn't understand . . . and he let Jamie know it.

"You know, Mose, it's like you're supposed to prove you didn't actually do anything wrong. How can you prove that you're NOT a murderer? It's impossible."

Jamie stood there, still in a stupor trying to sort it all out. Then he remembered this conversation all began by him mentioning that he wondered what Mose and Shelby's Tyrus were talking about.

"Why are you telling me about this now, Mose . . . after your solemn talk with Tyrus?"

"Remember, Master Jamie, when you tried to teach me and Jed how to play the game of chess? You said, 'It's a game about war . . . where men of different rank try to capture another man with the idea of huntin' down and killin' the king.' You said even the lowest rank on the board could put the king in 'check' . . . and he'd be good as dead. Well, I thought about what you said after my talk with Tyrus. You see, Master Jamie, I think you and me got a way to put Mr. Lancaster 'in check'. And if he don't wanna settle for being

346

'in check' then we might jes be in a place to slay that pole cat and string up his hide fer all the white folks . . . and blacks, too, to spit at."

"What do you mean, Mose? How can we prevent Father from being destroyed? And what does Tyrus have to do with your plan?"

"Master Jamie, I told you the devil's been workin' his way with me . . . and I gots to tell you what I got in my mind wuz shore 'nough put out there by the devil himself. But the way I see it, we're dealin' with another squatty, little no-good devil by the name of Shelby Lancaster. And followin' the devil's plan is the only way to strike back at him. You know, it's like fightin' fire with fire. We gonna be fightin' the devil with the devil. Are you up to that, Master Jamie? Cause if you ain't, then I kin understand."

Jamie looked into Mose's eyes like he'd done hundreds of time before. And, sure enough, he could see the devil looking out at him from deep inside the black man's pupils.

"Okay, Mose, count me in. How are we going to 'checkmate' that no-good weasel?"

\* \* \* \* \* \* \* \* \* \*

"Master Jamie, if you really trusted me you wouldn't be axing all these here questions you been pepperin' me with. Besides, there ain't time to waste while I splain to you ever little detail of my plan to checkmate Mr. Lancaster. There jus ain't enough time."

Jamie couldn't argue with the family's slave. He had entrusted Mose to lead their scheme and he felt bound to follow. After all, the "ignorant, illiterate darkie", as Shelby had characterized him, had uncovered this extortion plot when no one else ever could have done it. And, somehow, Jamie knew that Tyrus was instrumental to any chance of a resolution. But since the two had mounted their horses and had ridden down the Memphis Road about one mile, Mose kept them moving at a fast clip. He veered into the woods just beyond the short bridge at Clayton's Creek. They tied the horses to a tree deep in the thicket. Then the two pushed ahead on foot. Mose headed toward the south until they came to a small green glen that looked oddly out of place.

"This is the place. This is the place Tyrus told me about, Master Jamie. And look up there. It's the tree stand . . . built high up . . . jes like he said it'd be."

"Where are we, Mose. And did Tyrus tell you to come to this place?"

"Tyrus told me Mr. Beaty owns this land. He cleared the trees and brush and he planted the grass so deer would stray from the woods and graze near the salt lick you can see over yonder. Mr. Beaty fancies bow huntin', so he comes here at twilight and spends the whole night time sleepin' and waitin' up in that tree stand for deer to slip out at dawn . . . and into the open for a taste of sweet, green grass covered with dew."

"So how does Tyrus know about this place? And why are we here?"

"I can tell you most of what you wanna know soon as we shimmy up the tree into the stand. Let's move . . . fast."

Within a minute Jamie Cabell and his black friend sat on the floor of the shelter. The four plank walls stood more than five feet high. Along the top ridge of the walls there were scattered slat openings built along the parapet. This allowed a hunter to stand up . . . almost entirely out of view from a deer. The gaps afforded him an opportunity to aim his bended bow and strike at will. Jamie could see it was the perfect cover for a deer hunter. But he still hadn't learned what sort of "game" he and Mose were hunting this Saturday afternoon.

"Now, Mose, can you tell me what you're up to?"

The Negro spoke with a muted, soft voice. Mose held up his index finger in front of his mouth and mimicked a silent "shhhhhh" at the impatient white boy. Then he spoke . . . and when he began, Jamie was certain he wouldn't stop until all his questions were answered.

"We ain't huntin' fer deer today, Jamie. But I spect we're likely to bag us a big ol' skunk. And I spect our prey will look mighty familiar to you. I spect this skunk is gonna be Mr. Shelby Lancaster, the same skunk dats tryin' to ruin your Daddy.

"Tyrus told me bout this place. He say he been here before with Mr. Lancaster – most always while he be drivin' the squire back and forth to Memphis. It hurt like hell for him to confide in me 'bout this open spot in the woods . . . and he don't know fer sure that we gonna be hidin up here. But, I think he knows. I think he knows."

Tyrus had belonged to Judge Robinson, who gave his son-in-law the slave as a belated wedding gift. Over the past year Jamie noticed Tyrus had been almost tethered to Shelby . . . performing all sorts of small chores Shelby needed done in Memphis. Rarely did Shelby drive his own carriage any more. It was always Tyrus at the reins.

Tyrus was a striking looking man. He was the sort of slave one would give a second look . . . to figure out what set him apart from the others. He was about twenty two or twenty three years old. He stood just over six feet tall with a lean build that indicated both strength and agility. He was curiously quiet and he was pensive – the sort of slave who recognized Mose's wisdom and sought out his advice.

Mose once talked about Tyrus to Jamie when the two were visiting Raleigh one weekday. He said Tyrus took another slave of Judge Robinson as his wife when he was about seventeen and she was fifteen. They had a daughter who was now six and the woman had lost two babies since her birth. Tyrus said the little girl, Essie, was his pride and joy. Both Essie and her mother were also gifted to Shelby, but they continued to live on the Robinson plantation. Tyrus could only visit them when he carried Shelby to Raleigh.

"So what makes you think Shelby's going to stray off the road and come to this secluded meadow? I don't understand, Mose."

Mose kept peering through the narrow openings between the planks, but he felt safe giving Jamie an answer to at least one more question. He spoke in even a softer voice than he had employed before. "Tyrus told me Mr. Lancaster was in a meetin' at the Court House and, as soon as he could get his hair cut at the barber shop, our skunk told Tyrus to be ready for the trip home to Memphis. That's why we had to hasten our pace . . . and secure our lookout as soon as possible."

There was silence once again. But in a few seconds both men heard the muffled sounds of leaves and twigs being crushed by turning wheels. Shortly thereafter, a carriage emerged from the woods and passed over the low mound that bordered the grassy open space. It slowly paraded around the green glen's outer perimeter for one full revolution. Tyrus hesitantly pulled on the reins and the vehicle stopped.

Shelby stood up and called for Tyrus to jump off the bench as his master remained standing. He surveyed all around him - paying particular attention to anything unusual in the thicket outside of the clearing. He spent a long second eyeing the deer stand carefully. Shelby acted just as cautious as a skittish doe might be after leaving the safety of the forest. But the hideout was constructed so cleverly, a deer or even a low-down, human skunk couldn't spy anyone lurking inside it.

Tyrus seemed very nervous. He moved to the back of the carriage and opened the tool box sitting on the back board. He pulled out two ropes and tied one end of each to the metal brackets attached to the top corners of the rear seat. Meanwhile, Shelby walked toward Tyrus and soon he began a series of acts that Jamie considered to eerily resemble a ceremony – a dark ritual that had been practiced often over time.

Tyrus began to unbutton the cuffs of his long sleeve shirt followed by the buttons in the front. He slipped the shirt off his arms and placed it on the left rear carriage wheel. Then he used the wheel for balance as he removed one shoe and sock . . . followed by the others. He took his appointed placed standing at the middle of the back board. He raised his left hand and Shelby pulled the loose end of one rope around Tyrus' wrist until a knot was formed and fastened around it. He raised his right arm and soon it, too, was secured by the other rope. Tyrus never looked at Shelby. He raised his head up toward the horizon. He appeared to be trying to transport his conscious thoughts far, far away from the scene of whatever was to follow.

Shelby moved to within inches in front of the bound slave and the white fingertips from both his hands began a calculated slow descent from Tyrus' shoulders downward across his muscular chest and his well delineated, firm abdomen . . . until they rested over the tops of his trousers. Then he quickly opened each button of his fly. Next he kneeled and pulled down Tyrus's pants so that one foot . . . and then the other could step out of the pant legs.

And there stood Tyrus . . . standing with his arms spread outward like an ebony crucifix glistening in the afternoon sun. As horrified as Jamie was at this macabre sight, he was struck how . . . through it all . . . Tyrus managed to retain a presence of dignity that transcended his humiliating predicament.

Shelby held out his riding crop and lifted up his victim's member above his pubic hair and then he jiggled it playfully over and over. He got no intended reaction to his maneuvers. So, he grasped it in his hand and fondled it . . . vigorously enough that, finally, blood began to flow into the organ and it grew firm. Shelby seemed quite pleased with this plump transformation that stood at attention . . . like a soldier awaiting inspection.

Neither Mose nor Jamie could say a word, yet each could almost hear the other crying out in sympathy about Tyrus' predicament and the pathetic villain who was responsible for it. Both men squatted in the deer stand and put their heads between their knees. They couldn't bear to see any more. But they knew exactly what was happening down below. They couldn't possibly gawk at this unspeakable travesty . . . even if their eye-witness testimony might mean Tyrus could be eventually spared further degradation in the future.

Later, when Mose and Jamie finally heard the carriage jerk forward and the sounds of its turning wheels faded into the thick woods, they were free to speak.

"I'd have killed that sawed off fiend . . . right there in the open if he ever even tried something so perverse as that with me. I'd have killed him, I tell you, Mose."

"And I gots to remind you, Master Jamie, that you ain't no slave. And you shore ain't Squire Lancaster's slave either . . . lest I gots to remind you 'bout that."

"Slave or no slave, I'd still take that riding crop and strangle the bastard."

"And I say you wouldn't, Master Jamie. You wouldn't do nothin' but the same what Tyrus gots to do out there . . . whenever Squire Lancaster wants to have his way with him. Maybe I needs to splain it to a white boy like yerself. You be too smart to act so dumb, Master Jamie."

Then while the white boy and his daddy's slave still sat there in the tree stand, stunned with grief about what they had seen and heard, Mose "splained" it all to Jamie. He spared no detail about all the reasons why Tyrus passively allowed Shelby to humiliate him almost every time they traveled the Memphis-Raleigh Road. It was the dirtiest laundry list of threats and intimidations and disregard for human dignity that anyone could have ever imagined.

Mose told him Shelby had his way with Tyrus because he threatened to sell his daughter and her mother if he didn't comply. Once, when Tyrus resisted, Shelby ratcheted up his intimidation several notches. He said he would take Essie away for several days and rape her repeatedly unless her father had the good sense to spare her the pain.

Jamie felt like a fool, a stupid white fool, for forgetting what disgraceful acts Tyrus likely endured as a slave. These were issues he'd never had to face. After duly considering Tyrus's plight, he had to admit that if his owner were a brutal bastard like Shelby, then he, too, might try to shift his mind a million miles away and just accept his fate . . . all the while wanting to kill that horse-face devil."

Jamie stood up and he started to climb down the wooden rungs tacked to the tree trunk. He didn't say another word until Jamie and Mose were about a mile from home.

"Mose, you tell Tyrus something from me when you think it's appropriate. Now, mind you, you don't have to tell him we were spying on him today . . . although, I have no doubt he knew. You just tell him this. And this is a promise. You just tell Tyrus that Jamie Cabell says when a man gets unmercifully kicked like a dog . . . and I don't care if that man's a white man or a black man . . . then you just remind Tyrus to remember that every dog has his day.

Mose had never seen his white friend so angry . . . so vengeful. Jamie was tightly clenching his jaws together. His face had turned beet red and the muscles along his jaw line actually swelled up from the angry blood coursing through him. His lower teeth ground against the upper level and Mose could only imagine what the boy was thinking.

Finally, Jamie spoke again, but the words were forced through his clasped teeth. He was like an animal which had taken down its prey . . . and had clamped his teeth so unyieldingly at its neck that he wouldn't release the grip . . . even when he knew asphyxiation had long ago been achieved. Jamie appeared relentless in his hatred of Shelby.

"You talk to Tyrus, Mose. You tell him that EVERY dog has his day. Even the lowest kind of cur dog gets a chance at leveling the scorecard. You tell him I said he can bet on it. Yes sir, Tyrus, EVERY dog has his day."

# CHAPTER

# 24

October 1837

Mose missed Jamie so much it hurt. Sometimes he wished his friend had never grown up and left for college.

At that point in the nation's history - out of necessity - one had to return back East to receive a respectable education. Mose knew the Cabell's family's roots were in Kentucky and he had heard them talk about Jamie one day enrolling at Centre College. Jamie's stalwart black friend mulled over his painful emotions and he began to evaluate why he felt so lonesome. Then, the answer struck at him . . . like a lightening bolt.

"Jamie's not just going to college for a few years. He's never coming back to Memphis."

Jamie told Mose about the letter his father received from President Young. It arrived six months before classes began. He paraphrased it to Mose as best he could.

Dear Mr. Cabell,

I trust you'll remember I wrote earlier and expressed my hope then that your son, Jamie, would one day become a student at Centre College.

I know the time for his college education is approaching. I write to tell you his cousin, John Breckenridge, will enroll this fall. John's sister is my wife, Frances. She and I have told his mother we wish for him to reside with us in our home while he is a student.

Please know that Mrs. Young and I both hope Jamie will, likewise, enroll here and live with us and with his cousin. I think these two young men will be excellent students and I know their already fast friendship will strengthen and grow from this shared experience.

I await your response. In the mean time please give our warmest regards to Mrs. Cabell. We both hope Jamie's time with us will cause you to initiate a return trip to the Bluegrass. We sincerely hope we shall soon enjoy a visit with you here in Danville.

With Fond Devotion,

John C. Young

Mose sadly remembered the morning he drove the wagon with Jamie and his trunk of clothes to the wharf. There sat the 'Lucky Lady' ready to push his young white friend up the river all the way to Kentucky. Mose helped carry the trunk across the gang plank and into Jamie's cabin room.

The captain of the vessel was a man in his sixties with a long white beard that framed a welcoming smile. He greeted Jamie and, soon thereafter, there was a dazzled excitement in his eyes.

"Did you say your name is Cabell, young man?"

"Yes, captain, my name is James Barry Cabell. But everyone calls me Jamie."

"Young man, would your father by any chance be known as Calvin Cabell?"

"Yes, sir, that's my father. Do you know him, captain?"

"Indeed . . . indeed, I do. And all these years after meeting him and sharing a few heartfelt experiences together, at last, I have the honor of piloting his son up the Mississippi."

The old captain realized his young passenger hadn't the foggiest notion who he was.

"The name's Captain Moore, sir. I'm at your service and it's a high honor to have you aboard, Mr. Cabell. I had the distinct pleasure of transporting your father to Memphis when you were a wee lad and he was making his first visit

354

to this bluff. For reasons relating to what's happened in my life since then, I've not seen him in all these years. And today, I see you're the spitting image of your father."

Mose was standing at Jamie's side hearing everything Captain Moore had to say. The captain wrapped his arm around Jamie's shoulder and told him he wanted to show him the pilot house up above. But before Jamie allowed the captain to commence his tour, he turned to Mose one last time.

"I'm going to miss you, Mose."

"Yessuh," came his abbreviated acknowledgement.

"I want you to teach Jed all the remarkable lessons you've taught me. In the mean time, I've got other lessons to learn at college – or, so they tell me."

"Yessuh," Mose responded again. Mose was a tough old bird. He could take just about any punch life might swing at him. And the Lord knew he had already taken many a blow to his heart and his soul. But the resilient black man who stood before Jamie . . . with his hands hanging limply at his side . . . wanted to illustrate his devotion to Jamie. He didn't need to speak. Jamie could see the love in his eyes.

Those whites encircling his chocolate irises were splotched with red blood vessels that shot out from the sides . . . like lightning explodes in the black night sky. But, for the first time, Jamie saw tears that formed and clung to Mose's eyes. They almost blinded Jamie with their bright glistening. Yet, not one teardrop descended past his lower lashes to roll down toward his chin. These clear liquid reservoirs stood rigid and resolute so as not to expose the broken heart Mose was feeling inside. They were steadfast. They were Mose's tears . . . and the tears of such a noble man would never succumb to gravity.

Jamie broke loose from Captain Moore's welcome and the young white man wrapped his arms around Mose. He had never done that before. It felt so good to him . . . so comforting. But, it also felt very sad . . . all at the same time.

No other goodbyes passed over either of their lips. Mose turned about and descended the plank. The Captain realized this black man shared a close bond with his young passenger. And, as the slave walked toward the wagon at the top of the bluff, he didn't turn back – just like his master, Calvin Cabell, had resisted turning about to look at Captain Moore many years ago

Jamie watched his friend trudge up the incline. He had a lump in his throat the size of a watermelon. Then, he turned to his father's former confidante.

"Captain Moore. I very much would like to inspect your pilot house. Shall we go now?"

\* \* \* \* \* \* \* \* \* \*

Most of the time Mose never gave a moment's thought that he was a slave. But occasionally his mind would wander into unbridled moments of imagination. These daydreams activated all of his senses. He could sniff the air and smell freedom. He could lick at the wind and taste liberation. He could touch the skin on his face . . . and be assured his was the face of a free man. And, he could hear the angels singing a chorus of thanksgiving praises that proclaimed he wasn't obligated to anybody's will anymore . . . except the Lord's.

Even if the fantasy illusion lasted for just a few seconds, he relished every one of them. During those fleeting moments, he was unable to feel the abiding sense of bondage. He knew what it was like to feel free.

But hallucinations like these were always short lived. When he eventually opened his eyes, they inevitably revealed the harsh truth. Mose had always been a slave. Moreover, it seemed unlikely Calvin Cabell was going to ever sever the chain that tethered him and his family to the Cabells.

One evening at Valley View, Calvin instructed Mose to make a trip to Somerville the next morning. He said there were two English saddles and some tack he had ordered and they were ready to be picked up. Calvin told him to take the wagon.

Somerville was a good twenty-five miles east of Raleigh. So, Calvin wanted Mose to get started before dawn . . . as he thought the round trip could be accomplished in a day – one long day. Mose was thrilled. He'd have a whole day to think – to consider about what possibilities might lay ahead in his life.

He was already passing through Raleigh's streets as beams of sunlight began to creep across the eastern sky. And, sure enough, three miles from town he lapsed into a trance, one of his daydreams about being free. There was a very good reason.

Mose came upon a stage stop that also served as an inn. He saw a black man sweeping the front steps. The man looked up at him and he smiled broadly.

His eyes locked in on Mose's eyes. The man held the broom in his left hand and he began to raise his right arm in the air. He started to wave as a clear sign of welcome and hospitality. Mose responded by pulling the wagon over toward the friendly fellow. He reined the horse to a stop.

"Howdy, my friend," greeted the black man with the broom. "Welcome. Won't you come on in and refresh yourself with some spring water?"

There was something wrong with this picture so far as Mose could tell. How in the world did this man feel comfortable extending such a hospitable invitation?

"I wonder what this feller's owner thinks about this uppity nigger," Mose thought as he slid off the wagon seat.

Mose warily approached this solicitous individual. And, when he got close to him, the friendly black man held out his palm to offer a welcoming handshake.

"The name's Joe Harris. Pleased to meet you."

"This here's Mose. I'm on my way to Somerville for my master."

Mose couldn't figure out what sort of conundrum was at work here. So, he spontaneously spoke up to get a better handle on what was going on.

"Harris, I declare, if I didn't know better, I'd think you be actin' like you own dis place. Where's your master? Gone away for a spell, has he?"

Great gales of laughter came from the sociable man with the broom. At last, he managed to get control of himself. "Well, Mose, it seems you need to follow your first instincts. As a matter of fact, I DO own this place. Ain't no master here . . . or anywhere else on my property . . . 'cept for me."

"You're a free man? . . . a free BLACK man . . . that operates an inn? Is that right, Harris?"

"That's right, sir. But I don't "operate" this inn. I OWN it. Now, please call me Joe. Most folks know me as 'Free Joe Harris'."

"Don't know dat I ever met a freed Negro before . . . much less one dat owns property." Mose was perplexed. "You sure you own dis property?"

"Indeed, I do. I come to Shelby County in '33 . . . and I bought this inn with my savings. Me and my family live and work here. We're always happy to see strangers stop by . . . and spend a little money, of course."

Mose was overtaken by this incredible situation. "Is I dreamin', Lord? I do think I died somewhere back on the Raleigh Road and I've come upon Glory Land." He shook his head almost as furiously as if he were a coon dog shaking off rain water. His mind seemed clearer now. He was beginning to believe the man might be speaking the truth.

"Come along, now, and let's sit a spell, Mose. Grab that gourd over there and scoop up some water. There's the colored gourd. You can use it. The white man's gourd's hangin' over yonder."

"How come you to be free, Joe? And how'd you get the money for this place?"

"I come to Shelby County from Virginia. My father, you see, was also my master there. His name is John Harris and, bless his soul, he freed me four years ago . . . in 1832. By that time I'd already married a woman slave on a nearby plantation. She was owned by the Leake family. So, when Mr. Samuel and his brother, Mr. Richard Leake, pulled up stakes and moved their families to West Tennessee – naturally, I had to follow them . . . 'cause they was takin' my family with 'em.

"My wife, Sally, and I had four kids by that time. Of course, they were slaves of the Leake's . . . bein' the offspring of Sally.

"I'm blessed to be a craftsman, Mose. I was able to make a little money here and there and I stashed away every penny I could in a glass jar. By '34 I was able to purchase Sally and our baby daughter from the Leakes. I bought 'em for three hundred dollars. I paid one hundred and fifty up front and the Leakes secured the remainin' hundred and fifty with a mortgage on this place here. Of course, Mose, I got three other children still belongin' to the Leakes. Soon as I pay off Sally's debt, I'll start savin' to buy the rest."

Mose couldn't believe his ears. He never heard such a tale. The prospects of a free black man here in Shelby County were slim enough. But for a freed slave . . . to own an inn . . . and make the kind of money it takes to support his wife and daughter . . . and, all the while, he's saving to buy his children still in bondage – well, it was all very hard to believe.

"I got to tell you, Free Joe Harris, the smartest part of me says your master owns this inn . . . and he's been a fool to leave you in charge whilst he's tendin' to some errands. And here you is . . . sitting here feedin' hog slop to some innocent nigger that come down the road. Ain't no story like that gonna be true. You're a pullin' my leg, Mr. FREE Joe Harris. You're a pullin' on my leg, for sure."

Free Joe laughed a light hearted chuckle. He knew the story he had recounted was difficult to believe. But it was HIS life he was talking about and, unless his life was just one long fairy tale dream, he sure was telling the truth.

"Now, Mose, you see . . . you jes got to believe me, cause I'm a Baptist preacher, too. Been one since 'fore my Daddy freed me. Do you believe that, Mr. Mose?"

"I don't rightly know what to believe. But I think if a man lies that he's a preacher man . . . when he ain't, I 'spect the Lord'd swoop down a bolt of lightnin' and fry his gizzard . . . right here in front of me. That's what I think."

"I think you got that right, man. I sure ain't about to claim I was a man of the Lord unless it was the truth – the Gospel truth. You can bet on that."

Free Joe could tell his visitor was beginning to believe what he was being told. "So, Mose, I'm here sittin' and talkin' to you . . . and I'm tellin' you I ain't jes a preacher. I'm telling you I'm a free preacher, a free Negro preacher. And I'm also tellin' you I own this place. Now, what you got to say about that?"

On one hand, Mose felt his burden had been lightened . . . just by learning there was a free black man in Shelby County. Here stood a liberated Negro . . . who owned property and a business. He was a freed man who had already managed to purchase part of his family. Moreover, he was clearly bound and determined to eventually purchase his other two children . . . the ones who still belonged to the Leake brothers. Here was a living, breathing model of the man Mose ached to be one day.

On the other hand, this unexpected revelation saddened him. At present he could only dream about being free. He wanted to believe Calvin Cabell was going to grant his freedom one of these days. But he hadn't done it yet. And his master still hadn't even discussed the terms and conditions for freedom like he had said . . . like he had promised . . . several years ago.

Mose had finally seen for himself what a free black man looked like. Yet, when he honestly evaluated his own situation, it just seemed implausible that he might one day be able to ride out to Free Joe's place and tell him he was no longer anybody's slave . . . along with his wife and his son.

Mose could still dream. But, thankfully, he now had a real, live black man to mold his dream around.

He got up and went to ladle out another drink of water from the "colored gourd" at Free Joe's business. The water was especially refreshing. He tipped his hat to acknowledge his thanks for the hospitality he had been afforded . . . as well as to acknowledge his appreciation to have heard Joe's story.

"I got to get on down the road, Free Joe. It's been quite a treat visitin' here with you. I don't know when Mr. Cabell's gonna want me to go to Somerville again. But I do hope to see you sometime again. And when I shake your hand again, I hope you're shakin' the hand of a free black man.

"I hope so, too," Free Joe said in return. "I sure do hope I'll be shakin' a freed man's hand when I see you again."

# CHAPTER

# *25*

Christmas Eve   1838


"Put your gloves back on, Cassie . . . and this time, don't take them off."

The temperature was in the low fifties, but it felt much colder in an open carriage moving sprightly down the Cherokee Trace.

"Remember, I only agreed to bring you along if you remained snug and warm under the blankets. That also means you MUST wear your gloves. I promised your mother you wouldn't come down with pneumonia on Christmas Day."

Calvin turned about often from the driver's bench to ensure Cassie heeded his command. It was Jamie who was at the reins today. This excursion was his son's idea. At first, his father resisted. Eventually, however, Jamie prevailed. Calvin considered his acquiescence should count as a bonus Christmas gift to his son. A trip to who-knows-how-far out of town to see the Cherokee wasn't the plan Calvin had in mind for this Christmas Eve.

Jamie and John Breckinridge held within them a passion about Indians. Jamie's interest first blossomed when, as young boys, he and Cousin John would roam Cabell's Dale. They meticulously examined every tuft of grass . . . hoping to uncover old arrowheads, beads, or any other Indian paraphernalia they might be lucky enough to find. Now that the two were classmates in college, they carried on their treasure hunts in the Danville area. Over the years the cousins had accumulated a fine collection of Indian artifacts.

Jamie was home from college until after the New Year. Today he wouldn't be seeking souvenirs from the past. Jamie wanted to observe Indian history being made . . . today, in the present. He had pleaded with his father to tell him everything he could about Sam Houston living the life of a Cherokee

Indian named Raven. Houston was presently making history out in Texas and Jamie regretted he never had the opportunity to meet him. He had been too young to interview Houston and Crockett and the many other historical figures his father had known.

Now, here were the Cabells . . . traveling to observe, first hand, the great forced march of the Cherokee nation. It was the perfect time for Calvin to remind Jamie that Houston back in 1819 had foreseen the inevitability of the U.S. Government's relocation strategy - to rid the nation of Indians who lived east of the Mississippi. Jamie and many other Americans disapproved of this national agenda. The Cherokee had always been a valuable ally to the white settlers and to the nation. They battled with Jackson against the Creeks and the Seminoles. Many of their warriors were killed fighting as allies of the Americans. Andrew Jackson made a great fuss at the time to make certain everyone knew the Cherokee should be considered valued friends of the United States . . . instead of being considered its enemy.

Unfortunately, the Cherokee were the primary example of a Native American tribe that had become acculturated to the White/European ways of the United States. They dressed like American settlers. They adopted Christianity as their religion . . . and they called themselves by American names.

But, there was one aspect of their "American" acculturation the tribe absorbed in the early 19th century which was shocking and off-putting to many of those who supported them. Indeed, Jamie thought, they had perhaps become a little too "American". Many Cherokee who had earlier fled to Arkansas now owned slaves and they greatly prospered from the free labor.

Perhaps it was an innate sense of political insight that made Houston caution his adopted Cherokee father, Chief Oo – le – te – ka in 1819. He told him a momentum was building within the U.S. Government. There was a growing determination in Congress the Cherokee should move farther west. Calvin informed Jamie how Sam Houston told him face to face that he didn't regret initiating the tribe's move to the northwest corner of Arkansas. He only regretted Arkansas wasn't far enough to escape the greed of the White man.

Calvin turned up his voice's volume to make a point. "He told me he was wrong – so very wrong - he couldn't foresee white migration would move so far west. By the middle of the 1820s he knew white men would soon stake their claims in Arkansas - and far beyond. Did you ever consider why this road is called the Cherokee Trace, Jamie?"

"No, sir, I never gave it much thought," the young man replied.

362

"The name comes from the fact this is the route the first wave of Cherokee took west . . . back in 1819. The Cherokee up ahead of us, no doubt, wish they had trod this trail back then . . . without the military scooting them along."

"Father, isn't President Jackson at the root of this forced migration we're about to witness? What happened that caused him to change his mind and break his promises to the Cherokee?"

The answer was simple. Yet, it was so simple that even the brightest of young men – like Jamie – would have a difficult time understanding it.

"President Jackson did what all politicians think they have to do. He relented. He double-crossed people he said he admired and he loved. He caved in to the great demand swelling among the white man to take the Indians' land and deed it in their own names."

Jamie shook his head with despair for the Cherokee. "So, now those Cherokee who didn't follow Sam Houston's counsel are being rounded up and force marched across the country. What a shame. What a despicable shame."

Calvin looked back into the carriage once again to check on Cassie. She was having a marvelous time breathing in the cold air and observing all the plant and animal life she spotted along the way. The air was clear and the glistening winter sun hovered low on the southern horizon. It made the shadows of the horses and carriage on the ground dark and distinct . . . like sharply cut, black silhouette shapes on white paper.

"Father, they're just up ahead. Look."

Calvin turned around to face forward, once again. His sight followed Jamie's pointing finger. Sure enough, the mass of people he saw ahead had to be the Cherokee.

Jamie slowed down the pace of Star and Bluegrass to a fast walk. He didn't want to appear charging at the encampment. Besides, the Cabell carriage was being approached by a soldier on horseback. The man in a blue Army uniform was mounted on a rather ordinary dappled horse. He raised his hand in a manner that indicated the carriage should stop. Clearly, it was his intention to ask the Cabells a few questions.

*No Coin for Charon*

"Greetings, folks, are you on your way to Germantown . . . or to other points in that direction?"

"Private, my name is Calvin Cabell . . . from Memphis," Calvin responded, "My son and daughter and I have traveled out here to see the Indians. We heard your contingent was on the outskirts of town and we wished to offer our friends at home a preview of what they'll be seeing as you make your way to the river. May we proceed farther, private?"

"Yes, but just a bit closer, sir. I'll have to check with my commanding officer for permission to visit the encampment. Come . . . follow me."

The mounted soldier's horse walked at a slow pace as he remained side by side with the Cabell carriage. He didn't appear threatening at all. In fact, there was a tone of courtesy and hospitality to his manner.

"Mr. Cabell, my name is Private John Burnett and I'm from East Tennessee. May I wish you and your family a Merry Christmas?"

"And a Merry Christmas to you, also, Private Burnett. We appreciate your escort . . . and your hospitality."

"Thank you, sir. Isn't everybody hospitable at Christmas time?"

Cassie was fascinated and she cheerily looked up at the private and said, "Merry Christmas, Mr. Burnett."

"Merry Christmas to you, young lady. And, by the way, might I know your name since you know mine?"

"My name is Cassie Cabell."

"Well, Miss Cassie Cabell, I have a young brother just about your age and I know he'd enjoy meeting you."

"I don't think we can travel as far as East Tennessee to meet him," Cassie cracked back.

Private Burnett laughed a barely audible chuckle. First he looked ahead at the encampment about a hundred yards away . . . and then he turned again to Cassie. "You wouldn't have to travel to East Tennessee to meet him, Miss Cassie. He's here on the trail with me. I know he'd like to wish you a Merry Christmas. He hasn't spoken with a young white child in several months."

"You have a brother Cassie's age accompanying you on this long trek?" Calvin was incredulous. "Is it customary for our U.S. Army to draft thirteen year old boys to serve our country?"

"Well, Mr. Cabell, ours is an unusual situation. I can explain, but now I need to talk with Captain McLellan about your request. I'll return in a moment."

Burnett cantered toward a group of officers and the Cabells could see he was talking with one man in particular. After a short time this officer craned his neck over the others and glanced toward the Cabells. He appeared to give an approving response to Burnett's question. Soon the private turned his horse about and rode back.

"Most of our Indians are situated along the sides of the road. Captain McLellan told me it was alright for your carriage to pass through. Then, after you reach the end of the line, you may return here. You're in no danger among the Indians. But, please show signs of respect."

"Jamie, take the carriage and let Cassie sit up front with you. I think I'll linger here with Private Burnett. I don't think I need to add anything to his instructions. You will respect these people . . . as they are humans, too, just like your friends and family. You will observe their plight, so you can teach others at home all the lessons you'll, no doubt, learn today."

"Yes, sir, Father, I'll do just that."

Suddenly a boy approached the carriage. Private Burnett beamed a big smile and he waved his hand as if to say, "Come on over here." The boy, however, bore no smile. He walked forward with his head bowed low. John Burnett could tell the lad was contemplating some deep, troubling thoughts.

"Where've you been, brother? I've been wondering when you'd show up."

"I just dug two more graves by the side of the road. Two squaws fell ill yesterday. I guess they figured they couldn't hold out 'til Christmas."

"Bless your heart, Josh . . . you must've buried six Indians this week. I know that casts a pall over Christmas. But try to snap out of it. There's nothing you can do except what you've been doing. And remember. I'm mighty proud of you. You're a fine young man. Now, try to cheer up. There's somebody here I want you to meet"

Josh looked up. He seemed to have shrugged off his dreary experience. John began the introduction just as a smile began to appear on Josh's red cheeked face. "Mr. Cabell, may I introduce my brother to you and your family?"

Burnett put his right arm across his little brother's shoulders. The boy stuck out his right hand to Calvin, who was standing on the ground with the private. "Howdy, friends, I'm Josh Burnett and I'm mighty pleased to meet you."

Calvin was struck by the boy's manners, his presence, his maturity beyond his years, and his outgoing friendliness.

"Private Burnett, would it be acceptable for your young brother to ride with my son and daughter? I think he might be of some guidance to them. He also might have some information about these people that could instruct them. For my part, I'd appreciate it if I might remain here . . . and visit with you."

"Climb aboard, Josh. These folks from Memphis can use your help. Will you join them?"

Josh didn't reply with any message except a broad, affirmative smile. In a matter of seconds he climbed on to the carriage. Calvin said, "Cassie, with Josh now along for the ride, would the two of you sit in the carriage? Jamie, you continue to drive."

"Come aboard, Josh." Cassie pulled a paper bag from underneath the blanket on the carriage seat. She held it up with great satisfaction. "I used my Christmas money to buy some candy for the Indian children. You can help me pass it out. Okay?"

"Sure, Cassie, I know these boys and girls and they'll be mighty happy to get some sweet treats. I can tell you, your candy will be all the Christmas these Indian kids will know."

In a matter of seconds the youngsters bolted forward along the road. Their pace was slow as Josh and Cassie carefully culled through the blanket covered mass of humanity looking for children. When they spotted some on either side of the road they cried out to them while holding a piece of candy in their hands. With great joy they tossed the confections directly to them.

Cassie, as usual, was her highly verbal self. "Merry Christmas and please enjoy our Christmas candy . . . Merry Christmas, little girl."

As the carriage proceeded through the crowd, Calvin turned to Private Burnett. "Isn't your brother far too young to be a member of the United States Army, Private Burnett? Or . . . is the Army so desperate for escorts for these Indians they accept anyone who's over four feet tall?"

Burnett smiled at hearing a sample of Calvin Cabell's dry sense of humor. He tried to think of a clever witticism, but none came to mind. "Josh is with us on the march, Mr. Cabell, because I was assigned to this prolonged duty. There's no other family member to care for him. I'm all the family he's got."

"Well, why couldn't you be granted a hardship reprieve from this particular duty?"

"I was specifically ordered to serve on this march, because I'm the only soldier who can speak the language of the Cherokee. When I pointed out my responsibility to rear Josh and I pleaded for a pardon, Captain McLellan thought about the situation for a minute. He said, 'We need you on this assignment, Private Burnett. Your country needs you. And if that isn't reason enough, these Cherokee Indians desperately need for you to accompany them to the Oklahoma Territory. To these Indians, your presence would be a God-send'.

"Then Captain McLellan put his hand to his chin and massaged it while he was thinking. He said, 'Private Burnett, on behalf of the United States Army I'm willing to appoint your young brother to the position of drummer boy on this assignment. Now, he wouldn't have to tote around a drum or even carry drumsticks, but he can earn a little money and you can keep watch over him for the next three years. That, Private Burnett, is my best offer. I trust you and Josh will find it acceptable and worth your time'."

Calvin was stunned to hear such a proposal. He wanted to make sure he had the facts straight. "You'll be away from home for three years? Why so long? And how is this lad going to be educated during that very prolonged term of service?

"Well, sir, it'll take about seven months for us to complete the trip. And then, when we reach Oklahoma, it's my responsibility to serve as a liaison between the Army and the Indians. They figure it'll take two years or so for them to make their adjustment. They're going to need a patient interpreter to ease the transition. As for Josh's education, I suppose he'll be qualifying for a degree in 'Indian Science' or something along that order. Learning to read and write in English will just have to wait."

Calvin shook his head in a manner that illustrated his consternation at what he was hearing. Here were these two brothers far from home on Christmas Eve. And the only prospect ahead of them was several more years of military service. That meant three years of Josh's life would be wasted. It seemed important for a bright young kid like Josh to learn how to read and write and to learn about math . . . and all the other things that Calvin thought every child should have the opportunity to experience.

About that time the two men could see the carriage making its return trip through the crowd. This time all the Indian children moved up to the side of the road and held out their hands in hopes there was enough candy for these white folks to toss yet another peppermint stick. They were in luck. Cassie and Josh were still throwing out hard candy and both of them had a huge smile stretched wide on their faces. Jamie looked pleased as punch to serve as the liveryman for such a happy Christmas task.

All this while, Calvin was processing what he had heard from Burnett. He was wondering if or how he should respond. He couldn't get over Burnett's poignant story. But one thing was certain. Calvin wholeheartedly agreed that John Burnett was a blessing to these poor Indian souls being force marched across much of a continent.

"Private Burnett, might I have the opportunity to speak with Captain McLellan?" Calvin inquired. "I'd like to wish him and his men a Merry Christmas. I'd like to offer whatever assistance I can when this massive crowd of wayfarers passes through Memphis."

"I'm sure the Captain would be happy to make your acquaintance. And I'm certain he could use your advice about how we can best move through your city and get across the Mississippi. Please, feel free to approach him. He's over there at his tent. I think I should remain here to welcome back our Christmas candy carriage"

No one could hear what was said between Captain McLellan and Calvin Cabell. But all could see their conversation was peppered with friendly smiles and a few jolly pats on the shoulder. Every now and again Calvin and the Captain looked over at the Burnett brothers and the Cabell kids. Then, they both began to walk toward the carriage, talking lightheartedly along the way. When they arrived, each man was wearing a satisfied smile.

McLellan spoke. "Private Burnett, I've thoroughly enjoyed meeting and talking with Mr. Cabell here. And, I've got to tell you . . . Jamie, Cassie, and Josh . . . you've distributed more than candy to our Indian friends. You've been spreading Christmas joy . . . and that sort of Christmas spirit is what I want to talk to you about."

Calvin was grinning proudly as McLellan kept talking. You could tell that McLellan was soon going to get to the point he wanted to make. The youngsters just didn't know what it was or when it would come.

"Josh and John, Mr. Cabell here has asked me to grant him a Christmas wish. And when I learned what he was wishing for, I didn't have to think one second before I knew I should grant it."

Captain McLellan enjoyed his role as a master of suspense. All the young folks as well as John Burnett were clueless about what he was going to say. "I'm granting you Burnett boys a Christmas leave. Mr. Cabell has invited you to be his house guests this evening and to join him at the Cabell Christmas feast tomorrow. He says there's a hot bath waiting for you and clean clothes that would fit you both. Of course, in return for granting this wish, I'm going to require compensation be given as tribute for my graciousness. What I want in consideration is for you Burnetts to bring me a turkey leg when you return tomorrow evening. Mr. Cabell assures me there will be one to spare. Does an arrangement like that seem reasonable to the two of you?"

Both of the Burnett brothers' jaws dropped so low a turkey leg could have been stuffed inside each of their gaping mouths. And the reaction from the Cabell children was sheer joy. As for Calvin, he was pleased as punch that this leave could be granted and the Cabells could share their Christmas with two folks who would otherwise go without one.

Calvin wanted to get this festive celebration started as soon as possible. "I hear no objections from anybody, so I think it's reasonable to assume we need to hustle . . . so we can get home to Memphis. John and Josh, you two run and get your gear together and meet back here in five minutes. And, as for transportation, John, we'll need for you to ride your horse into town. The rest of us can fit in the carriage. Captain McLellan wants you to meet the troops by eight o'clock tomorrow evening at wherever they'll be camping along the highway. He predicts the march should be just outside Memphis by then."

Josh looked up at Cassie and Jamie. Both were delighted to hear their father's invitation. Jamie sensed there was lollygagging going on, so he tried to hurry things along. "Well, let's go fellas. It'll be dark in ninety minutes.

369

We've got some cleaning up to do and an eleven o'clock church service to attend. Time's a wasting."

John turned to Mr. Cabell and shook his hand heartily. Then he turned to Captain McClellan and he did the same. "Thank you, captain . . . and thanks to you, too, Mr. Cabell. What a surprise this Christmas has turned out to be. Let's go, Josh. We need to fetch our gear as quick as a bat flies."

And with that challenge, the two Burnett brothers high-tailed it back to camp. Calvin had never seen such a speedy dash.

Before they got out of ear shot he called out to them. "Hey boys, bring all your dirty clothes. We'll send you back tomorrow with them freshly laundered."

\* \* \* \* \* \* \* \*

Bettie, Mose, Jed, and Catherine were all beginning to be anxious why the family's Indian surveillance expedition hadn't yet returned. The sun set almost thirty minutes ago and Bettie expressed her concern that Cassie wasn't dressed warmly enough to cope with the winter evening's chill. "I fear she gonna catch her death a cold if she don't get in dis warm house soon."

Catherine got especially nervous when she heard her servant articulate the very same concerns which were popping up in her mind. She had considered all the worst possible reasons why her family wasn't home yet. "The carriage lost a wheel along the dark road. The Indians captured them for ransom and refused to let them go until they were assured the government would return their homeland to them. They've been robbed by a highwayman."

Everything she considered as a possible reason why they weren't standing with her right that instant was bad news. And bad news is what no one deserves on Christmas Eve.

"There they is," Mose called out pointing to the glimmering carriage lamps he spotted outside and heading toward the stable. "I do believe there's a soldier fella with 'em."

Catherine and the black folks were noticeably relieved. But, what about this "soldier fella"? This picture Mose painted still wasn't sensible. Now, there were new questions Catherine wanted answered before she could breath easily once again. She continued standing vigil at the window.

Soon she spotted Cassie walking toward the door. She was accompanied by a boy Catherine had never seen before. He was carrying a nap sack over his shoulder. Close behind Cassie, she could see Jamie, Calvin, and yet another strange man who also toted a nap sack. She darted to the back door as it opened. Cassie stepped inside with a big smile on her face.

"Mother, we've brought home a Christmas present for you. Daddy invited two soldiers to spend the holiday with us. Come out and meet my new friend, Josh Burnett."

"My Word, Josh, aren't you a little young to be a soldier? Well, young as you may be, we're pleased to have you with us."

Josh was about to give a polite "Thank you" to his hostess, but the door opened once again. Jamie, Calvin, and the man who actually resembled a soldier followed behind.

"Catherine, may I present to you Private John Burnett from East Tennessee. I see you've already met his young brother, Josh. We met these two soldiers at the Indian camping site and I invited them home so they can enjoy a proper Christmas."

"Well, I declare, this is a Christmas surprise like none I could have imagined. Welcome, gentlemen. We're all pleased to have you as guests of our family."

Bettie, Mose, and Jed stood ten feet behind Catherine. They were just as surprised as their mistress. Each knew there would be an extra chore or two they would need to complete for the guests. So, they awaited their instructions. Calvin gave the first one.

"Mose, we're going to need a lot of hot water. These Christmas waifs need a bath and I've told them they would return to their unit tomorrow evening with freshly laundered clothes. And, Bettie, we're all as hungry as Santa's reindeer the day after Christmas. What's on the menu for our Christmas Eve dinner?"

"I made rabbit stew, just like you like it, Mr. Cabell. And we got fresh dinner rolls to sop up the broth. And we got that fruit cake Miz Cabell bought from the bake shop. I'm gonna whip us some heavy cream and pile it high on each piece of cake."

"Excellent." Calvin turned to the Burnett boys. He could see they were almost salivating at the menu Bettie had described. "Sounds like good eating to me, gentlemen. Of course, I'm certain the U.S. Army serves a better meal than what we'll have. But they won't be gathering around a Christmas tree after supper like we will."

The mention of food caused Cassie to say, "Daddy, remember, Bettie and I made dozens of cookies and gingerbread men. What Josh and John don't eat here, they can tote plenty of them back to camp."

Catherine's anxiousness had finally been relieved. She was now smiling like this was going to be the best Christmas ever. "All right, gentlemen, we already have some hot water available . . . and we'll have some more ready in fifteen minutes. Why don't you two step in the wash room and strip down. There's a number twelve tub there we can fill about one third full. It's enough to get you soaped up. Then, by the time you're ready to rinse, I suspect the next bucket of hot water will be ready."

John and Josh looked at each other. They hadn't had a warm bath in over a month. Josh still was incredulous this was all happening to him. He had to pinch himself to confirm it all wasn't a fantasy.

"Mrs. Cabell, thanks so much. The last time we had a bath was longer than I reckon you'd want to know. I still can't believe all this. But until someone convinces me this is all a dream, then I want to thank you and Mr. Cabell for your hospitality."

Calvin was still beaming, but he thought these social niceties were going on a bit too long. There was a dinner to be consumed and an eleven o'clock church service to attend. He was already thinking about what sorts of gifts for the two brothers he could scrounge up.

"Let's get a move on it, lads. Mose, you get the tub filled with whatever hot water we have. And Bettie, you heat up as much water as you can. Now, Bettie, I know it's Christmas, but I think all of us here want these Burnett boys to return to camp wearing clean clothes. I trust you can wash whatever they've brought and dry them by the fire . . . so their clothes will be suitable when they head back about six o'clock tomorrow."

Bettie nodded her head, "Yes." Then she looked at young Jed in a manner that communicated, "You're going to have to help, son."

Calvin sensed everybody had their duties assigned. "All right, we've all got things to do. Let's not tarry. Christmas doesn't wait around, you know."

* * * * * * * * *

In their wildest imagination, the Burnett brothers never figured they'd ever be sitting at a long formal dining table covered with an embroidered lace table cloth. They looked in amazement at the finest China dinnerware they had ever seen. There was Sterling silver tableware and three silver candelabras that gave off more than enough light for everyone to clearly see one another. You could even look down at your plate and actually see what you're eating. The boys couldn't help but imagine what they would be eating tonight back at camp. Whatever it would have been, it couldn't begin to compare with everything they were experiencing.

Catherine never threw anything away. So, she was glad she hadn't passed on Jamie's outgrown clothes to someone else. She had almost donated them earlier in the month, but she never got around to it. The clothes fit Josh fairly well. Furthermore, John and Jamie were just about the same size. Consequently, John comfortably fit into his borrowed duds.

And then, there were these black servants. Neither of the boys had ever been waited on by a slave. However, it was Calvin who ladled out rabbit stew into the diners' bowl from a large porcelain tureen painted with hunting scenes. Each brother felt like he had been reborn . . . into another, quite splendid, life.

Before dinner the "squeaky clean" Burnetts joined the family in the front parlor. A fire roared in the fireplace and the marble mantle was draped with holly boughs so the red berries and dark green leaves glistened in the firelight. On the round table at the center of the room was a beautiful, painted porcelain crèche scene . . . complete with the three wise men, two camels, and several sheep. Each figurine was stalwartly keeping watch over the baby Jesus.

Calvin was serving brandy to John. And, for the first time, Jamie was offered a glass. John held up his Irish crystal snifter . . . half filled with its amber colored contents. He raised the glass, so he could look through it and see the fire. The beveled carvings on the glass made the liquid glow and gleam as the cut glass caught the fire's light and ricocheted its bright radiance in all directions.

Following the meal and the fruit cake covered with a mound of whipped cream that stood five or six inches high, the satisfied diners moved, once again, to the parlor where they took their coffee. Meanwhile, Jamie supervised Josh and Cassie lighting the Christmas tree. This was serious business. A candle not mounted properly on a cedar stem . . . strong enough to support it upright . . . could suddenly turn a majestic sight into a raging fire. So, to err on the side of safety, three wash pitchers of water sat on the floor in the corner.

Soon the stately grandfather clock in the great entry hall chimed the time. It was quarter past ten. Catherine instructed everyone, including the three slaves, to bundle up. They were all about to walk to the Presbyterian Church for its traditional midnight service. Calvin was going to help serve communion. He was also scheduled to read a passage from St. Matthew's account of the Christmas story in Chapter 4, Verse 10 – 18. It began, "Then the Lord spoke to Mary. And, lo, I shall bring unto you a child . . . and his name will be called Jesus."

The small children gathered at the front of the sanctuary and sang several carols accompanied by a respiring pump organ. Josh and John had never seen or heard one before. Each person brought his own candle. The last hymn was "Silent Night". Reverend Blair lit his candle from the most recently lighted Advent candle that was in the middle of the other four candles burning on the communion table. He proceeded to walk down the aisle, lighting only the candles held by the officers of the church. They, in turn, ignited the candles held by their family members and anyone else nearby. Jonas Williams' slave, Thomas, awaited Reverend Blair at the back of the sanctuary to light his candle. Thomas rushed up the stairs to the balcony . . . and soon all the slaves' candles were glowing, as well.

By the last verse of the carol, the sanctuary was aglow. Josh looked about, instead of singing along. He thought how he had never experienced such majesty. He wished the service would never end.

When the benediction was pronounced, "Now, go out into the world and share the message that Jesus is born. And tell the people that He brings to each one of them great tidings of comfort and joy." Everyone then joyously walked outside where a heartfelt "Merry Christmas" was exchanged between just about everyone gathered on the sidewalk.

However, Catherine unwittingly punctured one gaping hole in Calvin's Christmas cheer. She told him while they were dressing for church that she had run into Clarabelle Lancaster at the butcher shop. Clarabelle said Judge

Robinson was ill and he preferred to remain at home in Raleigh . . . instead of trekking to Memphis to spend Christmas with her and Shelby. In a thoughtless burst of Yuletide hospitality, Catherine invited Clarabelle and Shelby to join them for Christmas dinner . . . without first conferring with her husband.

Catherine could plainly see Calvin clench his teeth at the unwelcome news. But Catherine had no inkling of the animus between her husband and her invited guest. Despite the unwelcome news, Calvin was determined that nothing would spoil the joyful spirit of this Christmas. He pledged to himself he would somehow get through the holiday and he wouldn't let this bothersome rodent, Shelby Lancaster, sit at his table and spoil the cheer that was building . . . especially with John and Josh's inclusion in the celebration.

The Cabell clan walked home together singing, "Joy to the World, the Lord is come. Let earth receive her King."

Calvin Cabell pondered some things that Christmas Eve he had never pondered before. Sharing this Christmas with his unanticipated guests, his family, and his slaves warmed his heart and he felt particularly grateful. He looked up at the starry sky and offered a silent prayer of Thanksgiving . . . for his family, his guests, and for his slaves.

But when he spoke the word, 'slaves,' to himself in his impromptu prayer, the Christmas joy diminished. He recalled he had never – after five long years – talked to Mose as he had promised. He hadn't yet recited what the terms and conditions for his family's freedom would be. This realization made him eerily uncomfortable.

Calvin turned around and waited for the three black members of the household to catch up with him. When they did, he looked Mose and Bettie squarely in their eyes.

"Merry Christmas, Mose. Merry Christmas, Bettie."

# CHAPTER

# 26

CHRISTMAS DAY 1838

It was almost one o'clock in the morning when the Cabells returned home from church. Each person in the household that night was in a joyous holiday mood . . . no doubt, sparked by the heart-warming midnight service. It was now Christmas Day.

Catherine showed the Burnett brothers to their room. They hadn't slept in a bed – especially a bed with freshly laundered linens – for over a year. Both thought that a sound sleep, in a clean bed, within a Memphis mansion . . . was all the Christmas present anyone could ever hope for.

Meanwhile, Calvin collaborated in the front parlor with Jamie and Cassie. "We've got to come up with some respectable gifts for our two guests. What can we scavenge up on such short notice?"

After some ideas were suggested and discussed, the three devised a plan.

Calvin had ordered a crate of oranges from New Orleans. He said he would give both brothers two of them. Oranges were supposed to be a surprise gift . . . stashed before dawn in the children's stockings. But everyone knew Calvin ordered oranges every year. So, it was senseless for him to continue pretending the fruit was unexpected.

Jamie graciously offered to forfeit his pocket knife, so Josh would have a proper gift. He also thought it would be appropriate if he gave the boy his outgrown clothes.

John was harder "to shop for". After considerable discussion, Calvin came up with the idea of giving him the new horse harness and reins he purchased two months earlier. They were a fine example of hardware and leatherwork and

Calvin had bought the set at a premium price. He knew the gift would be much appreciated by John and, no doubt, the Army private would put them to good use.

"Well, I think we've managed to cobble together a respectable Christmas for our friends. Thanks, Jamie, for sacrificing your knife. I'm sure you know I'll replace it straight away. Would you mind, son, going to the stable and fetching John's gift?"

"Daddy, I've got to get hustling. We've got several packages that need wrapping."

"Yes, Cassie, I suppose we do need you and your mother to come up with some appropriate paper and bows. Let's get these chores done as soon as we can. We all need, at the very least, a few hours of sleep."

\* \* \* \* \* \* \* \* \* \*

"Mornin', Mr. Cabell. Merry Christmas to you, sir."

"Thank you, Bettie, and I wish you a Merry Christmas, too. I smell biscuits baking. Mind you, let's not feed everyone like field hands. We're going to have our Christmas dinner at noon, sharp. The Burnett boys probably need to leave about four-thirty. By the way, will their clothes be clean by then?"

"They're just about ready, Mr. Cabell. All three of us worked late out in the kitchen building. Right this second the clothes is washed and they is dryin' by our cabin's fire."

"That's excellent. Thanks, Bettie. That's excellent work, indeed."

Mose walked into the room and poured some water from the servant's pitcher into the white ceramic wash bowl. He began to lather up his hands. "Mr. Cabell, all the fires are stoked and hummin' away. Anything else you need doin', sir?"

Calvin walked to the pantry and pulled out a box from under the lowest shelf. He scooped up nine oranges using both his hands. "Merry Christmas to the three of you. Mose. I hope you enjoy these oranges. There's a crate of apples that was supposed to have arrived by now . . . and you can be assured that we'll soon be sharing them with you. Where's Jed? I want to give him three oranges."

"He's out in the summer kitchen, sir. I'll give three oranges to him and tell him 'bout what you said."

The stairwell abruptly became the epicenter of thundering, clomping sounds. Calvin reasoned all of his family and his two guests were bounding downstairs - everyone at the same time. He moved toward the hall to greet them.

"Good morning, everyone. Merry Christmas to you all. John . . . Josh . . . it's a Cabell tradition to open our presents before we sit down to a Christmas breakfast. Come along everyone. Let's gather around the tree."

Calvin put his arm around John and directed him while Jamie did the same for Josh.

"Mercy me," Cassie exclaimed. "There's a present here labeled 'John Burnett'. And, look over here. I see two presents under the tree labeled, 'Josh Burnett'."

Catherine and Calvin insisted the Burnetts open their gifts first. John was speechless when he discovered the leather harness inside its colorfully decorated gunny sack. And Josh's eyes widened gleefully when he found some shirts, some pants, and one splendid coat in his package. The two guests offered their grateful thanks to everyone. John assumed the authority to speak for both of them.

"Mr. and Mrs. Cabell, these gifts are so unexpected . . . so, unnecessary. We've already had the finest Christmas experience we'll probably ever have. These presents are simply too much. We talked about this last night. Both of us think we've been tossed into a glorious dream . . . and we need to wake up and get about our regular daily lives."

"Nonsense," Jamie responded. "You've made OUR Christmas very special – very special, indeed."  Then he pointed to one particular wrapped gift. "Look, Josh, there's still another present under the tree. And it's got your name on it. Here, open it up before it vanishes . . . when you wake up from your dream."

Cassie stooped to pick up his present and she placed the wrapped box in Josh's hands. "Now, open it, Josh. We all hope you'll like what's inside."

Slowly and methodically the boy peeled back the box's wrapping paper as if he were planning to use it again. Then he lifted the lid. He couldn't believe his eyes. There in the box was a bone handled pocket knife. It was the finest carving tool he had ever seen. With eyes still wide with disbelief, he lifted up the knife and he slid his thumb along the sharp metal edge as if he were honing it.

John wore a broad smile. He was so pleased for his brother. Josh had wanted a knife for the longest time. And now, by total chance, he held a spectacular carving tool . . . in a place where twenty four hours ago neither he nor his brother would have ever imagined they would be. Instead of being parties to a gruesome Cherokee relocation, they were here - amid a fine and a loving family who lived in a house that was the closest thing to a mansion John had ever seen.

Josh looked appreciatively at Calvin . . . and then Catherine . . . and, finally, at Cassie. "Thank you ALL for this gift."

Then Josh focused his grateful eyes on Jamie. "I especially thank you, Jamie." He knew where the knife had come from.

After the Cabells opened their gifts, they rifled through the Christmas stockings. There were two extra ones nailed to the mantle for their guests. Josh and John found two pair of socks in their stockings as well as two oranges. It appeared to them the magic might never end.

They all sat down again at the dining table and enjoyed Bettie's hot biscuits, bacon, and an assortment of jams and jellies that gleamed brightly in small cut glass bowls. Each variety of fruity preserves was impaled with a beautifully crafted silver spoon. They ate so heartily, Calvin admonished everyone. He reminded them the Christmas dinner would be served in several hours.

Everybody was excused from the table to go outside in the brisk sunshine. Josh wanted to find a soft piece of wood to whittle. But John lingered at the table with Catherine and Calvin. They were both very curious to learn more about their guests and about the cruel relocation of the Cherokee.

John was happy to answer their questions. He told his hosts about growing up in Sullivan County and how his mother died when Josh was six. He said his father spent most of the time after that carousing around the region for days at a time. He was ultimately killed by a man who shot him for getting too fresh with his wife.

The brothers became orphans when John was fourteen and Josh was eight. John had kept the two of them fed and clothed ever since his mother died.

"Daddy was still alive, but he was worthless. He just wanted to sit and be served . . . like Mother had always done for him. I got fed up with him. After awhile, Pop left one afternoon saying he wouldn't be home for supper. I guess he got that right. We didn't hear another word from him . . . or about him . . . 'til we got word he'd been killed in Sevierville. That was about the time I started settin' out for huntin' trips that lasted several months at a time. I really needed to get away from everything home started to symbolize – nothin' but heartaches, hunger, hard work, and our worthless Pop."

"So if you were out on hunting trips that lasted for months, who looked after Josh?" Catherine's motherly instincts were showing and she was relieved to hear John's answer.

"Mama's sister took him in and raised him the best she could. Of course, you could say she took me in, too. But by that time I was sixteen. I was determined to set out on my own. Then, one day several years later, I came back from one of those trips of mine and learned she had died, too. She took to a fever. Josh said he did the best he could for her for two or three days. Finally, she just closed her eyes while Josh was holdin' her hand until he couldn't feel the blood movin' through her veins no more.

"That's when I decided the two of us were gonna have to make it . . . all by ourselves. We lived just outside of Pigeon Forge and Josh started choppin' wood he could sell to the widow Jemison and anybody else who made it worth his while. I had learned to be a respectable gunsmith from my huntin' experiences. So, I took to working on firearms of any sort. We made it okay, I suppose. And then, of course, there's the Army that was a callin'."

Calvin asked John, "How did you come to know the Cherokee language?"

"Well, sir, on these long huntin' trips I became familiar with many of the Cherokee. I hunted with them by day and slept around their fires at night. That's where I first learned their language. They also taught me skills like trailing animals or building traps and snares.

"Back in 1832 I was on one of my hunts when I found a wounded Cherokee. He'd been shot – just like a dog – by a band of white hunters. The Indian was hidin' in a cave. He was wounded . . . and afraid to come out.

He recognized me and he says that's when I did my doctorin'. I cleaned the wounds as best I could. He was weak from a loss of blood and it was several days since he had any water to drink. I built a shelter out of bark I peeled from a dead chestnut tree. I fed him chestnuts and roasted deer meat. Then when he was well enough I helped him get returned to his home. What a sight his homecoming was. Everyone in the village had given him up for dead. But there he stood – alive. The Indians claimed I saved his life."

"This is all fascinating, John. And it sounds so familiar. I'm an acquaintance of Sam Houston. You know, Governor Houston spent several years living with the Cherokee. He told me it was the best part of his life."

"Yes sir, you're not the first man to tell me about Governor Houston's time with the Cherokee matchin' my own experiences. Sometimes I wonder what Sam Houston would've done if he walked in my shoes in the past few months. I've seen Cherokee villages destroyed, innocent men shot in cold blood, and folks herded into stockades like they were barnyard animals.

"You see, I thought President Jackson was on record sayin' the Cherokee were our friends and our allies. I've got to tell you, I knew all along he was set on carvin' out a good part of Indian Territory . . . and I reckoned he'd give it to white settlers. But I never thought he would give his approval to the kind of abuse . . . and this inhuman march the Cherokee have endured."

Calvin tried to put things in perspective. "But John, I don't think President Jackson was the primary official in the government behind all of this?"

"Well, here's what I can tell you about Jackson. You can reach your own conclusions. Early this year an Indian boy had a gold nugget he sold to a white trader. Well, word got out. And all of a sudden, the area was overrun with fortune hunters . . . claimin' they was government agents. Crimes were committed that were a disgrace to civilized people.

"Mind you, all these horrors were set on the Cherokee over one piece of gold. Why anybody sportin' a brain knows there ain't no gold to be found in the Appalachian Mountains.

"Now, Chief Junaluska was personally acquainted with President Jackson. Old Hickory had assembled five hundred of his Cherokee scouts to assist him at the Battle of Horseshoe Bend. The Cherokee lost thirty-three men that first day – all in the name of the United States. And Chief Junaluska personally drove his tomahawk into the skull of a Creek warrior. Everybody seems to agree that if it weren't for the Cherokee, Jackson would've likely lost that battle.

"So, with all this 'good will' the Cherokee thought they had nurtured with Jackson, Chief John Ross asked Chief Junaluska to go visit Jackson and get him to stop all this senseless mayhem. But Jackson dispatched Colonel Winfield Scott to secure the area. And that's exactly what he did. He ordered innocent Indians to be executed . . . just to let 'em know who's boss.

"Now remember, Mr. Cabell, Chief Junaluska had saved Jackson's life. He was expecting to meet with a man who would help the same folks who'd helped him. Jackson reluctantly agreed to meet with Junaluska . . . and he heard his plea. Then President Jackson looked the chief straight in the eye and he said, 'Sir, your audience is ended. There's nothin' more I can do for you.'

"The Chief came home and reported all this to Chief John Ross. He wailed . . . and cried out, 'Oh my God, if I had known at the Battle of Horseshoe Bend what I know now, American history might have been differently written.'

"Junaluska looked at Chief John Ross and predicted it was just a matter of time before the Cherokee were going to be rounded up or killed. He was so right."

"Yes," Calvin remarked, "Governor Houston saw this land grab coming back in 1819. He convinced as many of the Cherokee as he could that they should voluntarily move to Arkansas."

"I don't know if any place is gonna be far enough, Mr. Cabell. This trip has been long and hard. Many Indians have died along the way. I know, for example, of a night when twenty-two of the Cherokee died. There are hundreds of shallow graves dug along the side of the road. And soon we're gonna be crossing the Mississippi with hundreds of miles to still go in the dead of winter. Sometimes I wonder if any of 'em will finally make it to the Oklahoma Territory."

Catherine had tears in her eyes. There weren't any facts in John's story that indicated the white men in this nation had a reason to call themselves civilized. "John, your story sounds so bizarre . . . so unbelievable. Yet, I know every word is the truth. However, I've got to admit that I'm suddenly ashamed for the entire white race."

Then, Catherine – in this emotion ridden moment – said something that was astonishing. "The white man has pillaged and killed for gold where there's none to be had. And the white man has murdered scores of innocent people out of greed. And the white man has no compunction about owning slaves to do their work. There appears to be no end to the travesties of our race . . . and I deeply regret that."

Suddenly, it was as if a bell had rung in Catherine's consciousness – a huge bronze church bell that ordinarily might have been heard for miles. All three people around the table instantly sensed the bell Catherine had just rung was pealing straight and true. They knew her observations about the "white man" would be life changing. Those bell peals were reminding her that she, too, had been a party to some of the same sins of the "white man" which she was now almost cavalierly condemning.

"John, I know you're obligated to serve in the U.S. Army. But does the same obligation apply to Josh?"

"No, Ma'am, Josh is just along for the ride . . . so somebody can look out after him."

"He seems like such a nice boy. He's on the cusp of shaping his life experiences and molding himself into the man he'll soon become. How much schooling has he had?"

"Next to none, ma'am. You see, I can speak Cherokee. But I can't read much in English. So, there's no way I can teach him on the road the kind of learnin' I know he should have. But it looks like he's primed to serve in the Army. A body doesn't have to read and write in the Army."

"Well, he certainly seems to be a very bright boy," Calvin commented.

"Yes, sir, you're right about that. Why, he picked up speaking Cherokee just as good as me by the time we got to Chattanooga. He's smart as a whip."

Catherine and Calvin's marriage had gone through some rough times. Catherine was emotionally unstable. She often wouldn't come out of her "sitting room" for days. And Calvin had all but given up the notion that they would ever have a love life again. Then there was Jamie. While he was sometimes irritating whenever he used his gift of superior intelligence, he nevertheless had moved out of the house – probably forever. The Cabell place was beginning to feel a little empty – a little lonely.

For a moment around that table Catherine and Calvin shared a oneness with one another that hadn't been discernible for years. They both had independently thought of the same plan. It was a plan to rein in the growing dysfunction within the Cabell household.

"Are you thinking what I'm thinking, Mrs. Cabell?"

"I'm certain of it, dear. I have no doubt that I'm certain of it. Would you do the honor?"

Calvin turned to Private Burnett as he took a sip of water from the glass Bettie always poured as an antidote to her strong coffee. Then, he cleared his throat.

"John, you've done a noble job raising your young brother. It's clear to us you've done the best job possible . . . given the circumstances. But, as you say, Josh is a very bright youngster. And it seems a shame that he's not been given the benefit of a respectable education. I know you say he could join the Army when he's grown. But wouldn't it be terrific if he had other options ahead in his life?

"I wonder if you'd consider letting Josh stay here and live with us for awhile. That way he wouldn't be forced to witness any more death along the road . . . and he could get some much needed formal education. I'd be more than happy to pay for that . . . as well as any other expenses his stay might require. I think it's fair to say we would welcome Josh into our home and treat him as a son. With Jamie away for good now, we could use another son around here. How does that sound to you, John?"

The question called for serious introspection. John had grown up dirt poor . . . caring for a mother who died . . . and then he cared for a father who was as useless as teats on a boar hog. He had escaped temporarily from all that chaos by retreating into the wilderness. Just like Sam Houston, those years were the best part of his life. But now he found himself still scraping to get by and still caring for his brother. But, despite his best efforts, he wasn't able to do much for him. Instead of learning to read and write, Josh had to dig shallow graves almost every day for Indians who were no longer able to take another step along this long, treacherous trail of tears.

"I can't believe what I'm hearing you say, Mr. Cabell. And, yet, I know you mean it."

John looked quickly at Catherine. "And I know you have Mrs. Cabell's support. But, you do recognize, don't you, I'm obligated to stay in Oklahoma for two – maybe three years?"

"Yes, John, my husband speaks for both of us, although I must admit he speaks more eloquently than I could. John, we'll do everything we can to allow Josh to grow into a fine young man. Here, he'd have a mother and a father, once again. Cassie could work with him on his reading skills and, in no time, I'm sure a bright boy like Josh will be reading at the level of other boys his age."

Calvin knew John was feeling overwhelmed, so he spoke . . . trying to be reassuring.

"We're not going to keep him a prisoner. He could leave whenever he might choose to do so. Of course, we wouldn't allow him to go anywhere without your permission. Then, when you're released from military duty and you pass through Memphis on your way home, you, too, can stay as long as you like. You might even want to make Memphis your home. But if you want to take Josh with you and if he's of a mind to go, then the two of you can be reunited and be on your way. On this, John you have my word."

"While you and Mr. Cabell were talking, ma'am, I've been running through my feeble mind a list of all the benefits as well as the bad things about what you're offering. So far I've only managed to think of the benefits. I suspect I could consider this proposal for days and the ledger would come out the same."

John Burnett was a man who had witnessed far more tragedy in his young life than should be allowed. Now he was a man who was duty bound to the U.S. Army. He was  destined to serve the Army's needs first . . . and his brother's needs would have to be addressed with whatever time and resources he had left. And that, probably, wouldn't amount to much.

"Well, Mr. and Mrs. Cabell, you've treated Josh and me like family ever since we've been here. I have no doubt you'd treat Josh that same way . . . forevermore. And, I'm sure it's in his best interest if that could happen."

John paused for a moment before stating the obvious. "I think Josh should have some say in this, though."

"Absolutely," Catherine said. "This decision should be made by Josh, too. After all, it's not like we're buying a slave who has no say in the matter."

386

Once again, that big heavy bell within Catherine's conscience was set pealing. It was cast large and its clanging timbre reverberated with ominous, ear-piercing sounds. Those peals shook her to the core.

 "I think I'll go outside.  Josh and I can take a walk and discuss all of this."

"Excellent, John, you take a walk - as long as you want. And be sure to accurately express the sincerity of Mrs. Cabell and me."

"I will, sir. Now . . . if you two will excuse me, I have a speech to make."

"You're excused, John. But we'll take no excuses if Josh turns us down."

All three shared a chuckle at Catherine's sense of humor. John arose from his chair and placed his linen napkin by his plate – just like he might have been taught by a refined mother. He moved to the front door and closed it behind him. Within two seconds, Catherine and Calvin heard him shout out,  "Josh, where are you, little brother?"

There was silence at the table. Everything had been said regarding this proposal about Josh that needed to be said.

But those wake-up bells ringing within Catherine's soul continued their clanging. They kept nagging at her. And, even though she had wanted to bring up the subject time and again, it still remained unspoken.  She could no longer put it off. She had to get it out.

"Mr. Cabell, have you ever had that conversation with Mose . . . like you promised?"

*No Coin for Charon*

# CHAPTER
# 27

Christmas Day 1838

Calvin sat imperiously at the head of his imposing dining table and quietly studied each person seated around it. He winced inside when he made eye contact with Shelby. "Why did Catherine feel compelled to invite the Lancasters?" he whined to himself. "If she only knew how Shelby had threatened me. Of all the rotten luck . . . having him seated as a guest on what was supposed to be the most glorious Cabell Christmas ever."

He arose regally from his chair and tapped his crystal water goblet with a sterling silver table knife. He held a firm grasp to its stem so its clinking sound easily resonated throughout the dining room and beyond. Its clear message was that everyone within earshot should fall silent and give his or her full attention to the master of the house.

Then, when his command had been duly answered and all eyes were fixed on him, he placed the knife and glass back in their proper table setting. He held nothing in his hands. But there was much he held in his heart. And, he wanted to share it this Christmas Day.

"Friends and family, it gives me great pleasure to welcome you to my table to share this Christmas dinner. We hope each of you will fondly remember our meal as the Cabell Christmas feast."

There was a low murmur of giggles around the table. Everyone appreciated Calvin's exaggerated pretense of portraying the Cabell family as a clan that customarily functioned with an air of pompous grandeur.

"Mrs. Cabell and I are delighted each of you could be with us today." Then he turned toward his wife and offered her a courtly bow. "And, Mrs. Cabell, we're all grateful for the lovely table you've set for us. You've made our home a model for gracious entertaining. And your hospitality is appreciated by all who pass through our doorway. We bask in your unmatched brand of domestic glory."

Once again, the dinner guests snickered at their host's sense of humor. It was clear he was in a playful mood and the dining experience would be highly congenial.

"Our son, Jamie, has returned home from Centre College for Christmas. We had hoped his cousin and best friend, John Breckinridge, could have joined him so he, too, might be sitting here with us. But, alas, John found it necessary to remain with his own widowed mother and grandmother. Jamie, we're grateful for your safe trip to us. And we wish you 'God speed' when you return to Kentucky later this week.

"To my daughter, Cassie, you're an especially honored member of the family. Your generous and loving spirit was manifested yesterday as you sought to bring just a smidgeon of Christmas joy to the Cherokee children who are camped presently outside our city."

Cassie's father painted a perturbed scowl on his face before he continued. "And, in the process, Cassie, you've also given great joy to Arnold Edgewater's Candy Store. Your compassion – funded with my money - increased the store's December gross sales at least fifty per cent over what Mr. Edgewater had anticipated."

Now genuine laughter erupted around the table. Then Calvin carried on and chided, "I shall be withholding from your monthly allowance a portion of the cost of your extravagant Christmas largesse until the amount is paid in full. I suspect your debt will be cleared sometime before the end of summer."

Calvin knew he had to face the inevitable task of greeting the Lancasters. He, essentially, bit his lip before proceeding with the expected social niceties. "We Cabells wish to extend a warm welcome and our great gratitude that Shelby and Clarabelle Lancaster chose to accept our invitation to join us here." He couldn't dog cuss Shelby in his remarks, although he would have preferred that option . . . if it were possible. Then, he had an idea. He could thrash the bastard with his wit.

"Mrs. Cabell and I debated whether we should invite the Lancasters at the last minute. We wondered if there would be enough food. But Catherine reminded me of Shelby's diminutive size and the logical extrapolation . . .

that he wouldn't eat much. So, she calculated there should be plenty of victuals to go around."

At first Shelby turned red with either embarrassment or anger. Then he looked around and could see all the laughter that abounded was not spiteful. It was in good fun. And it appeared to affirm that Calvin's remarks were made out of fondness for him. At least, he convinced himself this was his host's motive.

"Now, Clarabelle Lancaster's appetite is not known to us. And we feared that . . . if it was anything like we've heard it to be . . . then her food consumption would cancel out the savings we were counting on achieving with Shelby."

The volume of laughter grew with each barb Calvin poked at everyone around the table. After all, Clarabelle Lancaster was thin as a rail. But he wasn't through with her yet. "Now that you are knowledgeable, Clarabelle, of the logic we employed as we considered our guest list, I ask that you restrict yourself to just two servings of each dish on the menu."

Clarabelle fidgeted the same nervous fidget Shelby made at his own teasing tongue lashing. Then, she also smiled and joined in the growing merriment.

John and Josh looked at each other while they enjoyed the fun as well. Each wondered if they would be the next victims locked in Calvin's sights.

"And we're especially pleased that John and Josh Burnett were able to join us. Of course, they wouldn't be here – once again – if it hadn't been for Cassie's unbounded compassion and charity. She has, as you all know, the natural instinct to drag home every stray cat she sees. So, it's only rational she would follow those instincts and drag the Burnetts home to our Christmas dinner."

Calvin had summoned up a devilish grin at every grilling he had dished out this afternoon. He was rather pleased with himself and with the joyous laughter he managed to spread around his table. However, his expression became more serious and genuine. In Calvin's judgment, the Burnett brothers deserved more than a mere quip or two.

"Actually, Josh and John, Mrs. Cabell and I have heard you state several times how beholden you felt to the Cabell clan for inviting you to spend Christmas with us. We both want you to know that we are, in point of fact, beholden to you for making this Christmas the most special any of us might have hoped for. As we've gotten to know you, we've come to admire both brothers. We're so very appreciative that you would grace our holiday table. We thank you for accepting our invitation."

In a few short seconds Calvin had managed to transform tears of laughter into the kind of tears that well up from deep inside . . . from great, heartfelt sentimentality. The guests and family members became hushed. Their silence was a tribute to the Burnetts and to Calvin, who so eloquently summarized the way all of his family felt about these two new soldier friends. Then, with impeccable timing, Calvin seized just the right moment to speak once again.

"Ladies and gentlemen, I would like to propose a toast. Would each of you rise? And, please, raise up your glasses of sherry?"

"To our new family members, the Burnett brothers – John and Josh: You've traveled a long and arduous journey that has led you to us today. You gentlemen have witnessed great hardship and much injustice. You've seen man's capacity for inhumanity to his fellow man – when his only difference is the hue of his skin. And you've done all this while still withstanding the natural inclination to let these experiences harden your hearts.

"As our Lord hath said, 'Blessed are the merciful, for they shall obtain mercy.' And so it is that you both will most surely be blessed by God Almighty.

"So, we wish to honor your steadfastness and your determination to uphold the human spirit. We wish you safety on your continued journey in the coming days and months. May you grow in your spirit and in your faith. And, as part of that faith, keep mindful that we around this table today shall keep you forever in our hearts . . . and, in our prayers."

The speech sent chills up and down the spines of everybody. It embodied the spirit of the season's promise for "peace on earth and good will toward men." Calvin's touching way of recounting the past, the present, and the future warmed everyone's heart. He raised his sherry glass above his head.

"To John and Josh Burnett: May your journey in life be fulfilling. And may the road you travel be laid flat and firm with the wind always blowing against your back."

"Hear . . . hear," came the cries . . . almost in unison. Cassie and Catherine moved from their places and hugged both Burnetts. Catherine punctuated her warm feelings by planting a kiss on each brother's cheek.

Then John and Josh walked toward Calvin and offered him a hearty handshake. They both expressed their gratitude for his kind words. While everyone at the table was chatting with one another about Calvin's teasing and his toast, Calvin guided the Burnetts over to the buffet. He wanted to speak to them alone – out of his guests' earshot.

"Josh, your brother's told me you're of a mind to linger here with us . . . as a member of the Cabell family. Is that so, son?

"It IS so, Mr. Cabell. Words can't express to you how honored I am at your proposal. I don't feel worthy to be called a member of your family. But I promise I'll do my best to live up to your hopes and your expectations."

"What joyous news," Calvin exclaimed in a muted voice - so the others couldn't hear him. He placed his right arm around Josh's shoulders and gave him a firm hug.

"May I have your permission to announce this wonderful news at the end of the meal?"

"You may, sir. You have my permission."

Then Calvin disappeared into the kitchen. Two minutes later the dining room door was flung open and he led a procession that included Mose, Bettie, and Jed. Calvin carried a large silver platter covered with a shining silver dome adorned with artfully crafted escallops around its base and its top. Bettie and Mose carried bowls of vegetable dishes to accompany the turkey that was still concealed beneath the platter's lid. Jed brought up the rear carrying a basket of steaming dinner rolls.

Calvin placed the covered serving plate at the center of the buffet table and the black slaves put what they carried on the buffet, too.

All eyes were on Calvin. He took advantage of the attention to dramatically raise the ornate dome to reveal a huge golden brown bird. The guests clapped with delight at the bountiful meal. Then, Calvin once again commanded the diners to be silent.

"Ladies and gentlemen, our Christmas dinner awaits us. I'm sure we're all mightily grateful for it. So, I ask that we stand - hand in hand - around the table so that we might offer our heartfelt thanks to our Lord."

Hands were clasped together forming a chain around the table and everyone bowed their heads as the black family quietly moved toward the kitchen.

"No . . . No . . . we need a circle of prayer here that's complete," Calvin cried out. Mose . . . Bettie . . . and little Jed . . . please come forward and join hands with us."

Mose and Bettie emanated a look of amazed consternation at Calvin's invitation. Or, was it his command, each wondered? Naturally, they followed their master's orders and, with Mose pushing Jed forward before them, the trio respectfully approached the table.

The Cabells began to move backwards behind the seats. They were expanding the circle to accommodate these three dutiful slaves. Soon they, too, were incorporated into the prayer ring. Mose held the hands of Calvin and Catherine. Bettie held the hands of Catherine and Cassie. Jed uncomfortably stood between Cassie and Jamie and he reticently placed his small hands in theirs. Without notice, each person bowed his head.

"O Lord, who made the heavens and the earth, in Your infinite glory . . . You made the sun and the moon and the stars overhead and everything that roams on the planet below. This day we celebrate that You had Your son come down to earth to live among us and to teach us the love You have for all mankind."

Calvin considered his prayer was going well. Indeed, one could say it bordered on being eloquent. But the master of the house had his arch enemy seated around his holiday table. He wasn't about to miss the opportunity to goad him with his guile. This was a chance to speak to Shelby . . . as well as to the Lord.

"Lord, we are all sinners. I know that my sins and the sins of my fellow man will one day be judged by You. We humbly ask that You graciously forgive us from those transgressions and that You take notice and smile down upon us when we attempt to atone for them. We all err. And, when we err, You have given us the opportunity to make things right, as our Lord Jesus taught us.

"We behold the bounty you have provided within our world. We, perhaps, are especially mindful of the Christmas feast you have provided all those around this table. May this food give nourishment to our bodies and enable us to serve Your will . . . more nobly than we have in the past. All this we pray in the name of our Lord, Jesus Christ. Amen."

"Amen" was echoed simultaneously by each person. The black people were noticeably uncomfortable being links in this white ring of prayer. And when the "Amens" had been said, each slave backed away. His parents guided Jed along until the family passed behind the dining room door, once again. All three moved considerably faster than when they processed into the room.

Then the door closed behind them. The curious mingling of the races had been remedied and made right . . . and white . . . once again.

* * * * * * * * * * * * *

"Catherine, the meal was divine. And the turkey was the most succulent I've ever tasted," Clarabelle Lancaster proclaimed to her hostess across the table.

"Now, we need to give credit to Mose and Bettie. Mose shot the bird and Bettie cooked it . . . and, rather beautifully, I must say."

"And your array of desserts was overwhelming. Why, each one of them was more delicious than the last."

"Well, I'd like to give Mose just an ounce of credit for the desserts. But Bettie should be acknowledged as the one who's responsible for each of them."

The door to the dining room opened and Calvin emerged from the kitchen . . . once again with the three black servants in tow. Just as before, it was clear they were commanded to do so. They stood at attention against the wall behind Catherine's seat. And, just like the last time they were called into the room for prayer, each one appeared very uncomfortable.

Calvin, once again, tapped his water glass to signal everyone's attention . . . which he speedily got except for the diners' occasional slurping sips of coffee.

"Friends and family, I stand before you once again to tell you how pleased we are that each of you is here. As I examine our guests, it's apparent your appetites have been satisfied. We've all enjoyed our sweet desserts. And, while you might think you've experienced all the delectable trimmings for the day, I believe I can convince you that isn't the case.

"As I commented before the meal . . . and as I memorialized in my toast, Mrs. Cabell and I have been blessed to have the Burnett brothers join us this

Christmas. Private John Burnett was granted his holiday leave with the understanding he would return to his post by eight o'clock this evening. We shall regret losing him. But our regret is tempered by the blessing that he could join us at all.

"And now, speaking of blessings . . . John, Josh, and I have spoken with one another and I can now announce our mutual agreement concerning an important matter. Josh Burnett has kindly agreed to remain here with us as his brother rejoins his company and fulfills his military obligations."

There was great excitement around the table with everyone simultaneously offering their congratulations to Josh.

"Now . . . now, dear friends, remember this is my table and I have not concluded what I intend to say. Josh is a bright, kindhearted young gentleman. He will be incorporated into our family as if he were our own. He will enroll in Mr. Magevney's school and we expect by Christmas next year, he can and will read to us from the Holy Scriptures . . . all by himself.

"Josh, we welcome you and we're thrilled to have you as one of the Cabells."

Great applause broke out. Josh stood up from his chair and shyly acknowledged this outburst of affection with a smile and a nod of the head that meant, "Thank you. I'm pleased to be among you."

"Now, ladies and gentlemen, I ask that you focus your attention on the three familiar people standing against the far wall. They are our devoted servants, Bettie, Mose, and their son, Jed. These folks came to live among us under most unusual circumstances. I must confess there was money exchanged for them for reasons that seemed valid at the time.

"I had a conversation with Mose far too long ago in which I promised him that it was my intention to compile a ledger which would tally all the services he and his family performed. And, I indicated after the purchase amount had been fulfilled, I promised to withdraw my lien on them. They would then be free.

"But I never got around to formalizing that promise. I'm sorry about that, Mose. It was unconscionable of me to be so inconsiderate and fail to live up to my word. Nevertheless, Mose, was quietly – no . . . make that 'silently' – patient with me. If he harbored any animosity or disappointment at my apparent betrayal, then I'm sorry for that and I apologize to you, Mose, with these folks as my witnesses.

"Now, speaking of witnesses, I wish for those around the table to be able to verify in the future what I have to say next.

"Mose . . . Bettie . . . I've hastily written a ledger similar to the one I long ago promised. Mrs. Cabell and I were inspecting it last night. We are unanimous in our opinion that the slate is now clean – that you have conscientiously performed what was expected of you. Consequently, on this Christmas Day I hereby grant the three of you your freedom. No longer shall you serve in bondage – in this household . . . or, in any other."

While there were broad smiles growing around the table, Calvin clearly indicated he wanted to continue with what he had to say.

"Now, as free people, you're able to go anywhere and do anything that you choose. That also means you're free to flee this household and make your home far, far away. But Mrs. Cabell and I want you to know we would be pleased and honored if you would remain with us as valued employees. The terms and conditions I can spell out for you, Mose, later this evening.

"Friends, these three black folks have become an integral part of our family - just as we now have also extended our family to include Josh. So, as Christmas presents to you three, we formally give you your freedom . . . and we give you our grateful thanks as well."

Bettie could be seen exhaling a sigh of relief as she raised her eyes heavenward. Mose, however, remained his impassive self. Jamie and Cassie rushed forward to hug and congratulate them. And every one of the people around the table found this grant of freedom just about the most perfect Christmas gift one could imagine. Everyone was pleased . . . except for Shelby.

As the diners moved to the parlor to mingle, Shelby sidled up to Calvin in a way to subtly gain his attention. He spoke quietly. "Calvin, may I have a word with you?"

He looked about surveying who was near . . . and then he returned his focus again on Calvin. "May I have a word with you . . . alone? I think we should step into your study."

* * * * * * * * * * * * * *

"You're going to have to say that again, Shelby. I know for certain I must have misunderstood what you just told me."

"Calvin, you know you heard me loud and clear. Bettie and Mose are the only two slaves you can free. You have no ownership of the little boy. He's still a financial asset of Mercer Watkins."

"This can't be true, Shelby. I had you draft those papers, the Bill of Sale between me and Mercer Watkins. How could you have been so careless to omit their son in the transaction?"

"I promise you, Calvin, I wasn't the one who was negligent. You never told me that Mose and Bettie had a son who was an asset Mercer Watkins wanted to sell to you. Hell, Calvin, I didn't even know they HAD a son until TODAY. I drafted the papers just like you told me."

Calvin and Shelby were standing face-to-face in front of the large glass window in his study. He looked out at the grounds so he could think clearly and sort though all the pertinent issues.

Calvin Cabell used all of the memory he had in "my numb skull head" and he tried to recall every detail that led up to these black folks "coming to live with us."

"Damn it. There you go again, Cabell," he silently scolded himself. "I just used one of those horrid euphemisms I hate. These three people didn't 'come to live with me.' They came to be my slaves. I bought them lock, stock, and barrel."

Calvin was tense. He despised Shelby and he now wished he had never assigned him the task of drafting the paperwork. Yet, he couldn't venture into a tirade with family and guests just beyond the closed study doors. And his temper was also tamed by a sensible dose of practicality. Much as he would prefer to rail at this incompetent rat, Calvin kept conscious the fact that berating Shelby likely wouldn't accomplish anything. In fact, it might irreparably cripple any chances of clearing up this horrible error. His objective had to be focused on the needs of the three Negroes and not his desire to give Shelby a piece of his mind.

"Shelby, it appears it won't help those three freed Negroes . . . I mean, those TWO freed Negroes . . . by calling you 'incompetent' or by accusing you of 'mal-practice'. But I don't flinch for a moment at reminding you what a conniving sidewinder you are. And, like any slithering snake in the grass, I know a snake can stick out its forked tongue, smell the mood in the air, and devise a lie that can cure this legal chaos. And that's what I'm asking you to do . . . ever-so-politely . . . this Christmas Day. What can you do to fix this mess?"

"Well, Cabell, you can't seem to shed your hypocrite ways. You've always been so self-righteous when you tell folks how much you hate hypocrites. You stand there all pious and pompous and tell me what a snake I am. I dare you to say I'm also a murderer . . . a philanderer who dispenses communion to simpletons in the pews . . . who ignorantly consider you to be a significant cut above every Tom, Dick, and Harry in the congregation. It's a cold blooded murderer who's offering them a bite of bread and saying, 'I am the body of Christ. Take, eat, and go and sin no more.' I can expose your hypocrite ways to everyone out there in those pews. And if you want to persist with this assault on my integrity, then I'll be more than happy to follow the course of action you apparently are forcing me to employ."

Shelby's harangue hurt. Calvin didn't know if his gut was writhing in pain from the threat he made or the truth he spoke. But there was no time for self-examination. "I'll make it worth your while to fix this Shelby. I know you can draft up a codicil or forge a paper. I'm sure I could persuade Mercer Watkins to execute a post-dated document that will clear this up."

"Well, isn't that rich. The Clerk of the Session, the paragon of Christian values wants me to forge a document, because I committed an egregious act of mal-practice. You never want to take responsibility for your own faults . . . your own sins . . . do you, Calvin?"

"I said I would make it worth your while, Shelby. I'll pay you handsomely to ensure Jed is freed along with his momma and papa. Surely you won't let your hatred of me get in the way of saving a little boy from the chance of being torn away from his family."

"You know, Calvin, Christmas makes a man real nostalgic. It brings to mind memories from long ago. And let me tell you the memories I recall. I'm reminded of a unique riding coat button that got pulled from YOUR overcoat by a barmaid struggling with her assassin. And, I can clearly see a worn, ladies purse . . . and even a receipt from the Barry Merchandise Store in it. And, I especially remember the unforgivable ways you and your friends used to treat me. 'Unforgivable'? Yes, I believe that pretty much describes the ill-treatment you dished out to me . . . time and time again.

"And I recall more recently . . . actually, quite recently . . . that the button and the purse and all the other evidence that links you to that murder back home are insignificant compared to new evidence that not even you are aware of."

Shelby's ruddy complexion had turned red as summer sunburn. He was angry. And the bile that made him sizzle like a blacksmith's forceps had been stewing within him for a long, long time. He knew his uncle, Governor Shelby, idolized Calvin and . . . at the same time . . . he always belittled his own kin. Shelby was a man who was prepared to take Calvin down. He would relish the chance to see the stunned faces of folks in Memphis when they discovered the citizen they admired and respected the most . . . is the man by whom they were most deceived. Calvin Cabell was NOT a Godly man . . . and one day all would know it.

It was a delicate standoff. Calvin knew he had said too much . . . been too harsh. As for Shelby, he knew his temper had gotten the best of him many times before . . . and he knew that what he really wanted was to forget a lifetime of being marginalized. But that was never going to happen. It was an elusive dream. That was a dream that would never come true.

And then Shelby remembered Mose and Bettie and Jed standing there in the dining room a few moments earlier. They had a dream. And it had come true . . . all except for Jed. And Shelby realized only he could save Jed . . . save the whole family. Because, if the boy wasn't free . . . neither were his parents. He had a choice to make. His pound of flesh was his for the taking. He could bring Calvin down. But the other choice he had was to lift up three decent people. He could lift them out of unending despair . . . and into the lofty status of freed men and women. He had the capacity to make either choice happen. He was a veritable God.

"Calvin, you get Mercer Watkins into my office tomorrow morning. I'll come up with something that should work. But mind you, I'll do this . . . this 'slithering sidewinder' will do this - not to help you - or to make you look like a savior in their eyes. I'll do what I can do for that little boy out there. You see, I've been a little boy much like Jed for as long as I can remember. I've spent a lifetime looking for a step up . . . a chance at freedom, if you will. I'll do it for the little black boy. And later . . . well we'll have to wait and see what I'll do with you."

"I'll go see Mercer first thing tomorrow morning, Shelby. I know I can convince him to do his part to straighten out this mess. The two of us will meet with you afterward . . . say, at about ten o'clock." Calvin felt relieved and just a little part of him wanted to feel sorry for Shelby. But, while Shelby offered to stretch the ethics of contract law, he had punctuated it with the caveat he was set on dismantling Calvin's reputation . . . soon.

"But, as for you and me, it appears we'll either have to work things out or thrash things out between us. If you think I'm going to admit I killed anybody back in Kentucky, then you'll have to think long and hard about whether you can prove it. And if you can't . . . and, I repeat, you won't . . . then you'll have to be prepared to slip out of town in the dead of night – just like you were forced to do back in the Bluegrass."

"Just remember, Calvin, my father-in-law, Judge Robinson, runs this county and I cast Judge Robinson's shadow here in Memphis. And someday I'll cast my own political presence over ALL of Shelby County. Don't get caught in that dark shadow, Calvin. It can get mighty cold when you find yourself deprived of the warmth of daylight."

Calvin moved toward the double doors of the study and he began to open them. The others were intent upon talking about this Christmas and Christmases past and no one even spotted the two men who had sequestered themselves.

"Won't you join the others with me, Squire Lancaster? They're talking about joy and good will to men. It's a more fitting theme, I think, than the talk of petulant retribution. Shall we mingle, Shelby? And . . . before I forget it . . . have I wished you Merry Christmas, yet?"

* * * * * * * * * * * *

"What a bittersweet day," Calvin moaned to himself as he opened his watch. It was almost five o'clock.

"What a bittersweet Christmas Day. The last rays of sunshine had been spent. The day had come to an end. And now John had to return to camp – but this time, not with Josh. I know John's overjoyed with our agreement. But he's made a sacrifice. He's taken care of his brother the best he could. If anybody is bittersweet this afternoon, it's got to be John Burnett right about now."

Actually, John's departure went smoother than Calvin had feared. John obviously had a big lump in his throat. But he left no doubt that this was the right thing to do. He considered Calvin's proposal nothing short of a miraculous gift.

401

Private Burnett wore a satisfied smile as he mounted his horse – laden with clean clothes in his pack and several dozen cookies Cassie had kept aside for him. But the cookies weren't for John and his Army buddies. Cassie asked him if he'd do his best to distribute them to the Indian children. She said she couldn't bear to soon see them march through town on their way to the river.

"I'll stay indoors. And, John, after I tell my friends what I saw Christmas Eve, I'll tell them to stay indoors, too."

Josh had a lump in his throat, also. And the Cabells were all confused how to comfort their newly adopted son. He was too young to go with John and join the Army. And, he was too old for Catherine to give him sloppy kisses and console him by holding his hand.

Josh handled it all like the man Calvin had predicted he would become. He was stalwart. John promised to get one of his literate Army friends to write letters to Josh. He proudly predicted to his brother that soon he'd be capable of writing him letters all on his own from Oklahoma.

Calvin made it clear to John that, when his tour of duty was completed, he had an open invitation to return to Memphis and be reunited with his brother. Calvin assured him there would be a decent job waiting for him, too. John smiled at his Christmas host and, now, the full time guardian of his brother.

He said, "Many thanks, Mr. Cabell," as he pulled hard to the left on the bridle and reins that were his Christmas present. That tug on his horse's mouth pulled at his horse sharply and soon the animal was cantering eastwardly on Adams Street . . . heading for Poplar . . . and on to the Cherokee Trace.

Then, Calvin headed toward the slave house. He had debated all evening whether Mose and Bettie should know what he had learned from Shelby . . . or, should he choose not to upset them and spoil the joy they were feeling. He even briefly debated whether he should just sweep the bad news under the rug for a while. As he walked he still wondered what he should tell the darkies. He knocked on their cabin door and asked to come in for a chat. He also asked if Jed might go outside and play for awhile. He wanted to keep what he had to say restricted to Jed's parents.

He laid out everything . . . just as it was. He left no stone unturned - including his assurance that he would take care of purchasing Jed as soon as it was possible. The two parents were stunned at the news when Calvin first told them. Bettie was especially emotional. She cried many tears, but she didn't cry out. As a slave, she had learned it never did any good. However, as he was about to leave, he thought Bettie was calmer and less anxious. But Mose, like always, appeared passive and enigmatic.

When Calvin walked out of their cabin, Mose had his arm around Bettie . . . trying his best to give her comfort.

"Ever thing gonna be all right, Miss Bettie. Ever thing gonna be just fine."

\* \* \* \* \* \* \* \* \*

Calvin stood at the window of his downstairs study where he and Shelby had retreated for their after dinner talk. He looked outside. Even in the dark he could see Jed. He was holding a lantern in his left hand and a handled reed basket sat on the ground nearby. He was picking pecans off the ground. Every time he stooped down, he placed two or three more in his basket.

Calvin was struck by the realization that the pecans he was picking weren't for his family's baking benefit. After Bettie would make a pecan pie or a pecan roll, it would be served to the Cabells. The black folks on the property would get the leftovers – like always had been the case since Calvin made his deal with Watkins. Even freedom wouldn't change that fact of life. Right now, Mose and Bettie desperately wanted Jed to be free – just like them. Calvin knew he had to fix it this unforeseen situation.

"Mercer Watkins," he called out loud. "I'll go see him first thing in the morning."

# CHAPTER

## 28

December 26, 1838

It was highly unusual for anyone to knock on the Cabells' front door at seven in the morning. Calvin had come downstairs about six o'clock. He wanted to ensure that someone from the household would be stirring about and available to greet Josh. He didn't want the boy to wander into the kitchen and find only Bettie there to bid him a "good morning". These East Tennessee brothers had shown they were, at the very least, uncomfortable being served by slaves – even freed slaves. Calvin wanted to ease Josh gently into the new life he would be leading in the Cabell home.

The master of the house was groggier than usual, because he'd been awake all night. He tried to sleep, but sleep successfully eluded him. He couldn't purge from his mind how bittersweet the Christmas dinner had been. Everyone seated about the table was in a joyous mood. Catherine seemed her old self for a change. Jamie told stories about his experiences with Cousin John at Centre College. Cassie was always excited and self-assured. That was especially evident at Christmas. The way she talked and acted at the dinner table served notice to one and all that she was transforming from a gangly school girl into a clever young woman. Her father was proud as punch.

But it was the Negro contingent of his family that mostly kept Calvin stirred up and sleepless. He poured brandy in his crystal snifter at midnight, at one-thirty, and again at three-thirty. Then he washed down this last and stoutest drink of liquor with a glass of milk. "Surely," he thought, "milk and brandy are a sure-fire concoction to promote restful sleep."

However, the spirits and the milk were no panacea to quell the scattershot thoughts that exploded in his mind throughout the long night. He still couldn't believe Jed was omitted on the Bill of Sale. Calvin was the kind of man who rarely got angry with others. His anger was reserved for himself in almost all instances. For example, if a crew at the mill cut lumber that didn't

405

meet the customer's specifications, Calvin placed the blame on himself and categorized it as an example of his poor managerial supervision.

Likewise, in the case of this botched Bill of Sale, his tendencies were to blame himself for not reading – not even once – the papers Shelby drafted for him. As hard as he'd been on Shelby and as intensely as he had despised the man, even Calvin didn't think it was fair to lay all the blame on him.

"I'm responsible for this mess. Shelby made an understandable error. And I was negligent when I defined the scope of the property conveyance. It is I who is responsible. It is I who must bear this burden."

But Mercer Watkins was another matter. All night long Calvin dwelled on him and he carefully dissected his role in this mess. "I was nervous as a man can be that afternoon. I couldn't hand Mercer this Bill of Sale and the cash fast enough. I was only interested in signing the document and getting out."

His thoughts always returned to Mercer Watkins' responsibility in the exchange. "I can't believe Mercer didn't read that Bill of Sale. His back was squarely up against a wall. Getting this conveyance handled 'just so' had to be important to him. And, if he recognized – as, surely, he did – that Jed wasn't being conveyed, then why didn't he contact me? Surely he knew the oversight should have been remedied.

"I don't know these answers now, but as soon as everyone in the house is up I'm going straight away to the Watkins' place to sort all this out. And I won't leave without a sense of satisfaction."

But, at quarter to seven Calvin found no one but Bettie active in the house. She poured a cup of coffee for her "master", her "boss", or whatever name which he should now be called. She was confused. Yesterday's pronouncement of freedom was meaningless to her. If Jed was still in jeopardy of being taken from her as chattel because of Mr. Watkins' money problems, Bettie was still shackled. She was still a slave.

In her heart she knew she should be overjoyed and grateful. However, without Jed's freedom, she considered her proverbial glass wasn't even half full. It was empty – empty of all joy . . . and empty of any faith that everything would eventually be resolved.

Just as Calvin was pouring some cream into his coffee, a sudden pounding at the front door startled him. The knocking was relentless and its noise rapidly grew evermore frantic His first reaction was to check the time. His watch said it was six fifty-five.

When he opened the front door he was startled to see Eloise Watkins standing there. She was shaking - no doubt from the cold. But she also appeared to be shaking because she was scared. Even at first glance, Calvin recognized she was agitated about something.

"Mrs. Watkins, what a surprise it is to see you this early in the morning. Where's Mercer?"

"That's what I'm trying to find out. Mercer's disappeared, Mr. Cabell. And I don't even begin to know where to look."

"When did you last see him? And, by the way, have you walked here from your home?"

"Yes, I've been up all night and I waited until daylight to seek you out. I last saw him yesterday afternoon at about four o'clock. He'd been in a real dark frame of mind for the past three weeks. And he'd been drinking throughout Christmas Day. He's been drinking way too much, Mr. Cabell. But to overdo it on Christmas Day was just horrible. I can't tell you how horrible it was."

"Did the two of you have a fight?"

"No, I was grief-stricken that he would try to drown his sorrow on our Lord's birthday, but I never had a cross word to say to him. The fact of the matter is I've been afraid of him for several weeks. He has so much anger bottled up in him. I'm sure he drinks to appease his demons. But the fact is his intoxication only serves to get Mercer and those demons all riled up and ready to strike out at anyone who's nearby. I have no doubt he knows I love him deeply. But he doesn't want love. He wants vengeance."

While Eloise was frantically talking to Calvin, he had managed to lead her slowly into the front hall. "I've not even seen Mercer for almost a month. You should have told me about his behavior earlier. I might have given him some counsel . . . or some comfort to get through this rough patch."

"The only thing he wants is revenge. You know, don't you, this bank ordeal has been eating away at him for several years. Yet, during the past four weeks his nerves seem to have frayed beyond repair."

Calvin all the while was thinking what should be done and if he could help. He recognized he needed more specific information about Mercer's disappearance . . . instead of just hearing his wife wail in his hall about her husband's demons and his drinking.

"When did you last see him, Mrs. Watkins? Do you remember if he said where he might be going?"

Eloise was sobbing now and her speech was erratic. There was a need to repeatedly wipe away her tears with the lace bordered handkerchief she was clutching. "All he said, sir, was, 'I'm going for a long walk. Don't worry if I come home late.' Then he put on his overcoat and wool scarf. But he left without his hat. You know how peculiar that is. He always wears a hat. I fear he's caught pneumonia and he's collapsed in a stupor somewhere in the cold."

"How can I help, madam? I can get Jamie and our new family member, Josh, to help in a search. We can even get Mose and Jed to help us."

"Actually, Mr. Cabell, Mose is the main reason I've come here. I've wandered about our property and searched every out building three or four times. But the shed is locked. I can't get in there. I remembered Mercer and Mose kept a spare key to the padlock hidden somewhere. I thought maybe Mose could tell me where it is hidden. Would you ask him for me . . . please?"

While Eloise was talking, Calvin heard the back door swing open and close again. He also noticed Bettie peering once or twice through the pantry door. Now he was sure he could hear Mose and Bettie talking low. No doubt, she was telling him who was at the door and what might be going on.

"Please sit down, madam, here in this chair while I hunt for Mose. I'll call for Jamie and Josh, too."

Just as Calvin told Eloise everyone he would be enlisting in the search, Jamie and Josh hung their heads over the upstairs railing. They had heard Jamie's father say he would fetch them for some sort of help. But that's all they heard. They knew nothing about anything else Mrs. Watkins had told Calvin.

"Here, Father, we're up here. Do you need me and Josh?"

Calvin moved to the foot of the stairwell and craned his neck upward. He saw both boys' faces stretched far over the banister and staring straight down at him. "Yes, both of you get dressed for an extended search outdoors. I'll go fetch Mose."

But Calvin didn't need to look far for Mose. He stepped outside the pantry door into the dining room . . . in clear sight. "You lookin fer me, Mr. Cabell?"

"Yes, I am. Come here, Mose. Mr. Watkins is missing and Mrs. Watkins tells me you might remember where the extra key to her storage shed is hidden. Then, we need to spread out and comb the area until we find him."

"Yessir, I do recall those spare keys. They should be hangin' on a nail hammered into one of the rafters in the stable. Master Watkins had an extra key to all the out buildings and put 'em on the same ring."

"Excellent, let's all go over to the house and we can begin our search there. Mose, go hitch up the wagon and I'll get the boys ready to go."

"We're ready, Father." Jamie and Josh bounded down the stairs while putting their arms through sleeves of winter hunting coats. They had the look of bewilderment on their faces, but they were prepared for whatever was expected of them.

"Hurry, son. Help Mose hitch the wagon so we can rush over to the Watkins' place."

Just as the two boys were almost through the kitchen and out the back door, Calvin had another order for them. "And fetch all those cow bells on the shelf in the stable. We can put them to good use in the search."

Both boys froze their flight when they first heard Calvin calling out these orders. When he finished they bolted out the door as Jamie hastily responded, okay, Father."

Catherine and Cassie were both making their way down the staircase wondering what was going on at this hour on the morning after Christmas. Catherine was startled to see it was Eloise sitting in a parlor chair weeping inconsolably. Calvin spotted his wife and daughter and he called out to them as well as to Eloise. "Mrs. Cabell, let Mrs. Watkins tell you why she's here. We're getting the wagon ready now and she needs to be in front of the house in three minutes."

Calvin dashed out the back door as Catherine and Cassie did their best to calm down their bereft friend.

\* \* \* \* \* \* \* \* \* \* \*

The wagon was hitched in record time and Star, the Cabell carriage horse, was soon trotting down Third Street toward the Watkins' home. Cabell had taken the reins and Eloise sat at his right side. In the pit of the wagon sat Mose, Jamie, and Josh. It was cold. Both boys were relieved they had bundled up so well on such short notice.

Mose sat silently throughout the short trip. But Jamie knew Mose's mind was never silent. He was sitting there percolating and processing thoughts. Jamie sensed his black friend concealed more than an idle premonition. There was a stoic look on his face. Yet, there was also a sagacious look in his eyes that hinted Mose knew where Mercer Watkins might be found.

Calvin reined Star to a halt in front of the Watkins residence. Everyone got off the wagon. There was little said as the posse walked around the house toward the out buildings in the rear.

Mose said nothing, as usual. But when he led Jamie and Josh toward the stable, all knew that he might as well be saying, "I'll get the spare keys for you."

As the three exited the stable and walked toward the shed, Mose was examining the key ring he held in front of him. He was sorting through the collection to find the one that unlocked the shed.

As if they were silently summoned, Calvin and Eloise gravitated toward the slow moving threesome. They stopped behind Jamie and Josh while Mose stood alone at the front of the shed door. Only the chain which fastened the two large doors was exposed. Someone had threaded it through the hole in each door. The padlock secured the premises from the inside. Mose was able to pull the lock through the large opening on the right until he could finally clutch it. He fiddled with the rusted device. As he tinkered with it, Mose peeked through the narrow opening between the two hinged partitions. The padlock seemed reluctant to respond to its master's key.

The clasp that had been so oppositional to Mose's jimmying finally relinquished its will to secure the premises. He lifted the lock off the rusty chain and, at the same time, he gradually began to swing open the two shed doors. Even as the doors parted, the shed remained so dark inside that no one could see much of anything.

But at the far end of the out building . . . where slivers of winter daylight poured through the gaps in the south wall and the dilapidated shake shingle roof . . . the sun's razor thin beams illuminated a lifeless body . . . visible only through slanted stripes of daylight.

The specter they spotted was Mercer. His head was lifelessly tilted far to one side. The bulk of his body was suspended by a noose of hemp rope he had stretched around his neck. He had tied its long end to the last rafter. A five foot high step ladder lay haphazardly on the floor. It obviously was toppled by the last living kick of a desperate man.

The five live souls on the premises stood motionless outside the shed's broad opening. Each was uniformly stunned by the discovery. Eloise finally fainted into Calvin's arms while screaming out an ear-piercing shriek. Jamie and Josh both held their hands to their faces. Jamie covered his mouth to prevent crying out. And Josh covered his eyes – all the while thinking he wasn't really peering at a suicidal death. He thought surely he had merely imagined seeing this hanging corpse . . . and when he, once again, opened his eyes . . . he hoped he would realize it was all only an apparition.

But Mose didn't make a sound. Nor did he cover his eyes or his mouth. He gazed at the light striped body for several seconds. Then, he quietly walked to the end of the shed, picked up the fallen ladder, and set it upright next to Mercer. Mose always carried a pocket knife in his overalls. He withdrew it and held it in his teeth as he climbed one step . . . and then another. At the top rung he held the knife in his right hand and he used his left hand to stabilize the taut rope below the wooden brace. He began to saw at the rope with his knife in a manner that could only be described as reverential.

"Jamie . . . Josh . . . go help Mose bring Mr. Watkins to the ground."

The two boys walked tentatively side by side through the shed . . . like a pair of acolytes processing behind their archbishop. Their heads were bowed. They were silently solemn. Tears began to flow from both sets of eyes.

No words were spoken. Everyone knew his disagreeable duty at hand. So, when Jamie and Josh heard the sounds of Mose cutting into the rope, both stepped forward. The sawing sounds meant the cord would soon relinquish its load . . . and it did. They reached out and grasped the other's hands. Then they locked them under the dead man's torso and accepted his lifeless body

411

into their waiting arms. Mercer's still-opened eyes gauzily glared up at them. Jamie was noticeably shaken by the sight. They slowly lowered Mercer and placed his remains upon the building's dirt floor.

Mose observed it all peering down at the scene from above. He gazed at Mercer. And only God and Mose know what he was thinking. After he stepped down on to the floor he squatted down and closed the dead man's eye lids while he fixed his own eyes on his former master's face.

Jamie employed his keen natural ability to peer into another person's mind and soul. He sensed Mose's memory was skimming and scanning through the catalog of experiences that peppered his long relationship with this limp remnant of a man.

Was Mose bitter at the man who paid good money for his flesh, but who could never have accumulated enough money to purchase his soul? Was he grateful to Mercer Watkins for trying to save Mose's family from being split up? After all, fracturing the family would have brought him top dollar. Was Mose thanking him for bartering his family away to become the property of the Cabells? Or, was Mose cursing Mercer under his breath . . . remembering how his former master had failed to convey Jed to the Cabells in the Bill of Sale?

Any one of these deliberations might have been crossing Mose's memory. But Jamie thought the smart money would bet that ALL of these thoughts were emanating from the black man. Here was Mercer Watkins' former slave looking down on his dead body . . . as if Mose were God up in heaven . . . contemplating whether or not to grant salvation to the deceased.

"That's it," Jamie silently cried out deep inside that omniscient gut of his.

He remembered his father telling him the uncomfortable encounter that took place the afternoon he took possession of this proud black family. He said Mercer was uncontrollably crying tears generated from a nagging guilt. He said when Mercer and Bettie exchanged goodbyes, Bettie told Mercer she would probably see him again at the Pearly Gates in the "bye and bye". But her optimistic prediction only served to squeeze at Mercer's guilt all the more. Mercer told Bettie he thought she, for certain, would get to heaven. But he doubted that his soul would be evaluated kindly by St. Peter. Mercer said heaven's gate keeper would likely reject him . . . and send him away . . . to hell.

"Mose surely is looking into that dead person's face and trying to decide if this white man's soul is headed to heaven or hell. And . . . he can't quite make up his mind."

Calvin had caught Eloise Watkins when she fainted. Fortunately, he prevented her from collapsing to the ground. While he held her, he shook her gently and tried to revive this newest widow in town. She had turned away from the horrid sight . . . and she clung to Calvin's breast. She was too distressed to be reconciled. Her tears flowed down Calvin's coat. At first they were saturated into the woolen cloth. However, when the water drenched coat so it could absorb no more, the droplets quickly slid down his outer garment . . . and fell at Calvin's feet.

Calvin began to lead the grieving woman away from the gruesome scene. He led her around the house toward the wagon as Star was curiously looking at them and winnowing.

"Jamie, I'm going to take Mrs. Watkins home to your Mother. She can care for her there and, hopefully, console her. Mose, would you supervise putting the body inside the house? I'll send word for Lassiter's Mortuary to come and take away the remains."

Then, almost as an afterthought, Calvin seemed ashamed. He had momentarily forgotten something. He turned about with Eloise Watkins following suit - still under the control of his guiding arms. Calvin realized he owed these two young men some praise.

"Boys, thanks so much. You're both champions. Nothing we can do in life is more honorable than how we care for our dead. You will both be blessed."

Jamie thought that was about the highest praise his father had ever given him. He could recall myriad ways Calvin Cabell had let him know he was disappointed in him. But he sensed this day . . . and this death . . . might just serve as a turning point in their father/son relationship.

* * * * * * * * * *

Jamie and Josh walked into the Cabell residence about two hours later. Jamie saw his mother and father and Eloise Watkins sitting in the front parlor. His mother sat with Mrs. Watkins on the mole skin sofa. His father sat in the maroon wing back chair facing the women. He noticed Catherine was stroking Eloise's hand – just like Bettie had often sat and caressed her own

413

weak hands . . . when she couldn't climb out of her black, emotional hell hole.

During the time Eloise had been under Catherine's care, she had calmed down dramatically. Jamie thought the scene seemed especially odd - seeing a newly minted widow sitting in a room where festive Christmas decorations were still spread all about.

"I guess I always knew folks die at Christmas . . . like any other day of the year. I suppose there's no way to prevent it," he thought.

Jamie carried two envelopes in his right hand as he approached Calvin. "Mr. Lassiter found these two envelopes in Mr. Watkins' inside coat pocket. One's addressed to Mrs. Watkins and the other's addressed to you, Father."

Jamie's news startled everyone. Eloise Watkins seemed terrified to learn whatever might be written in her envelope. Her anxiety spiked to such a level, it was impossible to shed any more tears. There was the look of terror in her eyes.

Catherine was taken aback and anxious, also. She and Calvin locked their sights on each other. Without uttering a sound, they were both communicating, "What should we do?"

"Thank you, Jamie. Why don't you give the envelopes to me for now," his father said.

Josh stood several feet behind Jamie. He appeared emotionally exhausted. The boy looked like he had concluded he should remain detached from what was happening. Calvin thought it was appropriate that both lads relax and process everything they had seen and done this day after Christmas – the day after Mercer Watkins killed himself.

"I'm sure, Jamie and Josh, that Mrs. Watkins joins me in saying, once again, how gracious you both were this morning. Confronting death on any account is difficult. And discovering Mr. Watkins' death was especially hard for the two of you. But, again, I assure you that your mother, Mrs. Watkins, and I appreciate all you've done for us . . . and, of course, what you've done for Mr. Watkins."

Catherine and Eloise nodded their heads in agreement and Mrs. Watkins' managed to smile touchingly at Jamie and Josh to illustrate how pleased and grateful she was for their help.

Calvin offered a suggestion he hoped would shake away the boys' blues.

"Why don't you two saddle Star and Bluegrass? And, Jamie, why don't you give Josh a riding tour of Memphis? Introduce him to some friends. We're delighted to have him as part of our family and he needs to know the lay of the land as soon as he can."

"Certainly, Father, and . . . Mrs. Watkins . . . please know you have my deepest sympathy."

She nodded her head and managed another smile.

"Mrs. Watkins, I've only been here for one day. But I'm glad I was here to help you out . . . however I could."

"Thank you, Josh. You've been enormously helpful."

Then, the adults all refocused their attention on the two letters Calvin still clutched in his right hand as Jamie and Josh turned about and headed for the stable.

* * * * * * * * * *

"What should we do?" Calvin asked Eloise, who sat erect on the sofa with a glazed look in her eyes.

Catherine didn't think she had any say in the matter. The answer to Calvin's question was solely up to Eloise. Her husband's somber expression silently communicated to the Widow Watkins that he, too, considered whatever happened next . . . should be her call.

"I want you to read them, Mr. Cabell. I want you to read both of them out loud – yours and mine."

Eloise seemed self-assured. She knew what she was doing. Calvin at first wanted no part of reading either of the envelopes out loud. But he considered Eloise had the right to trump him under the circumstances. So, he said, "Very well, I'll read both of them to you . . . and I'll begin with yours."

Calvin cautiously separated the glued flap from the envelope using his thumb's nail. Then he removed the letter from the envelope. He reverently unfolded the stationery and held its three pages before him. He pulled his

415

reading glasses from the right side pocket of his coat and began the process of strapping its stems around each ear. All the while he was perusing the letter as best he could to get a preview of what was to come.

"All right, madam . . . here goes. It's dated yesterday."

My Dear Eloise,

I don't need to tell you how unconscionable my behavior has been for the past three years – and, especially during the past three weeks. I've tried my best to conceal from you all the pressure I've been under since I was defrauded when I co-signed that bank note.

I've done everything imaginable to delay the threats of the Bank of Hernando. They've continuously put the squeeze on every asset I know of . . . and some they've pointed out to me, I didn't even know were mine.

I've cooperated with them to a fault. The bank established a repayment plan so we could continue residing in our house. I've paid them their due month after month. That obligation has left you without so many of the things you deserve. You're entitled to have a comfortable, peaceful life. And you deserve to have a husband who can provide for you and give you the loving attention you warrant.

But in the past thirty days, the bank has notified me it will start repossession proceedings on our home and all the personal property therein. They've made it clear that every cent I now claim as my own will be confiscated. So, now I'm faced with a burden that goes well beyond the shortcomings I've mentioned above. You should live in a comfortable home. And you don't merit being thrown out to scrap for a pauper's living with a man like me who lives his life with a black cloud continuously hovering overhead.

The point is this, Eloise. You deserve more than I will ever be able to provide you. The fact is clear. You would be a lot better off without me.

I hope you will ask your brother, Eli, in Holly Springs to take you in so you can begin anew in a fresh place. Hopefully, the cumbersome baggage I've packed and carried around for far too long won't follow you in a new town. Eli's made a fortune as a planter and I'm certain he will care for you royally.

I'm even so strapped for money that I've got to ask Calvin Cabell to pay for my burial. I know he will willingly and happily do this. I've also asked Calvin to convince you to move and to live with your brother.

Know this, my Love. It's best for everyone that I depart this life and cope with our Lord's judgment about whether or not I ever get to heaven. It seems doubtful to me. But this just illustrates all the more my valid reasons to leave you now. I'll never be reunited above with you and with our precious daughters who died so young.

I hope it's not you who finds my body. And I know you'll hear stories that are probably more outrageous than things really are. Please forgive me for causing this dilemma. Take assurance that burying my cursed corpse will be the last indignity you will have to face on my account.

You've been my true love. And I continue to love you so very dearly. I hope shedding me as a liability will cause the last days of your life to be free from the pressures and pain you would surely endure if I were alive.

Your devoted husband,

Mercer


Calvin sat bewildered. Eloise and Catherine appeared to share the same reaction – although, he could detect a steam of anger beginning to stoke up inside Eloise. But what surprised Calvin the most was the fact he was able to read Mercer's suicide letter without coming apart himself. He thought he owed it to Eloise to steadfastly plod through the recitation without unnecessary emotions. He had succeeded.

"Mr. Cabell, I thank you for reading the letter so eloquently. I shall not ask you to read it again. I shall destroy it . . . and I plead with you to speak of it to no one. How dare he try to ship me off to Holly Springs to my brother . . . as if I had just won a bonus prize from this hideous suicide. It makes me furious. And to think I was mourning him just ten minutes ago. His letter, however, succeeded at one thing. He managed to curtail my grief."

Both Cabells thought Eloise should speak her mind. And, she did. At first, there was nothing they could say or do to soothe her sorrow. There was, likewise, nothing they could say or do to diminish her hurt . . . and her hatred. But Catherine devised an appropriate strategy to end the silence which had cast a pall over the room.

"I thought you read that very well, dear. I don't believe anyone could have done a more masterful job."

Eloise had sat there through it all, silently mulling in her mind what Mercer had written. Suddenly, her brooding ceased. She now had something to say, as well.

"Mr. Cabell, would you now read YOUR letter aloud? Then, you can decide if you choose to do with it what I intend to do with mine – to burn it."

Calvin wasn't going to argue with this disconsolate widow who was becoming angrier and angrier. Besides, he thought if he was capable of reading Eloise's note with some composure that came from who knows where, then maybe it was best to get over all of this unpleasantness at one time.

"Very well, I'll open mine . . . and then we'll all soon have this episode behind us."

This time he didn't try to catch a peek or a preview of what Mercer wrote. He rather briskly unfolded the stationery, placed the written words before him, and he began to read.

Dear Calvin,

I write this letter on the 21$^{st}$ of December. I've pretty much decided to kill myself, but I still might change my mind. Christmas this year won't bring with it any seasonal joy to my household. Furthermore, I don't think there will ever be any joy again . . . so long as I'm around. In any event, if I go through with it, I'll need all my faculties to write to Eloise how much I love her and to explain how not having me to burden her any longer is a huge blessing to the both of us.

Something happened four weeks ago that caused my already precarious plan with the bank to crumble. I was traveling the road to Jebediah Wilson's house. He's an up-and-coming planter just south of Whitehaven. I had some whiskey with me . . . which is always snugly sealed in my leather valise. I had every intention of holding off taking a drink until I concluded my business with Wilson. But that day I was in a frightfully melancholy mood. I thought a few sips might fend off feeling worse . . . and keep my body warm, to boot.

418

Shortly, I spotted my nemesis. Approaching me was a carriage driven by Charles Garthwright, the President of the Bank of Hernando. I had consumed half the bottle and, consequently, I was feeling empowered, for a change. Garthwright spotted me about the same time and it appeared to me he wanted to scoot past by my buggy lickety-split. All the while Garthwright was focusing straight ahead . . . like he didn't see me. Or, maybe, it was because he fancies himself too superior to take a quick look and speak . . . even just a word or two to me. All the while I'm remembering that I'm the man who's trying to hold on to my home by paying this holier-than-thou banker an enormous amount of money each month. And it's all to reduce a debt that I don't even truly owe the bastard.

Well, all sorts of feelings started coursing through my veins. And I took two long swigs of whiskey . . . licking my lips and all the while figuring how I can teach this pompous good-for-nothing a lesson. So, just when he was about to slip silently by me, I turned my horse sharply to the left to block his passage . . . and he had to stop.

He said, "What are you doing, Watkins? You're blocking my way and I won't stand for it."

So, I stood up and said, "Well, then, if you 'won't stand for it', how about 'standing up' for a lesson I know you desperately need to learn."

He just sat there - haughty as a prince - with no apparent intention of stepping down to the ground as I had already done by then.

I was screaming at this devil. Finally, I grabbed his left leg and proceeded to pull him from the buggy – out there on the road with me. The bastard didn't say anything. He just stared at me condescendingly for a few moments and then he let loose with a shot of spit that hit my left eye . . . hard. And, as it drooled down my cheek, it got colder and colder. That was it for me. I commenced to giving him a good beating and he only fought back in the most pathetic manner you can imagine.

One of my uppercuts caused him to fall to the ground. It appeared he either wouldn't or couldn't get up. So, I decided if he wouldn't stand up and take his whipping like a man, then I'd give him a thrashing right there on the ground. So, I pulled him upright and I took to flailing him with my horse whip and its six foot long line. I striped his sorry ass over and over. And each time I snapped the whip at him, I did it with more anger-fed energy than the snap before.

Then, a thought struck me . . . just as sharp and painful as each whip lash I was laying on Garthwright. I realized I was about to kill this man. And any jury in Tennessee or Mississippi would surely send me to the gallows for the crime. So, I stood over Garthwright for a few seconds. And then I reached down to help him up. I didn't say anything. I just stood there breathing fast, heavy breaths . . . with sweat pouring down my face that turned into steam in the cold winter air.

But Garthwright had lots to say. He knew I was no longer a danger to him. So, he moved toward me and wagged his finger in my face so hard that I thought it would surely strike my nose. Garthwright was furious. He told me he'd been far too patient collecting the money I owed the bank. He said the monthly payments I'd been making amounted to just chump change compared to what I could really afford.

He said he wasn't going to have me arrested for this beating. He said if he did that, he'd never get his money. Instead, he was going to seize every asset I've got. He said he personally would see that I spent a long, long time in debtor's prison. He said that's where I belong – along with other scum like me.

And then he said something that bothered me. And I think it will bother you. He said he was going to go over the books with a fine tooth comb and uncover even the assets I might never have known. He said he'd repossess every red cent. Calvin, I believe he really means every word of it.

I know the Bill of Sale I gave you didn't include little Jed. Several times I thought to point this out to you. But each time I figured it was all nothing that would ever amount to anything. And I didn't want you to think I was begging you for more money. Now, during my final days on earth, I'm not so sure if I've destroyed my copy of the Bill of Sale or if Garthwright took it. I only know I hope this oversight never gets uncovered by his blood suckers. If you're ever asked about this, I believe you know better than I that a man of your stature and integrity can brush them off somehow.

I still can't purge from my mind Bettie and Mose and Jed's last hour with me. And I can't forget the unintended prophecy she spoke that afternoon. The human flesh that I bought and sold will survive their lives of hardship. And they'll pass on - to be with our Lord. But I don't stand a chance, Calvin. And I know, too, that I don't really deserve a crack at heaven.

So, it's my last written wish that you protect Mose and Bettie and Jed from harm and from heartaches. While the threat of losing Jed isn't certain, it's sill a real threat, nevertheless. And don't think for a moment that you can clear up this matter by simply offering a more than reasonable cash payment for Jed. Garthwright despises me now. I don't think even a king's ransom would buy Jed his freedom. I'm sure of it. So, please keep this information concealed from everybody.

Again, Garthwright means business. I've just received notice my house and its contents will be sold to the highest bidder during the second week of the upcoming year. I can't bear to see everything I've worked for carted away. I want to ensure that Eloise doesn't experience it either.

I've never been much of a man, Calvin. But I have appreciated your friendship. I beg of you to use your mind and your financial means to keep Eloise and the darkies safe. And so, with much gratitude I ask you to understand what's about to happen . . . and to pray for me. My own prayer is simple. "May God have mercy on my soul."

Mercer


Calvin kept his eyes fixed on the letter he held. He didn't dare peer over the stationery. He couldn't bear to observe what effects this astonishing correspondence had on Eloise and his wife. Secondly, he had an enormous lump in his throat . . . and he was squinting his face muscles harder than he had ever flexed them. He was trying to keep from developing tears, because . . . once they began to flow . . . they would pour out of him like water seeps through a sieve. He reasoned he might stand up and stretch. Maybe that would help him stay composed.

But he made the mistake of looking at Eloise and Catherine sitting together on the sofa. They were both silent and he could see no tears. However, they were both looking up as if to be saying, "How can one man hurt so many mortals who were devoted to him . . . all at one time?"

It was a worse sight than seeing Eloise cry. Calvin broke down . . . and he wept hysterically. After about a minute he turned his red, wet eyes toward Mrs. Watkins and he spoke.

"Madam, I can't talk about this now . . . and I know you don't want to talk about it either. I've got to get control of myself and go to Mr. Lassiter to make burial arrangements. Mrs. Cabell and I insist you stay with us as long as might be required. We will bear this grief together. And we'll get through it together."

421

Then Calvin picked up the letter and glanced at it for just an instant. However, his composure disintegrated, once again. He sharply turned and aimed his stride toward the stairwell. As he climbed the first step he managed to loudly mutter through his tears.

"I don't want to talk any more about this 'til tomorrow."

\* \* \* \* \* \* \*

Calvin sat alone in his bedroom . . . like he had done each evening for far too many months. There was a wall between his room and Catherine's "sitting room." Oh, how he despised that room's name. It was her "BEDROOM". She hadn't slept with him in ages.

He sat in his leather chair . . . eyes fixed on the dancing flames of the fire Mose had built for him. And he did what he had done so many times. He fixed his stare at the flames. He was convinced the leaping flames had a life all their own – a force of their own. He wondered whether he still had any energy – any power within himself – to remedy the fractured situations within his own home.

And he thought how there was merely a thin plaster wall that separated him from Catherine. Yet, that wall might as well be a mile thick.

Admittedly, he had never tried to scale the wall or try to tear it down. He had simply grown resigned to the emotional and sexual breach between them. He knew it would never be restored. The wall might as well be an impenetrable fortress.

He wondered. He dwelled on how the Christmas experience had played out. Any of their guests at that dinner table would leave thinking Catherine and Calvin enjoyed a deep spiritual connection . . . fueled by endless love and affection. It was all a charade – a ruse. It was a lie. Calvin reasoned he was living his life in a manner which only perpetuated that falsehood. He decided he was becoming sick and tired of living a lie.

"Maybe, though, there's still a slim possibility I can cure the breach. My conscience says I've, at least, got to try and restore this mess of a marriage."

He decided he had to make an effort – one last effort. He walked down the hallway and knocked lightly on Catherine's door.

"Who is it?"

"It's me, my dear wife. May I come in? I thought we might talk about the day . . . talk about Christmas."

There was stillness on her side of the door. "I'm feeling very tired, Mr. Cabell. Could we wait until tomorrow to discuss all this?"

Calvin soaked in every sound . . . as well as the nuance of every word she spoke. He was resolute this time. He wouldn't give up. "Mrs. Cabell, please open the door. I want to talk with you now . . . right now."

There was no answer.

"Darling, what I have to say can't wait until tomorrow. Again, please won't you let me in?"

There was still no answer, so Calvin began to assert himself. "Madam, I want you to open your door and let me come in. I demand it."

There was no reply – at least, no spoken reply. Her only response was communicated by the sound of metal striking against metal. As she locked the door from the inside, Catherine was locking out her husband. And Calvin knew she was sealing more than the door to her room. She was padlocking her heart. She was permanently blocking the chance to revive their lives together . . . when they were a genuine, married couple – a functioning husband and a wife.

Calvin realized the click of that door lock signaled his doom. It meant that he had to make a choice. He could remain living a life devoid of spousal understanding, companionship, and affection. Or, he could make a decision that might allow him to move forward with his life . . . and to address his needs.

Right there, standing outside his wife's sitting room door, he made his choice. He picked the latter one. The first one was Catherine's choice to make. She had made it. But he reckoned he was still too young for a significant part of him to die.

"There's a brand new year coming," he thought. "There's a fresh new year for me to start all over at living – living MY life . . . under very different terms and conditions."

*No Coin for Charon*

# CHAPTER
# *29*

December 28, 1838


"It's a miserable day for a funeral."

Calvin Cabell stood on the fourth step of the Presbyterian Church . . . under the metal overhang that was supposed to protect worshipers from inclement weather. But today's rain was continuous. A wet wind blew horizontally at him from the south. There was shelter only for those standing on the top step . . . and even this perch looking down on Poplar Avenue afforded minimal protection from the elements.

"And it's a miserable time of the year for a funeral, too."

"Well, Father, should we make it illegal to die during the Christmas season? That might solve one of those nagging problems. Or, perhaps, we should just stack up all the deceased for burial after the New Year."

Jamie Cabell was feeling his oats after one term away at college. He had acquired his father's style of very dry humor. Today he put it to use . . . hoping to offer some relief from the dreadful task they both faced this morning. But, immediately after he spoke, Jamie recognized he might have stepped over the line of father / son propriety. But, to his surprise, his father didn't sneer at him. Instead, he let a muffled chuckle slip out of his mouth . . . as if he genuinely appreciated Jamie's droll humor on a day like today.

Jamie and Calvin were waiting in the rain for the hearse to arrive carrying Mercer's body. During the past two days Eloise's anger had subsided a bit. She decided to return to her own home - despite the invitation to remain with the Cabells. But she insisted on burying her husband today. She said she couldn't bear the thought of a wake - either at home or at Lassiter's Mortuary.

"My home is no longer MY home according to Mr. Watkins' letter. Besides, I couldn't stand receiving friends on the very premises where he hanged himself."

One way to expedite the funeral service was to secure pall bearers right away. Eloise didn't want to be rejected by men of the church who might resent escorting the body of a weak Christian who committed suicide. She feared there were many men Mercer knew who shared that attitude. So, she asked Calvin, Jamie, and Josh. Moreover, to everyone's shock and consternation, she also asked Mose to be a pall bearer. No one had ever heard of such a thing. A Negro worshipping downstairs in the church was anathema. Consequently, a Negro serving as a pall bearer was an affront to everyone . . . at least, according to several church members when they heard about the arrangements.

Her reasoning made sense – especially in view of the fact that nothing about this predicament seemed to make any sense. Eloise thought the four men who found Mercer with her were the only men she could trust. In the end, they agreed to the widow's wishes out of respect for her . . . and her, alone.

Naturally, Josh was perplexed and apprehensive about being asked to serve. After all, he had only been a member of the Cabell household for three days. Furthermore, he had never even met Mercer Watkins. Seeing that limp body hanging from the rafters was the first time he ever laid eyes on the man. And now . . . here he stood in the rain . . . in a place he never imagined he would be just seventy-two hours ago. It was enough to make any boy's head swirl with confusion.

He told Jamie, "I guess since the two of us together lowered his body to the ground in the shed, then I suppose we could lower his body one more time into his grave."

Needless to say, Josh's admirable character traits had made a huge positive impression on the three pall bearers who stood with him. The boy seemed so stable and so mature for his years.

Eloise personally asked Mose for his help. At first he was reticent and unwilling. But, as she persisted, Mose kept remembering how his family's life might have been ruined if Mercer Watkins hadn't arranged for their sale to the Cabells. Perhaps, accepting Mrs. Watkins' request was a way of thanking him. He had never done that during his life. This was his last chance to pay his respects. He was prepared to disregard any of the finger pointing that was sure to take place.

Calvin thought Eloise's plea to Mose was "delicious", as he put it. Calvin Cabell was going to be acting like a new man – a man freed from the prim and proper farce that had been his demeanor during the past decade. What better way could he have imagined to put Memphians on notice that they should expect a much different Calvin Cabell. He was resolute about playing out his own definition of a man during the coming year?

From the church steps one could peer to the west and catch a glimpse of the Arkansas side of the river. The rain made this view blurry - like looking through steamed window panes on a cold day. But he knew he was looking in the direction of Hopefield, Arkansas . . . and the Pedraza Hotel.

He spent most of last night thinking about the Pedraza. Every time he had considered a trip there, his day dream always ended in the same cold sweat caused by a fear of being spotted and exposed as a philanderer . . . a cad.

"Delicious" was the only word he could think of to define a trip across the river.

Nothing seemed to be going right in his life. He felt as though he had been suffering from stomach influenza for many years. And now, he had the urge to vomit up all of this nauseous madness . . . right there in front of the church.

"There it comes." Jamie was the first to spot the hearse making its turn on to Poplar from Second Street. It was a glass enclosed wagon trimmed with shiny black, wood panels. On its top a large black plume ruled over the vehicle. No one knew the symbolism of this icon of death. But, even without an explanation, Jamie thought it was a perfect accessory.

He offered his own explanation. "I think it looks like a vulture . . . ready to pounce on the body once the mourners at graveside have left."

He and the others could see Mercer's casket inside. The liveryman pulled up to the church doors and Mr. Lassiter, who sat to the driver's right side, jumped down from the bench. He wasted no time. Without speaking, he motioned for the four pall bearers to join him at the rear of the hearse where he was pulling open the doors. The men moved with haste, but not such haste that they appeared to be irreverent. After all, there was a constant drizzle and they needed to get into the warmth of the church . . . lest they, themselves, catch a cold and die from pneumonia.

Calvin and Mose paired up to carry the front of the casket, while Josh and Jamie positioned themselves at the rear. Soon, they had mounted the church steps and were walking down the aisle to the bier that was set up in front of the communion table.

It was ten minutes after ten and anyone who cared to view the body before the funeral was invited to do so beginning at ten. But not a soul had arrived. And Calvin sensed there would be few, if any, visitors who turned up until the funeral began . . . which was scheduled for eleven o'clock. Mr. Lassiter made some small adjustments to the draped cloth that hung from the bier. He straightened a few creases crumpled when the casket was placed over it. Then he wasted no time. He opened the lid of the casket and, after inspecting his handiwork, he reached down to straighten Mercer's tie.

The four men stood in a row facing the body. Each had his hands clasped in front . . . and all four lowered their heads to pray. But there was no prayer offered – even a silent one. They just looked down at the remains. And in every man's mind all they could think about was the experience of discovering him . . . illuminated in the shed's darkness only by thin stripes of light that pierced through the raggedy roof above.

One by one Josh, Jamie, and Mose retreated to their assigned seats in the front pew. But Calvin continued to stand vigil in front of Mercer. Anyone could see he was deep in thought – puzzling thoughts. After about three minutes he reached into his right pants pocket and he pulled something out of it. Jamie was the only one who saw this movement.

He didn't know what sort of item was retrieved. Calvin held it in his hand. He was still deep in thought. Then, in a calculated manner, he stepped forward, leaned over the casket, and he placed his hand on Mercer. His back blocked Jamie's view. But his father's hands clearly remained in contact with the body for almost half a minute. Jamie wondered if his father was also putting his own finishing touches to Mercer's tie knot.

Finally, Calvin slowly backed away from the casket. Then, he bowed his head – this time in unmistakable, solemn prayer. And, whatever he had to say to God lasted about thirty seconds. Afterwards, he smartly pivoted himself around and joined the other pall bearers in the pew.

Jamie counted just six people who approached the casket to pay their respects before the funeral service began. Later, he turned around as folks were rising to sing "God of our Fathers" and he estimated there were only about twenty people in the sanctuary. Eloise sat in the front pew to their left

. . . next to a man and his wife. He reckoned the man was her brother from Holly Springs – the one with whom Mercer suggested she resettle and begin her life anew.

The homily was short, but respectful and thought provoking. At last, it was time for the pall bearers to rise and take their positions at the casket. Eloise declined to step forward for one last look at her husband. So, Mr. Lassiter closed the lid and fastened it shut with its metal clamps.

Every eye in the church zeroed in on Mose as the four men carried Mercer out of the church and into the waiting hearse. Reading their faces was easy for Jamie who always had the gift of figuring out things like this. Some were aghast at what they considered to be a sacrilege to both the church and to Southern society in general. Amazingly, Jamie interpreted that many folks were thinking the mix of pall bearers was just fine.

Jamie heard one attendee confirm his conclusion. The comment came from the wife of a wealthy planter. "It makes me wonder if my Harold might want to leave instructions for his Rufus to help carry him to the grave. I certainly will suggest he consider it when I see him tomorrow morning."

The funeral convoy to graveside was abbreviated . . . when measured by conventional standards. The hearse led the way, followed by just two carriages. The first contained Eloise, her brother, Eli, and her sister-in-law. The second one carried the pall bearers.

To everyone's surprise. Mr. Lassiter's tiny cortege faced a huge logistical problem - one that threatened to block his party from reaching the grave yard, altogether. The funeral procession had to cross the road that connected Ft. Pickering with the route of the Chickasaw Trace. There, in the gray mist just south of town, the mourners were confronted with an overwhelming site blocking the route.

Indians filled the roadway as far as anyone could see . . . to the left and to the right. They moved tentatively, like an endless herd . . . clumped close together, as if their collective body heat on this cold day might be absorbed by the weakest among them. It was an impenetrable barrier of humanity blocking Mr. Lassiter. He didn't know how to cope with this unanticipated obstacle.

Eloise's brother got out of his carriage and stomped angrily toward the wretched procession. He was indignant that "Injuns" and "savages" were "blocking the way for white folks mourning the loss of a loved one and trying to bury their dead."

He pushed his way forward . . . right into the mass of Native Americans. He apparently expected them to part their cordon for him . . . like Moses parted the Red Sea. But the Cherokee didn't push back. And they didn't look at him . . . or say anything, either. They just trod along, shuffling one foot after the other . . . oblivious to this white man's hostile demands.

The pall bearers were upset as they watched the ensuing confrontation. Josh jumped out and looked up and down the road trying to spot his brother. But the front of the march was far out of his sight and he knew John was surely at the lead. He quickly gave up the slim hope he might greet him. The two Cabells also ran toward Eloise's brother . . . to subdue the ranting white rogue. They had visited these Indians just four days ago. They had witnessed how forlorn and sickly they were. It incensed them this white scoundrel was treating them like animals.

"Eli, please get a hold of your self. Calm down," Calvin pleaded.

"I want these savages to stop . . . and let us through . . . and to show us the courtesy we deserve. I won't stand for this sort of impudence while we're trying to show respect for Mercer . . . and, most especially, for Eloise. She doesn't deserve this kind of treatment.

"The cemetery board wouldn't sell her a plot among the existing graves. She's already been humiliated that her husband's resting place has been relegated to the edge of the property's perimeter . . . almost in a corn field and all because Mercer took his own life.

"But Eli, I'm asking that you calm down and show a little compassion for these Indians. They've lost all that's dear to them. Their land's been taken along with everything they've ever grown or grazed on it. Most have lost loved ones. They've had to be buried in shallow graves along the road. Let's show some dignity to our fellow man. We can get to the other side without all of your histrionics. Again . . . I ask you to calm down."

"What's the problem here, gentlemen. What's all the fuss about?" The questions came from a sergeant who appeared on horseback out of nowhere.

"Sergeant, this gentleman is the brother-in-law of the deceased whom we're trying to bury. I know he's upset and he's got good reason to be. But, regrettably, he's taking his frustrations out on these poor souls. I wonder if you could help create a passage way along the crossroad here . . . so we can proceed to the cemetery.

"Say, aren't you the man who visited our encampment on Christmas Eve?"

He caught a glance of Josh standing about thirty feet away. The boy was overwhelmed at seeing the same Indians he had helped shepherd along the way. He had buried their sons and daughters as well as their elderly mothers and fathers. He had left a part of himself out there along this trail of tears . . . and he didn't want to relive the memories he thought he had shed.

"And that's John Burnett's brother over there. John says he'll be living with you, Mr. Cabell . . . getting an education and everything."

"We're blessed to have him, sergeant. And we were blessed to visit the encampment Christmas Eve. We were deeply moved by the plight of these Cherokee and we mean no disrespect to them. We just wish to bury our own dead. If you could assist us, I'd appreciate it."

The sergeant's horse swung toward the Indians and whinnied ferociously . . . so as to breach a gap in the throng. When he had opened a passable space and sat on his mount blocking those in the rear from progressing, the sergeant waved his hands at Lassiter . . . urging him to scoot through the opening.

"Come along, folks. I can't keep this swell of humanity still forever. Please proceed."

The funeral vehicles moved forward and slowly made their way through the gap while Calvin, Jamie, and Josh just stood there . . . immobilized by the monumental history they were witnessing. Jamie took special note of what he saw. He knew he'd be telling his grandchildren about the day the Trail of Tears passed through Memphis.

The Sergeant called out to Josh over the sounds of the wagon wheels. "Josh, I want you to know these Cherokee children really appreciated the cookies you sent back with John. They were sweet . . . and I'll betcha any amount of money those Indians will remember the many other sweet kindnesses you've offered them . . . all along the way."

Josh stood still . . . processing what he was seeing and what he was hearing from the sergeant. Tears filled his eyes. He knew some of them came from releasing the pent-up memories of finding Mercer West's body and from being separated from John. But mostly, he was shedding tears, because these

Cherokee were too noble to shed for themselves – even under these incredibly unjust circumstances.

The sergeant observed Josh's emotions pour out for a spell and then he was forced to cry out again. "Are you coming, Josh? I can't hold this opening forever, you know. This march has got to carry on."

And that's when it struck Josh. "Yep, he's right. Life's got to go on . . . even when death and human injustice is all around you. My life now is tethered to the folks in the carriage . . . on the other side of these Indians. Like the Cherokee, I've got to march on, too, and bury a man I never heard of two days ago.

"There's one thing, for sure, I've learned along this trail. Death's just a part of life. And I've got to get to that other side . . . 'cause that's where my life's journey has taken me."

\* \* \* \* \* \* \* \*

The pall bearers were drenched by the time they completed lowering the casket using two thick, purple velvet ropes. They looked forward to going to Eloise's house to dry off by the fire and sip the hot sassafras tea she promised to brew. It was only when they returned to the Watkins' house that anyone had the chance to relax, to dry off, and to warm up.

Calvin turned to his newly freed servant and whispered a suggestion. "Mose, let's you and me go out on the back porch . . . and discuss all the things we need to talk about."

"Yessir, Mr. Cabell. I'll go with ya. I knows what needs to be said."

The white man and the black man stood outside Mercer's house on the open back porch. They were sheltered from the drizzling rain, but their breaths belched out spurts of steamy condensation as they talked out there in the cold. Before them was the shed. The two doors remained wide open . . . just as they had left them two days earlier. Mose noticed the spare key ring he had recovered lay on the porch's wood floor. No doubt Mrs. Watkins had cast it there in a fit of bitter frustration.

"Mose, I've given this matter a lot of thought since I read Mr. Watkins' letter. I've given it a LOT of thought. And I haven't come up with a sure-fire way to solve this problem about Jed."

432

Calvin's words elicited no response from Mose. Then he felt silly expecting one - considering Mose's station in life. It appeared Calvin would have to carry on . . . solo.

"I've met this banker fellow from Hernando. He has a short fuse on a bad temper. It seems just about right he'd be so mean-spirited and bitter toward Mercer that he'd claim Jed as a seized asset. He'd do it, just so there'd be one more reason for Mercer to rot in hell - until Garthright joins him upon his own death. I don't think he'd sell Jed to me at any price. Out of spite, he'd take less cash from a planter . . . expecting to get a life time of work in the fields from a young black boy just beginning to get his strength."

Calvin took stock of what Mose might be thinking . . . about what he just said. Then he realized he'd probably never know. Mose would never tell him.

"So, all of that leads me to reason this, Mose. No one should mention this situation to a soul. Where there's no information about this oversight, I'm just about certain there will be no harm done."

Calvin again tried to read Mose's thoughts. But, divining what transpired in this man's mind was futile. From the day he had bought him, Mose had always appeared inscrutable.

"Now, you should find great comfort that I've already spoken to Mrs. Watkins about a strategy such as this. She assures me she would never mention Jed's predicament to a soul. She said she'd take the secret to her grave. I believe her, Mose. I truly believe her."

"That leaves just you, me, Jamie, Josh, and Mrs. Cabell who know what Mr. Watkins' letter contained. It's unimaginable that any one of these people will ever speak of this. I've already secured their pledges to remain silent. Of course, Josh is the one we know the least, but I think he's a kid of great integrity. I'm sure his word will be his bond. About that I have no doubt."

For the first time, Calvin sensed what Mose was pondering. And what he surely had concluded in his mind was, "This plan will never work. This plan will ensure that my only son will eventually be taken from me . . . and sold." Calvin was certain of it.

Then Mose raised his head to look him squarely in the eyes. His white rimmed eyes amid a black face had a layer of moisture covering them. There was a thick sheen of tears.

433

"No, Mr. Cabell, you ferget somethin'. You ferget 'bout Mr. Lancaster. He knows. He knows."

A dagger might as well have been plunged into Calvin Cabell's heart. Suddenly his chest ached with pain. He thought he might vomit out this toxic brew of secrets along with the pungent knowledge there are people you can and cannot trust to keep them. Isaac Shelby Lancaster was one who could never be trusted. Mose was right.

"Oh, how I wish I never allowed that pig to attend Christmas dinner. If ever there was a Judas at my table, it was Shelby, the guest who would, more than likely, sell his soul to the devil."

Calvin grew exceedingly pensive. Mose read his face and looked at his forlorn eyes. He could see how despondent he was. Any fool could have read him like a book.

Calvin raised his head and locked his eyes with Mose's wet eyes . . . shimmering on a layer of glistening tears. "He's given me his word on that matter. But you're right, Mose. Squire Lancaster cannot be trusted. I'll go to his office right away and talk to him again. He asked for a meeting with me and Mercer. If I have to bribe him . . . or threaten him . . . or kill him right there behind his desk, I'll do it. I'll do what I have to do to save that boy of yours.

"Unless there's something in this equation I've overlooked, then this is the only plan we have. We all need to do a lot of praying, Mose. Surely, the Lord Almighty will reach down and protect this innocent child and his loving parents. If God is about love . . . if He sent His son into the world that we might repent and be saved . . . then, He knows I've repented for my many sins. And, I think Mr. Watkins repented, as well. Surely God will recognize both of our pleas for mercy - two slave owners unworthy of grace. And He'll show His love by keeping Jed safe."

He looked at Mose, whose head was as hang-dog as he had ever seen it. Calvin greatly admired this black man who had enriched his life as well as the lives of his family. He held out his index finger and he gently used it to lovingly raise Mose's chin . . . so their eyes met, once again.

"Mose, you know . . . that I know . . . you've been through plenty of tough times. There've been plenty of days when change was in the air – change that was sure to adversely affect you and your family.

"Remember the day I picked you up, right here, at Mr. Watkins' house? You didn't have any assurance how your family's lives would unfold with me. And I remember what you said, then. And I remember Mercer telling me you also said it to him . . . after he broke the news the bank would soon seize you and all his other assets.

"Mose, you turned to him . . . and you turned to me . . . and you said, 'Ever thing gonna be alright'."

Calvin paused. He wanted to emphasize the positive resolve Mose had illustrated time and again. Maybe he could generate some more of that same faith . . . here . . . and now.

"Mose, remember? You said, 'Ever thing gonna be alright.' That's what you need to be saying now, Mose."

"This time I don't know 'bout dat, Mr. Cabell. This time . . . I don't think so. Things ain't never gonna be alright. I know it . . . for sure."

Calvin wrapped his arms around the black man whom he'd just freed. And, wrapped together as if they were one living organism, both men began to bawl. Calvin kept pondering. He kept paining about what Mose had said.

"This time I don't know about dat." Calvin quietly quoted Mose's assessment over and over in his mind.

Calvin confessed to himself that he didn't know either. But he pledged he wouldn't sit passively until the answer eventually revealed itself. He was prepared to wage war to resolve this dilemma.

*No Coin for Charon*

# CHAPTER

## 30

Calvin flung open the front door to Shelby's law office like a raging bull. He bellowed at Matt Clemons, the law clerk, "GET OUT. Leave these premises . . . now."

The young man jumped up from his chair and obliged Calvin's demand. He backed himself toward the door ever-so-cautiously. Clemons kept his eyes riveted on Calvin's . . . as if they were fixed upon a mad dog, whose foaming mouth might soon take a bite out of him without warning. Once outside, he stared back through the door's glass . . . incredulous at what had happened.

The commotion summoned Shelby who opened his office door. He looked stunned and he appeared reluctant to pass beyond its threshold. His initial look of surprise quickly evolved into a stance of angry defiance. He folded his arms and planted his feet firmly in the doorway. He glared at Calvin omnisciently. He always knew this moment was inevitable. And he was ready.

"Buried ole Mercer, I see. What an ignominious end he devised, Calvin. You must have been the perfect lead pallbearer for such a wasted life. Did you look down at his casket and get a glimpse of yourself – a murderer who'd played out his ruse of righteousness until his family and friends finally found out he'd been living a lie all along? So, do you intend to scrape off the gilded veneer now, Calvin? Or do you want to cooperate with me and live on . . . with only you and me knowing you're really a low-life fraud?"

Calvin gritted his teeth and moved toward the office door. Shelby wasn't intimidated. He casually moved to Clemons' chair and sat down. He held out his arm in a courtly manner which invited his enemy to take a seat, also. Shelby knew Calvin was capable of killing. But the lawyer was fearless . . . so long as the two men sat so folks passing by might look through the front door's large glass window and witness whatever might be the worst result.

"Now, Calvin, as I recall . . . you allege you've got a claim against me – professional malpractice, is it? Well, as I've communicated to you Christmas Day, I'm quite certain I drafted paperwork which was entirely accurate . . . given the limited facts you asked me to incorporate in the Bill of Sale."

Shelby took note of the temperament in the room and concluded he still wielded the upper hand. "And, as I've also communicated to you, you have no legal basis and, certainly, no moral standing to effect the changes you seek. It would be highly unethical of me to draft a codicil that remedies the original agreement so your young Negro's freedom is secured. In fact, he still remains the property of Mercer's estate. Consequently, as a conscientious member of the Tennessee Bar, I will NOT abdicate the law."

Calvin still seethed with rage, but he was willing to listen. He knew he had no choice.

"Now, Mr. Cabell, there IS one avenue toward a remedy that I foresee might possibly clear up . . . not only the so-called 'injustice' you're claiming . . . as well as the sundry other injustices which fate has thrown together into one rather bitter brew. Would you like to hear them recited . . . as well as my ideas how they could simultaneously be resolved?"

Calvin could sense a veritable sledge hammer getting ready to slam down upon him and shatter his life. But, he held no status here. Shelby had all the clout. "Carry on," he murmured.

Well, Calvin, I've taken on a new client. He's brought a very interesting case to me that cries out for a just remedy. He's a young man from Kentucky – Harrodsburg, as I recall. He relocated to Memphis several weeks ago. In fact, I believe he's secured employment at your mill. Do you recall a strapping lad of about eighteen with reddish hair and a rather serious demeanor? My client's name is Mr. Nelson – Timothy Nelson. Do you, by any chance, know this young man?"

"Somber demeanor, indeed," Calvin thought. "The young man Shelby described frequently seemed to be staring a hole in him – like he was sizing him up. Whenever Calvin crossed the lumber yard, he could sense this lad observing his every move. Calvin didn't think it broached the realm of impertinence. Nevertheless, he had mentioned this odd situation to Sperling who said he would keep a lookout.

The young man was an impressive specimen. At about 6'2" he weighed probably one hundred and ninety pounds and he seemed strong as an ox. Just last week when the weather was unseasonably warm, he noticed Nelson groan as he single handedly placed his end of a log over the saw pit. It took three men to manage the opposite end. Nelson had removed his shirt that afternoon . . . leaving only his suspenders stretching up and over his torso.

Calvin recalled his muscles swelled beneath his chest and abdomen. They tightened tautly while the pained grimace on his face illustrated he was capable of enduring considerable strain. He illustrated he could summon up sufficient strength for almost any physical task. Calvin remembered also thinking there must surely be great anger pent up within the man's body. His grunting and flexing and his physical strength appeared to be energized by a fury within.

"I know who the worker is. What about him, Shelby? He has no role in any of this."

"Ah, but I think you'll soon agree he does, Calvin. In fact, I'm sure of it. You see, Mr. Nelson has lived a life of egregious hardship . . . due to the criminal actions long ago of a despicable man. It all happened when he was a mere toddler . . . when someone back in the Bluegrass murdered his mother – in cold blood.

"Can you imagine? A highly esteemed man . . . with every possible advantage in life willfully snuffed out the life of a poor single mother whose work ethic was solely devoted to providing for her illegitimate child. After his mother's death . . . ah, her MURDER, I should say . . . Mr. Nelson was raised for a time by the woman who lived in an adjacent outbuilding. But she, too, passed away when he was seven and he was left to fend for himself.

"Mr. Nelson is quite certain he knows the identity of his mother's killer. He's pieced together information he learned from the local sheriff and – as it so happens – I happen to have additional, solid information which corroborates his speculation. Mr. Nelson would like to see this man hanged to death - even after all these years."

Shelby was certain Calvin had already pieced this puzzle together. Yet, he had just hit his stride. He was determined to enjoy this performance.

"But Mr. Nelson's a practical man and I've advised him that a cash settlement might be arranged in consideration of his egregious loss. Surely, such terms would be an appropriate act of atonement by the murderer . . .

who must have been sorely burdened by this guilt for almost two decades. Wouldn't you think, Calvin?"

"I wouldn't know, Shelby. I wouldn't know. But, what if a settlement can't be reached?"

"Well, that would, indeed, be unfortunate . . . and likely to be perceived by Mr. Nelson as yet another act of arrogant hostility. Therefore, in the event a lack of cooperation by the murderer were the case, I'm prepared to file a criminal inquiry back in Kentucky . . . and a civil complaint here in Tennessee . . . to bring about a just resolution.

"You know, Calvin, I remember once telling you early on after I arrived here that I've always been amazed there is no statute of limitation protecting a murderer. I find it heartwarming that our society values the life of each and every citizen so greatly that the law prescribes a murderer can never escape culpability . . . as well as a jury. He'll always get hunted down . . . eventually."

"I don't know what you're getting at, Shelby. Besides, I'm here to right another wrong."

"I think you DO know what I'm getting to, Calvin. I think you know the bull-of-a-man you've seen working hard at your mill is the same little boy whose mother you molested . . . while her son slept less than six feet away. I think you know that outbuilding where she lived and you know her neighbor, Rebecca, was witness to your presence that evening. She was so sure of it she signed an affidavit before her death that describes you. And your familiarity with that poor victim is further confirmed, because you registered as a guest at the White Oak Inn that same night. You remember the White Oak Inn, don't you? And you surely remember being a guest one January night back in '24."

"Such an affidavit, if it exists at all, would be worthless in court. You know that."

"Well, first of all, the affidavit does exist. And, fortunately for Mr. Nelson, it's secure in my office safe – right back there in the next room. But more importantly, there's another affidavit in the safe. That one is signed by me. You understand, don't you, that I was an eyewitness the day Mr. Nelson's mother came to you pleading for justice You reluctantly obliged by giving her money – which she put in her lavender purse along with a sales receipt from the Barry Merchandise Store. I picked that purse up off the ground. And

440

I was able to inspect it. That same purse was tucked in her dress pocket when her body was pulled from the Kentucky River. There was a man's coat button in that pocket, as well. The sheriff reasoned the woman yanked the button from her murderer's coat as she struggled for her life. He showed me that fancy, brass fastener . . . and that purse, Calvin. The button belonged to you. And the purse belonged to your victim."

"So, if you were so certain all this evidence pointed to me as the bar maid's killer, why didn't you spill the beans to the sheriff when he presented it to you?"

"My memory must have lapsed that day, I suppose. I figured "knowledge is power" and the knowledge I had about this murder might one day pay off . . . handsomely.

"And, speaking of lapsed memory, isn't it odd you recall the victim was a bar maid? You knew her quite well, didn't you, Calvin? So, Mr. John Calvin Cabell, that leads one back to what I was saying when you rudely barged into my office. What sort of memory will this community have about you when YOU'RE finally laid to rest like our disgraced friend, Mercer, was today?

"What will your family think of you as they peer down at you . . . one last time . . . as you lay in your casket? I think everyone will come to the same unfortunate conclusion. 'Here is the rotting flesh of a man whose arrogance . . . was premised on his perverted brand of religious dogma that God almighty had predestined him to rule with impunity over his fellow man. Yet, all the while he was portraying himself as a mainstay of the church. What a no-good hypocrite he was.' That's what they'll think about you. That's what they'll forever remember about you. And that's why I'm certain you'll want to settle your debt with Mr. Nelson . . . straight away."

"And what amount of money does Mr. Nelson . . . or, should I say, how much money do YOU seek? You DO get a nice cut from this flagrant extortion, don't you, counselor?"

"I only seek to bring about a just remedy for my client, Mr. Cabell. Of course, as his attorney, I will receive professional remuneration . . . in the amount of half the proceeds."

Shelby's face noticeably revealed he was jogging his memory. He had forgotten to point out something of significant importance. "Oh, I forgot to answer your first question, Calvin. Mr. Nelson believes $15,000 would amount to the sort of settlement that would illustrate contrition by his

441

mother's killer . . . and, therefore, an appropriate payment for all his damages."

Calvin stood up and held his hat in front of his chest – seemingly, so the leather brim might serve as a shield protecting him against any further verbal assault Shelby might throw at him like a sharp javelin. And his fears weren't unfounded. Shelby struck with one last lunge – one final demand.

"Now, Calvin, I trust you'll agree that my delicate negotiation of such a volatile legal and criminal matter warrants a special consideration on your part, as well."

"What do you mean, Shelby? What other trick do you have up your sleeve?"

"I just think any reasonable person would conclude my professional services on behalf of my client are, in point of fact, restricted to any potential civil claim he has. My fee from his proceeds wouldn't even begin to account for the redemptive services I'd be granting to his mother's killer. This man would be getting something else in the bargain – something of great value."

Shelby couldn't contain a seditious chuckle swelling up inside of him. It grew into a sly grin . . . that blossomed into a slanderous smile. "You might say, Calvin, that what this criminal might be getting was . . . well, he'd be getting away with murder."

Shelby's intolerant quip ended just as quickly as it arose. The little man with the ruddy complexion and the forward thrusting horse teeth . . . who had wormed his way out of one ethical infraction after another . . . and had married the daughter of the most powerful political tyrant in Shelby County . . . that maggot was ready now to up his ante – to sweeten his corrupt honey pot.

"It seems to me, Calvin, the murderer would find it prudent to pay the broker of such a sweet deal the sum of another $20,000. That seems a nominal settlement for "getting away with murder". Shelby let out another muffled chuckle. "Of course, I'd be willing to take payment over several years provided the agreement was reduced to writing and the note's payer wrote out his confession to the crime. That way – in the unlikely event that I should precede the debtor in death – there would be a lingering liability to his estate that needed to be reckoned with."

"Twenty thousand dollars is robbery. It's extortion. It's illegal as hell."

442

"And so is murder, Calvin. So is murder."

Calvin turned about and headed for the front door. It was still dreary weather and the atmosphere mirrored Calvin's mood. He had to plod on through many murky thoughts before he could make his decision. He needed to think on it . . . and even sleep on it for a time. Yet, he knew he would experience little sleep in the days ahead.

He had one parting question. "I suppose even the most outrageous extortionist would want to ensure that a little black boy who innocently got caught up in a legal mess might emerge from such a deal knowing that he was free . . . freed from bondage and freed from the threat that his life was bound up in a future lien on chattel."

"I think that would be a fitting end to all this compensation, Calvin. I think that would be a splendid idea . . . and one I would happily facilitate."

As he squeezed and turned the brass door handle Calvin muttered, "I'll get back to you soon, Squire Lancaster. I trust the law can sit on this matter for a while."

"Sure, Calvin, there won't be any action until the New Year. That's in three days' time. I need to hear from you before we all begin to use our 1839 calendars. However, that's the limit, Calvin. You've got three days to save your hide."

Calvin noticeably had winced at the short time frame he was being afforded. Three days was just seventy-two hours. And his head already was filled with a maelstrom of dark demons from all the unexpected tragedies that had exploded in such short order. And now, he had just three days to decide if he could . . . or would meet Shelby's demands.

There was, of course, another choice. He could follow Mercer Watkins' suit and put an end to all his dilemmas . . . with a pistol . . . or a rope . . . or a short jump off a fishing boat into the Mississippi. At the moment he envied the peace Mercer must be enjoying right now. Five feet of dirt finally covered his casket and served as a permanent barrier to the miserable life that fate had forced him to endure . . . above earth. "Maybe Mercer made the best choice after all," Calvin muttered.

"Don't forget, Calvin," Shelby cried out one last time - almost mockingly.

"Always better to start the New Year with a clean slate."

\* \* \* \* \* \* \* \* \* \* \*

Jamie's sixth sense had been honed razor sharp since Christmas Eve. A year ago he learned his father had killed a woman . . . 'a whore' . . . as Mose recounted from reading Shelby's letter. And during the course of the past two days Jamie had fathomed the pain Mercer Watkins carried within him for far too long. He had witnessed how Mr. Watkins passed along that pain to Mrs. Watkins. Now that he knew the story, Jamie couldn't help wonder if, maybe, Mercer had made the best choice.

"Maybe . . . come spring . . . Mrs. Watkins' sap will rise and her spirits will be renewed again . . . along with the dogwood and azalea blossoms."

He didn't know for sure. However, he sensed his father must be in a real pickle about now. And he sensed that Shelby Lancaster was at the core of his malaise. He was certain his father's meeting with Shelby would cause all these issues to fester. About three o'clock he decided it was time to act on the information only he and Mose knew. If he didn't, he could foresee yet another suicide . . . followed by another funeral.

"What does Josh think right about now?" he wondered. "I'll bet he wishes he was over the river with the U.S. Army . . . still trudging toward Oklahoma with John and the haggard band of Cherokee."

Jamie hadn't quite made up his mind what to do. He thought it was prudent to keep formulating a plan - even while he made his way to Shelby's office. Time was wasting away, as Shelby's law office would close in an hour or so. That's when he saw his father. He was just twenty feet ahead and he was making his way along the Main Street's boardwalk toward Jamie. His head was bent down . . . and his hat brim nearly covered his face. He was very deeply entrenched with somber thoughts . . . which Jamie was certain involved desperate decisions that he needed to make very soon.

Calvin passed by his son . . . directly in front of Court Square. He was completely unaware of Jamie's presence. The highly disciplined, unassailable man Jamie always thought characterized his father seemed just as lowly and mucked up by life as Main Street's mire of wet mud and manure only a few inches below the raised wooden walkway.

"Father," he called out after Calvin had already passed by him . . . "Father."

Jamie's call brought Calvin out of his trance and he turned about. But he was still in a daze just as foggy and murky and dark as this late afternoon atmosphere in December . . . when the sun sets before five o'clock. It was uncompromisingly dreary along Main Street. Yet, it was not so bleak and hopeless as the sorry existence Calvin Cabell was living. He still didn't speak. So, Jamie took the lead.

"Father, life's been difficult for you the past several days. Nothing's gone right. And, from my vantage point, it appears things aren't about to get any better. How about sitting a spell with me here in Court Square?"

"Things aren't about to get any better?" Had he heard his son correctly? Did Jamie know more than he let on? Calvin was always wary of his son's intuitive nature. Many times Jamie's insightfulness actually frightened him. And, this was one of those times.

"What do you mean, son? Why would you say 'things aren't going to get any better?' How do you know about anything that's of concern to me?"

"Come with me and sit over there on the park bench, Father. It's secluded from everyone . . . especially on such a foggy evening. I'd like to talk about what's been going on. Maybe you could help me sort through some things. And maybe I could even help you sort out some issues."

Calvin followed his son toward the bench and they sat down with their bodies slanted toward one another. Jamie placed his right arm over the bench's back. Calvin sat erect . . . with his hands clenched in two fists resting agitatedly on his lap. The rain had let up and the city was presently enveloped in a cold, moist fog – the kind that sticks to your skin and chills your bones during winter time in Memphis.

"Father, when we sat down in the pew after we carried Mr. Watkins' casket to the bier, you remained there . . . all alone. You were in deep, heavy thought for quite a while. And I saw you lean forward and touch Mr. Watkins one last time. I figured this was something about – well, about something very personal you had to say to him before the casket was closed."

Sure enough, Jamie's sixth sense had been right on the mark. Calvin was amazed at his perspicacity.

"Please, tell me, Father. What were you doing to the body? What were you thinking about? I believe it was significant. I think you did something that

445

was noble and gracious. I think it separated you from ordinary men. And I'd like to know for sure if my hunch is right."

"Jamie, when you left for college and took the steamboat upriver, Mose came back home and told me the boat was the 'Lucky Lady'. He told me a friend I met on my first trip to Memphis was still the captain of that boat."

"Yes . . . yes, that's right. I remember the captain said he knew you and he wanted a full report about your achievements. He was genuinely honored that your son was a passenger on his boat."

"That sounds just like him. Captain Moore and I shared an experience on that first trip that prompted both of us to speak very candidly about life . . . and death . . . and about the 'hereafter'. He told me his only son was playfully chasing his dog along the deck of his keel boat. He accidentally fell into the ink black river and drowned. At first, Moore blamed the dog for the tragedy. He despised that dog even though it was his son's best buddy. Finally, Captain Moore shared something I've never forgotten.

"He reminded me about Charon, the mythological ferryman who carried the deceased to Hades. That's the place in the after-life where the dead can live on . . . forever. Folks back then thought heaven lay on the other side of the river of death – the River Styx. Of course, Charon performed a valuable service . . . and he expected to be paid for it."

"Yes, I know about the legend of Charon."

"Well, Captain Moore told me after his son fell overboard, the Christian faith he would have sworn to be alive . . . through Jesus . . . was nothing more than a pile of crap. He couldn't imagine his Christian God letting something like this tragedy occur. As he looked out over the river shimmering in the moonlight, a vision came to him . . . a memory of the way folks living before Jesus handled the death of a son . . . just like his.

"He said the river reminded him that night of what the River Styx probably looked like . . . and he thought he could see Charon, the ferryman, poling his carcass laden boat to the other side. He remembered Charon always looked under the tongues of his customers and, if there was no coin stashed away for him, he left the body behind . . . destined to roam the earth as nothing more than a ghost. Captain Moore feared his son would be left behind – and he'd never make it across the river to heaven.

"So he muzzled the animal after placing two coins in his mouth. He said, 'Now, go fetch Robert and take these to him. There's one for him and one for you.' Then he tossed the dog into the river . . . and just hoped and prayed he'd done the right thing.

"You see, the captain didn't want to offend his Christian God . . . but, he didn't want to miss a bet that maybe what he thought he believed . . . was bogus.

"You see, Jamie, the captain was desperate. And I've got to tell you we all become desperate at one time or another. Sometimes everything we thought we believed in up until that time . . . well, it's suddenly no longer a tenet to our faith. We have doubts. We reject most of the things we've ever professed

"You see, Captain Moore was willing to defy what he'd been told about God, about Jesus, about sin, and about salvation – you know, everything about getting to heaven. He was a desperate man that night . . . and very much alone in the world. The captain would have shaken chicken bones in a bottle . . . even in the presence of Almighty God . . . if he thought those bones might possibly bring back to life the one he loved so dearly.

"So, this morning I stood there in front of Mercer and I got to thinking, too. I know I'm considered to be a pillar of the church . . . cut from staunch Calvinist cloth . . . and a man of unimpeachable faith. But everybody, Jamie, reaches a point where, at least for a moment, he's not quite sure of his own religious bearings. Every now and again a man's likely to leave the fold of his religion - to embrace a belief that other folks might consider heresy. You know, like it would be a mortal sin and that 'Doubting Thomas' would rot in hell if he strays just one Bible verse from the church's orthodoxy."

"Yes, Father, I know what you mean. Sometimes we all find ourselves in desperate straits."

"That's right. This morning I was looking down at Mercer Watkins. And I was thinking about how lots of good Christians believe that a person who takes his own life has no chance at all of getting to heaven. They believe a suicide means you go straight to the fire and brimstone of hell. Well, son, I just don't believe that. At least, I don't believe that anymore. And, recently, there's been more and more about religion I don't think I believe any longer."

Calvin stopped speaking and Jamie could tell his father's mind had all kinds of thought and emotions rushing helter-skelter through it . . . like bats pouring out of a cave at nightfall.

"And then, I remembered Mr. Watkins was an owner of slaves . . . just like me. He once told me he thought that was reason enough to be banned from heaven.

"Now, I know Mr. Watkins was a sinner . . . like the rest of us. But, I also know he had a tender side about him and a sincere respect for his fellow man. I stood there calculating whether or not I believed he had even a slim chance of being reunited with his Lord and Savior . . . given his spotted soul.

"All of a sudden, I wasn't sure if the doctrine I acknowledge in church . . . is what I REALLY believe. So, I thought there was no harm in covering the bet . . . with an insurance policy. I needed to do whatever I could to allow Mercer to get to heaven . . . or to Hades . . . or wherever we go - assuming we've got a shot at anything other than rotting in a cold grave."

Jamie listened intently to every word his father had to say. He knew exactly how this scenario would end.

"Like I said, the ancient Greeks used to put a coin under the tongue of their departed loved ones. It was Charon's ferry fee. Now, the point is I don't know if there IS a Charon and the River Styx and Hades. But I don't know for sure if there isn't. And what's got to be said that I'm not so sure the way to heaven . . . or Hades, is through following the Bible and believing in Jesus.

"So, I pulled out of my pocket a five dollar gold piece. I thought Charon would find that to be a more than a fair fare. I lifted up Mercer's tongue and I tucked that coin under it. I didn't want him to get to the bank of the River Styx and have no coin for Charon.

Jamie had heard several adults talk about their relationships with their father or their mother late in life . . . when they start to need special care. It struck him when one of those adult whose father was old and weak turned to another and said, "It just goes to show you how life turns you upside-down. My Pop cared for me when I was a baby. But now the tables have turned. Now I'm the adult and he's the baby who needs MY care."

That's what was happening to Jamie, the child, and his father, the adult who had cared for him. Tonight the relationship had been turned topsy-turvy. Calvin was the child who was afraid of the dark and Jamie's role was to reassure and console him. It was an moment of epiphany and Jamie wasn't about to let his father down.

"Son, I've done things in my life that I'm not proud of. Maybe – just maybe - those sins are significant enough to prevent me from reaching the Pearly Gates. Only time will tell. So, before you lower me into the grave, I'd appreciate it if you'd put a gold coin under my tongue, too – just in case. I may need it for Charon. And make sure no one at my funeral in the Presbyterian Church knows about it. That's an act of 'heresy', you know."

Jamie was as proud of his father as he had ever been. He was admitting that even the pious pillars of the church have doubts. They have fears that can't be quelled by reading the Bible or reciting the catechism. For the first time he realized his father, the illustrious Calvin Cabell, was far from a perfect human. No one is.

Jamie patted his Father on the shoulder. There had been plenty of tears shed that day, but the two Cabell men shed a few more sitting there on the park bench . . . in the sort of night mist one might imagine in the netherworld. Those tears joined them into heart-rending communion with one another . . . for the first time Jamie could ever remember.

Jamie decided he couldn't spoil the moment. He couldn't begin telling his father everything he knew, how he knew it, and how he intended to employ it. Telling him would be a sure sacrilege under these conditions.

"Now if you'll excuse me son, I've got to go have a chat with your mother. I'm not looking forward to it." Calvin wiped tears from his cheekbones as he arose from the bench. He looked down at Jamie with an oddly quirky smile.

"And remember . . . when it's appropriate . . . about Charon. Don't leave me to rot in a hell on this side of the Styx River. Put a coin under my tongue . . . please."

* * * * * * * * *

Matt Clemons had waited patiently out in the mist during Calvin's unannounced meeting with Shelby. He was scared to death by Mr. Cabell's aggressive behavior. Because Clemons was forced to make a hasty retreat, he left his overcoat on the coat tree inside the law office's front door. Consequently, he got soaked by the cold, wet moisture suspended in the night air. He didn't dare return to retrieve it. Instead, he chose to stand vigil across the street . . . never taking his eyes off the office door's glass window and the two enemies he could see inside.

He was sure he was going to be a witness to violence . . . or even a murder. And he was almost certain the victim was going to be his boss. He finally ventured back inside several minutes after Calvin departed. He acted as if nothing had happened . . . like he had just stepped away from the office for a minute to buy a newspaper.

Clemons was, once again, diligently working at his desk when he heard the front door fling open. The sound was more boisterous than when Calvin Cabell had burst in. He looked up and saw Jamie Cabell coming inside.

"Where's Shelby Lancaster, sir?" Jamie inquired in a tone that indicated it was his right to a quick and honest response. Clemons found his bearing oddly impudent for one who had just recently left home for college. But this young man WAS Calvin Cabell's son. And Clemons muted his initial reaction . . . remembering that rank does enjoy privilege.

"I'll see if he's here, sir. If you'll take a seat, I'll be with you soon." Matt Clemons was startled and confused. He thought, "First the father . . . then, the son barges in. What in tarnation is going on around here today?"

The whole place seemed to shake as the young man's loud voice reverberated, "SHELBY." Jamie again screamed as loud as he could. "SHELBY LANCASTER, you have a visitor and I need to see you straight away "

Shelby soon stormed through his office door. When he saw it was Jamie Cabell standing there, his natural reaction was to modulate the hostility he had posed in the doorway. But Jamie felt empowered by the moral advantage and the brutal knowledge he wielded. Yet, he surprised himself when he nearly roared, "Shelby, you and I need to talk . . . and, we need to talk right this instant. I recommend you chase away your boy."

"Your BOY," Matt Clemons kept hearing echo in his mind. Matt knew Shelby was sure to set this young whippersnapper straight. He even relished the next scene in which the Cabell offspring would be soundly thrashed for calling him Shelby's "boy". But, just as sufficient steam built up inside Shelby so as to erupt in a caustic tirade at Calvin Cabell's son, Jamie spoke again . . . and Clemons observed his boss's angry attitude suddenly melt . . . into meek submission.

450

"Shelby, we've got a lot to talk about . . . about what's gone on here this afternoon with my Father. And, I think we should begin by talking about what one can see from the vantage point of Mr. Beaty's deer stand . . . in the dale off the Raleigh Road."

Every drop of blood seemed to flush out of Shelby's face. His jowls were as white as flour paste. Jamie knew then and there he'd be dealing with a smarmy little worm.

"Mr. Clemons, I wonder if you'd be so kind as to leave me and Mr. Cabell alone for awhile. In fact, considering the time, why don't you just call it a day. I'll see you first thing in the morning."

"Yes, Squire Lancaster, but I'm almost finished with the opinion you asked for. I can have it on your desk in about ten minutes."

Jamie had his penetrating eyes locked on Shelby's and . . . even without a word being spoken . . . Shelby knew what those eyes had seen and what words were soon to come spouting from his lips. Shelby didn't dare flinch at his young visitor until his clerk had left the premises.

"I said that will be ALL for today, Clemons. I need to confer with our unexpected guest."

"That's right, Clemons. Move along, please. This is a confidential meeting," Jamie said.

Clemons swept up his coat and hat and the afternoon newspaper he still hadn't read. Without putting on a single outer garment he once again dashed out the front door. And this time he wouldn't be standing vigilantly across the street awaiting a crime. He was headed for home.

"Shelby, I think you need to take a load off your feet and sit here . . . in Clemons' chair," Jamie suggested without a challenge from the attorney. His short frame settled low in the seat and Jamie magnified the difference in stature between them by sitting directly on Clemons' desk so his eyes looked down at the meek little man - about a distance of three feet. Shelby was shaking. And though he didn't let on, Jamie was shaking inside, too. "Where to begin," he thought. Then, he just opened his mouth and it all spewed out . . . beautifully.

"Shelby, a number of us in the community are quite concerned about you. And being the year is almost gone and it's time for New Year resolutions, I thought now was a good time to sort through some issues. I guess you could say there are many people who are concerned that you have a distorted view of the world . . . and your highly exaggerated role in it. I, for one, think it's time to correct all that . . . and recast you in a more proportional player in the scheme of things."

Jamie was stunned at how well this trip to the wood shed was going. He had suspected a standoff of sort . . . a cat and mouse game in which he would have to prove he had the upper hand . . . and Shelby would deny, deny, and then deny some more. All was going well. He also was pleased with his oblique references to "a number of us". In fact, the number of folks "in the know" totaled two - just him and Mose. And, to Shelby's viewpoint, Mose was just an ignorant, illiterate, former slave whose son's future Shelby controlled . . . like a puppeteer pulling the strings of a black-faced marionette.

"Now Shelby, you don't seem inclined to say a lot sitting there. I understand. Believe me. But it might be a good idea for you to say now you know about Mr. Beaty's deer stand."

A lump in Shelby's throat obstructed any reply. He tried to clear it once. Then he choked a little as he tried for the second time. One more effort finally cleared the passageway. "Yes, I believe I've seen Mr. Beaty's stand . . . from which he hunts deer with a bow."

"That's right, Shelby. It's a beautifully laid out hunting spot. But it appears there's more prey out near Raleigh than just deer to take down. I know it's ironic, but some of the animals out there are even weaker and more easily lured . . . and slaughtered than . . . say, a little fawn.

"You know, some creatures are more at risk to predators than others. They've got far less control over their lives and their destinies than the animals scurrilous men hunt for food . . . or to satiate their sick pleasures. For example, you take a man . . . even a shackled slave man . . . who's got a child he loves and he would do anything for her. That man might be an easy mark if there was a spineless abuser out there with moral ethics as putrid as pond scum. And, if such a pathetic excuse for a man was hungering to have his perverse way with the father of that child, I suspect the only way such a snake could pull it off is if he threatened to have that little girl raped or sold off . . . to God knows who . . . or where.

"It just seems logical to me, SQUIRE Shelby Lancaster - whose namesake is someone highly revered by my father - that anyone who had the despicable urge to . . . say, rape that father . . . even though God Almighty has forbidden it in his Holy Word . . . well . . . that man should be stripped, tarred, and feathered, and then set ablaze.

"Now, don't you think such a feeble excuse of a man would be doomed to hell, Shelby? That poor, pathetic sort of a man might as well start living in his own hell . . . right here on earth . . . even though Gabriel hasn't yet blown his horn summoning the bastard home . . . or to hell. Wouldn't you say that's about right, Attorney Lancaster? That sort of scum's a stinking scoundrel, isn't he?"

Shelby was on the verge of crying. His lips were quivering and his eyes were cast downward . . . toward hell. He couldn't look Jamie in the eye while such disgusting chunks of his life were being so vividly recounted. But he knew he had to speak . . . even if it was barely audible. "Yes . . . yes, Jamie, that would be about right."

"But you know, Shelby, what's even more intriguing about all this purely hypothetical thinking about such vile men – men who have a soul constituted of barnyard excrement - is this simple, logical extrapolation. Let's say such a pile of shit, who would molest another man under such disgusting circumstances, were the son-in-law of the most powerful politician in the county – a man who is widely known to despise creeps like the ones who strip men naked in Beaty's meadow and have their way with them.

"What if, for example, this father-in-law – who, for the sake of argument, we'll say is a judge? Well . . . what if this judge was known to have actually sentenced men to the gallows who had violated these same laws against sodomy . . . established by Man . . . and consecrated by God? By the way, Shelby, didn't Judge Robinson hang three men a couple of years ago – men who raped a teenage boy? Does my memory serve me well, Shelby?"

Tears were welling up in Shelby's eyes. He wanted to get this tongue lashing over with as soon as possible. And he knew the only way to conclude this humiliating grilling by a mere college youth was to cooperate. "Yes, sir, Judge Robinson hates queers. Everybody knows it."

"Well, a number of us (Jamie was pleased he had pulled this nebulous phrase from his arsenal one last time) think that someone who's such a pathetic pervert would want to make amends to his fellow Man . . . and to his God. I thought you might see it the same way. And here at the cusp of another year, it might be a good time to settle some accounts where others might have been accused . . . rightly or wrongly . . . of things they've also done . . . and for

453

which they might also have great regret. But, God forbid . . . under these circumstances . . . if there's some fatally flawed bastard out there who's standing in the way of a decent person's chance at redemption."

"I think you're right, Jamie. Here at year's end, it might be a very appropriate time to grant reprieves to those who seek them . . . and who deserve forgiveness."

"I thought you might see it that way, Squire Lancaster. Consequently, why don't you get some quills . . . and some ink . . . and some paper. I think you've got a letter you'll want to write . . . for posterity's sake. It'll be a letter that my father will keep . . . with the clear understanding it could one day be pulled out of his safe and used against its author. And it's you, Shelby Lancaster, who shall be the author.

"It's like my father always told me. We need to begin the New Year with a clean slate."

\* \* \* \* \* \* \* \* \*

Jamie Cabell walked out of Shelby Lancaster's law office without the bluster he had summoned up on his way in. It was quarter to five and it was pitch black outside . . . except for the gray mist illuminated by the gas lamps. He held five pages of documents Shelby had penned. And every word he had inscribed was written *ver batim* from what Jamie had dictated to him. As he reflected on what was written on the papers, he was pleased he had covered all the important points . . . as well as some that weren't so important.

For example, Jamie ensured there would be no retribution against Tyrus or his daughter . . . or his wife . . . or to anybody to whom Tyrus might have confided. Mose was also protected. However, Shelby still didn't have a clue it was Mose who had read the terms of extortion Shelby levied against Calvin or that Mose devised the scheme to catch Shelby red handed out at Beaty's hunting stand. After all, Shelby still considered Mose to be an ignorant, illiterate nigger.

And the most important Negro of all that Shelby's letter addressed was Jed. Shelby had written a clear statement which served notice he had made a huge mistake by not including Jed as property transferred by Mercer Watkins. It cited the fact that Jed had been "inadvertently deleted" from the original chattel exchange and it stated that "good and valuable consideration" had already been paid by Calvin Cabell for Mose's son. Shelby wrote that he assumed responsibility for this amendment – even any potential financial

454

responsibility - and he said he would forever warrant the fact that due consideration was paid for all THREE slaves.

But the main prize was what Shelby memorialized about Jamie's father. Isaac Shelby Lancaster would no longer be a threat to Calvin, who had been so forlorn earlier, during their visit. Jamie was excited about showing him the terms of exoneration. But he had to pick the right opportunity. His mother couldn't be privy to any of the good news. Jamie turned on to Adams Street and began the trip home. He knew Mose was going to be overjoyed his son was no longer threatened by a seizure of Mercer's assets. He wanted to share the good news with him first.

\* \* \* \* \* \* \* \* \* \* \* \*

After Jamie left, Shelby sat motionless in Clemons' chair for over ten minutes. His mind was numb from the whipsawing he had endured. At three o'clock he had been in command of his own life . . . as well as the captain of the fate of others. Furthermore, he had plans to make a sizeable financial windfall from it all. Two hours later he was humiliated and broken. Where he once had others at his beck and call, now he was nothing more than Jamie Cabell's dummy . . . living with the constant threat a mere college lad might pull a string and he would be exposed. He would be ruined.

He finally got up from the chair and began shutting down the office for the night. There were two lamps in his private study that needed to be extinguished as well as three in the front office. He was puffing at the second flame when the front door opened, yet again. The light was dim, but Shelby could see it was Timothy Nelson.

"I just got off work, Mr. Lancaster. A friend reported he saw Mr. Cabell leave here earlier. He said the old man looked like he'd been beaten up pretty bad. I figured you had a report for me . . . a very good report, no doubt."

Shelby snapped at his client. "Who told you Calvin Cabell was here? I want to know. I can't have you spying on every person who comes in and out of this office."

"Easy, Mr. Lancaster, nobody's spying on you. I just heard what I told you . . . and I knew you'd have good news for me."

Now Shelby had a new predicament to deal with. And in some ways working his way through this one was going to be just as prickly as contending with the two Cabells. Shelby picked up the one lit lamp and he walked toward

Nelson. He stood face to face with him . . . so the lamplight equally illuminated both men's face. Timothy could see Shelby's expression was troubled. He figured that meant he was about to give a disappointing report.

"I don't think I'm going to be able to pull off this negotiation like I thought I could, Mr. Nelson. I think you need to forget the prospect of Calvin Cabell ever standing trial for the murder of your mother. It's just not going to happen."

"So, you arranged for a settlement instead?"

"No, there won't be a settlement, either. It appears Mr. Cabell's going to go free."

"But you said . . . you assured me that between the hard evidence I brought you combined with what you already had on him, there was sure to be an indictment . . . or, at the very least, Cabell would squeal so loudly about being caught he'd beg for a cash settlement to save his hide. That's what you said, Mr. Lancaster. That's exactly what you told me."

"Things change, my boy. Circumstances change, too. It's just that I've decided today . . . we don't have a prayer."

"But you also said if he wouldn't cooperate with us, you'd still file a civil suit here in Shelby County anyway. You said when the allegations were made public, Calvin Cabell would be a ruined man. You said he would lose his family over the scandal the law suit would cause . . . just like I lost my family to HIM sixteen years ago."

"Well, there won't be any law suit filed . . . by me or anybody else. I'm afraid you've misunderstood what I told you and you've built up your hopes way beyond what's reasonable. I'm telling you, you need to put this all behind you and get on with your life."

Shelby recalled what most folks said about red heads having a short fuse to their tempers. Timothy Nelson was seething mad. Shelby had already escaped physical harm by both the Cabell men. Now he wondered if this Kentuckian was going to wring his neck. Instead, he had to settle for another tongue lashing.

"They told me back in Harrodsburg you were a spineless maggot . . . who'd been run out of town for your lies and your greed. And that's just what I've found you to be . . . a lying scoundrel who'll say anything to anyone if it

456

means you can put a few coins in your pocket. But I came down here anyway. I was foolish enough to think that a piss ant like you would jump at the chance to strike out at the same sort of distinguished gentlemen who's been kicking your butt around all your life. And now I've exposed my backside to you . . . and it's you who's kicking my butt instead.

"I'll get you for your treachery . . . and your lying, Mr. Lancaster. You can bet on it. And you can bet that in the mean time I'll be dealing with Mr. Calvin Cabell by myself. There's more than one way to bring a man to justice for what he's done. There's more than one way to skin a cat, you know."

"I'm very sorry, son. Life is rarely fair to everyone. And the law's the same way. We picture that blind lady holding up the scales of justice and we see hope that the legal system and those who practice the law are fair minded. That's not always the case. And, if I've been unfair to you, then I want you to know I'm sorry. But life's not always fair to me either, you know. And this has been one hell of an unfair day. You can bet on that."

Even in the faint lamp light, Shelby could see the blood vessels in Nelson's neck stick out and pulsate. He was thinking. He was brooding. He was brewing up a plan. That's when Nelson noticed the glimmer of something white on the table to Shelby's right. He caught a clear glimpse of it and Shelby could see the young man had hatched an idea.

"Whose dueling pistols are those in the display case over on the table? And have they been cleaned? Do they fire?"

"They belonged to a client of mine – a former client. He foolishly decided to try to dodge a bullet in a duel . . . all over saving face about a comment he should have never made. He didn't jump fast enough."

The reason this vengeful young Kentuckian posed these questions suddenly popped into Shelby's mind. "Why do you ask, Mr. Nelson? Are you in need of pistols for a duel?"

The red headed man with this tense, muscular body stood still and said nothing. He kept his eyes fixed on the set of dueling firearms. Shelby still held the lamp between them and, because Nelson was so much taller than he, the illumination coming from below the man's shoulders cast black, eerie shadows on this cheated son's face. His eyes had disappeared and, in their place, Shelby could only see two hollow caverns of darkness. But Shelby knew precisely what the man was seeing through that pair of black holes. He was also certain he knew what his client was thinking.

"You think you can get your pound of justice by slaying Mr. Cabell in a duel, do you?"

Nelson's shadow strewn face slowly nodded in reply . . . and, after several seconds, then he confirmed his answer.

"Mr. Lancaster, you've lied to me. You know that. You set me up . . . and then, you let me down – hard. It seems to me those pistols aren't doin' nobody no good just settin' there looking pretty. I wonder if you'd let me borrow the set. I can return 'em tomorrow . . . or New Year's Eve at the latest."

Shelby's mind was racing with delight. His luck had suddenly turned. Jamie had neutered the little man's chance at retribution. But here stood Nelson . . . volunteering to settle the score for him. However, lots of folks had seen his pistols exhibited on the table. They often remarked at the beauty and craftsmanship of their pearl handles. Almost anybody would trace these weapons back to him and he would surely be implicated. Then, Shelby thought of a remedy. He could say Nelson must have stolen them. It seemed the perfect solution.

"I'll tell you what, Mr. Nelson. I think I'll let you borrow the pistols. I recommend you might want to just hold them for a spell tonight . . . that way you can consider the fact a duel wouldn't really solve your problem. Then I believe you'd see fit to bring them back tomorrow . . . still displayed in their box."

Shelby could tell Nelson was falling for his proposal. The Kentuckian moved toward the table and picked up the case. "I think you make good sense, Mr. Lancaster. I'm gonna dwell on all this while I fondle these beauties tonight. Maybe that's the key to getting over this legal setback."

"I'm glad you agree, sir. And I'm pleased you understand there's really not a chance of getting the satisfaction you seek . . . even if I were to try and humiliate Calvin Cabell in a civil suit. It wouldn't, in fact, accomplish anything."

"Maybe you're right Squire Lancaster. But fortunately there's more than one way to skin a cat. And skinnin' a polecat is what's on my mind right about now."

458

Timothy Nelson stuffed the pistol case under his coat – under his left arm pit so he could secure it walking down the street and no one would be the wiser. Without saying another word he opened the front door and stepped out into the fog. Three seconds later his powerful body melted into the mist.

Shelby wondered if his dilemma about how to finally triumph over Calvin had melted away, as well. His objective to bring Calvin Cabell to his knees was still alive . . . and, now, the final coup would be executed . . . by another man. Victory was at hand. And, he would be held blameless.

The twisted irony of it all tickled his soul . . . until he finally couldn't resist a muted laugh. "The boy's right. There's plenty of ways to skin a cat . . . even a polecat."

*No Coin for Charon*

# CHAPTER

# *31*

No one could see farther than twenty feet in the "pea soup" . . . as Bettie described the evening's fog to Jamie when he finally returned home. He inquired if his father had returned. He had. But Bettie said he had set out for the mill just three minutes earlier. Jamie realized he must have passed right by him out on Adams Street. They were both there, but on different sides of the roadway.

"Where's Mose, Bettie? I've got to talk with him."

"Here I am, Master Jamie." Mose replied as he stepped out of the kitchen into the dining room. "Awful messy weather out there, Master Jamie. Glad you come home out of it."

"Well, Mose, I think maybe one mess might've gotten cleaned up today. Step outside with me . . . on the veranda. I need to tell you all about it."

The two men walked to the corner of the porch in front of Calvin's study and sat on the stone railing. They could barely see one another. But Mose noticed a devilish smile on Jamie's face. He desperately hoped his friend brought good news.

"Mose, I did it. Actually, WE did it. I think I got the best deal we could have hoped for from Shelby Lancaster." He cracked open the left side of his coat and pulled out the small sheaf of stationery. He held the prize out and watched both relief and joy spread across Mose's face. Now, mind you, I decided getting Shelby to draft an official document that stated Mercer Watkins had already transferred Jed in the sale might cause more harm than good. It would involve forgery. And I think the bank would see right through it. But I can assure you Shelby won't ever open his mouth about it. The secret is sealed . . . and here's the insurance policy that'll keep him silent."

"Praise de Lawd, Master Jamie. Praise de Lawd. But, what about your Daddy? He left out a here mighty strange. Did you get the burdens off his back? I surely hope so."

"Yessir, I think so. I can't cleanse his soul. Only the Lord can do that. But I don't think anybody's ever going to know about his secret except for him and, of course, us. He's suffered a lot since Christmas Day. I think what I've got to tell him will be about the best belated Christmas present he could ever hope for."

"So, Master Jamie, what'd you say to the Squire? Wish I coulda seen the look on his face. And, what about Tyrus? Is he gonna be protected? What about his little girl?"

"Yes, I was sure to cover Tyrus' backside – same as everyone else. He's got nothing to worry about. Nobody's got anything to worry about except that weasel, Shelby."

Mose might be a freedman now. But he still was a black man – even in the sight of his good friend, his collaborator, and the individual had taken unseemly measures to right a wrong. He was still concerned about being impertinent to a white man - even Jamie. But he couldn't resist. "Well sir, Master Jamie. It appears ole Squire Shelby's done had the 'checkmate' whupped on him, for sure. That old king's been cornered . . . and not by a bishop or even a rook. I guess Mr. Lancaster, he been neutered by two little ole pawns. Ain't that a fact, Master Jamie?"

Jamie turned to Mose and recalled how fate combined with the trust each had in the other brought all these problems finally to a resolution that afternoon. He thought it was clever of Mose to remember Shelby's downfall was analogous to the game of chess he had taught him to play under the trees at Valley View. Mose was a smart man. In fact, Jamie thought he was about the smartest man he had ever known. But Calvin Cabell's son had something to add.

"Yessir, Mose, you're right about that. Old Shelby Lancaster's been neutered by two insignificant, piddlin' little pawns. And . . . if that isn't miracle enough . . . one pawn was white and the other one was black. How about that kind of checkmate, Mose? Sweet, isn't it?  So, how does it feel to be a deadly pawn that's just cornered a king in checkmate?"

"Sweet, Master Jamie. It feels mighty sweet."

\* \* \* \* \* \* \* \* \* \* \*

Suddenly Josh emerged out of the moist air. He came up the walkway and climbed the steps to the porch. There was a look of concern on his face.

"Jamie, I just passed Mr. Cabell about ten minutes ago. He looks mighty low tonight. I guess it's got something to do with burying Mr. Watkins today. He sounded real peculiar . . . real peculiar."

"What did he say, Josh?"

"Well, he spoke to me not like he was saying 'hello'. It was more like he was saying 'goodbye'. He told me he was so grateful I became part of his family, He said with you going back to college, the house was gonna need a man. He was almost crying. Why would he say the house was gonna need a man when he's still gonna be living here?

"And then I told him he looked real tired. And he said he WAS tired . . . tired as he'd even been. He told me again how much he appreciated me helping pull Mr. Watkins down from the rafters and helping in the funeral and all. Your father said he believed Mr. Watkins must've been just about as tired as he felt right about now. I sure wish I coulda done something to perk him up, Jamie."

Jamie's eyes were wide with panic. "Where was he going, Josh? Did he say?"

"He said he was going to the mill for a spell. Then he said, 'Goodbye, Josh. You're a God-send . . . a real God-send'."

"We've got to get down to the mill . . . right away. Father doesn't know I met with Shelby and got him to sign these papers. They solve all his problems. We've got to find him . . . fast. Come on, fellows, hurry along."

"You want me to hook up the carriage, Master Jamie?"

"No time for that, Mose. We've got to rush. Come with us, Josh."

Trudging through the "pea soup" atmosphere slowed them down. Josh tripped on a plank he couldn't see lying in the road and he fell crashing into the mire. Mose and Jamie helped him to his feet. He smelled of mud and horse manure all mixed together. But Josh was alright, so they sped along . . . although a little more cautiously than before.

They reached the mill in about eight minutes. Then, all of a sudden, Jamie held out his arms so as to silently signal something to Mose and Josh. He turned toward both and quickly curved the index finger of his right hand to his lips and made a low "shhhhh" sound which demanded their silence.

Up ahead he observed a murky scene. He saw a man whose front side was aglow from a nearby lamp. Jamie thought, it was a lantern that sat on the stump in front of his father's office. The three men stepped gingerly forward until they could finally be sure the man was Calvin. It was. He appeared to be in a conversation with someone else . . . someone who was still out of Jamie's sight.

Jamie ushered Mose and Josh maybe twenty yards forward. They could hear what was being said from that distance. Yet, because of the darkness . . . and the lamp light in Calvin's face, he couldn't possibly see them. The silhouette of another man stepped in front of Calvin . . . blocking the lamplight. And this silhouette carried a pistol which he held forward in a pose that indicated he might pull the trigger at any moment. Calvin's words could finally be heard and Jamie was quickly convinced a flash of gunfire wasn't imminent. His father apparently knew this man. He appeared to be asking for his forgiveness. And, most important, his assailant appeared to want to hear him out.

"I've thought about you . . . all these years. I wondered who cared for you . . . and if you were raised by family or friends . . . or if you lay in bed at night paining for your mother. I've wondered what you grew up to be . . . and what you looked like. And now I know."

"Oh, there was plenty of 'paining', all right. And Rebecca told me over and over she was certain it was you who killed my Ma. And, while I lay there grieving about my loss . . . about how I was robbed of my Ma . . . I kept my dark heart fixed on you, Mr. Calvin Cabell. I kept wondering what kind of a man considers himself so god-like in the Bluegrass that he can snuff out a mother's life . . . and carry on with his own life . . . like nothing evil ever happened."

"Well, Timothy, I can assure you I carried on . . . burdened by guilt . . . keeping this sin always eating away at my conscience."

"That's all well and good, Mr. Cabell, and I'm sure you might even have lost a few minutes of sleep before you slumbered off in your clean bed with your soft down pillows supporting all those sweet dreams that surely followed. But that was little comfort to me then . . . and it's absolutely no comfort to me right about now. I come all this way from Kentucky to see that justice got served. And here, moments before justice is finally measured out, all your talkin' ain't giving me no comfort at all. Only seeing you dead'll do that."

Jamie's heart raced at what the silhouette said. His blood went cold. There was a wet feeling inside him . . . the same clammy sensation he was feeling on his face and his hands. He had to do something. It had to be something that was a sudden surprise. He had a fleeting vision . . . in which he was attacking his father's assassin and throwing him to the ground . . . but, only half a second after the man managed to fire one shot squarely into his father's heart.

Jamie knew one thing for certain. He had to creep up on the pair alone. Mose and Josh tagging along would only risk the element of surprise. Their collective movement would put his father in dire jeopardy. He turned to Mose and mimed a motion that meant, "You wait here." Mose nodded his head in a manner that relayed back, "Okay, Jamie, but be careful".

The mill lot was covered with a thick carpet of sawdust. Fortunately, tonight the spongy layer was moist and it readily absorbed the noise of footsteps. But while the atmosphere provided him ideal cover, he remembered Josh had earlier tripped over the board in the road. So he paid special attention to anything lying on the ground that might cause him to stumble. Keeping his eyes peeled to the ground turned out to be wise for an additional reason. He DID spot an item . . . and it would have certainly stubbed his toe - enough to cause a tumble. But when he saw it, he immediately realized it was ideal for the plan that sprang into his mind. It was a brick . . . a solitary brick lying on the ground.

"Timothy, I'm not going to beg you to spare my life. Matter of fact, I came down here prepared to end my life . . . with the pistol I keep in my desk drawer. Why don't you let me go ahead with my original plan? It'll spare you standing one day atop the gallows. You see, with my way you could get the satisfaction of getting what you came down here to Memphis to get. You'll get your justice . . . and without the criminal liability."

"So, the high and mighty, Mr. Calvin Cabell, wants to end his own life? A man at the top of the heap in this town . . . and rich as anyone might ever hope to be? He wants to blow his brains out? I don't think that makes a grain of sense, Mr. Cabell. You must take me for a fool."

"You might see me . . . and others might see me . . . as 'high and mighty', but I've learned an important lesson in life, Timothy. One mistake . . . one momentary lapse of good judgment . . . or one urge to have your way with someone when . . . if you had just let the moment pass, the compulsion would go away . . . your life would go on without a hitch. But even one second or two of faulty thinking, foolish thinking, or arrogant thinking . . . can change the course of your life forever – as well as the lives of your family, your friends, and even people you never knew or might never have known . . . all because you momentarily lost your moral compass."

Jamie detected this deadly standoff just might be disengaged by reason . . . and by his father's heartfelt confession. But his optimism was soon dashed. Jamie heard Calvin say something really stupid . . . and incredibly senseless. He heard him say something that should've never been uttered. His father spoke these words just as Jamie picked the brick off the ground . . . all the while wondering how it could be put to use in this tense situation.

"You're a young man . . . and, yet, you're still a grown man, Timothy. You're just about the age I was when I met your mother. You've got urges that swell up within you. All men do. You've got to rein in those urges most of the time before you marry – when you're still a bachelor, like yourself."

"Yeah, but you were a married man the night you had your way with my Ma, weren't you, Mr. Cabell. All your urges could've been bottled up till the next day when you got home to your wife."

"Well, Timothy, sometimes those urges are whipped up by a temptress – a woman with no qualms about bringing a married man down by turning a cheap trick. There are whores out there, Timothy, and I suspect you've already encountered wicked women like that."

Jamie wondered if Timothy Nelson's body was going to explode . . . even before his dueling pistol blasted its fatal gunfire. The young man's rage instantly grew intense - instantly. Timothy Nelson's arm lifted up the pistol he bore and his stiffened arm trembled. But the quivering wasn't caused by weak nerves. It was fueled by the fury any man would feel when his mother was called "a whore" . . . by the very man who had murdered her.

Jamie held the brick below his waist and he deftly lobbed it high into the air toward its intended target – the shake shingle roof of Calvin's office. The brick landed with a loud thud and its impact resounded through the still night. It startled both Calvin and Timothy Nelson. Both men looked skyward and neither had a clue what it was or where was its origin.

Then Jamie sprang out of the fog and leaped high into the air. He landed on Nelson's back with his forearms choking the Kentuckian's neck. The attack buckled Timothy over and the pistol fell to the ground . . . just out of range of the lamp light. Jamie didn't say a word through it all. Instead, supernatural, primordial, guttural groans belched out of him. They filled the air with sounds so chilling they sounded as if they came from beastly demons . . . long repressed . . . but now set free on an unforgiving rampage. Indeed, Jamie had bottled up a lifetime of toxic emotions. And he remembered feeling purged of them, all at once, as he choked Nelson with all his might.

But Timothy Nelson was a powerfully built young man. And he, too, was energized . . . by his long awaited chance at vengeance. Jamie had tackled him valiantly, but he was no match for the red head. He bucked forcefully and Jamie flew to the ground while Timothy Nelson leaped toward the direction where the pistol had flown. He clawed in the dark at the sawdust until he felt it, once again, in his palm.

In a second he stood pointing the pistol at his victim. But now there were two Cabells before him instead of just the family patriarch. Calvin stood petrified from fear. A minute ago he was willing to die. He even wanted to die. But now he desperately wanted to live – if only to save the life of his son.

Steam arose from Timothy's sweaty shoulders as he aimed his pistol toward Calvin and Jamie. He panted laboriously . . . trying to catch his breath from the tussle. Between gasps of air he managed to stammer out a message. He intended for it to be the last words heard by either father or son. "You killed . . . my . . . mother . . . and now . . . you're gonna pay . . . for it . . . both of you."

Suddenly Jamie noticed Nelson was stumped by something he suddenly thought of. He was noticeably perplexed . . . as if a baffling conundrum had mucked up his plan. Jamie examined his face carefully. He easily read what was written on it. Timothy Nelson realized he held a dueling pistol . . . and dueling pistols fired just one shot. Nelson had two men trembling before him. Jamie knew what was about to happen. Nelson would fire at his father . . . and then he'll try to kill Jamie with his bare hands.

Nelson held up the pistol and then slowly lowered it to firing position with his arm extended ramrod forward. "I hate your guts, Calvin Ca . . . . . . "

The final harangue was cut short with a sharp "crack" that resounded from the back of Timothy's head. Calvin and Jamie saw what had happened . . .

467

clear as a bell. Fast as a bat flying out of hell, Josh Burnett had mightily swung a shank of firewood with a long, pointed edge hewn by someone's ax. The wedged side cracked open the back of Nelson's head. Like a great tree falling from the last blow of the axe, he crashed forward and fell with huge spurts of blood gushing from the linear wound. His head fell on the wet sawdust. It rested on its right side. For a few seconds his eyes looked up at Calvin and focused on him . . . leaving Calvin with an indelible image of horror and the missed opportunity at resolution which he saw in the eyes of Dolly's only son. The aggrieved son's skull was split open . . . and parts of his brain were oozing through the fracture. As blood-soaked sawdust formed a scarlet frame around the devoted son's face, his vengeful eyes closed . . . for good.

Mose, too, entered the filtered lamp light and the faces of four very disparate men all looked down at the corpse of the once vibrant specimen of a man . . . whose life had been squandered by an irresistible urge to even a score. And, almost in unison, three of the faces looked up at Calvin – the man whose idle evening years ago . . . bent on just a few minutes of sexual experimentation . . . had set all this human havoc into motion.

As the three looked at Calvin, something happened none of them had ever seen. Calvin Cabell began to cry. At first he merely whimpered. But in a flash, he stood looking at the dead man and he bawled - uncontrollably. He let go of hellish moans that pierced the still winter sky and his mournful pain must have been heard by every angel in the heavens.

Jamie wanted to hold and comfort his father in his arms . . . as if he were the sire and Calvin were the son who needed consolation and comfort. But Jamie had only known his father's secret for mere months. He couldn't imagine what it must have been like to carry this guilt-ridden secret for so long and know . . . and, surely his father knew . . . that one day he would eventually be exposed . . . and one day he would have to pay a price. Jamie knew the only consolation that could be afforded his father was from God Almighty. So, he just stood there and watched his father emotionally disintegrate . . . right in front of his eyes.

Someone had to break the trance. Remarkably, it was young Josh. And no one ever expected him to say what he said. "We've got to get rid of the body. Mose, get a flat piece of wood veneer out of the shed and put it under his head. Then keep his head squarely on it while I drag his body down to the river. That way there won't be a trail of blood."

Mose looked at the fourteen year old white boy in horror. Less than a week ago, Mose had just been freed by his master. Now a youngster living in the big house for only a few days was ordering him to help dispose of a murdered man's body. Even a freed black man would swing from a rope for such a deed.

Jamie sensed the moral quandary Mose was facing. He had to step in to save him. "I'll get the veneer, Josh. Are you sure you can tote the body all the way to the Wolf?"

"Right now, the way my muscles are surging from excitement, I could haul a horse to the river bank. I'm real pumped up after watching this man nearly kill your father."

"Alright then, Mose, get a shovel," Jamie instructed, "and start scattering saw dust on the ground? It's going to take quite a bit to cover up the blood. Go over to the shed and fill up some buckets with shavings. The sawdust piles there have been protected from the moisture. It'll be easier to handle . . . and it'll absorb the blood better."

Still, no one spoke to Calvin. They were too busy making the crime scene look unremarkable when the mill workers arrived for work tomorrow morning. Calvin was in no shape to help. In fact, as cover-up orders were exchanged, he began a new, heightened chorus of weeping. Mose and Jamie knew he was grieving that his own sin had sucked in others to commit crimes . . . and their intent was only to save him. The ghoulish workers who were feverishly trying to save his sinful hide were the men he loved and respected the most.

It was, maybe, one hundred and fifty feet to the Wolf River. Josh was right. He was super charged. He held the bulky corpse's feet tight in his hands and he tugged relentlessly at his load until, at last, he and Jamie stood at the water's edge. They both looked down and saw there was about a four foot drop to the water.

"Somehow, we're going to have to swing him back and forth until we've got the momentum to plop the body in the channel . . . maybe five feet out. The way I see things, if he surfaces at all, it'll be downstream in the harbor. With a wound like his, anybody's gonna think Nelson's just another hot blooded red head who got into an argument with a flatboat crew that turned violent. It happens all the time. If he surfaces next to a raft, the men are likely to just push the body out into the Mississippi . . . sort of like sweeping dirt under the carpet so company won't see it."

Jamie was struck at how blithe Josh was acting. He wondered if he had misjudged the new addition to the Cabell family. Maybe he was far from the wholesome lad his father had invited home for Christmas. Maybe Calvin was right when he said Cassie would drag home every stray cat on the streets of Memphis if she could. Maybe this young man had only the morals of a sinister, stray cat . . . and he was a budding murderer. Maybe he'd already killed a few Cherokee along the way . . . just for the thrill of it. But whatever hypothetical criminal profile Josh might fit, the fact was he was right about his assessment of the situation. And Jamie was more than willing to follow his directions.

"Let me grab his hands. And you take hold of his feet."

"Okay, Jamie, now let's swing him back and forth, real gentle at first. Then when I count to three we'll throw him up and out."

They proceeded with the plan. The body was limp and it was easier than Jamie thought to get a momentum going. When Josh started saying, "One. . . Two . . . Three . . . Let go, Jamie," the Kentuckian's carcass arched a foot or so into the air and then landed 'kerplunk' into the pitch black water. The sound reminded him of fat, old Marvin Brewster when he did a 'belly-flop' at the swimming hole near Valley View.

"The current's running pretty good now. So, I don't think anybody will find a body washed ashore for a good distance down stream," Josh predicted. Then he slapped his hands together several times . . . the way he might dust them off in the summertime . . . and he said, "We've got to get back up the hill, Jamie. There's more cleaning up to do."

"Mr. Cabell's sittin' in his office, Jamie. I told him to set a spell . . . and wait fer you. I brung out a lantern here and I been checkin' the ground. Don't see no blood . . . no sign of a fight. You can check it out yourself. See if you don't think it looks okay."

"I think you've done a commendable job, Mose. Josh, why don't you take the lantern? Hold it close to the ground. The two of you ought to look carefully. See if you can find anything out of order. And, Mose, what happened to the kindling wood that split him open? Where is it?"

"I took a hand ax to it, Master Jamie. I sliced at it and whittled it down to shreds. Then I took the slivers with blood on 'em and I cut 'em up real fine.

470

That little fire on the ground over there is what's left of 'em. Nobody gonna see anything out of order come mornin' time. You kin bet on dat."

"Good work, Mose. Alright, you two give me a moment with my father while you check out the premises one last time."

"Master Jamie, there's sumpin' else I spect you gots to know 'fore you go in there and talk to your daddy." Mose had a worried look on his face. He was staring at the ground.

"What is it, Mose? What else could there possibly be that I don't know already?"

"It's the pistol, Master Jamie. It's that duelin' pistol. First of all, your daddy says it come from Shelby Lancaster's office. He said he saw it there just this afternoon."

Then the black man got real tense. Jamie knew whatever would follow would be crushing news. "Then, if dat ain't enough . . . well, sir, that pistol didn't have no bullet in it. That Kaintuck boy coulda never got off a shot – try as he might. Ain't no way he coulda killed your daddy with us standing just out a sight. The pistol . . . it weren't loaded. Young Josh sliced open that man's head when there wasn't a bit a danger your Daddy was a facin'."

Jamie looked up and about twenty feet away he saw Josh gazing up into the air – like he was trying to look God in the face and ask Him for His forgiveness. He didn't know the pistol wasn't loaded. And Jamie knew neither Mose nor his father would tell the boy he had killed a man without cause.

Jamie remembered his talk with Calvin just three hours earlier. He had laid out everything that happened back in Kentucky . . . twenty years ago. Suddenly, he was struck at the irony of how Timothy's weapon had no ammunition in it . . . just like his mother's extortion threats to harm Calvin many years ago weren't backed up with "ammunition" either. He looked through the window . . . and he could see his father sitting at his desk . . . with his head braced on his upturned hands. Surely he, too, was contemplating the same cruel irony of it all.

Mose said nothing else. He moved toward Josh and the two appeared to fade into the fog as they began their walk home. When Jamie could see only a faint hint of Josh, the boy turned around and spoke in the gentlest of tones.

"Be strong, Jamie. And may God bless you . . . and Mr. Cabell, too. You just tell him everything's gonna be alright."

It was said like a blessing . . . a spiritual blessing that offered peace and reconciliation. The young boy who had just hauled a body and tossed it in the river . . . a body he'd gruesomely killed without knowing his name or that the deceased's pistol wasn't loaded . . . this man-child was offering his blessing. It made no sense. But nothing throughout the day made any sense either. Jamie was willing to accept blessings . . . even from the devil about now. He needed all the approval he could get. But this newcomer to the Cabell household . . . who had experienced more evil in three days than anyone should ever face in a lifetime . . . well, Josh was no devil.

Jamie responded with a sense of true gratitude. "Thanks, Josh, and you be strong, too. I hope you're right. I hope everything's going to be okay."

\* \* \* \* \* \* \* \* \* \*

Calvin read Shelby's affidavit in the faint light of the lantern. From time to time, he shook his head incredulously. He didn't look at Jamie or say a word until he finished.

"I just don't understand how you did it . . . or what you said to get Shelby to put these statements of exoneration on paper. If I didn't know you better, Jamie, I'd have to guess you held a gun to his temple while he wrote."

"Well, Father, as I always say, 'Every dog has his day'. And today I think I convinced Shelby Lancaster that maybe the Cabell bite was far worse than our bark . . . or something like that. I don't think that crook can ever be completely trusted. I know he can't. But that document needs to be kept safe . . . as well as secret. Sometime in the future we may need to pull it out and wave it in front of Shelby again."

"Your mother and I always said you had a sixth sense. It was scary. And I've got to tell you, I've sometimes been frightened of it . . . and of you. Somehow, I always believed that spooky sense allowed you to know all the haunting secrets of my life. If I've been hard on you . . . maybe that explains a lot. Now, mind you, I know Mose played an important role in all of this. But I don't know how."

"Father, most white folks think Negroes haven't got the sense God gave a goose. Yet, they're scared to death about one of them learning to read. That's never made logical sense to me. But I've learned their fears are warranted. You see, Father, Mose taught himself to read by listening carefully every Sunday to the reading of the lectionary. Then he spent all Sunday afternoon matching what he heard with words in the Bible Mother gave Bettie several Easters ago."

Calvin's expression changed in a flash. Suddenly he began to comprehend the meaning of events that occurred in the past. "So, when Shelby had Mose deliver those threatening ultimatums without securing them in an envelope . . ."

"That's right, Mose felt like the Lord helped teach him to read for a purpose. And this must have been the purpose. Never underestimate a servant. They know far more than they let on. Of course, Mose deeply regrets snooping at your personal papers."

"Jamie, I'd chuckle at your humor, except for what's happened here tonight. We've witnessed a horrible tragedy. And I bear the blame for it all. I'll never be forgiven for all the heartache I've caused. This secret's been at the root of the problems between your mother and me. She knew something was terribly wrong, but I couldn't tell her. You understand . . . don't you? I just couldn't tell her."

"I understand that Mother and Cassie are never to know any of what's happened tonight . . . or whatever happened back in Kentucky . . . or any of the other sordid stories. Mose will never tell Bettie and Jed. And Josh won't breathe a word to anybody."

"Except maybe in nightmares," Calvin interrupted . . . clearly with a heavy heart. He's surely set up for a lifetime of them. On one hand I wish he and John had never come home for Christmas with us. We've offered up nothing but heartaches to him. I'm going to make it up to him, Jamie. You'll have to help make this up to him. He's seen the worst in us. Now he deserves to experience the best."

"I will, Father. I will. Are you sure you want to get out of town. It's going to look mighty strange to folks . . . and even suspicious. What about the members of the church? They look up to you. They'll be wondering what's come over you."

"Jamie, I've reached the opinion the church is nothing more than an illusion. People believe what they want to believe. Always have. Always will. Look at me. Look at how I've deluded folks all these many years. They call me 'the pillar', but when I serve communion I've had the dirtiest hands in the congregation. I've lived a lie. And I've come around to believing the church has gotten by on lies and liars for all these years . . . probably always will."

"It's time, Father. Time's a wasting. You've got to get on your way . . . if you're determined."

"Oh, I'm determined, all right. But I've got to say goodbye to Mose and Josh and Cassie . . . and, of course, your mother. I suspect we'd better set out for home.

# CHAPTER

# 32

"Mrs. Cabell, I'm going to Arkansas. I don't know when I'll return, so don't let anyone get concerned."

"Why Arkansas, Mr. Cabell? You didn't say anything before about going to Arkansas. Is this about your business?"

Calvin thought for a few seconds about the question. The answer was "Yes". "Yes, madam, I've some pressing matters over there about some prospective timberland . . . and I don't know how long it will take."

Catherine Cabell felt wounded. This response and reasoning reminded her about their discussions in Kentucky when Cabell lied about visiting Memphis to investigate whether one of her father's stores might be established there. And it smacked of that night when he told her he was spending the night at Henry Caldwell's place while Henry was in Lexington. She knew he had lied then, too. This new 'Arkansas excuse' had a familiar ring to it.

"What about Josh? Jamie's headed for college in two days and the boy will be left here isolated – and just after being separated from John. My word, sir, we've already put him through hell - what with Mercer Watkins' suicide. How do you think Josh is going to feel when I tell him you've abandoned us – for a phony business trip that I'm sure could be delayed for several weeks?"

"Josh will be fine. He's a solid kid. In fact, Josh is going to take me down to the river. Besides, I should return in maybe a week – maybe more."

"A week? You'll be gone for a week? Mr. Cabell, you're just coming apart over this situation about Mr. Watkins. It's as if all Mr. Watkins' demons have congregated on your lap . . . biting your nose and taunting you with their wicked threats. You're acting like a man simply escaping his responsibilities."

"Maybe, that's just what I'm doing, Mrs. Cabell. Maybe I'm taking a much needed breather from my dreary life and my burdensome responsibilities."

Catherine tried to summon the indignant air of a "neglected wife" who had always managed to successfully debate Calvin early in their marriage. But, unlike the time they lived in Danville - when Jamie and Cassie were just toddlers and she challenged him relentlessly - this time she wouldn't argue with him. There was no longer any point to it.

"Very well, bundle up . . . and pack clothing for any kind of weather. You can never know what to expect on the other side of the river."

He thought how prescient her cautioning had been. He certainly didn't know what to expect in Arkansas . . . at the Pedraza Hotel . . . and beyond.

"I shall do that, Mrs. Cabell. I shall do that. That's good advice."


\* \* \* \* \* \* \* \*


One hour later Calvin Cabell sat in a rickety row boat with an impressive black oarsman at the helm. This ferry across the Mississippi was owned and operated by a man Calvin greatly liked and admired. He was Marcus Winchester's former slave, Isaiah. Last June, Marcus declared Isaiah's ledger had been repaid in full and the servant was freed. Marcus also financed Isaiah's purchase of his boat. He knew the loan would be repaid in full and, likely, sooner than prescribed.

Isaiah charged thirty-five cents each way. The river was covered with a thick ghostlike mist tonight. Calvin thought it hovered on the chilly water's surface like a gray, wet shroud . . . no doubt, hiding countless drowned souls languishing beneath the surface. He knew one of the names. He was a young man named Timothy Nelson. Isaiah wouldn't have made the crossing given the poor visibility for anyone other than his former master's good friend. He respected Calvin. And if this man needed to make a trip to Arkansas in the middle of an ice storm, then Isaiah would lean hard into the oars and row for all his might.

Calvin insisted on paying Isaiah a dollar fifty for the trip. He knew it was a premium fare. But he also knew he would benefit from sage counsel along the way. The price amounted to a bargain. Calvin said he wanted to go to Hopefield and the ferryman never hinted at the curiosity the destination aroused in him. However, he thought if a man of Calvin's stature wanted to go to the most sinful city within three hundred miles, at midnight, and in weather that would keep a fleeing convict's feet planted on the Tennessee shoreline, then he would gladly oblige.

Calvin's memory retreated back to the dense gray fog that hovered over the Lexington Road that April night . . . almost two decades ago – the night he stealth-like led Henry Caldwell's draft horse with Dolly's body draped over its back. The moist haze that evening concealed his crime.

And on this foggy night he was fleeing still another crime scene. Mose, Jamie, and Josh might consider what happened was an act of self-defense. But Calvin knew it would have never happened were it not for his own original sin. On this night of yet more needless slaughter, he felt the same way he felt along the Lexington-Harrodsburg Road – as if he were still on the run . . . with no idea when the chase would end.

Calvin Cabell was weary of running. His body and his soul were getting too old and too tired for it.

He thought about Mercer Watkins' body now resting in his wet grave. Only he and Jamie knew his remains concealed a gold coin under Mercer's tongue. If Mercer was going to hitch a ride with greedy Charon, Calvin thought it was likely Mercer was waiting for his boat on the banks of the River Styx right about now.

But it was he who was presently ferrying across a river and slogging through this opaque wall of moisture. It was just like Calvin had imagined the River Styx – eerie, very eerie. Tonight Calvin Cabell held out no hope that heaven lay on the other side of this river. He only knew there was more than just a little bit of hell he was leaving behind.

Sam Houston told him he was leaving his burdensome baggage on the east bank of the Mississippi. Houston understood he needed to travel light as he made a fresh start in life "on the other side". And Davy Crockett must have felt nothing less than exhilaration when he crossed this river and left behind a nation that was getting too crazy and too crowded to suit his needs.

Calvin Cabell was, likewise, feeling comfortable about breaking loose. It all just felt right. The only regret would have been if he hadn't taken his own dare to chart a different course in life . . . radically different than the one that had guided him thus far through such a series of unforgivable transgressions.

He thought about his rather pathetic record . . . his sorry slate, the life log that Captain Moore said got wiped clean each new day. Calvin shook his head. Down deep, he wasn't sure he was doing the right thing.

"There's a fresh start on the other side of the river. I'm sure of it. Houston and Crockett sensed it. And, so do I. Not bad company, Crockett and Houston. Not bad company at all." He unconsciously spoke these musings out loud . . . oblivious to Isaiah . . . as if Calvin were in the craft all alone.

Isaiah could tell his customer was mired deep in personal thoughts - thoughts only Calvin Cabell could wrestle with. He'd ferried many a passenger to the other side of the river and he knew many of them were struggling with demons way down deep. This familiar fare tonight had a demeanor . . . just like those. And experience had shown him these deep thinkers liked to be engaged in conversation. Isaiah found that talk usually broke the trance. So, he incorporated his cheeriest tone of voice before he spoke.

"Where'd you say you bound for, Mr. Cabell?"

"I'm heading to Hopefield, Isaiah."

Calvin was nervous. He had a compulsion to fill the silence with sound. "Did you know the Spanish explorers established a town at that very spot? They called it 'Esperanza'. It means 'hope' in Spanish."

Charon merely carried bodies to paradise. He offered no redemption to his fares. But Calvin Cabell was seeking a declaration of salvation from his ferryman this dreary night.

"You know Hopefield, don't you, Isaiah? And you probably know everybody who lives there or goes there for whatever reason. Do you think the Spanish got it right?"

"How's that, Mr. Cabell? Got what right, sir?"

Calvin paused thoughtfully. He was relieved Isaiah had broken the stillness. He needed to talk out loud about the important questions that stirred beneath his skin.

"Do you think there's any significance to calling a place 'hope', Isaiah – a place that maybe reaches out to lost wayfarers, welcomes them, and offers them a fresh chance . . . without knowing anything about them . . . whether they're sinners or saints?"

Isaiah pulled back hard on the oars he stroked with both of his calloused hands. The little boat on the big river jolted forward. The river current was tricky tonight. It was a challenge to any boatman. It was the sort of night when a passenger needed a skilled ferryman to safely cross the river. And Isaiah was skilled at more than just navigation. He was good at listening – a rare quality in a man these days.

Calvin remembered how sensible the sacrament of confession had seemed to him and Catherine when Tim and Sally Farley first told them about it. Calvin thought Isaiah would have been an effective Catholic priest. He would sit on the other side of that carved wooden confession screen and listen patiently. And when all the confessant's sins had been exposed, he would likely offer the supplicant a healing blessing of penitence – never harsh condemnation. Isaiah had the capacity to make a humble petitioner feel like the heavy load he carried with him into the confession booth had been left behind – right there on the sinful side of the screen.

Isaiah thought about Calvin's query for a while. The aging white man sensed there was great wisdom that resided in Isaiah's heart. After four long strokes of the oars, the black ferryman was finally prepared to answer his fare's question.

"I'll tell you what, Mr. Cabell. I believe there's something to what you be sayin'. Yessir, I DO believe there's hope out there beyond this fog. And I DO believes there's hope on the other side a dis river. Yessir, I believes there's jes gots to be hope . . . fer everbody out there – black folks and white folks, alike . . . on the other side of dis wily river."

Then the freedman - who just months ago was enslaved without any assurance of ever charting his life's own course – spoke with such unadulterated eloquence . . . it sent a shiver through Calvin's soul.

"And, after all's said and done, Mr. Cabell, if there ain't no hope ahead of us . . . out there beyond where none of us can see . . . well, sir, then I suppose there ain't no reason fer livin'."

*No Coin for Charon*

# Author's Notes

Author's Notes Concerning Characters and Historical Persons

---

Readers of *No Coin for Charon* might understandably assume most of the story's characters are fictional. This conclusion might be reasonable, in large part, because the novel's accounts about them seem (as the author has heard often) "stranger than fiction". Consequently, it is important to clarify fact from fiction with this brief statement.

The many recognizable historical characters in the novel have had their well-documented life experiences recounted accurately. Therefore, any of the story lines written herein about the lives of Davy Crockett, Sam Houston, Isaac Shelby, John Shreve, DeSoto, LaSalle, and the idealistic utopian, Frances Wright, her utopian mentor, Robert Owen, and her author friend, Frances Trollope, are all true.

Calvin Cabell and all the other Cabells are fictional. However, their cousin who is Jamie's age, John Cabell Breckenridge, is real and he plays a pivotal role in America's history before, during, and after the Civil War.

It should be noted Miss Wright was a "feminist" centuries ahead of her time. She was also a proponent of "free love". Therefore, her romance with Calvin is fictional, but could have easily happened . . . given her factual and his fictional circumstances at the time.

Abraham Lincoln did, indeed, make two flatboat trips down the Mississippi. The events and impressions he recounts herein about slavery which he observed during his first trip and the effects these experiences had on him are factual and proved to be indelible images about the horrors of slavery. What he saw during these river trips shaped his life – and, eventually, shaped the destiny of the United States.

Free Joe Harris was a real freed slave and the remarkable story of how he pieced his family back together through dedication and much toil are well documented.

Ike Rawlings's was an important citizen and an unforgettable "character" in the early life of Memphis. He became the city's second mayor. Everything written about him is true.

481

The story of how Memphians used "Little Vigor" to retaliate against the prostitutes from the Chelsea neighborhood is real.

John Burnett's story as a man who lived with and learned from the Cherokee is all real. Furthermore, he did, in fact, find himself escorting the very Indians he loved and respected along the brutal, forced march now known as the Trail of Tears. His brother, Josh, however is fictional.

Likewise, Marcus and Mary Winchester were real people and everything written about them herein is true. Marcus could have, without a doubt, asked for and received an important position in President Jackson's administration. However, Mary's lineage of mixed races would have been problematic and most people believe he loved her enough to pass up positions in the Federal government most men coveted to secure.

Marcus took to heavy drinking later in life. Many historians believe this "escape" through alcohol was rooted in his failure to join President Jackson in Washington, because Mary's racial makeup and her affair with Senator Thomas Hart Benton, essentially, blocked moving up into the mainstream of the federal government.

All the stories told along the way about the Roosevelts' lives, their experiences as steam boat entrepreneurs, and the earthquakes of 1811-12 are factual.

Hopefield, Arkansas, the Pedraza Hotel, and the gamblers who plied their games of chance there after being driven out of Vicksburg are also accurately portrayed

These characters in the novel were real-life men and women who all helped shape our Mid-South geographic region as well as our nation's identity in important and substantive ways. Nevertheless, the author and those who know their stories are incredulous – not so much that they lived – but that they did, in fact, interact with one another in a small town along the southwest frontier of America in the 1820s and 30s.

It is the author's sincere hope that readers will first visit the novel's web site (www.nocoinforcharon.com) to reinforce and expand their learning regarding these important historic characters and events. The author also hopes that any learning derived by readers from this novel will be vigorously discussed and passed on to others. We can simultaneously relish and learn from our collective past . . . so we might look to the future with a perspective of the people and their experiences which collectively shaped us into the society by which we are presently defined.

Printed in the United States
120644LV00005B/1-60/P